SHOCK THERAPY

ANGUS BLAIR

Troubador Publishing Ltd
Unit E2 Airfield Business Park
Harrison Road, Market Harborough
Leicestershire LE16 7UL
Tel: 0116 279 2299
Email: books@troubador.co.uk
Web: www.troubador.co.uk/matador

ISBN 978 1 80514 094 8

British Library Cataloguing in Publication Data.
A catalogue record for this book is available from the British Library.

Typeset in 11pt Minion Pro by Troubador Publishing Ltd, Leicester, UK

Matador is an imprint of Troubador Publishing Ltd

*For Charlotte and Elise, for all your ideas
and encouragement*

The possession of secrets acts like a psychic poison that alienates their possessor from the community. … [But] a secret shared with several persons is as beneficial as a merely private secret is destructive.

Carl Gustav Jung

PROLOGUE

Slouched at one end of a long table, the Deputy Rezident turned the pages of Captain Oleg Pinchuk's thick personnel file, taking his time, mechanically chain-sucking *semechki* – black-husked sunflower seeds. Removed from a rolled paper cone, kernel chewed, residue spat out onto a shiny anthill piling up in a red melamine Watneys ashtray. Pinchuk sat bolt upright, avoiding eye contact by focusing on this, the colonel's prize memento. With a pinhole microphone in the base, it had been carefully dropped in a smoky old pub in Gower Street, faithfully recording each evening shift of heavy-drinking MI5 men. The KGB veteran had judged four pints of bitter was optimal for the operation. British inhibitions gone but still just about coherent. He knew these people.

The colonel's eggshell bald head formed a flawless dome, save for a deep, shadowy dent below the right temple. Captain Pinchuk had plenty of time to speculate as the older man laboured over his file, running his stubby finger along each line. Shrapnel wound? Pistol whip? Or, most likely, the sharp corner of a committee room table after one fraternal vodka toast too many. Finally, the silence broke.

"You are pretty, Pinchuk. You will be popular with our British hosts." Delivered deadpan.

The colonel's gaze locked on to the young man's sharp blue eyes and then his shock of thick blond hair, too long by Soviet standards, the quiff verging on insubordinate.

The captain shifted uncomfortably. He stared straight ahead, trying to work out the game afoot. He was expecting a few test runs in the coming weeks and wondered what his new boss had planned for him. He knew that by tradition an officer starting his first posting at a large *rezidentura* like London would be expected to provide sport for his seniors. The more difficult and embarrassing, the better.

"Top marks from the academy. Congratulations, Captain. Four years studying the curious habits of the British from afar. And now you are here to try some of your clever tricks. We will get you started."

"I am ready to serve, Colonel."

The older man's face twisted somewhere between grin and wince. He swivelled around in his chair and pulled a newspaper from the top of a pile. It was pushed with some force across the polished table towards Pinchuk.

"What do you think of this, Captain? Did you read this journal in Moscow?"

The captain studied the red banner. Three bold letters: *NME. New Musical Express*. Below that, a picture of a pouting blonde woman with high cheekbones and spiky hair. The headline read, "The Revolution will be Peroxide".

"I read *The Times*, *The Guardian*, *The Daily Telegraph* and the *Daily Mail*. But I've never seen this before. Does it concern popular music?"

The colonel spat out a husk with some force.

"That's all I need. Another academy theorist. You probably think it's all cricket and cream teas here. You are about to find out otherwise."

Pinchuk tried to compose himself. This was certainly not the first time a senior officer of the service had faced him down. In fact, he was quick to recognise that familiar rage, barely contained, that came from another time and place. He had learnt all about it on the knee of his late, unlamented father. And then, as he grew, his education continued at the wrong end of his docker's steel toe cap. The old man always wore his four medals of the Great Patriotic War with pride, even inside the fetid one-bedroom Leningrad tenement that passed for home. May he rot in hell, thought Pinchuk as twenty-five years of experience kicked in. Freeze your face. Sit stock-still. Just listen.

"England is a midden. Degenerate. Turn to page seven. You see I have indicated your first mission. There, circled in red. Tonight. And a contact report on my desk by nine o'clock tomorrow morning, if you please."

Pinchuk bowed and withdrew in silence.

Back at his desk, he studied his mission. An advertisement for "Club For Heroes" at the Blitz in Covent Garden. No target from the Deputy Rezident. No brief. No chance to make his contact report a work of fiction. Pinchuk knew that operational protocol dictated one of his KGB colleagues would trail him. He would just have to do his best.

* * *

Ten p.m. and the young captain was ready; he was not going to fail on his first operational outing in London. The queue for the Blitz had moved slowly but he was now near the crimson padded doors. Ahead of him were three men dressed as nuns, behind a pirate linking arms with a highwayman. He himself had worn an open-neck purple shirt, its enormous lapels spreadeagled across the collar of a tweed sports jacket. He hobbled forward slowly, self-conscious of his limp. Pinchuk had been born with his right leg shorter than his left. In adulthood, he now sported a full two-inch differential.

"Only blondes tonight, darling." A hefty man with bright red hair turned a woman away at the door.

"No punks – now fuck off." Three more hopefuls spat theatrically on the pavement and then peeled away from the carnival parade. A trio of crestfallen cockatoos.

The KGB officer found himself at the front of the line, a couple of green pound notes damp in his hand. The academy had taught him to manipulate, burgle, forge, blackmail, blow up railway lines and even kill to order. But there had been no modules to deal with what confronted him now.

"Sid, come and look at this twat." The junior doorman called his boss over. A tall man with heavy eyeshadow and vibrant red lips sauntered up. The captain did a double take. What was going on? He was wearing a Soviet Army officer's cap, tipped rakishly to one side.

"My goodness, love, what have you come as tonight? It's so bad it's nearly good enough to get you in … but not quite."

"But sir, I am alone and for my first time in London. I am a student and want to make new friends."

The door manager laughed out loud and winked, every inch the pantomime dame. Without thinking, Pinchuk shifted from left to right foot, blushing as his lopsided gait went on full display. To his bafflement, for the first time in his life, the deformity drew an unmistakable, admiring appraisal.

"And you've got a deliciously gammy leg too, sweetheart. Well, you'll make a lot of friends if I let you in. Perhaps more than you bargained for." He tossed his head back.

"Where you from, darling?"

"Moscow, USSR."

"You're pulling my plonker. Really?" Eyeing the line, Sid pointed back to a hopeful-looking Cossack, complete with tall fur hat, harem pants and single oversized hoop earring. He dropped his voice.

"Listen, come back next week dressed like him and I'll let you in. Just ask for Sid."

Pinchuk was planning his next gambit when an imposing man with receding hair bypassed the queue and joined the discussion. He was immaculate in tailored white tie and tails, a crimson lipstick heart etched on each cheek. He held a black-and-gold cigarette holder in his right hand, its lit tip giving off the distinct perfume of cloves and heavy tobacco. Ten years older than the crowd, this was the sort of Englishman that the academy had prepared Pinchuk for – minus the face markings.

"Evening, Sir Jack. Lovely to see you."

"Hello there, Sidney. Frisky bunch tonight. Now, who do we have here?"

"A gorgeous Russian. Not sure ... maybe next week?"

"Oh, for goodness' sake. I shall vouch for him. He will be my guest tonight."

With that, the plush doors opened to the sound of David Bowie calling out for "Heroes".

There it was. Pinchuk's chance encounter which set him on the road to becoming the most successful and decorated Chekist of his generation. Beginner's luck? Perhaps. Forty years later, only seven living souls knew the full story of his exploits, of ABSALOM, but five happened to be the most powerful men in Russia. Quite a useful fan base.

1

TIME TO CONFESS

Henry Bradbury arrived at the Harley Street clinic in an uncomfortable, prickly sweat. The stroll from his chartered accountancy office in the City of London was ill considered, gradually accelerating into a power walk along Holborn and then finishing as a half jog, negotiating the dawdle of summer-sale shoppers that turned Oxford Street into a fleshy chicane. From under the sleeve of his Savile Row suit, a clever watch tapped at his wrist impatiently: eleven thousand steps taken today – only another thousand to go. The hefty twelve ounces per yard of cloth his tailor had recommended was proving a poor choice on this airless lunchtime. Why did he even bother dressing this way? Force of habit, laziness, lack of imagination? Nobody else at his office cared any more. Everyone else at Bonners LLP wore a uniform of chinos and casual shirts with infantile little embroidered animal logos where their hearts should be. But not Henry.

Also, he couldn't be late for his consultation with Nea. This hour had become the most important hour of the week, every week, and today was going to be the most important therapy session of all time. He had to get this one final thing off his chest. It was the big one, and it was overdue.

The ancient lift grumbled upwards, an interminable ascent to the top-floor garrets that gave him time to catch his breath and think. How much money had he spent with Nea over the years? A quick calculation and he easily got to the value of a family saloon car. Three years of couples therapy tried, and failed, to save his marriage with Jane. Twenty-seven years together, finished like that. It had been wise of Nea not to have charged on a success basis. Then followed twelve long months of solo help, picking up the shattered pieces, piecing back together the shards of his life.

Sweat trickled down his back, collecting in a lower reservoir God knows where, and a large wet patch formed on his chest, sticking blue poplin to pink skin. But it wasn't just the hottest day of the London season that was bothering Henry. Adrenaline was pumping, narrowing his blood vessels, a different kind of anxious, lipid perspiration. Both hot and cold sweat taps turned full on. But he was determined. Confessing all to Nea was the only way out of this mess.

Once in a while, if a therapy session with her went well, a moment came when she removed her glasses and rubbed her nose, signalling the adroit shift from

Nea, doctor and professional therapist, to Nea, Henry's venerable confessor. Her well-honed Socratic questioning stopped, and the consulting room walls closed in like a mechanical set change that gave him what he really craved: the security of a confessional box, complete with the ritual of absolution and finally her unambiguous edict.

Today of all days he needed Nea to breach her professional standards and just tell him what to do, tell him how to disentangle himself from this dangerous world of playing gentleman spy, an untrained Sunday league amateur tempting fate with Premier League professionals. Accrington Stanley versus Spartak Moscow. God help him.

The lift shuddered to a halt. He knocked loudly at the oak-framed door stencilled "Dr Nea Solomon MD MSc Psychotherapy".

A strong, clear mid-Atlantic voice responded. Half Brooklyn, half Maida Vale.

"Come on in."

He opened the door, conjuring his rictus grin in a pointless attempt to mask his nerves. Nea perched in the corner of her usual armchair, legs folded underneath her, dressed in her inevitable tailored black trouser suit topped by heavy framed glasses, complete with unblinking stare.

"Please, take a seat, Henry."

He sank into the increasingly off-cream leather sofa and removed his jacket.

"So how *are* you?"

"Very well, thank you for asking, Nea. A good week actually." Henry got ready for the familiar liturgy, versicle and response, playing for time.

Nea rose to her feet and lowered the heavy sash window which looked out onto the enclosed light well.

"Sorry to close this as I see you're warm, but I'm afraid conversation drifts between the consulting rooms. And you do have a habit of talking quite loudly." She smiled sympathetically, the spectacles greatly magnifying her dark, thoughtful eyes.

He wasn't going to be shouting his mouth off, now the moment of truth was here. That might be quite injurious to his health.

But Henry was going to stick to his decision. Over three long years, trust had put down deep roots, enough for him to now open his innermost chamber, let light shine into his pitch-black sanctum sanctorum. Unlike with Jane, with Nea his confessions didn't boomerang straight back into his face. And if she was judging him, she was a world-class poker professional at hiding it. Finally, she'd pulled off a remarkable sleight of hand. This therapist–patient relationship was no two-way street. He gave, she took, but as they sat there together, there was nobody else in the world he could feel safer with, although he barely knew her.

Early on he understood the unspoken rule: you never ask your therapist questions about themselves, their lives, their families. But over time Nea had on occasion talked to him about her early years in New York City. Henry came to realise that she, unlike him, was not given to blurting. In fact, he now realised everything his therapist said, did or asked was deliberate, calculated. Variously, he learnt that Dr Nea Solomon MD was born to British parents who emigrated to the United States from North London in the nineteen sixties. Mother of Jamaican descent, father from a Viennese Jewish family. She had been sponsored through Johns Hopkins Medical School by the US Army and then served as a military doctor around the world. As to where, the only clue forthcoming was when he asked Nea about an amulet she wore around her neck. The blue glass circle with a white inner and a black dot at the centre intrigued him. She didn't seem the superstitious type who might fear the evil eye. She told him it was a Persian *nazar* before quickly moving the conversation on.

Coming to London to pursue a career in psychotherapy was her dream. Her grandmother, also Nea, a collaborator of Carl Jung, had established a pioneering practice in this self-same Harley Street building just after the war. Thinking about it, Henry realised each of these meagre morsels was thrown his way to draw him out when he started to bring down the shutters on his soul. Clever.

Nea got the ball rolling.

"How's the dating going, Henry?"

He always liked this question. When he'd first met Jane there were no mobile phones, no internet. Telephone sex was in its infancy, but that was about it. Thirty years later the London online dating scene was proving to be a revelation.

"I've had dinner twice this week with a lovely, attractive woman. She's a Brazilian artist, somewhat younger than me, but her art seems very good – tropical, lots of bright colours … parrots, monkeys, fruit, that sort of thing. I think a big canvas might look good in my entrance hall, on the double-height brick wall."

He wasn't sure, but did Nea wince? She held his gaze, leaving just enough time for the silence to get uncomfortable.

"And she seems to like being with me." He trailed off weakly, unaccountably sad.

"Look, Henry, remember, we've been through this a number of times. What you need for the next leg of your journey in life is to walk hand in hand with a calm woman. Somebody you feel safe with, reliable. Somebody who is like you, who would fit into your life."

He nodded but must have signalled unspoken doubts to the all-seeing Nea.

"Henry, a calm woman can also be passionate in bed. Please do bear this in mind." This was said with uncharacteristic force, signalling the matter was now closed. He would have a good think about that.

He had readied himself to unburden, to come clean about Sasha, Roddy and Colin, beautiful Nataliya. But Nea began another comforting ritual which spared him for a few final minutes.

"Why don't we go through all the positive things you've achieved in the last year, beyond the tough stuff?"

"Well, I think it all wound up fine with Jane. That's an achievement. It's hurt a lot along the way, the feeling of failure. It gnaws away. But we kept it amicable."

"Good. Go on."

"The girls are still talking to me. They even helped me set up my online dating profile and sorted out my new wardrobe. Lots of black clothes and expensive trainers. I think the hoodies might be a bit too much though."

"Yes," Nea agreed, too emphatically for Henry's liking.

"I've got the new warehouse apartment in Shoreditch and kept the place in dear old Lisbon. And Bonners haven't quite fired me yet. I've joined the local amateur theatre group in East London, keeping up the acting. It's always been a great release for me, though I must say I did prefer playing leading man in the odd Agatha Christie at the village hall. All these new people want to do is sit on the floor in a circle, lots of silence, then we all have to shout a lot. I'll try to get the hang of it."

Nea smiled.

"I think you've got a talent there. And I know you always wanted to turn pro. I'd keep it up. There's always hope. And, you know, you can bring much more to the world than just thinking of yourself as a chartered accountant."

Henry sighed.

"And what else good is happening in your life, Henry?"

"The dating is a lot of fun … I never realised what was out there and my mojo is back, with a vengeance."

He was warming to the theme of the carnal pleasures of being a newly single man in London in 2019 when a glance at the clock forced his hand. It was time. He remembered his basic spy training and powered down his phone and smartwatch, arranging the two hopefully dead devices on the coffee table in front of him. Nea looked on at the inert objects with interest.

"Nea, can we please talk about risk? Personal risk. The risks men like me take when they're in my boat, a bit adrift, anchor dragging along the bottom."

She looked momentarily off balance, perhaps as surprised by his urgent tone as much as by the unexpected question. He had never seen this happen before and felt oddly pleased. He decided to play this out a little more, tables turned for once. Maybe this wouldn't be so difficult after all.

He stared at Nea in expressionless silence. There was still half an hour left on the meter. Today he was going to get his money's worth.

Nea gave her considered view, speaking slowly, deliberately.

"Over the years I've seen a lot of things go wrong for men like you. But I'm sure we can work this through together, like we have in the past." A reassuring smile, for once not reciprocated by Henry.

"You did get the vasectomy like I suggested, didn't you?" A nodded assent.

"I got the test results back on Tuesday. Not a sperm in sight." He had followed the instructions and triple-packed his sample, placed it inside a return-addressed envelope and squeezed it into the narrow mouth of a bright red pillar box in Mayfair. The testing laboratory was in a post-industrial town in North East England. First the mines and shipyard went, then the call centres; now it was first-class bodily fluids sent from the capital. He had felt a passing twinge of guilt.

"There are so many men I've worked with now playing unhappy families again, second time around, in their fifties and sixties. And there are young women out there who would see you as a good target. Always use your own condoms. They can put holes in them otherwise, you know."

"Not a problem for me now, Nea. I'm thinking of a different kind of risk."

This was becoming fun. He relaxed. The therapist stared out of the window, looking at the rusty, baking, blistered fire escape. He imagined that she was using each step as a line on her mental checklist of stupid things men like him had done. Luckily there were plenty of steps.

"You haven't bought a motorbike, have you?"

"Nope."

"I don't think it's a cocaine habit. You aren't the type."

"Correct, Nea."

"Online gambling?"

He briefly considered the odds of his new Russian friends sussing him, and the consequences of this significant gamble going against him, before putting that troubling thought aside.

"Never. I don't see the point in gambling. I've never met a poor bookie."

"Body piercings or tattoos? A Prince Albert or scrotum rings are absolutely fine as long as they are done professionally."

"I promise I won't try DIY. I failed my metalwork practical when I was sixteen." He couldn't resist a giggle. Nea laughed with him. Time to stop the game and use the remaining time wisely.

He cleared his throat portentously, leaning in and lowering his voice.

"Nea, I think you know I've told you everything – well, nearly everything – over the years."

Blank stare. A bit disappointing.

"But there is one thing I have held back from you. Something I badly need your help with."

The drum roll had no visible effect. The unblinking gaze continued. Oh well.

"Over the past year, I've been helping the British

government with some highly secretive and sensitive work. In plain language, I'm a spy. Well, sort of."

Silence. Henry felt compelled to fill the void.

"You know, I was flattered when they first approached me. Excited, alive again. I don't know why they chose me, an average chartered accountant, an average failure in life, really. But it felt like I was being picked for something special, that they'd spotted something about me that everyone else had missed."

Henry paused, realising he was talking too quickly. He willed himself to control his runaway nerves. Nea seemed to be watching his chest, its rapid rise and fall. He slowed himself down.

"The girls are grown up now and Jane kept telling me I was boring. You heard that from her. She sat right here on this sofa and said it. Remember?"

He patted the empty void next to him.

"I just wanted to prove her wrong. I haven't much to lose. It's made me feel, well, a bit sexy." Henry caught himself smiling coyly and then averted his eyes from Nea's steady gaze, wondering what she really thought of him.

"But I'm out of my depth. And they've asked me, in a nice British way, to hold my breath and dive one stage deeper. I don't know why, but I'm half terrified, half sorely tempted, both at the same time."

Oh God, he sounded pompous and histrionic. He should have rehearsed it more. He studied his therapist, willing her to remove her glasses and rub her nose.

"And it's not just about me. I'm putting others at risk too. But spying is like a drug. For me, it feels like an addiction."

A look from Nea he had never seen signalled something else was coming. Something new, unanticipated. Was she frightened? This was going wrong.

"Nea, look, I don't want to put you in a difficult position but I think our conversations are confidential. Doctor and patient. I've grown to trust you over the years. And, I don't know, I've really got nobody else to talk to about this."

Nea curled herself right into the back left corner of her armchair, shoes kicked off and bare feet tucked up under her legs. Making herself as small as possible? Maybe a reflex from the past, an instinctive attempt to disappear? She also looked like she was thinking hard, very hard. Staring out at the old fire escape, but this time looking for something else?

Several moments passed.

"Who are these people who've recruited you? And what is their mission?"

He was startled. His controllers – MI6 Roddy, and Colin, his MI5 oppo – occasionally lapsed into spook-speak, and "mission" was a favourite. Where had Nea just pulled that from? He replayed the last few minutes' conversation. He definitely hadn't said mission. Confused, he realised it was time to blurt. Big blurt time. Verging on a spew.

"Nea, I've been spying on Russians. All in a good cause. It seemed low-risk, safe-ish. But now I think it isn't."

Unbidden, he started to unload his story.

Roddy: sleek, persuasive and a complete chancer. The MI6 half of the double act from the "Joint Russia Programme". If Roddy worked at Bonners he would be on the widest of wide sales teams, with the confidence only an expensive public school can instil, finished off nicely with three years' idling next to one of the two great English power rivers, the Isis or the Cam. Roddy's colleague, Colin: soft spoken, with an unmistakable Birmingham lilt. The MI5 straight man. At Bonners he would have been in risk or compliance. Younger than Roddy, and probably quite a pleasant man when he wasn't burgling your house or standing over you in a windowless detention room at Heathrow immigration holding pen. Quite unremarkable, apart from a facial tick, an involuntary squeezing of the eyes followed by a spasmodic upward tilt of the head. It seemed to be triggered by nerves and, from the outset, Henry had wondered if this would excuse Colin from undercover surveillance duties.

Roddy's cryptic phone call had come out of the blue, and the invitation to breakfast at a smart West End hotel couldn't have arrived at a better time. Henry's week had been marked by record lows; the week when Jane declared their marriage officially dead, his long-time Bonners understudy, George, was promoted to be his boss, and, finally, his mother drew her last breath in that vile smelling nursing home he hated to visit.

Sitting at the starched linen table, the one furthest from the main door and closest to the kitchens, Roddy and Colin offered redemption. In fact, rebirth. And Henry seized it with alacrity.

His spy story started to tumble out to Nea. The cultivation of illegal Russian agent Sasha. The Russian Orthodox Church in Knightsbridge. Fat little archpriest Evgeny. His lovely Russian teacher, Nataliya, who always ordered flat white coffee and had the greenest feline eyes.

Henry paused the monologue that he had been directing at the coffee table and looked up, sensing the therapist was no longer in her chair. In fact, she was at the consulting room door. He had hardly got into his stride and Nea was signalling for silence, poking her head out into the corridor. A welcome breeze wafted in and disturbed the stale air. Other than that, nothing. Silence. Nea padded to the sash window. Cat-like. Light on her feet when she needed to be, he thought. First, she squinted up at the hazy blue London sky where a giant A380, inbound on its final approach to Heathrow, seemed to hang motionless. Then, a slow scan down the length of the fire escape followed by a peer into the litter-strewn, dark vortex below. She seemed to know what she was doing.

Nea sprang back across the grubby carpet, not to her armchair but straight at the sofa, sitting uncomfortably close. He was about to continue but the therapist raised her right hand in front of his dry mouth.

"Henry, be quiet and listen to me. It sounds like you might be tangling with the Russian Intelligence Service? Such a bad idea." His alarm went up another notch. What had she just asked? Not "the Russians", not the "KGB", not the "SVR", but the "Russian Intelligence Service". Again, pure Roddy and Colin. Only insiders said that.

He started to panic. Who was the real Nea? Doctor? Psychotherapist? Confessor? All of those, certainly. But was there a fourth, invisible string to her bow? She was about to tell him.

"Henry, I don't need to hear any more. I certainly don't want to know any more. I'm going to tell you my story. Please pay attention to this. This might well save your life."

He readied himself, but then she stopped, stone dead. A look of sheer pain melted her therapy mask, and she tilted her face downward so all he could see was her brown neck, tight pixie haircut and the crown of her head. He wanted to put an arm around her shoulders but stopped himself in the nick of time.

After what seemed like several minutes, she looked up, eyes damp and red. She had changed her mind.

"Henry, I care about what happens to you, believe me. But I can't help you anymore. I can't tell you why, but for your sake and mine, this is our last session. We're over now. This one's on me. I can recommend a good therapist colleague to take over, if you wish. Otherwise, it's goodbye and good luck." She inclined her head, indicating the door that opened wide onto the waiting world.

"Oh bollocks," Henry croaked.

2

DRY-CLEANING

LONDON, AUGUST 2019

Henry found himself blinking in strong sunlight, standing on the pavement where Harley Street meets Cavendish Square. A survival instinct appeared from nowhere as he made his way at a measured pace across the gardens towards the back entrance of the John Lewis department store. It was time to take stock, to make sense of what just happened in the consulting room. He had never seen Nea anything other than calm, collected, forensic. But his botched confession and the sudden onrush of her fear had spread across the room like an airborne virus, forcing Henry to stumble out towards the fresh air. Things had gone terribly wrong.

Roddy hadn't wanted to teach Henry the rudiments of dry-cleaning, spy talk for taking active anti-surveillance measures. He smirked when Colin suggested it at their second meeting.

"Listen, mate, if the Russian watchers are any good, which they are, you'll have no idea they are on your tail. Spotting them takes years of practice. And besides, Sasha suspects nothing, and if he ever did, we would know and take good care of you."

At this, Colin shifted awkwardly on the leather banquette, eyes scrunching and head suddenly tilting back. Henry began to spot a pattern. Colin had chosen an odd profession for himself: conflict always seemed to set off his twitch. Did he have the affliction before he joined up? Or had his work caught up with him? Right on cue, the waiter appeared at the booth with the drinks, giving the three of them a welcome moment of silent reflection.

Henry had already started to get irritated with this "mate" business. Whoever Roddy really was, he wasn't brought up matey. "Strangled by poshness" summed up Roddy, organically constricted vowels nurtured on the banks of the Upper Thames. On top of that, a mouth seemingly too full of teeth made for a strangely sibilant delivery.

He remembered a heated discussion with his politically woke daughter, Sophie, when he offered the opinion that the British class system was effectively dead and buried. She held a different view. They agreed to differ. But here it was in action, Roddy's studied attempt to find common ground with Henry hit his chippiness main nerve square on. As usual, Sophie had been right.

Colin usually deferred to Roddy. Mercifully this time he stood his ground. Roddy shrugged, slouched, and MI5 got their way. A training date was set. Henry was of two minds. He suspected MI5 standing orders required a bit of agent training, even if it was just to tick a box on the risk management file when Colin got back to the office. But he also detected an unspoken warning from Colin. This might not be as straightforward as Roddy's glossy sales pitch made out.

So now, as he entered the department store, he dug deep into the memory of that odd day out with Colin and his new spook friends. A day practising routines to spot surveillance by a team of eight watchers that Colin had rounded up at Thames House. It was exhilarating; the first time he felt he was what he quietly fantasised about, a secret agent for Her Britannic Majesty. Unpaid, untrained, out of his depth. Jane had got him so wrong. He was going to prove he could do this.

Now, as he sauntered through ladies' lingerie, he remembered the drills. Move at your own pace, don't hurry. Open spaces good, crowds bad. Don't make it obvious you are looking for surveillance – that's the worst thing you can do. Walk across the road away from the marked crossing points. That gives you a good reason to look around before heading into the traffic. See if you spot anything. Height is good too. Open escalators give you a chance to see if there is a team on your tail.

He stopped at the third floor and headed for the garden furniture department. A swing seat with a frilly canopy sat amongst a range of barbecues and afforded him sweeping views of the escalators as they switched back and forth, the open-plan arteries of the store. Nothing unusual down there, he noted, as he flopped down and began gently rocking back and forth. Lunching ladies wafting towards the restaurant. A dark-suited and booted

Chinese provincial government delegation with red lapel badges, skiving off their afternoon meetings in favour of rummaging through the sales tables. Two bored-looking security guards on the door. Apart from the odd burst of static crackle, a comforting silence coming from their walkie-talkies. Henry needed time to think, rewind how this had all started, scene by scene, look for clues, try to work out what had just blown up in Nea's consulting room.

So back to the beginning, a year previously, when he first met Sasha at a morning coffee break in one of the London School of Sociology buildings that dot Aldwych. The first session of the day had been even more tedious than expected and Henry was contemplating heading back to the office, having spent just enough time to claim the day for his annual Continuing Professional Development return. He hadn't opened a spreadsheet in years, so the first two presentations on "Predictive Modelling in Business Leadership", delivered in a monotone with a blinking cursor dragged across a twenty-foot-tall screen, weren't doing it for Henry. Not at all.

Packing his briefcase at a pedestal table whilst finishing a lukewarm instant coffee, Henry became aware of a giant hovering over his left shoulder. Looking up, he saw a beaming, open face, topped with a mop of brown hair and finished off with a bushy beard favoured by younger men in London. A large paw was proffered.

"Hello, sir. I am surely glad to meet you. My name is Sasha Orlov. Please, here is my card."

Sasha dug around in his backpack and, with a gracious old-world formality, presented his card to Henry with both hands and a slight bow.

Aleksander A Orlov, Doctoral Candidate
London School of Sociology

Henry reached into his top pocket and reciprocated.

"Henry Bradbury, Bonners Chartered Accountants," he muttered.

He had to crook his neck up as Sasha continued to beam down, studying Henry's classically embossed calling card.

"Oh, this is too great to meet you, sir. Bonners is such a famous company. Very old. I would love to demonstrate my work to you. I am not strictly academic. I am also a businessman. You will see."

And also, as Henry was soon to discover, a Russian Directorate S intelligence officer planted as an illegal agent in London.

Two days after the encounter, Henry's mobile rang. "Caller ID withheld" flashed up on the screen. It was that first cryptic call from Roddy. Breakfast arranged for the next day.

"Can I tell you a little about our Windsor range of garden furniture?"

A smartly dressed store assistant stood in front of Henry, a colourful brochure in hand. A black woman with a retro blonde beehive, home counties accent, hair and high heels giving her several inches height advantage. She smiled whilst studying him. How long had he been on the swing? he wondered. He received the pamphlet graciously, mumbled something about returning with his wife and headed for the exit. Non-existent wife, of course, but old habits die hard. He felt her eyes following him as he headed for the exit. He needed to control his breathing, stay calm.

He had three options now. One, head back to Bonners and finish his day at the safety of his familiar open-plan desk. Maybe find somebody to go for a drink with after work? But it was a Friday afternoon in August and the buzz would be all the young people in their twenties talking about clubbing, those in their thirties heading out of town for the weekend or in-laws, the forty-somethings would be starting out for the statutory two weeks of safari, Sandy Lane or Cornwall. No other fifty-somethings were left standing, except if you counted a couple of the security guards and old Ted who delivered the post around the office. Henry was the last man of his generation. Sad. So, scratch that idea off the list.

Two. Go home. That had a certain appeal. He could put on some vinyl, probably John Coltrane or Sérgio Mendes, crank up his new Vertere turntable twinned with beautifully expensive ATC speakers, pour himself a stiff gin and tonic over ice with a star anise stirred in, and put his feet up.

The hi-fi had at first seemed a pretentious extravagance but Roy, the personable salesman from Liverpool, was very persuasive. A few subtle questions exposed Henry's vulnerabilities within minutes. The aphrodisiac qualities of perfectly delivered late-night jazz were emphasised, together with the seductive styling of the hardware. That had him pulling out his credit card even before they left the confines of the soundproof listening room. Roy was wasted on Tottenham Court Road; he would be perfect for Roddy and Colin's purposes. Henry was determined to perfect the craft of getting under people's skin quickly, and as he thanked Roy for throwing in a set of gold-plated connector cables free and gratis, he silently acknowledged a greater debt. He would give it a try with Sasha next time they met.

And Roy had been right. The place in Shoreditch, the hi-fi, the minimalist furnishing, all proved a satisfactory backdrop to Henry's first faltering steps into online dating. And for that very reason, option two was a non-starter. Henry felt alone and didn't want to spend an evening in splendid isolation, wrestling with his secrets and the loss of Nea. No matter how comfortable.

So, to option three. A couple of hours meandering eastwards through the City of London, spy drills falling by the wayside at every twist and turn between ancient Ludgate and ultra-modern Bishopsgate. A curry and a few refreshing pints in his local pub were the short-term answer.

3

LONDONGRAD

It was there again. Sensed it in the half-light, and then saw it, standing at the end of the room. It just stares at me, not threatening, not anything. It is a void, a shape, faceless. It keeps coming back. Tried to raise myself up by my elbows, but nothing happened. Remained anchored to the spot. Tried to speak to it, to challenge it. As usual nothing happened. My mouth works but voiceless. It just stares at me. The line is disconnected.

HB's Dream Diary
Saturday, 31 August 2019

Henry awoke to sunlight streaming in through double-height ironclad windows wedged into industrial brickwork. Another warm morning in Shoreditch. He hadn't drawn the curtains and his suit, shirt and tie lay strewn across the ebonised hardwood floor.

He always set his watch to wake in time for his Saturday morning Russian lesson with Nataliya. But it wasn't on his wrist. Christ. Worried, he swung his legs out of bed and patted down his suit pockets. Mercifully, watch, phone and wallet all present and correct. Also, a crumpled receipt from a curry house in Brick Lane and a fairly extensive bar tab from the Pride of Spitalfields. After yesterday's Harley Street drama, a little local anaesthetic had evidently been in order.

He lay back on his bed, found his spectacles and turned on his phone. Eight a.m. Still enough time to ablute, scrub up, gargle and perfume away the evidence of the previous night. And still get to the café-cum-classroom in Sloane Square before the appointed hour, finish his homework and anticipate seeing Nataliya.

Reaching into his bedside table, he poked around and pulled out a small notebook. Black leather with *HB* embossed in gold on the front. The book had been Nea's idea, a diary to jot down his disturbing dreams, random thoughts he didn't quite get, questions he wanted to ask of her. He scribbled down what he could remember of last night's visitor, the dark figure who increasingly invaded his sleep.

Before he returned the notebook into the hidden envelope he had taped to the back of the drawer, he flipped to the final page and looked, as he always did, at two reassuring entries. One, an innocuous London phone number which was his own dedicated line to the Joint Russia Programme. And the other, the word

BRILLIANTINE. Both entries scored forcefully into the cream notepaper. BRILLIANTINE was his crash code, the word he would give if he ever found himself in danger or needed an urgent meeting. He had long ago committed number and codeword to memory, but just studying and then voicing them softly was balm for Henry that morning. His morning prayers.

The phone pinged and brought Henry back into the present. Fifteen hours' worth of texts and emails dumped from the ether into his inbox. He hadn't switched on the phone since yesterday's ill-starred visit to Harley Street. He yawned and scrolled through his digital postbag. A message from Rosemary, his executive assistant, reminding him of his upcoming appointments on Monday. Perhaps she was worried he had gone AWOL again? Then the usual dross, dross, more dross.

Until the last message. He sat up.

It was from Nea.

Henry. I've been thinking about our conversation. If and when you sort yourself out I will work with you again. but you've got to make your own decision. In the meantime take good care. Pls be careful. N.
Today, 06.32.

Henry dropped the coffee capsule into his shiny stainless machine and got the milk frothing. He caught himself whistling the theme from *Diamonds are Forever* and smiled.

Nea. Thanks for all your help and advice in the past.

*And for listening. You are right. I need to man up
and sort this out myself. Will be back in touch when
I have. Love Henry.* Today, 08.31.

He was about to press send and then caught himself. Shit.
Love. What was he thinking? Autocorrect or subconscious?
He needed to watch that.

* * *

Henry arrived early at the café in Sloane Square and
ordered his usual cappuccino and a pastry. He had calmed
down since yesterday's events but still took time to inspect
the sparse clientele. Evidently, on Saturday mornings,
Chelsea rose late. A young couple were speaking something
Slavic. Definitely not Russian. Polish? Czech? At least he
knew enough to be able to relax a little. Two older Arab
men, pastel linen suits and comfortable with each other's
company, switching between Arabic, French and English,
all within the space of a sentence or two. They unboxed a
backgammon set. That was it; London's warm, protective
amniotic fluid was settling his nerves.

While Henry sipped his coffee, he worked through
the pictorial Russian language exercise book. It seemed
to require him to place Mister Ivanov and his daughter,
Svetlana, together with their dog and cat, either underneath
or on top of a table, at the front door or peeping through
a window. He hoped Nataliya would arrive soon. She
wasn't Nea, but she was the non-prescription, over-the-
counter generic equivalent that might just help him. She
was also Russian, he formally reminded himself. That was

tricky. Her English was impeccable, but fifteen years in London hadn't made her a card-carrying lover of liberal democracy. Far from it.

Henry had first met Nataliya at Easter that year. More specifically, the Russian Orthodox feast of Pashka on Sunday, 28 April. And even more specifically, in the second row, standing in front of the glittering icon screen at the London church.

Henry's cultivation of Sasha Orlov had certainly broadened his horizons. He thought back to the Lenten lunch with his new Russian acquaintance, conducted under the watchful eye of the Joint Russia Programme. All cleared in advance with Roddy and Colin. It was a decent enough menu at an Italian place in St James's. Sasha picked his way through the observant vegetarian options, but fell head first off the hay cart when he ordered a goldfish-bowl-sized glass of a good Chianti. Henry was rather pleased.

Over a second sinful glass, Sasha had become increasingly voluble about the beauty and mysticism of his mother church. Henry wasn't just feigning interest any more. He'd grown to like Sasha, his enthusiasm and belief. Things that Henry was struggling to get back. But Sasha was an enemy of the Crown, he needed to keep reminding himself.

Henry and Sasha usually discussed literature. The Russian's passion for his country's classics was infectious and Henry had, half meaning it, promised to learn his language so that he could appreciate Pushkin, Pasternak and Bulgakov in the original. But that day, it was religion's turn.

Henry and Sasha were hard at it when the tiramisu

arrived. They discussed the Easter story. Though Henry knew that Sasha was an educated man, he looked blank when Henry spoke of the Last Supper, and Twelve Disciples. The mention of Judas drew a quizzical stare. The Garden of Gethsemane, utter puzzlement. Henry stopped the half test, half tease when Sasha shifted uncomfortably and averted his eyes downwards, sad.

"Sasha, I think you believe in your church and its teachings?"

"Of course, Henry; this is part of me, my life, being Russian. You do not feel the same about your church?"

"Well, I was raised Church of England, dragged to church every Sunday. I know the stories and the ritual. At Christmas, I join in the hymns and carols loudly and completely off-key. I'm pretty agnostic though. Never much thought about it, but I suppose I just follow our state religion."

Sasha had sighed and pushed away his non-compliant dessert. The mood was becoming too serious.

"Listen, Henry, I grew up in the ruins of the Soviet Union. My parents, teachers, uncles, aunts, nobody knew the Bible. There was nobody to teach us. This makes me feel bad, but it is not too late."

As often happened, Sasha brightened as an idea came to him. Leaning back, he beamed at Henry and tugged at his increasingly wayward beard.

"Let's go to church, Henry. Real Russian church. You will feel the beauty, the singing, the community, our soul. Maybe learn a little Russian too? Please say yes. Next Sunday, *Christos vaskres!* Christ is risen. I will see you outside the church at nine thirty exactly. Don't be late.

Every true Russian in London will try to get in, but I am friend of Father Evgeny. We will have no problems."

The date was agreed. This could be interesting.

Colin was expecting Henry's post-prandial call. Of course he should attend, if he could spare the time. Yes, the church was of real interest to him and his colleagues. Henry should know that the relationship between the Orthodox Church and the Kremlin had become very close and their mutual friend (names never used on the line, no matter how secure it was claimed to be) had no other obvious connections back to his masters in Moscow. Could Henry possibly meet the following Monday for a debrief? Usual hotel bar, one p.m.? Excellent. Their Easter services do go on a bit but the singing is divine. Enjoy it and keep your eyes peeled. Thanks, Henry. Click.

* * *

Henry made for the church on that beautiful spring morning. The walk across the royal park took him through drifts of daffodils. There was everything from washed-out pales to mimosas and then egg-yolk yellows, complete with orange trumpets. The palette extended for acre upon acre. It brightened his mood for his first ever Pashka and he rehearsed his part as he crossed the Serpentine. Just a walk-on role, a few lines, but he wanted to get it right. Dust down the old acting lessons.

At the end of their lunch earlier in the week, Sasha had enjoyed teaching Henry the Russian way to cross himself. Thumb, fore-finger and middle finger pressed together to represent the Holy Trinity, strictly crossing right to left. Franco, the restaurant's venerable major-domo, decided to join the fun, theatrically demonstrated his Roman version, emphatically left to right, whilst intoning a cod Latin blessing in a strong, sung baritone. Courtesy limoncellos had appeared to further lubricate the jollity, downed in a single slug, the Russian way. Henry decided to tip big time. After all, the Joint Russia Programme was picking up the tab. And, come Sunday, he hoped it would prove to be worth every last kopek to his handlers.

Flushed by their Lent-busting meal, Sasha had given his final lesson as they walked down Jermyn Street.

"Henry, at church on Sunday, when people say '*Christos vaskres!*' you just say '*Vaistinoo Vaskres!*' It just means you agree Christ is risen. Okay?" He had nodded his assent.

Sasha stopped abruptly, turning to face him, beaming down.

"Mr Bradbury, you are a good man and a true friend." His eyes were wet as he took Henry by both shoulders, stooped and kissed him three times.

"On Sunday you will be like a real Russian." With that the giant put on his battered fur hat and turned towards Piccadilly. Watching him amble away, Henry struggled with himself. Sasha was a decent bloke, for an enemy spy. Was he doing the right thing?

Turning into the tree-lined square in front of the church, Henry couldn't miss Sasha across the throng, towering above his fellow countrymen. Raising his fur hat in greeting, he beckoned him to join the queue.

Excusing his way through the hum of patient

29

congregants, Henry congratulated himself on his dress choice. The women, young and old, wore sober, shapeless coats set off with nondescript headscarves. As for the men, he blended in nicely. He had gone for head-to-toe black. Jeans, roll-neck sweater, soft leather jacket, trainers. The only things he had missed to complete his Orthodox Sunday best was a chunky gold chain and Rolex.

Sasha was chatting quietly with a few men ahead of him in line. He greeted Henry with a bear hug but made no effort to introduce him. One of the men was chewing something and produced a bag of black sunflower seeds. He offered a handful to Sasha who politely refused. Henry smiled broadly and cupped his hand. He needed to fit in. The thick-set man scowled and silently poured out a ration before turning back to his friends.

Sasha shook his head and whispered, "Henry. Please put the *semechki* in your pocket. This is a peasant thing. Not for people like you and me."

At that moment, he caught sight of Sasha's friend, Archpriest Evgeny Popov. As wide as he was short, with an impressive fair beard and sharp, watchful blue eyes, the priest stood at the top of the stairs. Women nearby ducked their heads in respect, though at this stage of the proceedings he wore a black hat and simple dark cassock with a plain wooden pectoral cross.

"Come, Henry. Father Evgeny will take us in. He is my, errr, *dukhovnik*." Sasha searched for the word. "My confessor," he said, relieved he could explain and evidently glad he was on the fast track to the sacrament of repentance.

"We all need one of those," Henry sighed as he tried to

keep pace with the long reach of Sasha's legs bounding up the marble stairs to greet the archpriest.

Sasha bowed his head in reverence. The fat little priest, standing three full steps above him, still had to look up to give his blessing. Sasha crossed himself and Henry decided to follow suit. He met Evgeny's unblinking gaze and smiled awkwardly. Nothing back. This was becoming a habit. Evgeny turned in silence and the two men dutifully followed through the church doors.

Inside, all was still quiet. Four or five vergers, women selling candles and communion wine, a young man setting up a camera on a tripod. Then a row of old parishioners already installed in chairs directly in front of the glittering icon screens, this morning catching the full force of spring sunshine through the higher windows of the church. Those were the only seats in the house. Otherwise, the eastern rite of standing for hours on end would need to be observed. Feet echoing, the priest indicated a privileged spot and Sasha placed his backpack on the ground.

"Please wait here and hold my place, Henry. I will now go to confess."

Henry looked around and saw what seemed like half of London's Russians filing in through the rear doors, dignified, unhurried, bowed, as if resigned to their fate.

Sasha joined a group of penitents waiting for Father Evgeny to robe up and reappear at the lectern to the left of the main screen. The increasing chatter rising in the church, together with a melancholy lone voice beginning sung prayer from an upper gallery, rendered Sasha out of earshot. But Henry had clear line of sight. He cast a nonchalant eye at Sasha now and again, cursing the fact that the Russians didn't seem to hand out prayer books; such a useful prop to flick through at times like these.

An apparition from nowhere, Father Evgeny was now at the lectern. Robes a riot of purple and gold, an elaborate enamel gold cross and a big hat that gave him much-needed stature. Swirling, sickly incense and a studied, theatrical serenity completed the tableau. As the line of confessants formed, he intoned a prayer. Then came the same ritual, one after another. Approach the priest, pray, explain your sins in front of your fellows, say your name, wait for the priest to place his stole over your head, receive absolution. Cross yourself and withdraw to join friends and family waiting in the nave.

Except for Sasha. Yes, the same routine, but with a deft embellishment that lasted less than a moment. A benefaction reserved only for him. Everyone seemed to miss it, except Henry.

The swap could have passed unnoticed when a large man blocked Henry's view by awkwardly removing an oversized sweater over his head at the wrong moment. But he just caught it. Unmistakable. As the priest reached up on his tiptoes to cover Sasha's head with the embroidered cloth, Sasha pushed a small buff envelope into a fat little hand and the priest reciprocated with an ancient black leather book which was slipped deftly into his coat pocket. Sasha really was getting special treatment, and Henry couldn't wait to impress Roddy and Colin with his surveillance skills.

Sasha crossed the aisle, found his place next to Henry and knelt. After a minute, genuflection turned to a full prostration with forehead touching the floor. Henry looked down, a little alarmed, and contented himself with a few novice signs of the cross whilst waiting for his Russian to resurface. He was taking his bloody time. And surprisingly agile for such a big man, Henry thought.

The church had filled up around him but half the congregation was still outside the handsome Victorian edifice when the service started. Full focus on the priestly sleight of hand had led him to neglect his new neighbours. He needed to watch everything if he was to progress from foundation-level spying. Annoyed with himself, he glanced around. Immediately in front was a young couple, blond and slim, with matching little son and daughter. Behind were four muscular men, each with hands folded in front of them, raised chins directed towards the altar. He clocked one as the sunflower seed man.

Finally, to his near right, a figure that he now realised for the past few minutes had been giving him his unconscious cues through his peripheral vision. When she bowed her shawled head, so did he. When she crossed herself, he followed suit. Now intrigued, he turned sideways, looking his puppet mistress full in the face, meeting her deep green eyes, almond-shaped and completely neutral. Not quizzical, not flirtatious, not annoyed, not friendly. Perhaps the passed-down legacy of countless generations of a people where one wrong expression could lead to oblivion?

He smiled at her. Third time lucky with the Russians? No. She just turned her head back to the icon screen and bowed to whatever she imagined lay behind it.

He should have been concentrating on the service, but he was now preoccupied with his neighbour. As MI5

Colin had said, the music was sublime. That was true. And the liturgical performance unfolding in front of him was astonishing. Lots of opening and closing golden screens, costume changes, hanging around for fifteen minutes whilst the bishop was sequestered, an ancient mystery kept well away from his flock. Screens suddenly thrown back to see the big man remove his crown to comb his hair in front of the altar. Seriously, what was that about? Precious little audience participation except for the odd "Amen".

On another day, Henry might have speculated whether the old Russian habit of public church confession he'd just witnessed might make their history of show trials that bit more understandable? Or if an ingrained habit of standing in awe whilst bearing silent witness to gilded opulence, enjoyed in elite male seclusion behind closed doors, might explain an acceptance of everything from the Soviet nomenklatura to London's oligarchs?

But he was preoccupied with his neighbour. Not impure thoughts. That wouldn't do in God's house. No. He was building a picture. She was Russian. Tall and shapely, heavy breasted under a long dress. Full shoulder-length chestnut hair. Lightly tanned. Forty? No make-up, glowing skin. Long, ringless fingers. God, he needed to stop this and concentrate on watching Sasha. That was why he was here.

Something was happening that brought Henry back to the here and now. The congregation was stirring, finally asked to participate. To his left he heard a strongly voiced "Sasha" and to his right the woman said, "Nataliya," loud and clear. Then the whole church hit the deck. Older worshippers on their knees, younger prostrate, foreheads on the parquet floor. Decision time. Sasha and Nataliya were already down on either wing and so he took the dive too.

He got down fine. Now came the tricky part. Prayers finished and a bell rang behind the altar. The congregation started to rise. Henry cracked painfully up onto one knee before feeling a strong hand under his right elbow, guiding him to his feet.

"Perhaps next time you should start on your knees? Ease your way into our prayers?" Nataliya spoke to him in clear, clipped English.

Henry blushed, cursing under his breath. Most distressing was that he hadn't said a word. He had been convinced that he was pulling off his undercover operation masterfully. Acting the part. Maintaining character. So how did she spot him? Damn.

The whispered conversation began.

"Sorry. How did you know that I'm English?"

"You are obviously English. You couldn't be anything else!"

"I'm sorry. But why?"

"Because you apologise when you don't mean it. Very English. And you keep smiling at strangers. For us Russians, only imbeciles smile at people they don't know. Are you an imbecile?"

This was delivered softly and without emotion, but Henry sensed four pairs of eyes burning into the back of his head whilst the couple in front glanced back at him. Only Sasha seemed oblivious, enrapt by the bishop's homily which was now in full swing.

"That's a bit harsh, Nataliya." Henry was angry, but couldn't muster anything stronger. He was out of his depth and surrounded by Russians. Also, fascinated by his ice-cold neighbour. But he had got one thing right.

"How did you know my name is Nataliya?"

His neighbour had said her name reflexively in the liturgy and her eyes were now less certain, thin with suspicion, and also intrigued.

"Just a wild guess. It was a choice between Nataliya and Svetlana. Fifty-fifty chance of getting it right," he whispered back.

A moment's pause, and Nataliya smiled for the first time. A beautiful smile, animated by the tinted sunlight straining through stained glass. Henry gulped. Note to self: a little rudeness goes a long way here.

"My name is Henry Bradbury."

"I know. Sasha already told me about you." Nataliya tilted her head to one side, clearly enjoying watching her little joke sink in. Touché, he thought.

"Anyway, time to take communion. See you outside, Mr Bradbury."

Henry left the church and waited for ten minutes in the shadow of a plane tree, watching the communicants file out and thinking back to the enforced Sunday services in the Yorkshire village of his youth. A jolly vicar bidding farewell, besuited parishioners with colourful wives, the trip to the Wheatsheaf before the Sunday roast. Henry was starting to realise that Russians did things differently.

Sasha and Nataliya approached him, talking quietly. How did they know each other? They came down the steps slowly, two feet apart at the shoulder, looking straight ahead towards him, not at each other. Henry wondered whether he should report Nataliya to his spy handlers. How close were those two? It was starting to bother him.

Sasha got to him first, beamed down and took Henry by the shoulders.

"*Christos vaskres*, Henry! Happy Easter."

Henry tried to remember the response. A hesitant "*Vaistinoo vaskres*" bubbled up, much to Nataliya's entertainment. She had removed the headscarf and gave a throaty, unbridled laugh.

"Sasha tells me I'm to teach you Russian. Or at least try to. A lot of work to do before you are reading our classics in the original, I think. But we will start this Saturday. Ten o'clock sharp. The French café in Sloane Square. Henry, don't be late for me."

Sasha stood between them, evidently approving the union.

"Nataliya Aleksandrova is the best Russian teacher in London. Everybody says so. She also teaches English to the children of the most powerful Russian family here. You will learn everything from her."

Henry noticed that she didn't demur from Sasha's opinion. His phone was halfway out of his pocket when he aborted the idea of a show consultation of his diary. All three knew he would be there on Saturday, as instructed. The mobile was re-trousered and he kissed both his Russian friends farewell. Nataliya held his gaze for an extra second or two. Maybe just a cultural thing, but he hoped not.

There and then, he took the decision that it would be better not to mention his beautiful new Russian teacher to Roddy and Colin. Not for now, at least.

4

RUSSIAN LESSONS

Henry ordered Nataliya's usual flat white coffee at 09.51, and at 10.00 it arrived, along with his flustered teacher. He watched her slip into the booth. She barely acknowledged the waitress or Henry as she took her first sip. Henry blew softly into his hand cupped over his nose, checking for booze fumes from the night before. To his relief, the mouthwash seemed to be holding up.

"Good morning, Nataliya," he said brightly.

"*Pa russkiy, pozhaluysta*, Henry. In Russian, please."

Henry was groggy, but it was five months since he had met his teacher at the church and the basics of the language were now there. So he tried.

"Sorry, Nataliya. I will now speak Russian. How are you today?"

"Not great, Henry, if you must know."

He was just about keeping up, nodding his understanding.

"I am meant to be going to a wonderful Russian party on Friday night. One of the most important London parties of the year. I teach English to the children of Boris Borisovitch Aslanov. You have heard of him? Very rich and famous. I simply must, must, must go."

He nodded along, getting increasingly muddled with some key words.

"I was invited as the children's teacher, but the old pig I was asked to accompany is now taking a younger woman. He is a friend of Boris Borisovitch. I can do nothing. Most humiliating."

He was now showing his linguistic confusion.

"*Kak svinya!* What a pig!" growled Nataliya, with bilingual spleen, though Henry had got the Russian without need of translation.

Snapping back into her profession, Nataliya translated what she had said.

"I am sorry to hear that, Nataliya. What an idiot!" he managed in Russian.

Her green eyes were blazing gloriously, her beautiful mouth half parted in exasperation. He spotted an opportunity for both his spying and, well, for himself. Too good to pass up. The promise to Nea to cease and desist spying crept into his mind, unwelcome, to be swiftly ushered out by a heady mixture of excitement coupled with desire.

Henry had got to know Nataliya over the months. Smart, proud, suspicious. A Russian woman. So, he decided on a subtle approach.

"Do you need a date? Someone to accompany you?"

Nataliya nodded.

"Perhaps Sasha could be your 'plus one' instead?" he ventured, a picture of innocence.

He knew the answer already. As expected, Nataliya looked insulted and incredulous. And any pretence of speaking Russian ceased.

"Don't be ridiculous. Sasha is a nobody. He talks about books and classical music all the time. Not business, vacations, property, fashion. He is not modern. He has no money. And look at how he dresses! Henry, this idea of yours is absurd!"

This was working a treat, but he felt an irrational urge to defend his friend, Sasha's top-secret service for Mother Russia, his noble sacrifices, his old-world values. Thankfully he thought better of it.

"Nataliya, is it just Russians at the party? Would the Russian conversation be difficult for someone like me to understand?"

He attempted a winsome smile and prayed Nataliya was getting there. She looked him up and down and then smiled.

"Henry, please give me your business card."

He obliged, a suitably embossed red-and-gold Bonners crest at the top with his impressive-sounding but wholly meaningless job title below. Nataliya studied the card in silence and finally put it away in her purse which poked out of the orange Hermès bag.

"Henry, you are going to be my charming Englishman on Friday night. You will dress like an Englishman, talk like an Englishman."

Henry tried, and failed, to hide his delight at the invitation. His tailored dinner jacket might just need letting out; he'd better check as soon as he got home.

"You will also explain which university you attended and whether you rowed or played rugby. Was it Oxford, or Cambridge?"

Panic set in, alarm bells rang.

"Err ... Oxford, yes. Hereford College. Yes. And a boatie. An oarsman."

Henry thought of the day in 1983 when he ripped open the letter from Hereford College. Another rejection letter, hammered out on an old typewriter, wishing him luck with his future endeavours. He'd received almost the same one from RADA the previous week. The backup plan, a northern English plate-glass university, unfashionably within humming range of a motorway, had served him well. But that week scarred him for life. He sighed. Always trying so hard; too hard, Nea had told him. The golf club membership, Bonners, the City of London ... MI6. He so wanted to be on the inside. Occasionally the door opened ajar, but mostly it was slammed shut in his face. Now that his foot was firmly wedged in, he was not a man to walk away. Not Henry Bradbury. He knew he had to act, in every sense of the word.

Nataliya scribbled out the address of London's best Russian restaurant. She added *7 p.m., Friday*, underscoring it three times. Handing it to Henry, she excused herself to wash her hands. Henry watched closely as she sashayed to the back of the restaurant.

As his teacher disappeared up the stairs, he made a show of dropping his exercise book off the table onto the banquette where Nataliya's bag sat. Reaching over to retrieve it, he flipped open her purse and looked for a UK driving licence amongst her cards. It was the first item that came to hand. Briefly placing it on his lap, he photographed it with his phone. It was back in place within five seconds and Henry admired his handiwork on the glowing small screen:

1. *ALEKSANDROVA*
2. *Ms Nataliya Antonova*
3. *11.11.1979 RUSSIA*

He scanned further down.

8. *Flat 58, Mafeking House, Sloane Avenue, London SW3 9QT*

By the time Nataliya returned, Henry had the Russian picture book open at the happy Ivanov family, pen poised, ready for the lesson to begin. His pulse was racing, a wayward pupil who had just played quite a trick on teacher.

Later, on the tube trip home, he had more time to consider his morning's work. At least three new boundaries transgressed with Nataliya. Namely: deception, impersonation, and rummaging through her crocodile-skin bag.

Just spycraft, he thought, casually absolving himself.

Truth be told, he wanted to be at the party as badly as Nataliya. And the time had now come to mention her to Roddy and Colin. How else could he further advance his services to Her Majesty's Government? By consorting with Boris Aslanov and his courtiers on Friday night. And what would Nataliya wear? She was already stunning in her weekend ensemble of joggers and trainers. Henry couldn't wait.

* * *

Monday morning, and Rosemary was waiting for Henry as he made his way across the acre of open-plan desks that now constituted the seventh floor of Bonners' head office, an expanse of young faces locked on to computer screens.

Henry had exchanged the 07.29 train from the suburbs into the City of London for a fifteen-minute stroll from Shoreditch. He didn't miss the grey-faced commuters, that woman who obsessively consulted her compact for the full forty minutes of the journey, the young chap who never stopped drumming his fingers on the table, the hard-masticating crisp eater who savoured every crunch until they pulled into platform twelve.

Now a free man, he was testing Bonners' new "agile working" policy to its very limit. For his youthful, ambitious colleagues, it was an early morning scramble to secure a narrow strip of desk for the day, or failing that, back to working from a small bedroom with noise-cancelling headphones for company.

But thankfully, he had Rosemary.

"Morning, Rosie. Thanks for getting me a spot sorted out. Not a bad one. Oh, and for setting up my computer."

She now worked "with" him as his executive assistant, as she had for the past ten years. But when they had first met, twenty years earlier, she worked "for" him as his secretary. A subtle shift in prepositions and job title, all part of the fake democratisation of their workplace. But Rosie was loyal and patient and this was one of those increasingly common occasions when Henry wondered whether, in fact, it was he who now worked "with" her.

"How was your weekend, Henry? We missed you on Friday afternoon." He detected a hint of both reproach and conspiracy.

"Oh, yes, sorry about that. I got some bad news and needed a bit of space."

All true, he thought. He was prepared to lie through his teeth to his Russian acquaintances, but his limit with Rosie was blustering British obfuscation. He had to draw the line somewhere.

"Things got better at the weekend. In fact, my Russian teacher invited me to a fancy party on Friday so I will actually get to practise. Wish me luck."

"That sounds fun. And speaking of Russians, you've got a Mr Orlov in the diary at ten. I've booked a conference room downstairs: tea, coffee and biscuits. Then your diary says you are meeting Mr Brown and Mr Jones at the usual place for lunch. Would you like a cab, or will you walk?"

They went through his diary for the week. It was sparse, Henry realised. He also suspected he was living on borrowed time at Bonners. And so, evidently, did Rosemary.

"Just one other thing, Henry. The new talent coach has asked for a touchdown. She's called Celeste and has apparently been assigned to you."

He felt his face flush and he scrolled across his diary, consulting a few dates in the following month.

"Sorry, Henry, but she wants to see you this week. She was quite insistent, pushy in fact. Apparently, she needs to review a few issues with you. Something like that, anyway. We've pencilled in a time for the two of you to meet in the Talent Suite."

Rosie was standing over him, smiling.

"Don't look so worried. I'm sure she won't bite."

When Henry joined Bonners in 1985, there was a friendly office on the fourth floor called Personnel. It had provided him with a steady supply of luncheon vouchers and also girlfriends sporting velvet headbands and wax jackets. But over the decades it had slowly but inexorably mutated, via Human Resources, into the now truly terrifying Talent, Respect and Inclusion Hub. Every time the lift stopped at the fourth floor, he now flinched.

Henry assented to the meeting with a shrug of resignation. It had been a good run at Bonners, he thought. Probably time for him to exit stage left.

5

A WEB OF SECRETS

Sasha Orlov arrived early for his meeting at Bonners and had already been ushered into the meeting room when Henry appeared. The Russian was hunched over a projector, connecting his laptop. An image appeared on the projection screen as his machine booted up. He whistled with relief and then sensed Henry behind him.

"Mr Bradbury. How good to see you in your place of work."

"Welcome to Bonners, Sasha. And you must remember to call me Henry here. In Britain, it is now illegal to use surnames at work."

Sasha didn't seem to get the joke, but grinned anyway. He towered tall, replacing his usual giant's hunch with a conscious display; shoulders thrown back, chest out, on parade.

"I am so very honoured to give my presentation to you at this most famous and prestigious company. I so hope you find my work valuable to your great organisation and your famous clients. This is an important day for me indeed, Henry."

As Sasha fired up his presentation, Henry poured the coffee and reflected on how to handle the meeting. At the outset, Roddy and Colin had set him two challenges.

Firstly, befriend Sasha, find out what he was up to, who he knew, what his vulnerabilities were, what might make him change his mind about serving Mother Russia and work for their British Crown instead.

Secondly, ensure he stayed in London, at least for a while. Roddy said Sasha needed money. Apparently, illegal Russian agents had to pay their own way to avoid detection. And also give him hope, instructed Colin; string him along, feed him with the promise of a contract with Bonners. Humour him whilst we prepare our endgame.

And that was what this morning was about. Sasha had wanted to demonstrate his research to Henry since they first met. He put it off for as long as possible. But the time had come, and this was Sasha's big break. He looked nervous, looming over the projector whilst leafing through a thick sheaf of handwritten notes.

Henry decided to take control of the situation.

"Sasha, come on, there are just two of us here and we're friends. Why don't you just sit down, drink your coffee, and we can talk through your model? That would feel more relaxed, wouldn't it?"

Visibly relieved, Sasha sat next to Henry. Henry tried to break the ice.

"Thank you so much for introducing me to Nataliya, Sasha. She's an excellent teacher and a great person."

Sasha looked troubled.

"Henry, she's a very good teacher. This is true. I am not so sure a great person. Please be careful with her. There are some stories I hear …"

Sasha's subsequent silence left him puzzled but cautious about digging further. That wasn't the objective of this meeting. And he wondered if he would rather not know.

Time to get down to the matter at hand.

"I think all businesses need to understand which companies have best leaders who will make big profits, and which ones have bad directors who will take risks and ruin business. Is this not correct, Henry?"

"Absolutely correct, Sasha. If you know how to work that out, you have struck gold."

Sasha grinned broadly.

"Then we will be rich men, you and me. For I have the answers here."

Sasha pointed at the white projector screen. A set of four graphs appeared. Henry couldn't make out the labels on the axes, but could see two lines following each other very closely on each graph. He was humouring Sasha, but was also now intrigued.

"I have studied the boards of directors of two hundred companies around the world. I study everything about them; sometimes I work twenty hours a day. It is my passion. I feel I know them all now," said Sasha with conviction.

"Fascinating," he answered, quietly wondering

whether his research might also be of interest to Sasha's bosses in Moscow. Useful profiling.

"I look at everything I can find and now I know how to predict who will win, and who not to trust. Who is good, who is bad. I predict from board history and can tell the future. Every time."

Sasha now had Henry's full attention. This was actually interesting and he might kill three birds with one stone. Sasha, happy and in place with a contract and some money. A delighted British intelligence odd couple. And something clever and new to take to Bonners that might save his job, at least for a while.

Sasha pressed on.

"Four things to look at, Henry. So, four graphs. Work every time, you will see. First thing. Experiences of directors. How many years, how much education? Graph one. More experience correlate to more profit, less risk. Bingo, as you English say."

Sasha was on a roll, sensing Henry's growing enthusiasm. Henry tested the work, asked a few questions. Sasha came through with flying colours.

"Second thing. Graph two." Sasha waved his shovel of a hand at the screen. "You know average number of boards that directors are members of, Henry? Number is four. So look at how other three businesses do. Good profit or bad risk? Good directors join all good boards, not crap ones. Again, perfect match."

He asked more questions and looked at the spreadsheet with Sasha.

"This is remarkable, Sasha. This really works."

Sasha gripped his arm a little harder than was

comfortable. He tensed as he wondered what that hand could do to his windpipe if Sasha realised his game. Colin had casually told him that advanced unarmed combat was part of the four-year SVR training for illegals. He was literally sticking his neck out here. He needed to keep this conversation on an even keel.

"It gets better. Now a new thing, nobody looks at this before. So, unique insight. Graph three. Height of board, Henry. Height of board!"

Sasha jumped out of his seat, huge and triumphant. Henry pushed his chair back, startled and confused.

"Sorry, Sasha. Maybe a little language difficulty. You don't mean height? H-E-I-G-H-T?"

"Exactly what is meant, Henry. Average height of all directors. Tallest boards, best leaders and profits. Shortest, bad decisions and lose money. Always. Iron rule."

He gestured for Sasha to sit back down.

"Sorry, Sasha, but how could you possibly know the height of a board?"

Sasha was obviously expecting the challenge and opened a new programme on his computer.

"Henry, this is the Phenotype programme. 'Phenotype' means things easy to see about a person: height, eye, skin colour, hair colour. Bald, or big hair. Beard. Moustache. Even lipstick. All boards like to take nice photos of themselves and put at front of reports. They love being in pictures. Makes it so easy for me."

Henry decided not to argue with that. Too right.

"Clever American Phenotype programme here. Look. Great for instant profile. Just put in picture of directors …"

Sasha smiled archly as he dropped Bonners' very

own board into a window on the computer. A bar started to build across the projector screen, and the word "Calculating" pulsated.

"And you see, your own directors' average height is … 178.2 centimetres. Congratulations, Henry! You have excellent bosses. Tip-top. Look. Bonners in top five per cent. A great board."

Henry slumped back in his chair, contemplating a picture of twelve white men in matching blue suits with tieless white shirts. They were grinning across a polished oak table twelve floors above where Sasha and he now sat. Two women flanked them, also in blue: the terrifying chief talent officer and the sad-looking company secretary.

This was going to be difficult. A lot at stake. He spoke carefully.

"Look, Sasha, this was going so well until now. Your first two board tests are brilliant. Just what we're looking for. I could sell that to my colleagues."

Sasha slammed his hand down on the table in triumph.

"But I'm sorry, the height thing is terrible. I can't show this to anyone, even if it is true. Which I don't believe for a second."

Sasha's eyes blazed. Anger? Frustration? He had to proceed with caution.

"But this is finest correlation I have. Two hundred companies studied. Two thousand directors. Totally accurate. I show you analysis. What is the problem?"

"Women are usually shorter than men, correct?"

Sasha nodded in agreement.

"So, boards with more women are on average shorter. Also correct?"

Sasha looked bewildered but had to agree.

"So, your work suggests that boards with more women make less money and screw up. Is that what you are saying?"

Sasha brightened.

"Henry, you have such great brain. Of course, you are right. I now understand why tall is good!"

Henry did all he could to compose himself.

"That is absolutely not what I am saying. All the other research I've read says that more women in leadership makes for better decisions. And, more importantly, I could get fired if I showed this to Bonners."

Sasha looked dejected.

"Dare I ask what the fourth graph shows?"

"Graph four. Happy boards, all laughing at camera, terrible. Serious boards, not smile, hard face, stare at photographer so he tremble, big profits and success. This also very true. But maybe you don't like this either, Henry?"

Henry contemplated the giant squeezed into the office chair right next to him.

"Look, Sasha, I suspect that is true. It's actually a very good insight, but it might upset a lot of senior people in the City who have progressed to the top largely based on height and a very good set of teeth. They would quietly like the height bit, but not the grinning insight."

Sasha missed the joke. He was evidently thinking hard. Then he dropped his voice and leant in.

"Henry, you are like my uncle. I must tell you a secret, a big secret, that I can tell nobody else but you."

Game on. This could be another tasty offering for

Roddy and Colin over lunch today. There would be a lot to discuss. And everyone seemed to have their secrets. He had one. Sasha had at least two; he was an undercover Russian intelligence officer, but something else was about to drop. Nea had a troubling secret. It sounded like Nataliya had a juicy one. And his two luncheon companions inhabited a swamp of secrets.

While Sasha gathered his thoughts, an intriguing question occurred to Henry. Were all these secrets related? He recalled a conversation with Nea when she had talked about the "lizard brain". He now sensed his inner reptile hissing at him. Put the secrets together and solve the puzzle, it mouthed.

"Go ahead, Sasha. I will help you if I can."

"Henry, I am in such trouble. I need a contract with Bonners. Not much money. Maybe" – Sasha hesitated – "fifteen thousand pounds, to do anything you want. Change model. You name it."

Henry stayed silent.

"I need money so I can stay in London and finish my work here. I don't spend much. Live like student. No girlfriend. But I have no money left."

Henry nodded encouragement.

"If I have to go back to Moscow, I failed. Here, I am protected and safe. But in Moscow, I owe some bad people money. Bad investment. Before I did my research."

"A short board of directors, by any chance?"

Sasha glowered and, to Henry's alarm, tensed his fists, knuckles whitening. Henry remembered Colin's advice, yet another euphemism from the Joint Russia Programme. If the Russian were to "make a scene", back off immediately.

He pushed his chair back on its casters, closer to the door. Then Sasha spoke.

"That is not funny. The people I owe are dangerous. Brutal. They will hurt me. I cannot explain more, but other people now protect me. If I fail here and have to go back home, these other people will, how do you say, *oblegchit sani*… lighten the sleigh?"

"They will throw you to the wolves?" Henry ventured.

The horror on Sasha's face suggested that this might be a real possibility.

"Sasha, thank you for being honest with me. Always the best policy. I think we can work on the model and get you the contract. Win-win, as we say."

Sasha stood and wrapped Henry in a bear hug.

"Henry, I feel I can trust you with everything. A true English gentleman."

He could only agree.

* * *

Roddy and Colin were deep in conversation when Henry handed his coat to the receptionist. Conversing, but both with eyes firmly fixed on the entrance to the restaurant. Were they rehearsing something?

Colin got to his feet and indicated that Henry should sit between him and Roddy on the plush bench. He felt a little trapped by the arrangement, and there seemed to be a mood change from his handlers. More tense. A glass of Rioja arrived and was set in front of him.

"Your usual, Henry," said Colin.

"So how did it go with Sasha?" Roddy enquired,

holding his gaze, mouthful of teeth bared. No pleasantries this time. Straight to business.

"An interesting morning." Henry stopped there. His patience was starting to wear thin. He could play their game too – he was learning. Lapsing into hard-faced silence, he was going to turn the tables on the men from the Joint Russia Programme. After a tense minute, it had clearly worked. Colin painted on a smile and did his best impression of congeniality. Henry was pleased. He could out-act these blokes any day of the week. He had put them in recovery mode.

"Henry, you're doing a fantastic job for us. And your country. We can't thank you enough. If there's anything on your mind, we're your mates. You just tell us."

There was something troubling here. The tone of his answer was somewhere between direct and brusque.

"Are you sure Sasha really is who you say he is? He sometimes seems more like a daft lad rather than a highly trained Russian illegal. And you guys aren't infallible, by all accounts."

"We are positive," Roddy shot back, all toothy smiles. "One hundred per cent. Can't tell you how we know. But we do."

To his left, Colin gurned, bristled at his colleague, then spoke firmly.

"I can tell you this much, Henry. My service found Sasha. A lot of painstaking work and cancelled holidays for me. Then we brought Roddy and our MI6 friends in to support *us*."

Henry made a mental note of that, particularly the emphasis on who was in charge. That was interesting.

Roddy sucked in breath and then continued.

"As for being a daft lad, a good spy is a good actor. Sometimes it helps to play dumb. And illegals like our man sometimes need to stay in character for years at a time."

Now back to Colin.

"The other thing to remember is that Sasha is out here on his own. Nobody to consult. No office to go back to. No money except what he can earn himself. Any contact with Moscow is a risk to be minimised. That's where their judgement fails and mistakes creep in. He is lonely and you have his trust. That's worth a lot to us. You spotted the drop at the church. As I say, you're doing a great job for your country."

Henry kept up the cool act, hiding his pleasure. The door to that inner room of acceptance had just opened a few more inches. Now to push it wide open.

"He's come up with a half-brilliant, half-crazy business idea that he wants me to introduce to Bonners. I know you want me to help him, but as it stands I could get fired if I get involved. But I think I can make this work for us."

"Mate, we have to keep Sasha in London. Get him fully under our control. We are relying on you."

Roddy bared his full mouth of teeth whilst rolling a cocktail olive around his tongue. He nodded towards Colin and Colin nodded back. Something was coming.

"If you help us pull this off then Colin and I might be able to put you up for a Queen's award. Through one of our ministers. Perhaps an MBE. At a stretch, an OBE. 'For services to British exports', something innocuous like that. It happens more often than you might think. How does that sound?"

It sounded bloody marvellous. Just the ticket. Roddy and Colin beamed and awkwardly patted him on both shoulders. The door had swung wide open. Time for him to explain Sasha's work.

"Look, he's developed four ways of studying boards of directors. Two are excellent. I can sell those to Bonners. Two are mad. Essentially Sasha thinks hard-looking, all-male boards always do better than smiley boards with lots of women on them."

He paused for effect. Roddy and Colin looked mystified. Roddy broke the silence.

"We aren't businessmen, Henry. But Sasha's work makes sense to me. What's the problem?"

Henry stared back, eyes wide.

"The problem is, the gender thing is simply wrong. It goes against every other piece of work I've seen. And even if it was true, nobody in their right mind would touch it with a bargepole."

Roddy considered this for a moment and then snorted with nasal laughter. Heads turned in the restaurant. He leant in.

"I've got it. I know what Sasha is up to," Roddy said softly. "The crafty bugger."

Roddy pulled his phone from a pocket and scrolled until he found an image. Keeping the device firmly in his hand, he showed the grainy picture to Henry. A group of men in a clearing in a birch forest, standing in the snow. Blue sky. Thick padded jackets trimmed with fur. About twelve of them, several with rifles, and a mountain of brown fur prone in the foreground. It was a telephoto shot but on closer inspection Henry made out the mortal remains of a huge bear. The men were posing for a photographer, but not this one as they faced about thirty degrees off to the right.

After a couple of seconds, the phone was safely back in Roddy's pocket.

"Don't ask me how we got the shot, it was quite the coup. This is the entire management board of the SVR, Sasha's ultimate bosses. Moscow Centre. And as you can see, tall, male, and not given to smiling for the camera."

Roddy snorted again.

"In fact, I'm surprised Sasha didn't also factor in the combined weight of the board. Those fat bastards would be world-class."

Henry joined Roddy's laughter as he watched Colin. He decided this was all news to him too. Roddy continued.

"MI6 'community away days' are now truly ghastly. Building things with Lego, and lectures on 'unconscious bias', whatever the fuck that is. Role-playing how to give women difficult feedback. All management bollocks."

Roddy nodded towards Colin, who was sitting in stony silence.

"And Colin's lot are even worse. To be honest, mate, I think our Russian oppos have the right idea. Old school. Get as many large mammals in your gunsights as possible, then lashings of vodka and a patriotic singalong around the campfire. I'm quite envious."

Henry sensed he wasn't going to get much help from his handlers so moved the conversation on.

"Okay, I'll get Sasha to just work on the sensible stuff and drop the nonsense. And I can get him his money. I'll organise it today."

Roddy and Colin ordered a celebratory round of drinks.

When the waiter was out of earshot, Henry was ready to continue. On a roll, wondering if his old morning suit would still fit him for the trip to the Palace.

"There are two more things I need to tell you. I think you'll be interested. First, Sasha let me into a big secret."

Colin leant forward and stared intently whilst Roddy stiffened and sat back, staring into the middle distance. He wasn't expecting that.

"Sasha is terrified of going back to Moscow. He practically begged for the money to stay. Apparently, he owes some bad people money for a deal that went wrong. He said something about failing in London meant losing protection and getting hurt. I was quite worried for him."

A minute's silence followed the revelation. Roddy continued to stare at the restaurant chandelier, seemingly deep in thought. Colin twisted his linen napkin around his fingers. Finally, Colin spoke.

"Henry, this is really important for us to know. It's a classic. It's just what we've been looking for. Sasha's vulnerability. We can work with this. We can turn him. But we will need your help."

Henry was about to explore this when Roddy jolted out of his trance.

"You said you had two things to tell us, Henry. What's the second thing?" The question was terse and urgent.

"I've been invited to a party being hosted by Boris Aslanov. This Friday night. Is he of interest to you?"

"My goodness, Henry. He is very much of interest to us. We can't get close to him, and an invitation to one of his events is nearly impossible to come by."

Henry preened, but only for a second.

"So how *did* you come by the golden ticket?" Roddy asked sharply.

"Oh, I started Russian lessons five months ago. Once a week. And my teacher invited me. They teach Aslanov's kids English."

He tried to look innocent but coloured up.

Colin's tick went into overdrive before he composed himself, then spoke.

"How did you find this teacher? Who is he?"

Henry knew this wasn't going to be easy.

"It's actually a she. Nataliya. Sasha introduced us at the Russian Church. She's a very good teacher."

Roddy grinned, exposing his teeth.

"*Tak kak pozhivayat russkiy, Genry? Naskol'ko ty ponimaesh seeches?*"

Roddy's faultless sounding Russian took Henry by surprise.

"I didn't know you were fluent, Roddy. And to answer your question, the lessons are going fine and I can understand quite a lot."

Roddy smiled. Colin glowered.

"I'm surprised you didn't mention Nataliya to us earlier. Especially if she was introduced by Sasha. She could be anyone. Dealing with the SVR isn't a game, Henry. We can only protect you if we know what is going on." Colin was angry and turned his face away to hide his twitching. On his other side, Roddy clenched his eyes tight and gurned theatrically, lips spittled, smirking towards Henry. He was evidently pleased with his little impression of his partner.

Henry reached into the breast pocket of his suit and

pulled out a folded single sheet of paper. It was a printed scan of Nataliya's driving licence. Colin made to take it but Roddy was quicker off the mark. He intercepted it, took a look and smiled again.

"Well, well, Henry. You're single, aren't you? Gadding about town? I can certainly see the attractions of the lovely Nataliya. If I was in the market for Russian lessons, one could do much worse. Very attractive." A gentle whistle escaped through his teeth, arranged like the ivory keys of a grand piano. He examined the page further before putting it in his pocket.

"I will get my people to check her out. But I'm sure she is as clean as a whistle. And I think we should in fact thank you. Learning Russian off your own bat and getting an invite to the court of King Boris Aslanov? You've had a busy time."

Henry gulped at his wine and avoided eye contact.

"Colin, how about a fair division of labour, mate? I'll take care of the Nataliya question, and you get Henry ready for his big night out. Perhaps get your boffins to sort him out with some new eyewear?"

Colin started by ignoring Roddy but then seemed to think better of it. He asked for Henry's spectacles and he obliged, blinking as he tried to refocus. Colin studied the round, thick-lensed tortoiseshell glasses. Then he started to polish them with his napkin.

"You need to get your prescription from your optician and call it in to me. The usual number. This afternoon. Then we'll meet on Thursday morning for a rehearsal, sound and vision check. Somewhere noisy so we can put you and the technology through its paces. I'll text you the meet details. And from now on, no cutting corners on security. Aslanov isn't a nice character. So the proper drills, please."

Colin returned the spectacles to him.

The bill arrived and Roddy produced the usual bundle of cash. He couldn't resist having the last word.

"One other thing, Henry. If you do get lucky with Nataliya after the party, and I sincerely hope you do, remember to leave your specs outside the bedroom. The last thing you want to do is give Colin and his deviant colleagues a live-streamed performance, now, do you?"

6

WAITING FOR MAURICE

Colonel Oleg Pinchuk packed away the hotel hairdryer and inspected himself in the vanity mirror. The blow-dry had given his hair the required body. Restoring his blond hair with dye had been the afternoon's project. Now he trapped it in place with a generous misting of hairspray. The manicure case was open in front of him and ten neat nail clippings sat in a coffee cup, together with a scattering of discarded black *semechki* husks. These remnants of the sunflower seeds he chewed constantly served as a Russian spy's hourglass. The bigger the pile, the longer he had been waiting for one Englishman or another to knock at his door. More often than not, they didn't come. Pinchuk calculated he had spent half his career in lonely hotel rooms. London, Lisbon, Prague, Helsinki. Waiting for an Englishman.

His suite was on the seventh floor and commanded views of both Helsinki's central railway station and harbour. Light was starting to fail and the car ferries banged and crashed metallically, loading up their cargo before heading off into the darkening Baltic. But the colonel was more interested in the train on platform six. The grey-and-red liveried *Lev Tolstoy* would be pulling out for Moscow in ninety minutes, and Pinchuk needed to be on it.

Time was running out for MAURICE.

He carefully arranged five identical brochures on the desk. In Russian, English and German, they glossily explained his company's full range of stationery products in excruciating detail. His business cards, also carefully stacked, made clear he was the Nordic sales manager for a leading Russian paper exporter. One of his six passports sat alongside the return first-class sleeper ticket. It was a standing joke amongst the clerks at Moscow Centre that the colonel insisted on a birth date at least fifteen years younger than his real sixty-six years. But what Pinchuk wanted, Pinchuk got.

Pinchuk was known as a stickler for operational detail. He insisted on being booked into a suite. Not for comfort but to double the difficulty for a hostile surveillance team. More doors to check, double the space to cover, double the trouble for MI6 or a local team to make an entry without falling into a counter-surveillance trap. And for a meeting like today's, he would usually have insisted on bringing a hand-picked set of watchers to secure MAURICE's route in. Not amateurs from the Saint Petersburg station nor, God forbid, the Helsinki SVR *rezidentura*. Only elite members of his own ABSALOM squad.

But now Pinchuk had taken a calculated gamble. For the first time in twenty-six years, MAURICE had signalled for a crash meeting. As agreed, a prearranged rant about immigrants in a thread in the online *Daily Mail*, posted by Derek of Ilford, had turned his entire ABSALOM team out of bed. And sent the colonel trundling through the Russian night, across the Finnish border. And, unless he was panicking, MAURICE knew the rules. Any sign of a problem, any bad feeling in his gut, and he would abort the meeting. At least, Pinchuk prayed he would.

Twenty-four hours alone with his own company meant no escape from his own thoughts. He should have retired at the statutory age of fifty-five. He could have gone a lot earlier. For plodding officers that was pensionable age. But the Centre gave true Chekists, the risk-takers, men like Oleg, three years' pension rights for every year served. They were good like that. And, of course, there were the bank accounts in Lugano and Malta. But Pinchuk wasn't in this hotel room for the money. He was here for ABSALOM, his life's work.

Englishmen. After all this time, they still had the ability to surprise. In countless hotel rooms, Pinchuk had laughed with them, cried with them, drank whisky with them, flattered them, threatened them, flirted with them and, as required, made love to them. Even killed them.

There was the absurdly pompous former Lord Mayor of the City of London. Nobody at Moscow Centre could quite understand why he offered to betray Britain's innermost financial secrets in return for dressing up and parading around Red Square. In SVR number one dress uniform, or as a Russian Admiral of the Fleet, together with a chest weighed down with service medals. But that was all he ever asked for. On his third visit he was interviewed by a panel of central bankers who swiftly concluded that he was a financially illiterate middle manager with nothing to offer. But they let him keep the uniforms all the same.

Then came the intense, awkward young Oxford graduate he had picked up at the Hungry Duck bar by the Kuznetsky Most in Moscow. The Wild East days of 1991. First the Russian girls were allowed in for two hours to drink for free. Then a horde of inadequate Western men were unleashed. Pinchuk's target had bad breath and didn't speak a word of Russian; all he wanted was a girlfriend. Pinchuk procured three for him. All at the same time. In the same bed. Long returned to London, the man with the disquieting stare and odd ideas remained eternally loyal.

But most repulsive of all was the Cambridge don. His visits to Russia always began with the ritual presentation of a painted icon. Then followed a candlelit dinner with a handful of underage boys. The next morning, the professor demanded a private service of absolution from an Orthodox priest. Thankfully, one of the SVR's in-house chaplains shared similar proclivities and was more than happy to oblige.

The colonel felt a trifle nauseous as he remembered his back catalogue of British traitors.

Pinchuk's stock-in-trade was understanding the British – their motivation, their manifest weaknesses. On reflection, even in his early days of Soviet spying, he didn't think he had ever met a radical Englishman. They might be able to mouth whole sections of *Das Kapital* or *The Communist Manifesto*. They knew the slogans. But get them drinking and talking and they just wanted revenge. Or to exorcise guilt. Usually both. Against their parents, their schools, their universities, their wives, their clubs. They wanted to pull down the pillars of their own temple.

And then came new Russia. A gift for Pinchuk, the KGB and British sybarites alike. The pitch got easier and there were plenty of takers. No awkward ideology. Just money, sex and advancement. ABSALOM started to ride high.

Pinchuk looked down through the gloam at the illuminated station clock. He would need to check out of the hotel in half an hour. This was getting tight. It would be Svetlana's fortieth birthday tomorrow. A party for two hundred guests at the house by the lake. Fireworks. All five of his children there. But not just that. Operational practice told him to start packing.

Pinchuk was a fastidious packer. Shoes in a separate compartment, the right ones built up by two inches, partly compensating for his short leg, helping him with his limp. Neatly folded suit and shirts. Two Hermès ties. Cufflink box. A black leather belt that concealed a handy, industrial-strength garrotte wire. Finally, his silver-framed family photograph. It showed Pinchuk with his arm around the waist of a short, fat woman of his own age. Dyed red hair. She's wearing a bright lime tracksuit and they are flanked by two oafish young men. The Centre's idea. Were they taking the piss? The sort of family a traveller in stationery might acquire. Repulsive people dragged in off the street. Pinchuk shuddered.

Svetlana was the third Mrs Pinchuk. Wife number one had been a mistake. Married young when he joined the KGB Academy. He had thought her kind, loyal and a little simple. She stayed in Moscow whilst he screwed his way across London. On his return from his first posting, Soviet divorce came easily. Later, Pinchuk heard that she had been seeing a KGB major in his absence and now lived a comfortable life with him in Monaco. Good for her.

The second Mrs Pinchuk was an altogether more complicated affair. Yulya. A talented artist, she splattered and scraped at enormous canvasses whilst the Soviet Union collapsed around them. She'd set up her workshop in an abandoned Communist Party office and attracted a wide range of artists, musicians and reformers to her salon. Her parties were notoriously wild. Hammer and sickle flags burned. A dub reggae version of the Soviet national anthem played. Pinchuk could stomach that. Just.

But the second Mrs Pinchuk's intimacy with a Georgian poet of her circle crossed a line.

Even by the standards of Moscow in 1992, the crime scene was grim. The Georgian, an ardent nationalist to the last, had expired on the wooden floor of the studio. Arms splayed and hands nailed to the boards, palms skyward. A flag with a red cross on a white field had been stuffed into his mouth. The flag of Saint George.

For her art, Yulya favoured a high-powered spray gun that delivered oil-based paint to canvas with considerable force. The results were spectacular. Not least when the gun drenched her and a flicked match followed. She had tried to get Pinchuk interested in performance art. The colonel thought back and smiled. Tied to a chair, she had given a remarkable seven-minute show that rounded off her career nicely.

Pinchuk had stood with the police sergeant as they surveyed the smouldering horror.

"The work of Chechens," said Pinchuk. The sergeant asked Pinchuk how to spell "Chechens", closed his notebook and offered a weary salute.

A Finnish Lutheran church clock near the hotel struck the hour. Pinchuk shook his head and locked his suitcase. He rose wearily.

Then the knock came. He would recognise that fist anywhere. It was MAURICE.

7

A RAINY DAY IN LONDON TOWN

LONDON, SEPTEMBER 2019

Sensed it standing by my bedroom window. Dense black mass in the shape of a man. It watched me and shifted its weight from one foot to the other. Then the smell. Sweet putrefaction. (Like when I left those lilies to die in the Tom Dixon vase and went away for the weekend). Then I made for the apartment door and sensed it following me. Couldn't open the door and rattled the security chain desperately. Think I tried to talk to it as it got closer. Over my shoulder. It just stayed in the shadows. Woke in a cold sweat.

HB's Dream Diary
Thursday, 19 September 2019

Henry hid the little book away in its usual place. Lying back on the bed, he listened to the insistent rain on the skylight above him. Brown leaves were making their way down the glass, caught in the rivulets that streaked the grey London sky. He wanted to see Nea. The dreams were becoming troublesome. And dreams were her thing.

It had been at the third or fourth therapy session when Nea asked Henry and Jane about their dreams. Henry went first and described a recurring scene. He was on a train that was about to leave the station when he realised that he hadn't packed his belongings before leaving his hotel. He went through a list of everything he had left behind, and panicked. It was nearly all his possessions. That was the point when he always woke. Jane had laughed at his dream. She said that her dream was checking in at an airline counter, one-way ticket in hand. When Nea asked how this made her feel, Jane threw her head back. "Ecstatic!" Henry remembered holding back the tears, knowing then that their marriage was finished.

The shadow had started to intrude on his nights around the time Roddy and Colin did the same to his days. This new dream subsumed the old one. He wondered whether it was their shadow, or his own? Or a third party. Person or persons unknown. The more the odd couple from British intelligence asked of him, the more risks he took, the more the figure appeared to him. Sometimes sitting at the foot of his bed, sometimes blocking his bedroom door. But always mute.

Nea had suggested that he speak to it, a cheery hello, even a hug. Make friends with the dark void. Easier said than done; it scared him shitless. And he wasn't sleeping well. But Nea would have to wait. He had his mission.

Henry steamed the milk into his cappuccino and

consulted the diary on his phone. The appointed hour with Celeste from Talent, Respect and Inclusion was there. Four p.m. today. In their lair, euphemised as "The Hub". Maybe that was what the dream foreshadowed?

Otherwise, he had blocked out this morning's diary with "Working from home". He was waiting for Colin's summons.

At 9 a.m. sharp, the text arrived from "Caller ID withheld".

Please board the westbound Thames clipper boat at 10.23 this morning from Tower Bridge pier. I will see you at the bar. Remember your drills. Really important now. C.

He needed to get moving. In the closet, he rooted around for his fluorescent helmet, bicycle clips and collapsible commuter bike. Then he chose his bright-yellow waterproof jacket from the coat rack. Finally, he packed a nondescript grey hoodie together with a dark-blue baseball cap into an old canvas tool bag that had been left in the apartment by the builders. The direct cycle ride down to the river should have been short, but events were intervening. The bad dream and then Colin's message had conspired to spook him. He thought through his route carefully.

Heading out from home, he mounted the wet pavement and darted the wrong way up several narrow medieval streets. Hanging Sword Alley, Oystergate Walk, Castle Baynard Street, all flashed by before he turned south towards the Tower of London. Speeding across slick cobbles into a long pedestrian underpass, he braked sharply alongside an unlit row of bicycle stands, part hidden in a niche in the tunnel wall. The bike was quickly secured and he doubled back towards daylight. A quick change, and the previously luminescent commuter now passed for a bricklayer or electrician on his way to work. He was pleased with his amateur dramatics as he walked down the pier and saw his boat pass under Tower Bridge towards him. The stage had always been his real calling.

As the boat shuddered away and began its turn into mid river, he gripped at the guard rail. Rain was sheeting down and bouncing off the muddy chop of the Thames. The ancient White Tower hulked above him as the boat spun on its axis. A water spout gushed out of a drain right next to the blocked-up arch with the words, "Entry to the Traitors' Gate". Was he really going to make Sasha a traitor? Was he himself treacherous? To Sasha and Nataliya? Food for thought.

Henry sighed. Abandon all hope, ye who enter here. He left the back deck to find Colin.

The boat's coffee tasted oddly burnt and he sipped it tentatively. Colin was all reassuring smiles as they sat on plastic bucket seats. They were on the open deck but under cover, facing back down the Thames as the City of London sped by. Colin conveyed Roddy's abject apologies. Called away on urgent business, apparently.

"Did you lose your bicycle somewhere along the way?" teased Colin.

He was pleased. They must have had an MI5 covert surveillance team reporting on his every move. But a downward glance from Colin put him right. He coloured up.

"Unless you always wear bicycle clips to keep your chinos neat and tidy," Colin joshed, and Henry's nerves reminded him that he was casting off into the unknown.

Colin produced a smart glasses case and handed it to him. Opening it, he found an identikit pair of spectacles to his own.

"Try them on for size. Then we'll do a signal check. This has to work tomorrow night. There's a lot riding on you."

The spectacles were a perfect fit. Colin explained the eyewear.

"A tiny camera and highly sensitive directional mic in the bridge of the specs. Undetectable. Keep the case in your pocket. It relays the signal to us. We won't be far away. Put the glasses back in the case after three hours. The case also charges them. Ten minutes and they'll be ready again." Colin had to raise his voice over the noise of the engines and the wash of the churning river.

"Now I'll go to the front of the boat, and you need to make some friends here on the aft deck."

Colin smiled at Henry's evident discomfort as he surveyed the handful of fellow passengers braving the elements.

"Don't fret, Henry. Good practice for Friday night. All part of our basic training, in fact, working a room. Or in this case, a deck. I'll go inside to check things with my technician. You should stay on the boat until Westminster Pier and then be on your way."

The reality of what he was about to do hit him for the

first time. He had read articles about Boris Aslanov. He could read between the lines. Powerful and ruthless. He was scared.

"What exactly do you want me to find out tomorrow night? At Aslanov's party?"

"Roddy will be in touch with a briefing before you get there. Aslanov and his ilk are his brief. But just relax, Henry. Follow the drills and absolutely nothing can go wrong." With that, Colin was gone.

Henry pushed the spectacles up his nose and nervously studied the deck. A young couple with oversized rucksacks sporting the Danish flag. A businessman in a Burberry raincoat. Was he Japanese? An older Black couple huddled together, laughing despite the driving rain. Or because of it? And a pretty young woman in a nurse's uniform under a purple poncho. This was it. His prey.

He stood up and lurched towards the back rail. The boat shifted under him and he was propelled, crab-like, towards the businessman. The choice had been made for him. Grasping at a stanchion with one hand whilst scalding the other with coffee. He came up just short of the alarmed-looking man, letting out an involuntary yelp.

"Christ. Sorry about that. A near miss. I'm afraid I haven't got my sea legs today."

The businessman looked bemused and studied Henry's reddening hand. He pulled a white linen handkerchief from his pocket and offered it to him.

"I think you might have burnt yourself. Please, wrap it in the handkerchief. You can keep it."

Henry offered profuse thanks.

"I'm not a regular on the river. Are you?"

The conversation went well. Mr Itoh was from Osaka but had worked as a banker in London for ten years. He loved England but not the weather. His children had become Londoners and he didn't really want to go home. He wished Henry the best of luck with his hand and politely suggested he take more care when moving around the boat.

Buoyed by his success, he made eye contact with the nurse. Blonde, late twenties. She moved towards him, holding the rail.

"I couldn't help notice your spill. Are you okay?"

He was on a roll.

He should run his hand under cold water for twenty minutes. And Emily worked at Saint Thomas's Hospital in the accident and emergency department. She was originally from a small village in North Wales but she found London much more exciting. Though she missed her parents and dog, Gelert. Her Italian boyfriend worked in IT. He was fun company but was now getting far too serious. He wanted her to meet his family and she wasn't ready for that.

Henry was starting to enjoy this and decided he was a natural. Acting was in his blood.

He was about to risk crossing the deck to charm the backpackers when Colin appeared from the cabin. Studiously ignoring Henry, he silently waved to Mr Itoh, Emily and the four other deck passengers. Laughing together, they joined Colin and disembarked at Embankment Pier. Henry watched them all get into a waiting minibus on the Embankment.

Very funny. He still had a lot to learn. But somehow this seemed like a valuable lesson in the theatre of espionage.

Henry knew his time at Bonners was running out. He just needed to secure a decent payout and be on his way. Was there an upper age limit for acting school? What about private medical cover and his mobile phone number? Henry acknowledged that his urgent summons to the feared "Hub" was overdue as he considered the green and blue beanbags. He plumped for the less humiliating velvet wingback chair instead. Framed posters on the wall showed a number of his youthful colleagues in various states of virtue. Picking up litter on an inner-city estate. Yomping up Mount Kilimanjaro for charity. Dancing on a Bonners' float during this year's Gay Pride parade. An enthusiastic rainbow of joy. A happy band.

But Celeste did not look quite so happy. Intense and northern English, she had the air of someone who would favour an exciting new psychometric test over a decent bottle of Rioja every time. She wore not one, not two, but three different security passes on a rainbow-coloured lanyard, projecting a sense of access to an inner sanctum that once would have been his by birthright.

She patiently explained her role, how she was looking forward to "reverse mentoring" Henry. He certainly wasn't an expert in body language, but sensed a dramatic dissonance between the talent coach's words and her posture. Nea had given him a useful crash course to help his dating – mirroring, matching, leading, following. Adapting a few of these to this "touchdown" with Celeste just wasn't working. The more he leant in, the more the young woman pushed her chair back. And then crossed her arms across her chest. She also studied his gauze-bandaged right hand with interest.

Celeste started with a question she already knew the answer to.

"How many times did you have to take the online 'Respect and Inclusion' course before you passed?"

His reply was, at best, a half truth.

"Four times."

In fact, he finally gave up and got Rosie to log in and complete it for him. Definitely worth the Jo Malone gift pack of delicious unctions he had left on her desk.

"Are some of these concepts difficult for you, Henry? Or is it that you don't agree with Bonners' policies and new direction?"

He spotted the trap and swerved around it. Time for some serious obfuscation. This was where Nea's brilliant idea of the little notebook would come to the rescue. As well as dreams, she'd asked him to write down words that he heard but wasn't sure of. His daughters provided a rich seam of these. As did Bonners. He had amassed four pages under the underscored heading "New Ideas". Nea had then patiently explained each mystery to him.

"Oh, definitely the former, Celeste. But I'm learning. I'm very interested in new concepts, actually. Never too late to adopt *new societal norms*." He enunciated his last three words loudly and swung his hand like an orchestra conductor for emphasis.

He began his incantation.

"Intersectional."

Celeste took a note.

"Neurodivergent."

Another note.

"Non-binary."

Celeste looked like she was relaxing.

"Heteronormative."

She was even smiling.

"Pansexual," he said with gusto. This was going well.

"Well done, Henry," encouraged Celeste.

"TERF!"

She looked suddenly confused. Henry was triumphant.

"Surely you know what a TERF is, Celeste?"

Her face darkened and she shook her head. He spelt it out in a sing-song voice.

"A Trans-Exclusionary Radical Feminist."

Now she looked irritated. Celeste opened her notepad and cleared her throat.

"That's all very impressive, but our senior management has determined that you will attend a pilot course we're trialling. Totally immersive, one week's residential, in one of the most deprived towns in the country. It's an opportunity for you to have some real, lived experiences. You'll be with people from walks of life very different to your own. You will work with them, talk with them, eat with them. Who knows? It could be life-changing for you."

Celeste grinned. He detected malice. He had had enough.

"Gaslighting."

She looked off guard.

"Gaslighting. Do you know what that means, Celeste?"

"Roughly. But do tell …" she sneered.

"It's a method of manipulation which slowly undermines the victim's perception and capabilities, until the victim finds themselves questioning their own sanity. It's a series of false assertions about the victim that build over time, making them question themselves and their worth. Making them a vulnerable outsider."

He slumped back deep into the comfy chair. Happy to have got that off his chest but also wondering what the hell he'd just done. He was about to find out.

Celeste smiled and produced a letter in a crested Bonners' envelope. She handed it to him.

"I'm afraid you don't fit the profile of a victim. At least not in my book. I've been authorised to give you this. It's an offer of voluntary redundancy. The terms are generous and, given your thirty years of service, we'll organise a fitting leaving party."

A swirl of emotions crowded in on him as he turned the sealed envelope in his hand. This was the final anchor of his old life being pulled up. Marriage gone. Job gone. Status gone. But also a welcome blast of freedom. A new horizon. Both fear and elation. He felt unexpectedly calm.

"Thank you, Celeste. Do I have any choice in this matter?"

Celeste looked down at her notes. She read, word for word, the response that had been approved by Bonners' legal team just hours before.

He could opt for the week in Burnley followed by a programme of regular "360-degree feedback" from junior colleagues. Bonners would also throw in a mandatory weekly performance improvement review with her. Or take the redundancy. A decision by Monday, please.

All eyes were fixed on Henry as he left the consultation. An open-plan sea of expectant faces. He intended to disappoint the lot of them. Shoulders back, head high, chest out, a cheery smile and a wave of manumission with the bandaged hand. Now it was his time to party.

8

AT THE COURT OF KING BORIS

Henry pushed the final stud into his dress shirt and adjusted his bow tie. The rain hammered on the skylight and he knew he was cutting things fine. He had heard nothing from Roddy. He had even resorted to putting on his magic MI5 spectacles and calling out to him through the ether. It had felt surreal and garnered no response.

Nataliya had just texted and made it clear that she didn't want to be announced at the party entrance without her escort in tow. He was to meet her in the restaurant lobby at seven o'clock sharp. A tall order with the rain; taxis would be hard to come by. But luck was on his side. As he stepped out onto the pavement, a London black cab immediately heaved into view, the welcome yellow glow of its lamp signalling it was available for hire.

He flagged the taxi down and gave the address. If the

traffic flowed, he would arrive just in time, but a line of stationary red tail lights ahead didn't bode well. Nataliya would not be happy.

"It's the rain, guv'nor. Not much we can do about it." The cabbie stared ahead. "What did you think of the footie last night? I thought Chelsea was a shocker. Diabolical."

Henry was irritated. He knew nothing of football and cared even less. And he needed to think through the evening ahead. He felt he could manage things without Roddy's briefing, but tension was building.

"Sorry, driver, but is there any way you can get me there quicker? I have to be there by seven. I'll double the fare if you can do that."

The white baseball cap with the England flag nodded.

"Gotcha. I'll give it a go, mate."

With that the taxi spun on its axis and headed up a narrow street at twice the legal speed limit. Then it took a right so sharply that Henry was slammed against the window. He gripped the door handle as the cabbie aquaplaned through a red light, catching the shocked faces of a couple who were about to cross the road in front of the cab but thought better of it at the last minute.

"Christ, slow down!" Henry shrilled.

The cabbie laughed. "But we don't want you to be late for Nataliya and Boris."

For the first time, Henry caught the driver's eye in the rear-view mirror. Roddy winked at him.

"Relax, Henry. I'll get you there in one piece. And in time for your party. There's a lot in this for me too."

The cab had slowed and Henry was getting his breathing back under control.

"You and Colin are developing a bad habit of messing with me. I'm getting fed up with it."

Roddy laughed, his full set of teeth shining in the mirror.

"You're in safe hands. I've done my Metropolitan police advanced driver's training. And the cab is one of theirs. They have four, in fact. Excellent for surveillance and picking up unsuspecting targets. Like you, for instance."

If Henry was meant to be impressed, he wasn't going to show it. He sat back in silence and watched the sulphurous lights of the city pass by.

"Anyway, we appreciate what you're doing for us. I've checked your specs and they are coming through loud and clear. Nataliya has only just left home so I will have you there before her. And the mission is straightforward."

Roddy had to shout through the glass partition. The noise of the wet road and honking of frustrated car horns was causing interference. He described what Henry should expect. British intelligence surveillance was out in strength tonight.

Sea buckthorn. Raspberry. Elderflower. Gooseberry. Chilli. Horseradish. The clinking of chilled bottles of infused vodka as crew-cut waiters in white jackets stock the bar before fetching the Absolut Crystal and magnums of Krug. But go easy, Henry. Strong stuff.

The kitchens would be frantic. Caviar with blinis and smetana. Roast suckling pig. Soaked crowberries. Pelmeni. Pirozhki. Coulibiac. Sashimi. Sushi. Lobster. Arctic crab. Honey cake. And a spectacular birthday cake, six foot tall at the highest point, with an edible gold-leaf dome; an uncannily accurate confection of the Kremlin.

Roddy smacked his revolting lips and leered back at Henry. He continued to paint the picture.

The maître d' would be fretting and sweating. Boris Aslanov, Roddy confided, was the ultimate beneficial owner of his establishment, no matter what was registered at Companies House. This was the finest Russian restaurant in London. And no chain of shell companies would put a safe distance between him and his master's wrath if even the smallest detail was overlooked. Roddy seemed to find this particularly amusing.

This was Pyotr's eighteenth birthday party, the eldest of Aslanov's four children. The younger three were his daughters, charming and well-schooled in English by Nataliya Aleksandrova. But for Boris, his son was the future of his dynasty. He was to continue building the empire in that powerful liminal world between Britain and Russia.

When he arrived, Henry would notice two liveried footmen at their positions by the entrance to the reception room. Ex-Spetsnaz. Resplendent in nineteenth-century high-collared frockcoats, if required they could switch to close protection of the Aslanov household with ease. Less subtly, four men in identical black Hugo Boss jackets would have quietly taken up their positions to oversee the grand arrival of the Aslanovs.

Henry was growing impatient and nervous as they drew close.

"Great, Roddy. But what exactly should I do tonight?"

"Henry, Boris Aslanov is a little piece of Russian history."

Roddy had grown serious, as if for the first time he understood the risks he was asking Henry to take.

"The KGB knew that the Soviet Union was going to hit a brick wall years before anyone else. Best placed, really. Also best placed to get billions in foreign currency out of the country before anyone noticed. And that's where Aslanov comes into the picture. A smart young KGB accountant. He knew where all the money was and then did a remarkably good job of staying alive. Uniquely good. That's his specialty. We don't know his exact kill count, but he's not someone to mess with."

Henry nodded. He had decided to take all this in his stride. The redundancy letter from Bonners lay on his bedside table, unopened. He would look at it later. He was now much more interested in his new job. He was learning.

"So, Comrade Aslanov washed up in London ten years ago. A huge figure in Londongrad now. But here's the curious thing. Whilst we know where nearly all of them sit with the Kremlin, Aslanov is a mystery to us. And probably to them. Half of the wealthy Russians in exile here are pro-Moscow, always welcome home. The other half are on the run. Or perhaps pretending to be. Here on a secret Kremlin licence. I need to know which he is."

"So where do I come in?"

"Take it easy this evening. Don't rush things. See if you can get an introduction to Aslanov through Nataliya. Find some common ground. Business? Your fictional love of Russian fiction? His children? Children usually work best. Anyway, the most you will get at first pass is some kind of follow-up. That would be a great result."

Roddy was turning the cab towards the brightly lit restaurant now.

"Just one last thing. Be subtle, but the more you can have your specs looking directly at Aslanov, the better. I want to pick up as much of his table talk as possible."

With that, the cab drew up outside the party and a doorman approached to open the door. Roddy stopped the fare meter.

"That'll be twenty-five pounds, sir," said Roddy loudly. And then softly, "Sorry, Henry, but we need to make everything look real."

Henry handed over the cash, wondering what was real about any of this.

Nataliya looked gorgeous. A long green satin dress and hair worn up. Heels gave her a few inches on Henry, but as she kissed him and linked arms, he didn't care. He was at peace.

As they approached the salon, he felt in his dinner jacket pocket to find the gold embossed invitation card. A moment's consternation as he realised it was still on his bedside table. But the stern-faced Hugo Boss jacket on the door helped out.

"Welcome, Mr Bradbury and Miss Aleksandrova. Have a lovely evening."

He recognised him as one of the heavyset *semechki* eaters from the Orthodox church at Easter. They were obviously expecting Henry.

At the door to the reception, a British Master of Ceremonies was announcing guests, every inch a retired Regimental Sergeant Major, slaughtering the Russian names at ninety decibels. He looked most relieved to bellow a simple "Mr Henry Bradbury".

The Aslanovs had formed a receiving line. First the

patriarch, splendid in white tie and tails, a diamond-encrusted double-headed eagle hanging from a blue ribbon at his neck. Then his wife, tall with the poise that signalled a retired fashion model. Then Pyotr, also in white tie, but dishevelled. Whilst his parents greeted their guests with clear voices, a handshake or a kissing embrace as appropriate, young Pyotr avoided eye contact, mumbled something surly and looked like he would rather be anywhere but here. Finally came the three daughters in descending age, bright-eyed with excitement.

For the first time, Henry remembered his MI5 glasses, imagining the surveillance team in a nearby apartment or van. Aslanov welcomed him formally, and with a practised movement, turned the handshake into a firm propulsion along the conveyor belt. Mrs Aslanov, however, held his hand for seconds, obviously intrigued by Nataliya's English friend. The son shuffled his feet and inspected his reflection in his patent leather shoes. The girls giggled and exchanged glances. In his wake, he heard a different welcome for Nataliya. Hugs, kisses, animated talk in Russian. Even Pyotr seemed to brighten and pull out of his slouch.

He fetched Nataliya a glass of Krug whilst he experimented with an ice-cold glass of sea buckthorn vodka. She stood close to him and he smelt her perfume. Leaning right into his ear, Nataliya whispered:

"I am so pleased you could come with me tonight. You are a wonderful man. I've grown very fond of you. You just need to be more confident in yourself. And with me. Be strong, Henry."

With that she gave him a playful kiss on the cheek.

Unthinking, he pushed his chest out, shoulders back and chin forward, like a heavyweight entering a boxing ring. Whilst Nataliya headed towards the board displaying the seating plan, he stood alone for a minute, watching her graceful progress across the room. And thinking about Colin and his MI5 listeners. Did they catch all of that? He rather hoped they did.

He began to survey the room, guests warmed by the glow from an overhead Murano crystal chandelier. There were a few familiar faces. Father Evgeny, gloriously enrobed, hovering by the kitchen door, ready to be the first to intercept the next silver tray of delicacies. One of the *semechki* quartet was huddled in the corner, deep in conversation with two cadaverous-looking men sporting enamel Russian flags on their lapels. Otherwise, it was a merry crowd of all ages, mostly Russian.

Nataliya beckoned him over. She was pleased with their table. They were sitting with Mrs Aslanov, Nataliya's three pupils, a famous Russian rapper, a fashion designer, and two senior diplomats from the embassy.

Dinner was a splendid affair. Father Evgeny said grace. Countless toasts were called for. Aslanov gave a stirring speech, something about Pyotr and the importance of family, country and God. A five-piece traditional folk group struck up on the balcony above the high table whilst Pyotr shuffled over to cut his cake. Krug flowed like water.

Henry enjoyed the table talk, one of the Aslanov girls on one side and the amusing Russian cultural attaché on the other. Yes, Miss Nataliya was a wonderful English teacher, Polina told him in a cut-glass accent. And Doctor Kirov reeled off lesser-known novels and short stories that

Henry absolutely must read. But he also kept his eyes fixed on his host. Aslanov occasionally looked over and caught his eye. That wasn't a great feeling, like a sudden draft of Arctic air crossing the room. But Henry persisted. This was his job now.

The assembly rose and mingled at the after-party. Nataliya stood with him, hand gently holding his elbow as they laughed with their fellow guests. He felt her warmth next to him and knew he might one day be happy again.

Suddenly, Aslanov was in front of them. It wasn't a customary gentle circling of the room that brought him there. The approach was direct and determined, with two of the *semechki* eaters at his shoulder. Henry faced him and remembered not to smile.

"I trust you have enjoyed Pyotr's party, Mr Bradbury?"

Henry unconsciously pushed his spectacles further up the bridge of his nose. He held his stare.

"Very much so, Mr Aslanov. A wonderful evening to celebrate the birthday of a special young man. Nataliya and I thank you very much."

He calculated that implicating her with him might soften whatever blow was coming. And he liked sounding like a couple.

"Henry, if I may, I think you are a strong man, not afraid. Also, a man of influence in your country."

Henry said nothing but nodded an imperious assent. He was getting into character, back on stage.

"You can look another man straight in the eye. This is an important quality."

He hoped Colin was getting all of this.

Aslanov acknowledged Nataliya.

"Miss Aleksandrova tells me you were educated at Oxford University. Hereford College. Is this correct?"

"Yes," Henry replied firmly, whilst imagining Colin's team rifling back through their notes, wondering what the fuck he was playing at. No turning back now.

"In this case you can help me. I should be most grateful to you."

"How can I help you, Mr Aslanov?"

"I wish Pyotr to study at Hereford College. PPE – politics, philosophy and economics. Please use your connections to help him."

Henry looked over the room at the forlorn young man standing alone by the crumbling remains of the Kremlin cake. Poor little sod.

"He will have to retake a few of his A-levels first. But this place at Oxford is most important to the future of my family. I think you understand me?"

"I understand, Mr Aslanov. We will see what we can do."

It was the first time Henry had seen Aslanov smile.

"Excellent, Henry. You shoot, of course?"

He nodded, as if it was a ridiculous question.

"In this case, please join us at my sporting estate for the first weekend of the game season. It's a little while off, but I think it will please you. My inaugural shoot, in fact. We can discuss matters further. And, of course, Miss Aleksandrova will be with you."

He felt her draw nearer to him, her breast jutting against his arm. His pulse raced.

Aslanov was turning on his heel when he stopped.

"Henry, I am trusting you with my family's future. This is most important to me."

Then he was gone.

Out on the pavement, the rain had stopped. Nataliya held his hands and kissed him fully on the lips. Her eyes were bright and she pressed herself against him. This was meant to be Henry's night.

He remembered what she had said earlier – be strong – and was about to make his next move when he heard a familiar voice.

"Taxi for Mr Bradbury! Hop in, guv'nor." Roddy was by his black cab, holding a name board.

Henry couldn't hide his irritation.

"Don't worry, darling. I have a car that the Aslanovs arranged for me." Nataliya caressed his cheek.

"You just need to wait until our weekend in the country." Nataliya laughed and kissed him again. Then she was gone.

He sat in the back of the black cab, spiralling into a sulk.

"Sorry to drag you away, mate," teased Roddy. "It looks like you had a good evening. In the flesh, Nataliya is really quite special. And, by the way, we checked her out. Nothing to worry us there, apart from an insatiable sexual appetite!"

Roddy winked into the rear-view mirror. He was still wearing his stupid England baseball cap.

"Just kidding. Anyway, Colin's given me a summary. You've really excelled yourself. Totally surprised me. You're good on your feet. More than a touch of Olivier, apparently."

Henry wasn't really listening. All he could think about was Nataliya. He wanted her badly. But was he doing the right thing?

"Look, Roddy, I'm glad you and Colin are pleased. But I'm not sure I want to carry on with this. Sasha is one thing, an enemy agent. But Nataliya is different. She's innocent. I don't want to drag her into your game."

Roddy exhaled sharply.

"I said there was nothing for us to worry about with Nataliya. That's factually correct. But she is far from innocent."

The cab was now halfway to Shoreditch.

"And the truth is, if you want to spend that shooting weekend with your new girlfriend, and time beyond, you now need us as much as we need you."

Henry thought about that.

"You played it very well tonight. But you've now got a couple of challenges, haven't you?"

"Go on."

"Well, do you shoot? And did you graduate from Hereford College, Oxford?"

He considered asking Roddy to stop the taxi so he could walk home. He knew he was about to be snobbed. And he didn't want the evening ruined with a humiliating reminder of why he wasn't quite one of them. But he also knew Roddy was right.

"You know I can't shoot and didn't go to Oxford. Happy now?"

Roddy pulled the cab over to the kerb and swivelled round to face him.

"I'm your man, Henry. I'll get you there in the next few weeks. What fun! It will be like *Pygmalion*."

Henry laughed mirthlessly, getting a joke that Roddy hadn't intended.

"So, tell me about your masterclass, Roddy."

"Two things on your programme." Roddy was now deadly serious. "I'll take you down to some shooting grounds in September. A day on the range will sort you out. They can simulate everything there – pheasant, partridge, woodcock, all with clays. I'll bring a pair of Purdey side-by-sides that have been in my family for generations. Twelve-bore. Concave ribbed. Chopper lump barrels. Lovely pieces. You can borrow them for your weekend."

"Sounds good." This might be an interesting start to his involuntary retirement after all.

"I've also got a colleague with a similar girth to you." Roddy wisely decided against a snide comment. "A keen shot. I'll borrow his tweed shooting suit for you."

"Thank you. What is the second thing I've got to look forward to?"

"Well, you played a blinder, you chose the right college. Hereford is my dear old alma mater."

Of course it bloody well is.

"We'll get one of our analysts to create your legend there. Insert you into college and university records. Old newsletters. The alumni magazine. The rowing club. Anything Aslanov is likely to search."

Henry liked the idea of his retrospective place at Oxford.

"Then you and I will head up and have dinner with the master of the college. A dear man. In fact, he started life with MI6 as luck would have it. So he will be only too willing to help. The connection will be important as you string along Aslanov and his idiot son."

The cab pulled up outside his building.

"No charge for this one, Henry. In fact, we owe you."

He watched carefully as Roddy pulled his cap down low and the cab disappeared into darkness.

9

THE SHOOTING PARTY

SOUTHERN ENGLAND, SEPTEMBER/EARLY OCTOBER 2019

Different dream last night, but same shadow. It was dark and I stood on a pier by the Thames. A small old barge moved quietly down the river, drifting towards Traitors' Gate. The arch was unblocked – open to the water – like in the old days. Could just make out Sasha and Nataliya sitting together on a bench in the bow of the boat. They seemed happy, laughing. Two other figures. The shadow standing at the helm, silent as always. Staring at me. Hard to make out the final figure in the stern with him. Nea? Tried again and again to call out a warning as they disappeared into the tunnel. But no sound came out. Then woke.

HB's Dream Diary

Henry rose late. His head throbbed. Mixing flavoured vodkas with Krug champagne now seemed unwise. Coffee in hand, he surveyed Shoreditch and the London skyline beyond his kitchen window. The rainstorm had passed through and was well into the North Sea. Crisp and bright, London felt like a new city. Cleansed.

He opened the Bonners' letter. Kind words. Much more importantly, a decent payoff. A new chapter. Nataliya, shooting parties. Perhaps invite her down to Lisbon? She would like that. An OBE courtesy of Roddy and Colin? Lovely.

He would resign on Monday. His only requirement would be a few days' consultancy from Bonners to supervise Sasha's project. He knew they would buy that in order to get him out of the door and on his way. Otherwise, next week would be dedicated to building his legend, his fictional days at Oxford, and to honing his prowess against a swarm of helpless game birds. If he could get through the weekend, Nataliya would be his. The dreams were troubling him, and he needed to see Nea. He would break with Roddy and Colin when the time was right. But not quite yet.

Roddy was waiting in the comfortable clubhouse at the shooting range, slouched in a battered leather armchair. The walls were festooned with regimental insignia and wooden boards stencilled with names of members who had fallen in battle. The MI6 man looked completely at home. Plus fours, matching jacket, college tie, polished black brogues. This was Roddy in his element. They drank lukewarm instant coffee and then Roddy fetched the guns whilst Henry changed into his shooting suit.

The day on the range was a success. Punctuated by a heavy lunch of steak and kidney pudding and claret, Roddy covered all eventualities. They blasted at clays, simulating every British game bird, together with rabbits bouncing across open ground. The two men stood shoulder to shoulder as flush after flush of targets darkened the sky. Henry's barrels got so hot with the amount of lead shot he was sending skyward that he needed a glove to open them. After a sloe gin together at the end of the day, Henry decided that Roddy was decent enough company when he was in his natural surroundings. As Roddy dropped him off in Shoreditch, complete with his Purdeys in a double gun slip and tweed suit in a carrier, Henry realised that he hadn't been called "mate" once all day.

But the trip to Oxford didn't end so well. At least not for Roddy.

* * *

On the drive up, Roddy waxed lyrical about his old college. He spent the journey inducting Henry into the arcane language of the place. Bulldogs. Scouts. Cuppers. Mods. Sconce. Subfusc. Then came the legends of the college. Henry's head was spinning as they pulled up outside the porters' lodge.

"Roddy, to pull off this weekend, what's the one single thing I need to remember about acting 'Oxford'?"

Roddy paused for thought.

"Oh, I don't know. Just act as if you own the place. Any place. That goes a long way, Henry."

The master of Hereford was solicitous and charming.

For "reasons of operational security", Roddy had advised Henry to introduce himself with a cover name. As he struggled to think of an alter ego, Roddy laughed.

"How about your porn-star name, Henry?"

What on earth was Roddy talking about?

"Simple formula. The name of your first pet and then the street where you grew up. Give it a try."

"Okay. It's a good one." Henry couldn't help chuckling. "This will work. Please meet Mr Monty Crompton."

After a tour of the college, the master, Roddy and newly minted Monty settled down for dinner together. Served by the college butler in the private dining room of the master's lodge, the candles flickered and the best of the cellars was brought forth. Those four medieval walls had been much privy to conspiracy and intrigue over the centuries. And tonight the three men held with the best traditions of Hereford. By the time the malmsey was served, the plot to lead Aslanov and his boy down the garden path was agreed and in play. An invitation to the college for the old man. The master would give his usual tour. Perhaps Mr Aslanov would be interested in knowing more about some of the opportunities to fund Hereford's ambitious expansion plans? Followed by a decent lunch. And, of course, young Pyotr would be welcome to come up to have an informal tea with some of the current undergraduates. Henry sensed the master had done this before.

Roddy and Henry took their leave and strolled across Middle Quadrangle towards the porters' lodge. Henry was deep in thought. Had he just stumbled into the life he should have had? The one he had always wanted. Or was he as fake now as Roddy was when he was playing a cockney-sparrow Hackney cab driver?

A sharp voice brought him back to the cold Oxford night. It emanated from a slow, stooped figure approaching them in the opposite direction.

"Samson-Brown?"

The old man waved a walking stick. They closed on each other.

"Samson-Brown! Rupert Samson-Brown!"

Roddy was avoiding eye contact. He looked like he wanted to change course across the frost-glazed lawn, but he was too late. The old man stood before them.

"Ah. It *is* you. If I remember rightly, you managed to get into the Foreign Office after those shenanigans in Moscow. Remarkable. Are you still there after all these years?"

The old man winked.

"Good evening, Professor Macindoe. Indeed I am. Still plodding on." Roddy shuffled his feet.

The professor looked at Henry, evidently waiting for an introduction. For once, Roddy seemed lost. Henry darted out a hand.

"Very pleased to meet you, Professor Macindoe. My name is Monty Crompton. Rupert kindly arranged dinner with the master. My son, Roddy, is thinking of coming up to Hereford next Michaelmas term, if he can get a place."

Where did all that come from? He was in his stride whilst Roddy looked like he wanted to sprint to the safety of the world outside the college walls.

"Oh dear, Mr Crompton. I am afraid family and old boy connections don't work like they used to. Not at all.

No help any more. In fact, they may well count against your boy."

He seemed to relish imparting the facts of life of the new world. The old man couldn't resist parting with the sting of a don.

"Young Samson-Brown here wouldn't have secured a place now, despite being third generation. Not a cat in hell's chance."

Then the coup de grâce.

"And, if I remember his performance correctly, Rupert would have been rusticated at the end of his first year ... anyway, goodnight, gentlemen."

With that he laughed, waved his walking stick in valediction and headed on to his rooms.

The journey back to London was difficult. Roddy silent, Henry riding high. Roddy sped down the M40 with his eyes fixed on the road.

Finally, Roddy spoke.

"Macindoe always was a nasty old bastard. Translated Pushkin fifty years ago and done bugger all since. Chippy grammar-school type."

Henry let that linger in the air, savouring it.

"Anyway, please do us both a favour and forget my real name."

Henry sighed.

"Happy to oblige, mate," he chuckled. "Though if you weren't a Roddy, you had to be a Rupert."

Roddy gripped the steering wheel and accelerated.

"Oh, just fuck off, Henry."

* * *

"Good afternoon, Mr Bradbury. Welcome to Martland Manor."

The housekeeper smiled thinly and spoke with a light West Country accent.

"You are in the Montgomery Suite. Pavel will take up your bags and shotguns."

She nodded to the *semechki*-chewing Russian who was fast becoming a firm fixture in Henry's life.

"Please settle in and join the shooting party in the bar for drinks at seven o'clock."

Henry noted that no room key was offered.

"Oh, and by the way, Miss Aleksandrova has not yet arrived. When she does, we will send her up to your rooms."

Henry composed himself. Just. Looking at the printed guest schedule through ninety degrees, he confirmed his wildest dream. It read:

Montgomery Suite. Mr Henry Bradbury and Ms Nataliya Aleksandrova. No dietary requirements.

Hurrah!

Pavel sullenly dropped off the bag in the dressing room and locked the Purdeys away in the gun safe whilst Henry inspected their quarters. A sitting room that looked out over the darkening lake and beyond. Gentle Berkshire hills and woods. He could hear duck families calling to each other across the still water, though the windows were firmly closed. Nightfall. The wood fire crackled in the hearth. Krug champagne in an ice bucket with stag antler handles. Two crystal flutes. A selection of canapes. He explored further, breathless.

Bingo. Only one king-size, four-poster bed! He was about to do his version of a mating dance. But then he composed himself, just as there was a knock at the outer door.

Pavel was back, looking more resentful than ever as he staggered in under the weight of Nataliya's luggage.

"Miss Aleksandrova will be up soon," he muttered.

Henry abluted in a rush. Marvis licorice toothpaste. George Trumper eau de cologne. A little four-sided blue tablet that he had tucked away in his washbag for just such occasions. He worked fast whilst running through his weekend duties. A weekend with the Aslanovs wasn't meant to be all fun.

First, Roddy and Colin had told him not to bother with his MI5 spectacles. Given the spread of the estate and Aslanov's tight perimeter security, they couldn't pick anything up. Second, his mission was to befriend Aslanov and his family, see how friendly King Boris really might be to Britain if the right buttons were pushed. And young Pyotr would be key to that. As Colin described it, "Do like you've done with Sasha, do whatever you have to gain Aslanov's trust. But this one isn't an untrained puppy. He's a full-on Doberman Rottweiler cross. Remember that."

Otherwise, British intelligence instructed Henry to enjoy himself. That shouldn't be difficult. And reassuring to have Her Majesty's Government's approval in the matter.

As he stood before the fireplace in his evening wear, there was a knock and Nataliya was ushered into the sitting room. Pavel then withdrew, a picture of malice. Without a word, she put her arms around him and held him tight. Her kiss lingered. Her scent enveloped him. After what seemed an eternity, she stood back a pace, dropping her fur coat to the floor. He wasn't sure what to expect. But the black cocktail dress did nicely. Nataliya slowly twirled. She moved like a ballerina. She also sang softly, beautifully, a Russian song. It sounded both joyful and melancholy, an odd but moving marriage, though he grasped hardly a word. He was aroused.

Nataliya woke from her dream and came back from wherever she was.

"Darling, please pour us a drink. We will take it to bed. Then you will go downstairs with the men while I get ready for dinner."

Holding each other in front of the fire, Nataliya sipped demurely at the champagne. At first. Then, her hand running through her chestnut mane, she took a full mouthful of Krug, placed the glass on the mantelpiece and deftly unbuttoned the flies of his trousers. The cocktail dress dropped easily to the floor. They didn't make it to the four-poster bed.

* * *

The dinner table was set for thirteen. But one setting, at the opposite end of the table to the host, was being hurriedly removed as the guests took their places. Henry guessed the reason why.

As drinks were being served to the six guns in the bar before dinner, Aslanov seemed agitated. All the other guests were Russians, now familiar faces after Pyotr's birthday. Three London-based businessmen and two senior men from the embassy. The conversation tested his language to the limit, but he didn't want to let Nataliya down. Everyone seemed to know and approve of his teacher. But when things got tricky, the conversation switched effortlessly to English for his benefit.

The two guns missing were young Pyotr and Lord Witney. Aslanov explained to the company that His Lordship could not join dinner tonight but would be at the shoot breakfast bright and early tomorrow. He was Aslanov's neighbour, if sharing a four-kilometre common boundary counted as such. The Russians laughed at their host's self-indulgent joke. Witney also ran one of the most prestigious shoots in the country, decidedly old money. Rumours of royal patronage. And Aslanov seemed desperate for a reciprocal invitation.

But where was Pyotr? He had just come of age so should be drinking with the men. Aslanov consulted his watch and whispered something to Pavel, as ever close to his master's shoulder. Pavel was dispatched and another heavyset man, Ilya, quietly took his place in the bar. Soon raised voices could be heard from another wing of Martland Manor. Two men and then a woman's voice joining the distant chorus. The guns studiously ignored the altercation, simply raising the decibels of their conversation and ordering more drinks from the butler.

Pavel returned and whispered into Aslanov's ear. Aslanov snapped. Crashing his vodka glass down with such force that it splintered on the chrome bar top, he made for the door, waving Pavel off as he tried to follow. Fifteen minutes of distant rage ensued. But as the conversation continued to flow as smoothly as the drinks, Henry decided that Russians had a natural flair for shutting out unpleasantness. Something they share with us British, he thought. He also wondered if the Oxford plan was now in jeopardy.

Aslanov returned, flushed and angry. Mrs Aslanov followed on, eyes red, but as elegant as ever. Then the other women guests joined. Nataliya was the oldest but, to Henry, the most beautiful and poised. The others were, he guessed, on average half their male companions' age. Attractive, hard-eyed and watchful.

Aslanov clinked his glass with a cocktail stirrer and, when he had their attention, formally welcomed his guests to his inaugural shoot to be held at Martland Manor. Henry just about followed the speech, and anyway, Nataliya stood next to him, translating sotto voce when he looked baffled. Ten thousand pheasant, red-legged partridge and mallard had been reared for this first season. There would be five drives tomorrow. The last was Aslanov's favourite. The guns would be towed on a pontoon into the middle of the lake whilst the security detail would "encourage" the duck skywards as they patrolled the lake in his teak-decked launch, imported from Venice. Otherwise, the "boys" would beat the undergrowth to put up the other birds. Aslanov assumed that the ladies would be happy to act as loaders for their men? Stuffing the two barrels with cartridges as they switched between their twin shotguns? The suggestion drew enthusiastic assent from all.

Finally, Aslanov drew his guests' attention to the fact that driven game shooting was an old English tradition. And, as such, as with everything English, came with some odd rules.

On cue, an Englishman of Henry's age was ushered

into the bar. Ginger-haired, red face etched with gin blossom, clad in a worn tweed suit. Aslanov explained that Donald was his head gamekeeper and would now describe what would happen tomorrow.

Donald had the bonhomie that comes with the job, but also an air of world weariness as he surveyed the room. He looked like a man who had seen it all over the decades. He cracked his usual jokes, asked the guns' names and made a vain attempt to say them back. Only when he asked what the ladies had planned for tomorrow did things take a turn for the worse.

Aslanov stared at Donald, who shuffled from one foot to the other.

"The ladies will be loading the guns for their men, of course. Two guns each. They will be very busy."

The crowd laughed. Donald looked uncomfortable.

"I wonder, Mr Aslanov, if it wouldn't be better for some of the under-gamekeepers to load instead? They are experienced and can maybe offer a little advice to your guests during the day."

Donald smiled feebly as Aslanov's eyes bore into him. Henry felt for him, though when his fellow countryman looked his way for moral support, he dropped his eyes to the Persian carpet.

"No. This is the Russian way. Men shoot. Women load. This is what we will do tomorrow."

"Very good, sir. I expect these gentlemen have all shot before anyway."

Henry nodded his head vigorously but all the other men stood stock-still. He revised his view. Perhaps old Donald hadn't quite seen everything before, after all.

Donald moved things to safer ground. He produced a ribbed leather wallet from his pocket. It contained silver pegs numbered 1 to 8. Carefully inverting and shuffling them, he solemnly offered them to the men, starting with Aslanov. The host pulled 7, the peg he would start on at the first drive tomorrow morning. The others followed suit. Henry went last and drew 8. He was pleased. That meant he and Aslanov would be shooting next to each other throughout the day. Two pegs remained in the wallet. Donald explained they would sort that out at breakfast. Henry wondered if Pyotr would even be there to pull his peg. And he hoped that the son would be as far away from his father as possible. For all their sakes.

The ornate French clock behind the bar struck eight as Donald started his safety briefing.

Hardly had his first words, "No ground game, please, gentlemen," left his lips when Aslanov interrupted him.

"Donald, please go now and prepare for our glorious day tomorrow. My guests are ready for dinner."

"Yes, of course, sir. I apologise."

Donald backed out of the room, head bowed, as if withdrawing from the presence of an oriental potentate. He would no doubt have a few stories to tell the lads in the Fox and Hounds tonight. And a serious warning to tomorrow's beaters and pickers-up. For Christ's sake, keep your bloody heads down.

Dinner was a tense affair. The Aslanovs avoided eye contact with each other for the rest of the night and Henry felt that the other male guests shared a common ambition with him: to get upstairs with their girlfriends as quickly as possible. Boris Aslanov proposed a few half-hearted toasts but when one of his business associates politely attempted to reciprocate, he was met with icy stares from the other men. Nataliya seemed to assume the position of senior female guest and instinctively stepped into the role abandoned by the catatonic-looking Mrs Aslanov. Nataliya was charming, funny and sexy. He wanted her. Again. And again.

By ten thirty Aslanov declared the evening over and suggested his guests get an early night before tomorrow's sport. Nataliya and Henry led the guests up the grand staircase, bidding every couple a hearty "*Spokoynoy nochi*" – "Sleep tight". But that night Martland Manor giggled, creaked and groaned into the small hours. The sport had already begun.

* * *

Donald and the under-gamekeepers helped the guests climb down from the tractor-drawn trailer that had pitched and heaved over rutted, ploughed fields to get to the first drive. The morning was perfect. The low sun was burning off a light ground mist and the woods above the shooting party were a glorious autumn palette of burnished gold, oranges and reds. A steady breeze would propel the birds above the treeline nicely, said Donald, making for a challenging day's sport. The unmistakable sound that precedes an English game drive filled the air. Hundreds of birds, calling to each other, already sensing danger, hearing the beaters and dogs as they scurried for cover in the dense undergrowth and trees.

Pyotr had arrived at breakfast, blueing around one

eye socket. The guests looked at each other in surprise. He wasn't expected. Ordering a breakfast of wholemeal toast topped with avocado further displeased his father.

"Pyotr is a vegan and cannot abide cruelty to animals. He has decided he is Buddhist. His father hates this," Nataliya explained to Henry under her breath.

"Then that should make for an interesting day, shouldn't it?" He smiled.

"Be serious, Henry. I and Mrs Aslanov are worried about things. Pyotr is kind and sensitive. He would never harm a fly."

Nataliya continued.

"Oxford. Shooting. The family name. This is all too much pressure for him. His sisters are each more capable of this. Each could go to Oxford. Run a business. Even shoot. But Boris Borisovitch cannot see this."

Lord Witney had drawn number 6, which put him next to his host. At breakfast, Witney had quickly spotted Henry as his sole fellow countryman and made a point of sitting next to him in the trailer.

"I saw you have a lovely brace of Purdeys. Had them long?"

In his early seventies, His Lordship was straight to the point. He needed to establish there and then whether Henry was the sort of chap who had to buy his own furniture.

"They've been in the family for generations," Henry lied. "My father gave them to me when I came down from Oxford. Perhaps as a reward for my third-class degree. Misspent youth and all that. Rowing and girls." He chortled along with his neighbour.

Lord Witney looked relieved. Now he could slot Henry precisely where he belonged in his English cosmology. And he had established he was no dangerous intellectual. All boxes ticked, so far. Now to test Henry's attitude to Aslanov and his friends.

Witney leant into him conspiratorially, just as the tractor took them down a precipitous slope and across a stream. Their flat caps bumped together, causing both men to lose them and laugh.

"I say, have you shot with Aslanov and his ... hmm, associates ... before?" A quiet but firm question.

He eyed the rest of the trailer. He, His Lordship and Aslanov were smart in their regulation tweed suits, plus fours, caps and calf-length leather boots. The others had clearly not read the invitation. They looked like a Sunday supplement picture he remembered: a ragtag of Russian special forces on the retreat from Kabul. A heady mixture of combat gear and paratrooper boots set off with bandoliers loaded with shotgun shells. Apart from Pyotr, that is, ever defiant in a pink hoodie, fluorescent baseball cap and gold trainers.

"Do you know, some of them have brought camouflage semi-automatics? Can you imagine that?"

Indeed he could. But instead he decided to mirror Witney's aghast look.

"Just wait until you see the loaders, Lord Witney."

As the men dismounted from the back of the trailer, three black Range Rovers swerved onto the field in tight formation. Pavel and his men were driving. Screeching to a halt, they opened the rear doors and helped Nataliya and the four other women down.

"My God! I've never seen anything like it!"

"Indeed, my lord. Russian women do carry off tweed rather well, don't you think?"

Nataliya and the other loaders looked ready for a photoshoot. Eschewing the traditional Englishwoman's androgynous top and long tweed skirt, sculpted and tight-fitting jackets with matching culottes to the knee were the order of the day. All set off with white linen shirts open by at least three buttons. And not forgetting tweed caps worn at a jaunty angle. And, of course, Hermès silk scarves to complete the ensemble.

Henry could sense that shooting etiquette might not be what Witney would remember the day for. Far from it.

Oversized lips were puckered and selfies taken as the noise from the undergrowth intensified. The Aslanov girls were there, each with their own black Labrador, ready to pick up fallen prey. Donald tried to organise the eight guns into a loose arc below the woods. One by one they were placed on a peg. Pavel was loading for Aslanov. Ilya was assigned to Pyotr. An under-gamekeeper stood with Witney. The two of them spoke quietly, urgently. They obviously knew each other and both looked nervously up and down the line as shotguns were pulled from their gunslips and loaders inspected their fingernails.

Henry took Nataliya through what was going to happen. The beaters would drive the birds through the wood. They would fly up in alarm and once he had a clear aim over the treeline, with blue sky behind, he would take a shot or two. He would then break the barrels of the gun, eject the spent cartridges and then hand it to her to reload. In return, she would return the loaded gun back to him. This would continue until a whistle signalled the end of the game drive.

Nataliya kissed him fully on the mouth.

"Henry, this is so romantic. It is fate."

He laughed at what he mistook for a joke. But, on studying her closely, he found no intent of humour.

"Henry, I mean it. This is exactly how my grandmother met my grandfather. The Third Battle of Kharkov, 1943. They were a mortar crew together. They would approve of us."

Nataliya welled up with tears and he was about to kiss her again when the battle front erupted. The whole line was firing as a flush of birds gained height and accelerated over their heads. He shouldered one of the Purdeys and downed a cock pheasant with his first shot.

"Good shooting, my darling."

One of the black Labradors, quartering in front of them, picked up and shook the flapping bird until it succumbed.

"Well done, Megan!" called Nataliya as the dog trotted back to one of her pupils with its trophy.

Things then moved quickly. A larger flush, the air dark with ascending birds, their two-note distress calls filling the woods. The guns were shooting wildly. Low, high, across each other. Into the trees. Branches splintered as they were peppered with lead. The only saving grace was that the snapping of highly polished fingernails was reducing the rate of fire. But every rule of the ancient sport was being broken.

Henry kept shooting in his own arc but was aware that Aslanov was taking no prisoners. Poaching through and down the line, with no evident success, Aslanov was shouting at Pavel, using an earthy Russian vocabulary that Nataliya had yet to explore with him. He caught his other neighbour's eye. Witney was ashen, expertly bringing down bird after bird but looking like he was ready to bury his face in the mud beneath him at a moment's notice. Further down the line, Pyotr stood with a beatific look on his face, trance-like. Had he taken something? Something strong? He had gently placed his shotguns on the ground in front of him whilst his burly loader, Ilya, looked imploringly at Pavel.

Aslanov threw down his gun in frustration and focused his wrath on Pyotr.

Marching towards his son, with shots still being fired, he was screaming.

"*Strelyay! Strelyay, mal'chik!* Just shoot, boy!"

After what seemed an eternity, the whistle blew. Henry and Nataliya picked up the fallen birds around them. One of the Russians even found a new rule to break, shooting a bird in the head at point-blank range as it tried to run across the ground for cover in the bracken. A pate of raw pheasant and lead was all that remained.

Witney made clear he wanted an urgent word with Henry, which was precisely why his fellow Englishman linked arms with Nataliya and headed back towards the other guns who were gathering by the vehicles.

Henry approached the party carefully. The safety briefing that had been skipped the previous evening now took on a greater significance. He carefully positioned himself between Nataliya and the men who still had their shotguns closed, possibly live, and were swinging them about with abandon. Stirrup cups of vodka were being poured and the group was fired up. Ready for the next drive.

Aslanov and Pyotr returned in silence with the security man trailing behind with the unused shotguns.

"Nataliya, this is actually quite dangerous. Somebody is going to get hurt. And what's with Aslanov and that poor lad?" Henry whispered.

Nataliya pondered this.

"Henry, you will know what to do. I believe in you."

So, the time had come. He drew himself up tall and walked over to Aslanov.

"Can we please have a word? In private." He held the angry gaze. Minutes seemed to pass.

Aslanov finally nodded and the two picked their way across the ploughed furrows with Pavel hulking behind, just out of earshot.

"Look, Boris Borisovitch, I really am grateful for the invitation. And it is wonderful to spend time with your family and Nataliya."

Aslanov stared coldly.

"And?"

"I've arranged for you to meet the Master of Hereford College and for Pyotr to visit."

Aslanov gripped Henry's elbow.

"Thank you, Henry. I am most grateful."

Henry scowled and shook his arm free of his host.

"But as soon as we get back to Martland Manor, I am cancelling everything, Boris."

The Russian looked stunned.

"Pyotr stands no chance of a place at Oxford feeling like he does. He needs to be himself. Think for himself. Follow his passion. That is what they're looking for. That is what they saw in me. Frankly, you're wasting my time."

Henry, Hereford College reject, smiled to himself ruefully. Aslanov thought for a few minutes and Henry allowed him his time.

"So what do you suggest?"

"Let me spend some time with Pyotr. Find out what makes him tick. Coach him. And as for today, how about a compromise? From now on, he loads for me and you let Nataliya take his place? His gun. Something tells me she'll be a natural shot. And then he stays in the field but without actually killing anything."

Aslanov smiled.

"I hope you are right, Mr Bradbury. So, let's give it a try. You are the first Englishman I have trusted."

As they walked back to the party, Henry really went for it.

"Boris Borisovitch, do you want to be invited to Witney's shoot?"

Aslanov laughed.

"You read me like a book, Henry. That is what I want. Dearly. And I fear you have further advice for me."

"Listen, this morning is not going well for you, but we can rescue this. A little humble pie is called for."

Aslanov looked blank.

"Before the next drive, ask His Lordship to be today's shoot captain. Let him make a speech about field etiquette. Take charge. Let poor Donald say his piece and get on and manage things safely."

"I can do that."

"We English are very odd. You know that. But we win. Wars, that sort of thing. And your people didn't take

Stalingrad and keep Leningrad by shooting wildly into the air, with no discipline. No targeting. Wasting ammunition. That is not Russian."

Henry had to work hard to supress a self-satisfied smile as he watched his host gravely nod approval at his preposterous speech. This was working.

"Nataliya is teaching you well. I think you understand us perfectly now."

Aslanov gave him a hug and kiss that did not go unnoticed by the field.

Henry quietly explained the change of plan to Lord Witney, who turned gammon-faced with delight. His world order had been restored. The mood of the shoot lifted. Aslanov stood on the tractor and made a short speech in calculated deference to His Lordship. Witney delighted in patronising the Russians in such strangulated English that Nataliya had to interpret. Clever as ever; her artful mistranslation kept honour served all round.

The day progressed as planned, until the final drive. The duck massacre.

Henry made the most of his time with Pyotr. The young man wanted to be a theatre designer. He liked the idea of pansexuality, but any form of sexuality would suit him nicely for the moment. He felt more English than Russian. He loved his father but was terrified of him. He begged for Henry's intercession, to smooth things. By return, Henry got an agreement that the boy would visit Oxford, act interested. He also got Pyotr to go through the motions of loading his guns in return for a promise to miss every bird he fired on, harder than Henry imagined with a sky thick with flapping and squawking.

As he suspected, Nataliya was an excellent shot. A natural. She only went for the high birds, the difficult targets. And they all tumbled to earth stone dead, clean kills. Witney talent-spotted her. And Henry spotted His Lordship making a fawning beeline for her between each drive.

The guns got into a rhythm and calmed down. Only Aslanov was having a bad day, visibly frustrated with his empty gamebag. Donald wisely folded and tucked away the individual scorecards he had been keeping. That was a secret to bury deep.

The light was failing as the guns were helped onto the floating pontoon. Towed into the middle of the dark lake, the seven guns spread out on the polished deck as best they could, planting their legs wide for stability. The girlfriends took pictures from the shore. Even the Russians had worked out the dangers of crowding too many people onto the barge. To Henry's annoyance, Witney had positioned himself right next to Nataliya. The peer had sheathed his gun and was standing close to her, mottled hand on her shoulder, close in, helping perfect her stance and gun mounting. With a tactility that he judged excessive. He thought how easily His Lordship might end up in the lake. An accidental brush would do it.

The still of the early evening ended violently. The throaty rumble of Aslanov's 1967 twin-engine Riva Aquarama fired up in its boathouse lair. Its mahogany hull nudged forward out into the water, slowly at first. The billionaire stood at the blue-and-white wheel. One hand steered whilst the other rested on the throttle controlling the Cadillac motors. He had abandoned his shotguns and changed into a black turtleneck sweater and racing jacket, topped off with superfluous sunglasses. His four bodyguards were squeezed, bicep to bicep, into the immaculate leather cockpit.

On the pontoon, Henry let out an involuntary giggle. Pyotr stood next to him.

"What's so funny about this, Mr Bradbury?"

"I don't really know. But I suspect your father is about to do fifty miles an hour. On a lake. In the half dark. Wearing sunglasses."

Pyotr laughed too. And sure enough, Henry was right.

Family after family of ducks took to the skies, some silhouetted against a rising full moon. Aslanov careened the motorboat up and down the water, pitching at forty-five degrees, exposing its white hull and whiter faces of his henchmen crew. The wake pulsed down towards the pontoon and made for some uncomfortable shooting as the guns tried to stay out of the water.

"Henry, this is terrible," croaked Pyotr. "The ducks have no chance. Every time they land back on the water, my father chases them up again. This is mass murder."

Bird after bird rained down. The dogs worked quietly in the water, retrieving what they could keep up with. But the bobbing, lifeless velvet green heads of mallards seemed to stretch as far as Henry could see through the gathering murk.

"Only a few minutes to go, Pyotr, before the final whistle. We've nearly lost all light."

Aslanov slowed his launch and came alongside, right by Henry and his son.

"Henry, hand Pyotr your gun. He will honour his

father by taking one shot and bringing home a duck for our supper." He removed his dark glasses and his eyes blazed.

Pyotr stood frozen. Henry thought quickly.

"Of course, Boris Borisovitch. But can you please put up one last flight of duck for us?"

Aslanov nodded, gunned the engines and tore away, describing a wide sweep around the pontoon. Henry handed a precious Purdey to Pyotr who meekly accepted it. He was in a trance.

"Pyotr, the gun is loaded. The safety is off. Pull it into your shoulder. That's right. Cheek against the stock. Point the barrels at the moon. No birds there. Squeeze the trigger. Before your father comes back. Take the bloody shot! Now!"

Things happened quickly. A crack and muzzle flash against the darkening sky. Pyotr let out a howl, fortunately drowned out by the engines of the Aquarama. He grabbed Pyotr's jacket collar as the gun's recoil propelled him backwards. Both men teetered right above the cold water before Henry recovered their balance in the nick of time. The Purdey hit the pontoon's varnished deck and was tumbling away into the darkness. He fell on it heavily just before it had time to escape into the depths.

Aslanov was powering back towards them. Pyotr nursed his shoulder. He had waved the stock of the gun an inch away from his collar bone as he fired, and was now paying the painful price. Nataliya sprang across the deck and pushed a beautiful dead drake, freshly scooped from the lake, into Pyotr's functioning hand. God, she's smart, he thought. He and Nataliya lifted Pyotr's good arm above his head, displaying the trophy. They whooped in triumph as Aslanov circled them.

"Pyotr got the last bird of the day," Henry shouted above the roar of the engines, "and he's an absolute beauty!"

* * *

Dinner that evening was a family affair. The other guns headed back to London with their girlfriends. Nataliya laughed as they dressed for dinner.

"The manicurists and stylists of South Ken will be busy on Monday morning. You are a lucky man, Henry. To have found a low-maintenance Russian. We are rare creatures. To be treasured, even pampered."

He laughed at her joke. And then they made love.

The couple were the only guests that night. Pyotr's arm was in a sling, which seemed to be a source of both amusement and pride to his father. The mood was light. Duck was served and even Pyotr's plant-based alternative, spooned up with his left hand, went unremarked by his father. The conversation revolved around the day's triumph, the dogs' excellent performance, and excitement about father and son's forthcoming trip to Oxford.

After dinner, Aslanov invited Henry to his library. Alone. Nataliya retired to their suite. Pavel stood guard outside his master's solid oak door. The host poured them two generous brandies and invited Henry to sit with him by the fire. Something was coming.

"Henry, you have proved to me you know your country. You have connections. You are in the middle of things. This is of great value to me."

Henry sipped the Louis XIII and remained silent. Had he really fooled Aslanov?

"You know Oxford. You know shooting. And I think therefore that you know other things. Other people. Your gentlemen of the shadows."

He tensed but knew he couldn't show it. The glass was heading to his lips for a long gulp, but he mastered himself just in time and put the brandy down.

"What kind of people, Boris?"

The cold stare.

"Spies. British intelligence."

His heart raced. He could only think of Pavel at the door and the other three goons lurking in the dark recesses of Martland Manor.

"I need to speak to them. Urgently. Make them an offer. And I think you can help me."

Henry leant forward. Conspiratorial.

"Perhaps I can help you. Again. Like Oxford. Maybe I do know somebody. But you need to tell me what this is all about."

Aslanov sighed.

"I have spent so much money on London lawyers. Accountants. Lobbyists. Just a waste."

Henry nodded encouragement.

"Trying to become a British citizen. Move everything here, where my family will be safe. But always blocked."

He had to think fast. Was this treasure? Or a deadly trap? He had one shot at getting this right. He thought of Nea. What would she do to extract a confession without giving anything away?

"I might know somebody, Boris. I can't promise anything. But what is your offer?"

Aslanov paused and stared through his amber glass at the flames beyond. He answered a different question.

"I want British passports for me and my family. I want help from the London financial regulators to move my assets here. And I want full protection of the British state."

"That's quite a shopping list, Boris. It isn't my world, but I imagine a lot will be expected in return."

Aslanov placed his glass down, stood up slowly and went to a bookshelf by the window. It was packed wall to ceiling with leather-bound Russian first editions. He pulled a volume off the shelf and returned to his armchair. After removing a single handwritten page secreted inside, he studied it for several minutes. In silence. Deciding what to impart. Finally, he spoke.

"I think you know I was KGB. When I was young."

Henry nodded.

"I was the accountant in the British section. In the nineteen eighties. Less boring than it sounds. I travelled all over Europe wearing money belts stuffed with cash. Francs – French, Belgian and Swiss – Deutschmarks, pesetas, escudos. But most of all, pounds sterling."

Aslanov paused to let this sink in.

"Please tell your contact I want to speak. I was the paymaster of all British operations. All British recruitment here. And also the British who came to Moscow."

Henry kept imagining Nea in the room with them. What would she do?

"Why do you think British intelligence would be interested? It sounds like ancient history to me."

"Not just history, Henry. Current affairs. I read the newspapers. What I can tell them is very topical. Most powerful. The investments we made back then must be paying off remarkably for the Kremlin now. Just tell them this and they will want a deal."

Smiling coldly, Aslanov replaced his note in the book, snapped it shut and returned the volume to its rightful place. Glasses were drained and no refresh was offered.

"So now I have work to do. And Nataliya is waiting for you upstairs."

Henry rose.

"Please understand, Henry, this is a matter of considerable urgency. I need your help. Quickly."

10

SHOCK THERAPY

"How long has it been? Since I last saw you?" Henry was thrilled to hear that comforting transatlantic voice again, drifting somewhere between New York City and London.

"Two months to the day. And we've got a lot to catch up on. I'm so relieved you've agreed to see me. I can't tell you how much I've missed our sessions."

Nea was curled up on her usual perch. The consulting room was the same, perhaps even a little grubbier than before. Or maybe it was the light. Summer had faded to autumn.

Nea listened carefully as Henry made his solemn promises. Directly after this session he was going to meet his handlers. He would tell them that he had done his duty. They would be disappointed and pile on the pressure. But he couldn't carry on deceiving people. Putting himself and others he cared for in harm's way. It had all gone too far.

He was now in full rehearsal mode. Practising his imminent speech to his handlers. But he had to be circumspect in what he told his psychotherapist.

"I've got one last present for them. It's a bombshell, I think. I hope that will keep them happy. Get them their promotions. And then I will be on my way."

Since the shooting party, he had worked out his exit plan. Pass on Boris Aslanov's offer. Hopefully it would mean something to Roddy and Colin. Bonners would pay Sasha so his work there was done. The spy wouldn't need to go back to meet his fate in Moscow just yet. Perhaps a last lunch with him to explain he had retired from Bonners and to wish him luck. He would miss the giant. Finally, a gentle question about the OBE. Nataliya would be none the wiser of what it was really for and she could come to the Palace with him.

Nea now spoke deliberately.

"Henry, you'll need to be really clear with them. Stick to your guns. They won't let you go that easily. You're too valuable and I know them. Be firm."

The last time he had seen Nea, there had been his confession. Her unexplained tears. Her secret nearly shared, but then withdrawn. She had given him his cue. Now was the time to ask.

"Nea, you seem to know something about this shadow world. And I think you nearly told me before. What happened to you? It might help me."

Nea removed her heavy glasses and rubbed her nose. The subliminal signal that the two were once again entering the confessional. But, for the first time, it was Nea's turn to come clean.

"I was recruited in London, as soon as I qualified here to practise as a psychotherapist. A discreet approach at the drinks following my graduation ceremony. A friendly Englishwoman told me I was an ideal candidate: honourable discharge from the US Army with the rank of major, British passport, medical doctor, experience of sensitive combat tours, good under stress. Then I passed all their psychometrics with flying colours."

Things started to fall into place.

"I worked for the same organisations that are running you, Henry. And a couple of others you won't even have heard of. Well paid and it got me started in my new career. Given four passports, five driving licences. I began with three clients and then my caseload cranked up."

He was in shock.

"Everyone in the British witness protection programme is offered a psychologist. And believe me, they need it. Buried in a strange town, newly minted identity. Sometimes another country. Cut off from friends and family … otherwise left to rot. The pressure on them is terrible. That's what I did for ten years, before I had to get out."

Nea paused for breath.

"Hardly any of them do this willingly. It's just that their alternatives are far worse. Long prison stretches or a life waiting for your old associates to catch up with you. These are serious criminals, Henry. Or Muslim informants. IRA families who've never left the Province before. Even the odd British intelligence officer."

Another silence as he digested this last piece of unwelcome news.

"That's why I finally got out. Finding there were British spies in the programme terrified me. They'd been compromised and passed on information to the enemy, or been paid for it. They would have to hide for the rest of their lives. I realised you couldn't trust anyone from their world. None of them. That's what I've been wanting to tell you all along."

Nea let that sink in.

"I think I'm tough, but it overwhelmed me. And I lost one of my clients too."

Nea told her story. A desolate, burly middle-aged Irish bachelor who had been removed from a border farm in County Armagh just minutes before an Active Service Unit caught up with him. Years of informing on cross-border IRA smuggling of fuel and cigarettes meant a 9mm bullet with his name on it was on its way. Then followed his purgatory in a series of small English towns. Nea saw him every week. First, drink driving cost him his licence. Then fights in pubs put him in the cells more than once. Whiskey-fuelled confessions in bars kept him on the move from safe house to safe house. Every week he cried when Nea had to leave him. She watched him disintegrate in front of her eyes. He missed his mother terribly and knew he could never see her again. Nea was seriously worried and raised it with her controllers. Hard-bitten and cynical, they suggested she file a report. She did. And then – nothing.

The door to the grey, pebble-dashed council house in Swindon was wide open when she arrived. Nea already knew what she would find. The Irishman hung from a rope tied to the top banister, head lolling. Purple bruising around the ligature. He was not long dead. The front of his grubby grey sweat pants was soaked and urine dripped onto a black-and-white photograph that had fallen from his hand to the floor beneath him. It was a picture of a young bride in her wedding dress. Beehive hairdo. Beaming. His mother.

"I tried to continue but I had a breakdown. I thought I could deal with anything. But I hadn't saved him. I failed."

Nea dabbed at her eyes as he looked on in stunned silence.

"That's just awful, Nea. But one question. Who else have you told?"

Nea sobbed.

"One other person. And now you. The life of a psychotherapist is all listening. Asking questions. Like a spy, I suppose. It can be lonely. But I feel better for talking to you. I think we're in the same boat, you and me. It's an odd bond, isn't it?"

They stared at each other for minutes. Finally, Nea broke the silence.

"You don't have to tell me, Henry. But what is your parting gift to British intelligence? What have you got for them?"

He tried to find the words. Impart enough without putting either of them in further danger.

"It's a message from a Russian. A powerful man. He says he has a big secret to trade with our mutual friends. He says he knows all the KGB operations in Britain. In the nineteen eighties. He hinted Moscow still has somebody in place. In a senior position in London."

He stopped. He had said enough. Nea was now back to being more measured than ever.

"Henry, there was only one person I ever met in witness protection who seemed happy. I settled her in a new life. Buried her, as we say. She seemed so grateful to be starting again. Couldn't wait to escape."

"Who was she?"

"I can't say. Just that she had been a senior MI6 officer. In fact, the most senior woman in the service. We became close but I never really got the story straight. Something went badly wrong for her. I think it might be related to this."

He sensed that was all he was going to elicit.

"I'd better get going, Nea. Thanks for the advice."

"Think twice what you tell them when you resign. You don't owe them anything."

He rose to leave.

"Be strong, Henry. You can escape too. Why don't we meet again on Friday? Same time. Somewhere discreet now. There's a café on Marylebone station. You can tell me how you got on."

* * *

Roddy loaded the shotguns into the back of the black Range Rover and the three men pulled off and headed north from Shoreditch. Roddy drove. Henry sat in the front passenger seat and Colin sat directly behind him. The mood was convivial. Roddy seemed genuinely interested in the day's shooting. The two spies laughed at his tales of Lord Witney, poor Donald and the glamorous Russian loaders. Roddy was alarmed when he heard of the near miss with his Purdeys but then saw the funny side. Henry felt quite the raconteur and forgot to ask where he was being taken.

Finally, they pulled into a pub car park, the car's two-and-a-half-ton chassis compacting gravel with a heavy crunch. It was not Henry's part of London but he recognised that they had arrived at a venerable coaching inn nestled by Hampstead Heath.

"Let's hear your good news first," said Roddy as Colin set three pints of bitter on the table. "We'll save your bad news for later."

Henry had given them the option between the two and was relieved at their choice.

First, he unpicked the weekend. The names of the Russian guests. Pen portraits of them too. The layout of Martland Manor. The staff. Security arrangements. The unhappy Aslanov family. Poor Pyotr – sensitive, vegan and bullied.

Roddy and Colin took notes while Henry pulled at his beer.

"What about Oxford, Henry?" asked Roddy.

"Game on. Though I had to make a deal with Pyotr. He'll go through the motions just to stay on the right side of his bastard of a father. He wants to study theatre, stage design."

Roddy laughed.

"Sounds limp-wristed to me. That won't please the old man. What else have you got for us?"

Decision time. Say nothing of Aslanov's offer and just walk away. Or perform one final service for his country. And perhaps save the Aslanovs.

"Gents, I've got one last thing to tell you about Aslanov, but then I want out. I think I have something useful for you. And then I've done my bit. Sasha is taken care of with the money. I'll take him for a last lunch. Apart from Nataliya, I'm swearing off Russians from now on. Signing off."

Henry gave a mock salute in a vain attempt to lighten the atmosphere in their nook of the pub.

"That's really disappointing news for us," sighed Colin. "I think we might need you to carry on with the Aslanov case, if you have something worthwhile for us. You're definitely heading towards that OBE at this rate."

Henry paused, weighing the gong against Nataliya and Nea.

"Look, I just want a quiet life. I want to really get to know Nataliya. Spend time down at my place in Lisbon. And I've neglected my daughters. I need to go back to seeing my psychotherapist without all this deceit hanging over me like a dark cloud."

He hadn't planned on mentioning Nea. The silence from his drinking companions had made him blurt.

Colin's turn. A rapid succession of eye squeezing and head tossing gave ample warning of what was coming.

"Do you see a therapist, Henry? Only we like to know these things. For security reasons. Like knowing about Russian girlfriends. Same sort of thing, really." The tone was sarcastic.

He felt himself colouring up, but shame was swiftly purged by a cleansing surge of anger.

"Listen, it's my bloody business who I see. I haven't taken a penny from you. I haven't signed the Official

Secrets Act. I've done everything you asked until now. I have a right to a private life. And, anyway, it's irrelevant. I've just quit."

He finished his pint and rose to his feet, starting to put on his coat.

Roddy had turned professionally emollient. He smiled his full set of teeth and gestured for Henry to sit back down. Against his better judgement, he obliged.

"Let's have one more round for the road. We've been through a lot together. Let's part as mates."

This time Roddy fetched the beer from the bar. Colin took a large gulp and wiped the foam from his mouth.

"That's better. You're quite right, Henry. About your therapist. I assume you haven't been silly enough to mention us. Anyway, it doesn't matter now."

Henry sat in stony silence. Roddy sank back down next to him, uncomfortably close.

"But could you please just tell us the final thing on Aslanov? Then you're off the hook. Roddy and I will take it from here."

Henry relented and explained. The drink in the library. The offer. What was wanted in return. Colin scribbled furiously and Roddy went into that middle-distance stare that he had witnessed once before. When he had imparted Sasha's secret.

"Henry, this is dynamite. You probably don't know what you've brought us. Thank you so much." Colin shook his hand. But Henry had something on his mind.

"Just one last question from me. Can you help the Aslanovs? To safety. Not the old man – he's a wanker. But Pyotr and the girls? And his wife?"

Colin nodded vigorously.

"If he has what he says he has, for sure. But you might need to help us as a go-between. Just one more trip to Martland Manor. That's all."

Before Henry could answer, Roddy shook his head.

"Henry is right. He's done more than enough for us. This should be our last meeting with him. But Henry, did you feel, really feel, that Aslanov had details about this? The old KGB operations? We are talking forty years ago, after all."

Colin didn't even try to hide his irritation with Roddy.

Henry suddenly remembered the sheet of paper that Aslanov had consulted in the library.

"Yes. Yes. In an old leather-bound book on a shelf by the window. Green binding with Cyrillic gold letters. I think it's all in there. On a handwritten sheet."

Roddy pounced. Which side of the window? Left? Right? Near the ceiling or the floor? Do you remember the title? Think, Henry, think.

He did his best but wasn't very clear.

Colin closed his notebook.

"That's brilliant. Roddy and I need to have a private chat about what happens next. But thanks again."

Henry was making his final attempt to part company when Roddy put his hand on his forearm, firmly. Restraining.

"Just a formality, mate, but what is the name of your psychotherapist? For the record."

He didn't have time to think. He just wanted to be gone and never see the pair from the Joint Russia Programme again.

"Dr Nea Solomon. She practises in Harley Street."

Colin spasmed and Roddy shook with laughter.

"Oh, for fuck's sake, Henry. You really know how to pick 'em. First, the dodgy Russian bird. And now you tell us about that pathetic American smackhead who should have gone to prison for a long time. Maybe do yourself a favour? Just steer clear of girls, at least for a while."

Henry clenched his fist and for a moment considered doing some ad hoc dental work on Roddy's pearly white set of grinning teeth. Without anaesthetic.

Instead, he got to his feet, stood tall, drained his pint, and left Roddy and Colin without a word.

* * *

"I don't know where to start, Henry. That chapter of my life is just a blur now. I've buried it very deep."

The café was empty and quiet except for the occasional Tannoy speaker announcing a train departure.

For once, Henry was in the therapist's chair. Nea continued in a flat monotone.

"You shouldn't have mentioned me to your controllers. That was a mistake for both of us. But we are where we are. And at least you ended things with them."

He watched her stirring her tea as she looked out of the window across the concourse. Empty apart from a delivery driver wheeling a stack of *London Evening Standards* on a trolley, ready for the commuters' weary home run.

"When the poor man hung himself, I had nobody to turn to. I wasn't in a relationship. My parents are three thousand miles away. I guess work was everything to me.

Travelling the country, council house to council house, a different identity for every town … one heart-wrenching case after another."

He trod carefully, sparing his therapist Roddy's colourful description of her.

"They mentioned the drugs, Nea. I suppose you were just self-medicating? It sounds like the whole witness protection programme was a mess."

"Well, they probably told you this anyway, but here goes. Another of my clients had been a major figure in organised crime. Hidden away in a terraced back street in Yorkshire now. Marco was like a lot of his type. Intelligent, charming. Off the scale EQ."

He guessed what was coming.

"I turned to him. He was understanding, seemingly kind. A good listener."

He held Nea's hand across the plastic table. She squeezed in reciprocity, gentle but strong.

"And, of course, a manipulative bastard."

A young blonde woman in a padded white jacket entered the café and ordered at the counter, texting with one hand and carrying a newspaper in the other. The chrome coffee machine hissed and Nea lowered her voice.

"We became lovers. He stayed at my flat in Maida Vale most weekends. I couldn't wait to see him when he came down. And he always brought me a little present of prescription drugs. Fentanyl. In the end I think it was those little blue pills I craved most. More than him."

The woman sat down three tables away and removed her jacket. Just out of earshot. She started typing furiously on her mobile phone.

"It was all so wrong. I was in a total mess. Breaking every rule, professional code. And an addict. But it was the only way I could get the image of that Irishman's mother out of my mind. In the end, I'm glad the drug squad kicked in my door that Monday morning. It saved my life."

Henry was listening intently, nodding encouragement.

"Of course, Marco couldn't give up his old job. I should have known that. I noticed he didn't exactly pack light when he came down to London. Sure, he was the best-dressed man in Doncaster ..."

He smiled at the joke.

"... but the five kilos of cocaine the police found was a better explanation."

"What happened to you, Nea?"

"I was fired. Avoided prosecution. Just. It would have been too embarrassing for them. The professional bodies are also none the wiser. I went through drug withdrawal on my own. In agony, locked away in my flat."

He watched her clench and unclench her brown fists as she relived the nightmare. The blonde woman put her phone away and was picking up the newspaper.

"Well, I would have been locked away – if the door hadn't been off its hinges. But you know the worst thing, Henry? I couldn't say goodbye to my clients. If I go near any of them, I go to prison. They made that clear to me. Anyway, here endeth my confession. Now you know everything."

But he had stopped listening. He was staring at the blonde woman. More precisely, at the newspaper she had just opened. Without a word, he released Nea's hand and bounded out of the café towards the man handing out the *Evening Standard* by platform seven.

He returned, ashen and breathless, staring at the front page in horror.

"Henry, what is it?" It was Nea's turn to reach over and touch his hand.

He looked down at the front page. Boris Aslanov stared back, those familiar dull eyes. And an inset photo of a row of sixth-form boys in blazers. Pyotr was there, his face circled by a black ring.

The headline read: "Russian billionaire shot dead at Berkshire home."

He shook involuntarily and pushed the newspaper towards Nea.

"Christ. I just spent the weekend with him. And went to the boy's eighteenth. I just can't read it."

Nea studied the article and then turned to a profile of the Aslanov family on page five. Henry sat in silence.

"What happened, Nea? What does it say?"

"It seems like a murder-suicide. Boris Aslanov was shot point-blank with a shotgun. In the back of the head. Then the son turned the gun on himself. They lived at a place called Martland Manor. Let me get you another tea. Just sit there, catch your breath, and I'll be back in a minute."

Nea returned to find him studying the article intently.

"Henry, was this your powerful Russian? The one with the secret to sell?"

He nodded.

"A complete wanker towards his son. A bully. Mentally and physically abusive."

Nea held his hand tightly.

"What do you think happened?"

He shook his head and reread the article. The bodies were found together in the library of Martland Manor by the Royal Berkshire Fire and Rescue Service when they were called to put out a blaze. A collection of rare books was destroyed. Thames Valley police had taken over the investigation.

"Pyotr wouldn't harm a fly. He told me he loved his father. They seemed to be getting on better by the end of last weekend."

"Do you think his father could have pushed him over the edge?"

He slumped back in the plastic chair, cradling his tea.

"I suppose so. Aslanov is a nasty piece of work. But Pyotr had damaged his shooting shoulder. He couldn't use his right arm when I left. It was in a sling. I don't see how he could've handled a shotgun in that state."

"So, what else might have happened?"

He thought back over the weekend.

"I don't know, but Boris Aslanov went nowhere without his goons. Four of them. Where the fuck were they? And why was the fire brigade there first, not the police or paramedics? And who set fire to the books? This is all wrong, Nea."

He sensed Nea reaching the same conclusion he was coming to. At the same moment.

"Did you tell your handlers about the offer? Aslanov's offer?"

He nodded.

"How did they react?"

"The man from MI5 was thrilled. The guy from the darker side went quiet. Then, when your name came up, it was as if he wanted to provoke a fight with me. Bonkers."

The café was filling up and four men settled into the adjacent table. Probably fathers of children at the same school, he thought. The volume of friendly argument about Brexit was cranking up, joshing the one who had voted to leave. No harm done. Let's see what happens. The sound of the suburbs.

Henry had to lean in close to Nea in order to be heard.

"Nea, don't you think we should talk to your friend, the MI6 officer you buried? To see if she can cast any light on this?"

Nea was firm.

"Absolutely not. She has a new life to lead. I would go to jail if she reported an approach from me. And I think you have dug yourself deep into a hole already. Don't you think it's time you stopped digging?"

Henry knew she was right. And now her counsel came.

"In fact, if you're thinking what I'm thinking, you need to lie low. Very low. I'm sure Lisbon is lovely at this time of the year. If I were you, I would be on a flight there this evening."

11

A NEW CHAPTER

Henry kicked up, broke the surface and struggled to heave himself onto the board. After several ungainly attempts, he finally flopped down heavily, rubber belly prone against epoxy resin. Looking down the line, only three other surfers were out so early. All waiting for that perfect wave. Henry would let them go first. His ability to stand was still hit-and-miss, and he didn't need to provide amusement to a youthful, tanned audience. Meanwhile, he tried to guess the time, squinting towards a thin winter sun hanging low above the hulking citadel of São Julião da Barra. He had given up wearing his fancy wristwatch soon after fleeing London, five months ago now, and didn't miss it. As the board rocked gently, he remembered the final line of Nataliya's letter. She had written it on blue Smythson's notepaper, the colour of the sky above him. It was in a beautiful Russian copperplate hand. He had needed his dictionary to understand the finer points, but now her final line, a quote from Turgenev, was in his mind.

"Time sometimes flies like a bird, sometimes crawls like a snail; but a man is happiest when he does not even notice whether it passes swiftly or slowly."

That was his life now. Henry stretched out on the board and smiled to himself. He was keeping busy in Lisbon but, for the first time that he could remember, only busy doing things he loved.

The letter had arrived several weeks after he'd settled into his Lisbon apartment. He had tried to call Nataliya from Heathrow Airport as he fled. No reply. Then from his Lisbon apartment. Still no reply. His emails and texts went unanswered. And so, what Nataliya had to say hadn't really surprised him. He knew there was a secret. Sasha and Roddy had both warned him. He just hadn't wanted to be privy to it.

Nataliya explained that she now lived at Martland Manor during the week, helping Mrs Aslanov and the girls pull their lives back together. She spent weekends at her apartment in London. After the terrible events following the shooting weekend, Nataliya had met a new man, a fellow Russian. Apparently, an old family friend of the Aslanovs – kind, generous and understanding. She apologised for not having told him before, but there it was. This news was delivered matter-of-factly and, in rather formal Russian, she had thanked Henry for his kindness and wished him well for the future. If he was ever back in London, perhaps they could meet at the restaurant in Sloane Square for a quick coffee?

His fellow surfers were up on their feet, arching forward in anticipation of the wave they coveted, the perfect crest, but for now he was content to flop on the board, rocking, rolling and thinking.

There was just one curious thing about Nataliya's letter. She had enquired why he had left England so suddenly. And if anything happened during the weekend at Martland Manor that she or the Aslanovs, at least the survivors, should know about? Fair enough questions. There was no hint that Nataliya suspected anything other than what was reported at the Berkshire coroner's inquest. A terrible unlawful killing and suicide. But then a Russian proverb followed, seemingly apropos of nothing. Just hanging there, underlined.

Про сéрого речь, а сéрый – навстрéчь.

At first, Henry translated it literally:

Speak of the grey one, and the grey one heads your way.

Puzzled, he had scribbled the quote into a notebook and strolled over for lunch at the Russian café by Lisbon docks. It was an occasional haunt, where he liked to practise the language with the owner, an old seaman from Odessa who had jumped ship in Soviet times and married a local woman. It was early and it wasn't difficult to persuade the elderly man to share a large cold bottle of Baltika beer. They talked about Russian culture and Henry edged towards folk sayings. An Orthodox crucifix always dangled over his host's threadbare purple sweater. Henry explained he had read a phrase he didn't quite understand, ripped the page from the notebook and placed it in front of his drinking companion. A sharp intake of breath, slow shake of the head and a reply in proficient English followed. He hadn't realised the old Russian knew the language.

"My friend, the grey one is the wolf. And the wolf is the name we use" – he dropped his voice – "when we don't want to name the devil himself. I think in English it is 'Speak of the devil and he will appear.' Something like that."

He wondered if the unexpected switch to English was the old man's way of avoiding stumbling into the pit himself. The mood changed and the page was pushed back towards him.

"Now, please excuse me. I have my work to do in the kitchen."

Henry had walked straight back to the apartment. The reply he had written to Nataliya was sitting on the secretaire – very British, amicable and laced with noble forgiveness. He reread it and then burnt it in the old blue-tiled fireplace in the corner of his study, raking over the ashes with a poker.

The breaker wasn't the best of the morning and he wasn't a gifted surfer. Rather graceless, he had to admit. He'd taken a week of lessons and, with a little luck, now just managed to stay on his feet as he was propelled onto the beach. Grounded, he carried his board up to the surf school where a hot shower awaited.

A pleasing Lisbon routine had unfolded. Days melted

into weeks, weeks into months. Sometimes a morning run beside the wide river Tagus, the promenade just a stone's throw from home. Then a quick *bica* at Ricardo's, the café on the ground floor of his building. Bica – strong, thick coffee favoured by the Portuguese. Back upstairs, turn on the BBC radio news whilst checking the morning's surf report online. Mostly done for fun – he couldn't believe he was now a surfer – but a couple of times a week he would put his outrageously expensive, overspecced board under his arm and walk over to take the surf train from the Cais do Sodre terminus. They left every twenty minutes, so he didn't even bother to learn the timetable.

Then Tuesday and Thursday evenings were spent at the drama academy, the other evenings given over to learning lines for the expat Lisbon Troubadours' summer production of King Lear. One hundred and eighty-eight lines, to be precise. Henry felt that he had been typecast, but he liked the eponymous role. It suited him, and his fellow expat cast members joked that his time in make-up would be minimal.

The morning after his fateful escape to Lisbon, Henry had resolved to change his life. Hiding out in Portugal was far from his choice, but he was determined to make the most of his Atlantic exile. Sitting on his balcony, he'd found a blank page in the little black book and started with three short notes:

1. *Get fit, lose weight (at least two stone), and change appearance*
2. *Learn to surf*
3. *Get acting skills up to professional level*

He had hesitated, torn, but then wrote down the final one.

4.   Toughen up and be ready to fight back – hard

He had sighed as he snapped the notebook closed, knowing that, sooner or later, that time would come.

* * *

As he towelled himself down, looking into the mirror of the spartan changing room, a different man stared back. At least different to London Henry. He'd done well with his objectives. He hadn't tended his beard since the day he parted company with Nea. White, wild and irregular, there was now something of an Old Testament prophet about him. The Atlantic winter wind had burnt his face and scalp. The pallor of thirty years' commuting was gone. He wondered if people might think he had been living rough, if he ever dared venture back to London. On the plus side, his designer wetsuit was now too big for him around the gut, tighter around the shoulders. He remembered the embarrassment of his first visit to the beach the previous year when, after a number of fruitless contortions, he had suffered the indignity of asking a young surfer to help him peel off the rubber straitjacket.

And now his twice-weekly boxing sessions with Luis, a former Portuguese Commando Regiment PT instructor, had worked wonders with his upper body. Ricardo had introduced them at the café and they trained under the jacaranda trees in a nearby park. Just pad work and circuits, but Henry's confidence was growing with every week that passed. After three months, he felt ready to ask Luis the big question that had been on his mind since the first practice round. His grey-headed, crew-cut instructor worked him hard, but had a surprisingly gentle way about him. He wasn't sure what his reaction might be. Getting his breath back, using his boxing-gloved hand to support himself against a trunk, he'd felt it was time.

"Sorry, an odd question, I know. But if I was attacked, do you think I'm now ready to defend myself?"

Luis's eyes had narrowed.

"Why are you asking this? I thought you wanted to get fit, not fight people."

"Yes, well, that's right. But just in case. I know it's unlikely ..."

His coach had slowly removed his sparring pads, tossing them onto the grass.

"Listen, Henry, Lisbon is one of the safest cities in Europe. And you aren't a street-fighting man ... But you will be fine if you learn just one move and practise, practise, practise, so it becomes your instinct."

Without any further warning, Luis's bare left hand shot out at Henry's chest, a lightning jab that stunned him. Almost simultaneously, his right fist powered in a cross to Henry's exposed windpipe. All in a fraction of a second. Henry recoiled, nearly falling backwards to the ground. His coach smiled.

"You are lucky I pulled those punches, my friend. But that will work for you every time. Remember. One-two. One-two. One-two. If anyone asks you, I never taught you this. It's very dangerous. I saw a man killed by this move in Angola. More than dead." He smiled, as if welcoming Henry to a secret club. "But we will make it part of your training from now on. Whoever you've got in mind, well, he won't be getting up after that."

* * *

Henry retrieved his valuables from the surf school locker, tucked the board under his arm and switched on his phone. A few sandy paces towards the station and he was stopped dead in his tracks. A ping, then a text appeared, an unwelcome reminder of another life.

> *Hello, my dear Henry. It is Sasha here. I will come to Lisbon tomorrow to meet with an old friend. Nataliya told me you are at your place there. Sorry for short notice but only just decided. Perhaps i can stay with you? We can discuss my work and have a good time together! I also have something important to tell you. Please say that will work? I miss you. S.*

Henry doubled back to the beach café which sat above the surf school. They knew him, and a bica arrived without him asking. He ordered a *prego*, a heavily buttered, sliced-beef sandwich that for some reason the Portuguese usually eat as a dessert. He had given up red meat months ago, but now he made an exception. He felt the need for brain fodder.

The last time he had seen Sasha was the day before his fateful meeting with Nea at Marylebone station. Henry had organised a lunch with the enthusiastic young analyst from Bonners who would now work with the Russian, helping develop his research. Probably his daughters' age, Priya had a doctorate in business organisation and data mining. Coupled with a brilliant reputation, which would usually be a good thing. But not that day. Lunch was a close-run affair. Priya was barely five feet tall and Sasha was on a roll. He didn't look at her once, beaming over her head towards Henry, stressing what a loss her boss would be to the firm. When Sasha started to expound his theories of board composition, Henry feared the worst. He hurriedly called for the bill and brought proceedings to a close. Priya had stayed friendly, engaged and charming. Professional to the end. But Henry didn't hold out much hope.

A prego, by tradition, is made from the cheapest cuts of meat and Henry was now chewing heavily, mechanically, considering his options.

A basic rule that Roddy and Colin had hammered home was to behave naturally, always stay in character. Act as if he didn't know that Sasha was a Directorate S illegal officer, one of the SVR's elite. Sasha should have no reason to suspect Henry of being an agent of British intelligence. And, come to think of it, he wasn't any more. That was finished. So that argued for welcoming the Russian with open arms. There wasn't much else in his diary, after all. And, as Sasha said, it could be fun.

But what if Sasha had rumbled him? Inviting a six-foot-seven-inch-tall, shovel-handed, highly trained enemy spy to stay under his roof might not be so clever. And what was the important news? What if he learnt something during the visit that obliged him to call London on his special number? Perhaps something that suggested Nea or Nataliya were in danger? The last thing he wanted to do was reconnect with Colin, not to mention that prick, Roddy.

The last visitors from London had been Henry's daughters. They spent Christmas with him in Lisbon and then New Year with Jane. They surfed with him, shopped, laughed together. His attempt to barbecue a turkey ended up with predictable hilarity. He loved their company, and by the end of the week he was sorely tempted to book a flight back to London. But something held him back. That odd line in Nataliya's letter. It wasn't safe. At least not yet.

He mopped up the meaty marinade with the last crust of bread and typed his reply.

Hi Sasha. Great to hear from you. Of course. You are always welcome here. Stay as long as you want. It will be good to catch up. See you tomorrow. HB.

12

TWO ENGLISHMEN ABROAD

LISBON, EARLY MARCH 2020

That evening, Henry made a point of locking up the apartment carefully. And then he double-checked, rattling every door and shutter. He had grown casual about security over the past few months but Sasha's arrival the following morning put him back on high alert. The clock from the convent up the hill struck midnight as he shuttered the windows and bolted the doors in his bedroom that gave on to a terrace with views over the old market and down to the wide river Tagus, flowing silent and silver in the moonlight. The beautiful deep, plaintive voice of Cesária Évora drifted up from the Cape Verdean bar down the street.

Henry occupied the top floor of his apartment building. The flats on the lower four floors were owned by foreign investors and he had never heard or seen a soul.

He lived alone in a building that was constructed in 1800, then gutted and gentrified in 2012. Until then it had served as a cheap boarding house, renting out rooms to mariners and fishermen. And, of course, as a brothel. As he climbed the worn limestone stairs, Henry sometimes stopped to touch the old tiled walls, to commune with the ghosts of the past. He tried to imagine what had happened behind them. All he felt was a strange peace, a building at rest.

Until fifteen years ago his was a street that decent Lisboetas avoided like the plague. A street for drinking, fighting and fornicating. The watering holes of the neighbourhood paid tribute to the sailors who exhausted their last escudos there. Bar Liverpool. Bar Rotterdam. Copenhagen. Viking Bar. Jamaica. Bar Oslo. But as soon as the docks moved down the river, the developers moved in. True, the old ladies in their widows' weeds still hung out of their windows alongside their washing. And the bright-yellow funicular continued to rattle up and down the steep cobbled street right next to Henry's place, its bell a reassuring reminder to him that he was far away from England and everything that had happened there. But now the passengers were well-heeled tourists, not dockers. At night the bars were techno clubs for Lisbon's new throng of residents, young digital nomads from northern Europe. By day the cafés served them oat milk lattes as they huddled at tables, coding and reprogramming the world.

Henry had learnt by heart every inch of his *bairro*, his adoptive neighbourhood. He saluted the shopkeepers, hailed the bar owners by name and recognised by sight the regular postman, street cleaners and patrolling policemen. Shoreditch had been a faceless mystery to him. Here, both time and inhabitants moved more slowly. The patterns of daily life were easier to study. And besides, something that one of his MI5 trainers had said kept coming back to him.

"Always look for the absence of 'normal'. If it doesn't feel right, it isn't. Trust your gut, Henry. Every time."

The following morning, he remembered that advice as he sat at a pavement table outside Ricardo's, waiting for the Russian giant to arrive from London. Nothing felt out of place. Tourists were thin on the ground in early March, though the sun shone and he drank his morning bica in cargo shorts and a Clash T-shirt. The regular drayman was delivering his beer barrels. The kitchen porter from the Chinese restaurant heaved a trolley laden with onions, peppers and sacks of rice over the cobbles from the wholesale market. José, an ever-patient Angolan, was directing cars into parking spaces, receiving a handful of small coinage for his troubles. Henry could hear the children playing in the yard of the school over the road.

He spotted Sasha before the spy saw him. He was shocked. The lumbering gait and sheer body mass signalled the Russian's approach. Otherwise, the young Russian was unrecognisable. His beard was gone and his hair was short and neat. He wore a plain navy blazer set off with a striped club tie and oversized black tasselled loafers. Henry caught sight of his own reflection in Ricardo's window and squirmed in his seat. He looked like a bum.

Sasha scanned the pavement tables and Henry had to raise an embarrassed hand of greeting. The Russian's own double take said it all. It had been a long five months for both of them.

He braced himself for the bear hug and kiss but was

offered a formal handshake instead. Sasha beamed but there was a strain, a new tension about him. Henry was now off balance.

"Welcome, Sasha. So, what brings you to Lisbon?"

The Russian ordered a morning beer and contemplated Henry before answering.

"I need to catch up with a friend. An old Englishman who lives out in Cascais." He continued to smile but his eyes were looking over Henry's shoulder. He sucked the beer down in a single draught and ordered another one.

Henry stayed silent and let Sasha continue.

"I met Jack at London School of Economics. He is very wise. Economic history."

He knew Sasha was lying. Against his better judgement, he was now intrigued. At least the spy wasn't meeting a fellow Russian.

"Yes. Jack is a gentleman. Just like you. But I am afraid he is quite ill now. So, I must see him, before it is too late. To tell him news and say goodbye."

Sasha sighed, produced the address of a bar in the Bairro Alto district and asked Henry how far it was. Apparently Jack was making a special trip into the city from his seaside home down the coast and the meeting was in an hour.

"Not far. I know it. A fifteen-minute walk up the hill. Let's take your bag up to the apartment and get you settled in." Henry had been relieved to see that his guest was travelling light. He didn't plan to stay long.

But Sasha didn't make to move and ordered his third beer of the morning. Henry sensed a heady mix of tension and elation. Something was coming.

"Henry. I have two important items to tell you. Wonderful news. And I have to thank you for everything. With all my heart."

Henry chuckled. Beardless and supported by the striped tie, Sasha's face looked like a huge slab of old English beef as he finished his beer.

"Henry, we must celebrate! We shall now drink champagne!"

Henry looked up at the clocktower of the old Lisbon central post office. Eleven o'clock. This was going to be a long day.

Ricardo opened the best sparkling bottle he had and poured two flutes. Glasses clinked and Sasha limbered up for his first toast.

"To eternal love."

"Can't argue with that."

"Please, will you honour me to be my best man?"

Henry gulped on the wine and unexpectedly found himself tearing up. Sasha was nervous, expectant and earnest.

"Of course. I would be delighted, Sasha. But why ask me? And who are you marrying?"

"Because you are the one who made my dreams come true. You introduced me to my darling Priya."

His brain went into overdrive. Priya? Priya? Christ, Priya!

"Priya? The girl—" he caught himself in time. "I mean, the young woman from Bonners? The clever one?"

He tried to grin over his incredulity.

"Yes. We have so much in common. We are made for each other. I am a such happy man."

Henry composed himself and resolved to proceed with caution.

"Congratulations, Sasha. Marvellous news. Do you have a wedding date in mind?"

"We are thinking later in the year. When I return to London next week, I shall meet Priya's parents to ask their blessing."

Good luck with that, he thought.

"They may not understand at first. But Priya and I, we are in love. We computer code together. Play chess. Solve puzzles. She is so good – almost Russian."

"It sounds wonderful. I'm very happy for you both. Will you be able to stay in London?"

Then the next bombshell. Sasha placed his hand on Henry's.

"The second news I have for you, Henry. Bonners has given me permanent job. I am so honoured. Thanks to you."

Sasha leant over the table and proffered a business card. He recognised the embossed crest instantly. It read:

Dr Aleksander Orlov
Head of Board Analytics, Bonners LLP

He studied the card for the polite amount of time and then pocketed it.

"That is brilliant news. Looks like everything is falling into place for you. Now, let's get you sorted out. You shouldn't be late for your friend."

* * *

Henry stood on his balcony and watched the sun's final flicker as it disappeared behind the blue-tiled building opposite. Sasha hadn't returned and the street below was coming to life. Friday evening and the locals were starting to come out. Nothing strange about that. The ornate, wrought-iron carriage lamps now glowed yellow and a tape of fado music played from the Bangladeshi-owned gift shop on the corner, forlorn music to lure in any tourists who happened by, looking for the real Lisbon.

He had considered a quick rummage through Sasha's belongings but then thought better of it. That world was behind him; and besides, if the Russian was following his training, he would have set a few traps to detect amateur interference, even if he had left buzzing with alcohol and excitement. He hadn't seen him drink like that before and, despite his enormous size, the beer and cheap fizzy wine had taken visible effect. Henry concluded he was drinking to calm his nerves.

At least Henry had time to take stock, but all he had come up with was a list of troubling questions. With no answers. What was the meeting with Jack really about? How on earth had Sasha and Priya got together? Would this wedding go ahead? More worrying, had Priya taken his place as Roddy and Colin's agent? She was keen and earnest, just the type. A girl guide who might be tempted to add an espionage badge to her sleeve.

So, should he warn her? And fuck, what about Bonners? He had faded away without a fuss. But they had just employed a Russian spy he had introduced. Sasha now had access to their systems, databases and secrets. The more he thought about it, the more of a mess he had left behind in London.

What to do?

His phone pinged.

Hey Henry. I am still at bar with Jack. Please come join us. It is fun. You will like him! We celebrate. Sasha

* * *

Henry stood at his hallway mirror, running a brush through his beard. Instinct had sent him to the back of his wardrobe and he now sported a pair of pink chinos, blue linen jacket, crisp white shirt and buffed black Oxfords.

A steep walk up the Bica hill behind his building brought him to the door of the bar. More museum than bar, in fact. He knew it, and its quirks. Hard to find for tourists and filled with endless nineteenth-century oddities – posters, toys, stuffed animals. Entrance required ringing a doorbell and then speaking through a small grille in the door with a bow-tied waiter. Inside, red plush velvet greeted him. And the sight of Sasha with Jack Somerset. They sat at the habitual spies' table, furthest from the entrance and closest to the kitchen.

Henry took in the scene as he approached the table. Sasha – florid, expansive and clearly drunk. His older companion – haggard, grey and unmistakably English. One look at him confirmed Sasha's prognosis. Henry's Yorkshire grandmother would have described him as "on his last legs", a description she reserved for, one by one, her departing friends, with the grim satisfaction of a born survivor.

Sasha stood, swayed and pulled up a stool for Henry. Jack Somerset looked languidly surprised. Then he tried to rise to his feet, still tall but stooped, gripping at the table as pain shot across his cadaverous face. Old British courtesies seemed nearly the last thing to die.

"Please don't get up, sir." Henry never called anyone "sir", but with Jack it came as a reflex, a deep impulse. He wondered why he had said that. He was about to find out.

He joined his two companions in a goldfish-bowl-sized gin and tonic as Sasha made the introductions. It was clear that whatever business brought the Russian spy to Lisbon was now concluded and, at least to his mind, he was off duty. Now it was time for the two Englishmen abroad to study each other in time-honoured fashion.

Henry decided to take advantage of the persona that MI6 had digitally fashioned for him. Hereford College, Oxford. Oarsman in the first eight. Career in the City satisfactorily concluded. Happily divorced. Now enjoying a bachelor's retirement in the sun. It all sounded plausible, not least because Henry had grown to believe it himself.

"Hereford, eh? I didn't send many of my boys there. In my day, Eton favoured older Oxford colleges." Jack sniffed. "But there was one pupil of mine, I recall. Now the master of Hereford. What is his name? My memory is shocking. Do you know him?"

Jack's eyes were milky and red-rimmed, but razor-sharp. Suspicious. Henry knew he couldn't fluff this. Henry reminded Jack of the master's name. First test passed.

"In fact, I had dinner with him only last year. A lovely

man. Seems to be doing wonders for Hereford. Did you teach at Eton College, sir?"

Second test seemed to be in the bag. Jack sank back into his chair. His long hands were bony and mottled purple as he nursed his drink.

"I did indeed. And please do call me Jack. I am afraid the old schoolmaster in me does bring out the schoolboy in a lot of men like you." Jack gave a shallow, rasping laugh. Then came the difficult one, bowled low, slow and deliberate.

"Tell me this, Henry. I am guessing you have had … professional dealings with the master of Hereford College over the years, have you not?"

Jack's stare was unblinking. The old man seemed to scent the taint of MI6 on him, lapsed or active, wafting across the velvet Victorian card table where the drinks were placed. In the nick of time, he remembered Colin's little trick. Focus on your interrogator's nose; avoid the eyes at all costs. At close range, your opponent can't see where you are looking. Helpfully, Jack's nose was fascinating. Aqualine, but shot through with angry blood vessels, white hair sprouting and a globule of something damp and yellow forming up in the right nostril.

"I've only got to know the master recently, Jack. In the last few months. I've time on my hands and volunteered to help raise funds. Put something back, you know?"

"That is very noble of you."

Henry wondered if his delivery was a bit too breezy. And was the response a tad sarcastic? There was a long pause, but then Jack seemed satisfied and turned his attention to Sasha.

"Well, Sasha, I think we should have a final toast to all your good news and then I must to bed. João will wonder what on earth has happened to me."

Glasses were raised, clinked and drained. Henry and Sasha helped Jack to his feet and a waiter was quick to bring his old covert coat and horn-handled walking stick. He spent a long minute catching his breath before shuffling forward.

Jack used the frame of the bar's front door for support, the yellowed fingers of his right hand trembling as the waiter scoured the street for a taxi.

"Henry, have you ever dined at the British Club in Cascais? They have hare in season at the moment. *Lebre com feijoa*. It's splendid."

Henry admitted that he hadn't.

"Then let's have dinner there tomorrow night. The four of us. João could do with an evening out. I must confess that Sasha somewhat surprised me with you this evening, the scallywag. But it's always a pleasure to meet a fellow Englishman like you. Important to reminisce at my time of life."

Henry and Sasha agreed to dinner enthusiastically. As the taxi pulled up, Jack had the valedictory word.

"Henry, when we meet tomorrow, please don't be surprised or offended if I offer very mixed feelings about our country. I will never see her again. Sasha might have mentioned, but the quacks give me a month or two at most. So I feel I have very little to lose now. I think I did the right thing with my life, I really do. But, like with the medics, a second opinion is always beneficial."

As the cab pulled away, Sasha looked puzzled.

"What did Jack say? Sometimes he speaks in a way I do not follow."

Henry had caught everything, crystal clear. Jack's delivery, in the style of a nineteen fifties' BBC Home Service continuity announcer, was the embodiment of authority and precision. At that moment he knew his peace in Lisbon was about to be shattered. But also that there was nowhere else to run to. Deep down he had known the time was coming, and now it had arrived, he felt oddly calm, ready for the trial ahead.

"I think he just wants British company. So, let's enjoy a decent dinner tomorrow night and make the old man happy. By the way, what's wrong with him?"

The two men started their cobbled descent back to the apartment.

"Lung disease. Very bad now. Jack always smoked. Still does. Dirty Indonesian cigarettes. And Balkan Sobranies. I always bring a tin for him from London." Sasha caught himself. The drink was talking and he was providing too much information. His visits to Lisbon sounded regular.

Sasha stopped and looked down the hill and out across the river. The last funicular of the evening was starting its trundle down from the peak behind them.

"Maybe you have already guessed, Henry" – Sasha was conspiratorial and solemn – "but I am afraid Jack is also homosexual."

* * *

Shadow again last night. Same odd thing as the last few months. It was there in the dream, but much further away than before. Looked out of the window and it was standing in the shadows, down the road, by the entrance to the market. And less scary. Neutral or even a friend. Waving. Connecting. Difficult to understand given what's happening to me. Really need Nea to help me.

HB's Dream Diary
5 March 2019

The sky above Ricardo's café was piercing blue as Henry finished his third black coffee of the morning. He was completing the entry in his little black dream diary when Sasha finally emerged from the front door of the building, blinking in the strong sunlight. Henry deftly stowed the secret book in his breast pocket as the Russian joined him at the pavement table, sighing as he squeezed his massive frame into the little red plastic chair. He smelled of Henry's purloined aftershave and stale booze.

"I've ordered you a coffee. How's your head this morning?"

Sasha leant back into his seat and it groaned along with its occupant. Henry was worried it might disintegrate under his weight.

"*Bog nakazyvayet menya* … God is punishing me." Sasha managed a weak smile. "What time is it?"

Henry pointed up to the clock on the old post office tower. Two minutes before noon.

"Maybe you want quiet night tonight, Henry? Perhaps not the British Club? Maybe see Jack Somerset some other time, after I'm gone?"

Henry guessed that sober Sasha now realised he had

made a mistake. A big one. And was offering all of them a way out. Henry didn't hesitate – he had already made his decision. Ever-smiling Ricardo breezed over with the next round of coffees.

"I wouldn't dream of cancelling. I feel as fresh as a daisy. And, besides, I don't know if I'll ever see Jack again."

Sasha shrugged, fatalism *à la russe*.

"As you wish. Seven thirty tonight at the club. You, me, Jack and his João. You need to wear jacket and tie." Sasha eyed Henry. "And maybe cut beard a little. Or at least wash it."

Henry laughed and Sasha joined him. The Russian spy and British agent understood each other.

"Okay. I give you Jack's number if you have problem. He doesn't have cell phone. This is his house." Sasha paused and again looked over Henry's shoulder into the middle distance.

"I need to do something first so will see you at the club." Sasha hesitated and then produced a small, square dark-green box and handed it to him. "Please, Henry, this is engagement ring for Priya. Please look after it for me, for now."

He took it and put it in his jacket pocket carefully, searching Sasha's bloodshot eyes for an explanation.

"Henry, you know this is duty of best man."

Henry nodded in sad agreement. "You have my word."

* * *

Henry cleared condensation from the grubby window with the sleeve of his linen jacket and then watched the lights of the anchored tankers and freighters reflect off the river as they passed them by. The Lisbon to Cascais train rumbled through his usual surf station, then penetrated the dark night ahead. It was early evening and the carriage was quiet. A few shopworkers heading home from Lisbon, tired and pallid under the unforgiving strip lights. He was the odd man out, but he didn't care. He wore his British ensemble from the night before with the addition of a straw hat and Hereford College tie as a flourish. He had bought it in a small shop in Burlington Arcade and its purchase, after his visit to Oxford, had been more nerve-wracking than anything he had done for Roddy, Colin, Queen or Country. His palms had sweated as he selected the cerise-and-cream tie. He was ready at any moment to be challenged by the shop assistant. He had rehearsed his bona fides, only to find the main hurdle was remembering his PIN as he panicked when paying. Tonight was its first public outing and he couldn't rid himself of the irrational thought that an old member of Hereford College, Oxford, might board the train at any moment and unmask him for the imposter he was.

The lights of the British Club shone a beacon across Cascais harbour. Housed in a mock Tudor mansion built during the war, Henry couldn't miss it. A nest of spies back then, tonight felt like the final chapter of an age-old game. The evening was chilly and, as he waited in the hallway to be seated, he was glad of the log fire after his walk from the station. The waiters moved glacially, wearing white double-breasted evening jackets, men of Jack Somerset's vintage. As he was led across the wood-panelled dining room, the carving trolley, crisp linen and small latticed windows signalled a time warp. As such, Henry prepared himself for a fateful history lesson.

Jack was seated by the window at a table set for four. His companion was a slightly built Portuguese, probably twenty years' Jack's junior. Henry's age. A full dark head of hair and with twinkling, playful eyes, João sprang to his feet and offered his hand. Jack rose painfully but Henry now thought better of stopping him. Pleasantries were made and dry sherry taken. Jack summoned the waiter and, without consulting either the menu or his dining companions, ordered stewed lampreys followed by hare with beans. The fourth chair remained stubbornly empty.

"Jack, have you heard from Sasha? He said he would join us here. I hope he hasn't got lost."

Jack played with the silver napkin ring, slowly twirling it around his fingers.

"Sasha knows where to come. I am sure he will be here soon. But he is young, and rather disorganised at present. I am sure he will learn better discipline as he gets older."

Interesting. He spotted his gambit.

"Does he remind you of any of your boys at Eton? He can't be that much older, after all."

The punch landed. Jack caught his breath, rasping, and João looked on anxiously.

"What an astute question, Henry. Terribly clever of you."

Henry wasn't sure whether he detected anger, admiration, or both.

"You know, I hated that place. The institution, the smugness, self-satisfaction, everything it stood for."

Jack threw his head back, hitting the hardwood high

chair as he gasped for breath. João poured him a glass of water. Henry knew not to interrupt the flow.

"But some of my pupils were different. I loved them. Exceptional talents. I taught history and I knew my subject. I think you do too. The miners' strike. Bloody Sunday. Thatcher. Mary bloody Whitehouse. Not much to be balanced about back then. I was a northern state-school boy. Just like you, Henry. I just hide it better."

Henry tried to object but Jack raised a hand to silence him. He looked indulgent.

"Henry, I've got your number. I've worked you out. I know you. *Gnothi seauton*. Know thyself."

For the first time, he saw Jack's naked charisma and imagined him in his prime, casting his spells.

"I think you just haven't been brave enough to come off the fence yet, work out whose side you are on."

The wine waiter arrived at the table and started with the required theatre, decanting a decent bottle of a full-bodied red Alentejo wine. But after fifty years at the job, he could sense the mood of a table like a human barometer. As such, he poured quickly and then backed away in silence.

"Forty years ago, every Eton College pupil entering the sixth form was able to approach a beak for personal tuition. Mentoring. Preparation for one of the great universities. Time given freely at weekends."

Jack stopped and pulled a white handkerchief from the breast pocket of his suit jacket. Three loud, spasmodic coughs and then a careful inspection of the contents. Jack looked down with the dispassion of a biology teacher inspecting a frog dissection, before carefully folding the linen and putting it away in his trouser pocket. Henry feared the worst for him.

"I say this with no particular pride, but I was heavily oversubscribed with requests. Well, if you can't be radical when you are seventeen, when can you be? But, can you believe it, some of the other masters who had no takers even complained to the headmaster about me? But I took them all on. All the boys. Bright, open-minded, vessels to be filled. And some have done remarkably well for themselves in later life."

Jack slumped back again, but now with a mischievous smile.

"So, Henry Bradbury, to answer your question. Could I have taught Sasha anything in the very unlikely event that he was a pupil of mine at Eton College?"

Jack struggled forward on his elbows and leant in. His breath smelt of cloves, tobacco and decay.

"Of course. Two things for that young man. Firstly, always play the long game – never cut corners. And secondly, a gentleman is never, never, off duty."

Jack thought a little more and then laughed.

"Though I think I would have pointed him to the rugger pitch rather than the groves of Academe. He would have made an excellent second row for the First XV."

With that, Jack raised a finger, signalling for dinner to be served.

* * *

Henry paid the bill. The fourth chair was still empty and he decided not to mention Sasha again. Conversation had flowed. João was a book editor and entertaining company. A mine of knowledge on Portuguese history and, as the three men walked slowly along the promenade outside the club, evidently an accomplished a cappella fado singer. Henry supported Jack's right elbow and João his left as his sad song of loss drifted on the February air. They reached the door of the couple's whitewashed cottage by the high sea wall of Cascais, and Henry prepared to take his leave.

But Jack gripped his hand tightly, with surprising strength.

"Don't go quite yet. Pop in for a nightcap. One for the road, I seem to remember. That's the expression. Yes. I remember."

* * *

Jack Somerset led Henry into the sitting room whilst João started to close the plain wooden shutters. The window at the far end of the room looked directly onto Cascais harbour, the lights of the British Club being extinguished just as the slight Portuguese locked and bolted it. Even closed, waves could be heard lapping somewhere below.

João poured three glasses of tawny port. Warre's 1970. Henry knew he was going to get the grand tour. It felt like a special occasion. The sitting room opened onto a small dining area, with a table for four, and a galley kitchen beyond. There was a pleasant smell of fried garlic mingling with beeswax. Bookshelves were floor to ceiling, mostly hardback, in English, Portuguese and a few old Russian titles. Two walls were left for photographs and prints. Jack's long life on display, not an inch of hanging space left fallow. Victorian and Edwardian sporting prints – huntsmen, dogs, polo, a solitary stag on a misty hill. An oil painting depicting a group of bekilted men taking aim at a flight of duck made Henry shudder.

But twelve narrow, framed photographs held pride of place. He inspected them politely under Jack's steady gaze. Eton College's sixth formers, 1977 to 1989. Serried ranks, white-tie uniforms. The boys' hairstyles progressed with the years, but he spotted Jack Somerset as the constant, tall and erect, receding blond hair, anchoring the third row, seated on the right, year in, year out. He lingered over the early nineteen eighties, confirming the boys that he thought he recognised in the hand-printed name guide below. Some famous names – and faces.

"You seem particularly interested in a few noteworthy years there, Henry. Quite a talented cohort, you'd have to agree, would you not?"

Jack wheezed triumphantly.

"It's my generation, Jack. And funny to see those youthful faces, knowing how they've all aged."

He was about to move on when his eyes were drawn, almost dragged, to a particularly familiar face, tall with a full mouth of teeth – 1987. Henry concentrated hard but was aware of the steady gaze of his host. Trying hard to mask his interest, he searched the legend to match a name. There it was: Roderick Samson-Brown. But, too tall for his Roddy. It was his older brother! A quick scan of 1989 solved the puzzle. Rupert Samson-Brown stared insolently back at Henry.

Henry could hear Jack's laboured breathing close to his left shoulder and turned to face him. Both men took one step backwards, re-establishing the required English distance. He knew he had to move things on.

"Are you still in touch with your students?"

Jack swayed on his feet and then seemed to ignore the question. Instead, he shuffled to the corner of the room nearest to the harbour, bending over a gramophone player that Henry now noticed for the first time. He switched it on and pulled an LP from a stack that sat above the old contraption. João was on hand to pull the shiny black disc from its sleeve, place it on the turntable and lower the needle.

The music started softly. As it grew, Henry grasped its significance.

"I am sure you recognise this?"

He knew Jack was being transported back to his Eton one-to-one weekend tutorials of forty years ago. Always challenging his boys. An education in a world wider than the Thames Valley. A chance to put his pupils down, break them in, only to pick them up as better men.

"Of course, Jack. Rachmaninoff. *Vespers*. Beautiful."

Jack smiled unhappily. He looked disappointed. Henry knew he had passed a test he wasn't supposed to, but Nataliya had introduced him to it after their meeting at the church. And now it was time to press home his victory.

"So, come on, Jack, are you still in touch with any of the boys? I suspect you were a great influence on them."

Jack drained his port and shuffled towards the entrance hall in silence. Henry and João put their crystal glasses down and followed on.

"Henry, a lovely evening. Wonderful to spend time with a fellow Englishman. But I am afraid that you might miss your last train back to Lisbon. And I am flagging."

As the three men reached the front door, Jack swung around with an energy that surprised Henry. He raised his hand and pointed to a black-and-white framed print, a medieval woodcut, hanging in the hallway. Henry had missed it on the way in. It was water-stained at the margin and its title at the bottom was in German gothic script.

"To answer your question, indeed I am in regular touch with the boys. We remain close. I am very proud of them."

Henry inspected the print. It showed a strong, heavy man hanging from a tree, caught by his abundant hair, whilst his horse escaped from under him just as his enemies approached, brandishing spears. The title read "ABSALOM".

Jack gasped for breath as he unlatched the door.

"My life's work, Henry. I confess I thought I might need a second opinion. But, as a matter of fact, I don't. I did the right thing. Now, goodnight to you."

13

BLOODY SUNDAY

Lisbon is old-fashioned when it comes to the observance of high days and holidays. Sundays are still a day of rest and restaurants are full of three or four generations of families lunching together. In every bairro of the city, the churches are thrown open for morning mass, while trade and offices are shuttered for the day.

Henry's phone pinged in his jacket pocket, waking him with a start. He found himself sitting bolt upright in his old wicker planter's chair which was turned to face the entrance hall to his apartment. He wore his club clothes from the night before, and the poker from his fireplace lay on the chair arm beside him. His tie was still knotted tight but at least he had removed his straw hat. Church bells began to peel as he gathered his wits.

He had returned to the apartment after midnight fully

expecting to find Sasha. First, he knocked tentatively on the bedroom door. Then louder, listening for snores from within. Nothing. The door was unlocked and he peered around it. The shutters were open and the moon was full, coldly illuminating an empty room. No Sasha. Bed unmade and roller case gone. Just a faint, residual fug of sweat and stale farts. He checked the other bedrooms and library. No note – nothing. He checked for Priya's engagement ring. Still where he had left it in the back of a small drawer in the secretaire.

He was worried. Something was wrong. He couldn't get Nataliya's warning about the "grey one" out of his mind. And then the other troubling image, mighty Absalom swinging from the tree by his luxuriant head of hair. Jack had presented him with a real secret, perhaps the key that unlocked all the others he had collected since that first call from Roddy?

Henry had made himself a pot of strong black coffee to help him with his night vigil. The last thing he remembered was the convent clock chiming four bells, and then suddenly the churches were summoning the people of Lisbon to morning mass. He stood up stiffly and cautiously approached the window with a vantage down along Rua de São Paulo. At first, he stood to the side of the casement, shielded by the concertinaed shutter. Gingerly, he peered up and down the street, minimising movement and conjuring his mental map of the bairro when at Sunday rest. He saw beer bottles strewn in the gutter from the night before, overflowing waste bins from the bars and cafés awaiting collection, but not a soul in sight.

He went to the kitchen and poured himself the last

of the black coffee, cold and thick from the night before. His palms were damp and sweat beaded down his neck. Leaning against the sink, he wondered if he wasn't just having a midlife crisis but a full-fat nervous breakdown. Was this what it would feel like? Or some kind of paranoid psychosis? Was it normal to arm yourself with ironmongery in the middle of the night and obsess about a Russian saying and a medieval German woodblock print?

His mobile phone rang and answered the question for him. A Lisbon number.

"Hello. Is that Mr Bradbury? Henry Bradbury?"

The voice was British, no nonsense. Classless, perhaps an undercurrent of Scots? Henry couldn't quite pin it down.

"Who is calling?"

"First off, sorry for intruding on your Sunday. I did try texting you earlier. It's an urgent embassy matter."

Henry remained silent.

"My name's Colonel Tim O'Driscoll. I think we've probably met at one of the British Club knees-ups?"

They hadn't. They both knew it. Henry detected a clumsy attempt at finding something to warm up a very cold call.

"Anyway, I'm the British military attaché in Lisbon. For my sins." He laughed weakly. Henry let another attempt at bonhomie fall flat on its face.

"Look, I'd be grateful if you'd come up to see me at the embassy, please. A government colleague in London needs to get an urgent message to you. Somebody you have kindly helped in the past."

Henry's silence was evidently unnerving him.

"He said to say 'BRILLIANTINE' to you. All capital letters. I hope that rings a bell? Means nothing to me. It's the highest priority signal I've ever received from, err, that lot."

The colonel sounded like this wasn't his thing at all. He wanted to get off the phone as quickly as possible. And on to his golf, Henry suspected.

"The embassy guards are expecting you and I am waiting in my office. Just give my name to the Portuguese police on the barrier."

Henry broke his silence.

"When do you want to see me?"

"Now. Right away. It's a fifteen-minute walk from your home. Or take the tram – number 25. There's one along in seven minutes; it's running five minutes' late, so you're in luck."

"On my way, Tim."

"Oh, and please bring your passport. Just a formality, but I need to check it before I read you the cable. Protocol, apparently. See you soon, Henry."

He drank the cold coffee down to the dregs and then rummaged in the secretaire for his passport. The colonel was very well informed. He knew where he lived, where he was at the moment. He knew he was in his apartment. Even the live tram times. He smiled with relief. He wasn't going mad, after all.

Springing down the three flights of stone stairs, two worn steps at a time, he swung open the door of the apartment building that gave onto black-and-cream limestone cobbles. Fresh graffiti had appeared overnight on the wall immediately to the left of his building. It hadn't been there when he got home, and he stopped and stood back to take it in. It was actually very good. Every time the landlord painted the wall, a fresh piece appeared. Lisbon was famous for it. This one was about five feet tall by fifteen feet wide and extended onto his front door. A striking young African woman with one eye open, one closed, and a silver fish head – perhaps a sardine? The paint was still tacky when he touched it, and at least seven different colours were involved. It must have taken hours. Four? Five? More? Perhaps the *grafiteiros* had been his unwitting nightwatchmen. Pleased with the idea, he placed his straw hat on his head and pulled the brim down low. The sun was already strong. He decided to walk, and something propelled him along with a brisk purpose. Adrenaline? A mission? A desire to untangle the secrets of the last year, once and for all? He knew he was getting closer.

The walk gave him time to think. Fact one, the colonel had indeed received a cable from either Roddy or Colin – how else would he know the crash code word? Fact two, Sasha had screwed up and led him to Jack. Fact three, Jack had got his big secret off his chest – to Henry. Then the conjecture, the tricky questions. After all these years, did Jack just need an audience for his curtain call? A jury of at least one of his peers? Confession and absolution? And how significant was ABSALOM? Surely a cable from the Joint Russia Programme was hardly a coincidence?

"Just find ABSALOM. And quickly," Henry ordered himself, under his breath. He knew what he had to do.

Never be rushed, set your own pace. Take your time. Colin's words of advice on anti-surveillance intruded on his thoughts as he turned into the long tree-lined street that led up to the British embassy. Colonel Tim could wait a little longer as Henry started his drills. The military attaché had been very exact about timings. Perhaps his military background? A desire to tee off as soon as possible? Or, as was seeming more likely, to walk him right into a trap? Anyway, the colonel wasn't going anywhere and Henry wasn't taking any chances.

He took a sudden detour into a square to his right where a kiosk was just opening and a waitress was chalking up the day's specials on a blackboard. He ordered a bica, the first customer of the day. Whilst the coffee was being prepared, he lent his elbow on the serving hatch and took in his surroundings, using the dusty mirror behind the spirits bottles to his advantage. A few older couples heading to church and a Senegalese vendor unfolding a blanket, laying out sunglasses and African carvings. So far, so good. But then a man in leathers on a powerful motorbike pulled up and dropped the kickstand. He kept his black helmet on, visor down, then pulled his phone out of his leather jacket, studying it intently. An old red saloon car with a young couple wearing sunglasses came up the hill – the same direction of travel as him. In the mirror, it came into view sauntering slowly, but as it passed him, picked up speed.

He pulled up a chair at a solitary table under one of the jacaranda trees and stirred his coffee. Searching his jacket pockets, he was relieved to find the handwritten note of Jack Somerset's home telephone number. He dialled it. Engaged. He was trying a second time when the same car slid back down the hill, driver and passenger looking straight ahead. The motorcyclist was still concentrating on his text. Henry scanned the square to his right. Two new characters had arrived, complete with a theodolite on a tripod. Both men wore high visibility jackets, dark glasses, and one had a clipboard. Both avoided looking in his direction. Everybody in the square was looking anywhere but at him.

The idea of Lisbon's city surveyors actually working a Sunday shift caused him to chuckle and then pocket his phone. He had the forethought to choose the table nearest to a steep, narrow set of steps that dropped straight down the hill to the river. Colin's other edict now started flashing up, in neon.

"Remember our MI5 golden rules, Henry. Once is an accident. Twice is a coincidence. Three times is an enemy action. No mission is too important to abort. Just get the hell out of there."

Henry didn't need telling twice. He moved calmly but with purpose. Within ten minutes he had descended to sea level. Hanging laundry fluttering overhead and the smells of Sunday lunch drifted through the labyrinth of narrow alleyways. Garlic and fish. He took a long look back up the hill – nothing except two young girls throwing a ball to each other. A black cat shot across his path as he maintained a steady pace. He tried to remember if that was a sign of good luck before deciding it was going to be.

The promenade by the river Tagus had come to life. A three-piece Brazilian ensemble had struck up a lively samba, setting a small crowd swaying, children hoisted on their fathers' shoulders. Sleek hydrofoils and old ferries zigzagged across the wide river, and a regatta of sailing dinghies was tacking midstream, taking advantage of the stiff February breeze blowing in off the Atlantic.

Henry needed time to make two phone calls and then plan his escape. Just a little time to think in peace. There was no sign of the red saloon car, motorcyclist or unlikely surveyors. But he knew his pursuers wouldn't be far behind.

Spotting a familiar two-masted yacht tied up at the end of a short pier, he made his decision. It was 11.47 and *Mystique* would cast off at midday for her regular two-hour cruise downstream, past Belém and then back again. It was a favourite outing with Henry's visitors and he had become well acquainted with the old skipper. He was a good host, keeping the plastic wine glasses topped up and conversation flowing.

He bought his ticket from the young woman on the dock, Cristóvão's niece.

"How many people today?"

"It's quiet. Two couples, probably Americans? But a beautiful day to sail, Henry. Enjoy."

She waved him goodbye as he hurried down the floating pontoon and was helped aboard by Cristóvão and his mate.

"*Olá*, Henry. *Bom dia, amigo.* How many times is this, my friend? I must be doing something right!"

The skipper slapped him on the shoulder and, without being asked, handed him a brimming glass of cheap white wine.

Henry raised his straw hat to greet his four fellow passengers ranged around the cockpit, before moving forward along the deck to the bow, out of earshot. The engine had started and the wind was whistling through the metal stays. He dialled Jack's number.

Third time lucky. João answered.

"Hi, João. It's Henry. Listen, thanks for the hospitality last night. I just wondered if you've heard anything from Sasha?"

Silence.

"It's just that he's disappeared and I'm a bit worried."

Silence.

"Sorry, it's noisy here. Can you hear me?"

"Yes, Henry, I hear you."

Cold. Stone cold.

"Has Jack heard anything?"

Pause.

"Jack is dead."

Henry gripped the phone tightly to his ear and looked about. The crew were making the boat ready, and out of the corner of his eye he sensed a man jogging down the pontoon towards *Mystique*, holding his hand up to stop Cristóvão casting off.

"Oh João, I am so, so sorry to hear that. He was a very special man."

He could hear João whispering to someone.

"I just hope it was peaceful."

Pause.

"Far from it. At dawn I found Jack at the bottom of the steps up from the sea wall. Fallen onto the rocks. Twenty-metre drop. His body was broken, but he'd still tried to crawl home. He made it to the steps. Must have been agony, his final moments."

More whispers.

"God, João. What happened?"

"I think you might know already. He took a phone call

181

shortly after you left us last night. He was agitated, got his coat and went outside. I tried to stop him."

Henry was thinking hard, looking at the man boarding the boat from the stern.

"Henry, you see, Jack told me he was going out to meet you."

Cristóvão held out his hand to help the latecomer board but was waved away. A slightly built, dapper man in his sixties sprang onto the aft deck. With spiky blond hair and an expensive-looking black leather jacket, tight white shirt and matching jeans, he didn't look like he had started the morning with sailing in mind.

"Where are you, Henry? You need to talk to the police."

Henry rang off and finished his wine in one swig.

His phone buzzed. He recognised Colonel O'Driscoll's number and declined. Five missed calls. A timely reminder of an apparently casual comment Roddy had once made, with a whiff of menace. He couldn't quite remember the context, but the MI6 man had warned Henry that intelligence agencies and the police can find you any place, any time, the moment you switch on your phone or tablet. The same with credit cards, airline boarding passes, border control. So, he would now allow himself one last call before heading home to England, fading to grey, running analogue. He was saying goodbye to the digital world until he found ABSALOM.

Mystique was now motorsailing away from the quay, Cristóvão at the helm and the mate pouring drinks in the cockpit. The Americans were taking pictures of each other, and the sprightly latecomer perched next to the aft hatch, laughing with the skipper.

Henry made his last call, standing with one hand on the foremast to steady himself.

"Hello, Nea Solomon." That transatlantic voice was the best thing he had heard in a long time, but he had to be brief. He shouted above the river.

"It's Henry. Can you hear me?"

"Just about. Good to hear from you. Are you back in London?"

A freighter sounded its horn – a long blast.

"No. All at sea at the moment."

Nea laughed.

"Nea, I've got to be quick. And I can't say too much on the phone. I know you understand?"

The boat was turning up river and Cristóvão was starting to heave on a sheet to raise the mainsail. The newcomer had volunteered to help him whilst the mate took the helm.

"You need to be really careful, Nea. I'm afraid you are in danger."

"Go on …" The voice was mill-pond calm.

"It's all turned to shit here in Lisbon. One dead body. Somebody else disappeared. Persons unknown following me."

Nea's silence triggered a question that he hadn't planned.

"You really got to know me, Nea. Professionally. Did you ever consider I might slip into mental illness? Like paranoia? Persecution complex?"

"Not really, Henry. Of course, you've got your issues to work on. But no. Why do you ask? Do you need help?"

He sighed with relief.

"I need lots of help. But I'm going to have to rely on strangers for that from now on. I'm about to go off-air for a while, for everyone's sake. I think I've got the kiss of death, or something like that."

He heard the engine die and turned to see the sail fill out and start to tug *Mystique* towards Alfama, Lisbon's oldest neighbourhood. The boat bounced gently over the chop of the river.

"The thing we discussed. It's real. I'm stuck in the middle of it. I need to solve it myself. It's my only way out. But I'm scared for you. And sorry if I've landed you in it too."

"That's okay, Henry. I can take care of myself. What are you going to do?"

"I need to solve a puzzle. Listen, does this name mean anything to you? ABSALOM?"

As soon as the name left his mouth, he caught a shadow crossing the white deck behind him. Turning, he saw the slight man heading his way, closing fast. He was relieved to see that both his hands were occupied, one with a polystyrene plate of bread, cheese and ham, and the other gripping the boat as *Mystique* tacked.

He rang off and powered down his phone. For the last time. Frustrating, but ABSALOM would have to wait. The snacks were swung in front of him and his companion gripped the mast, spare hand clenched right above Henry's. The heel of his small, tanned hand touched Henry's thumb.

"Come on, help yourself to food. And don't be a stranger, man. The party's just getting started in the back …"

* * *

Henry checked that he was quite alone below deck before picking up the polished brass dividers from Cristóvão's chart table. *Mystique* was nineteen fifties' vintage and had aged well, lovingly cared for. The mahogany panelling was rich and dark, the saloon wall barometer and ship's clock both proclaimed their Liverpool heritage with pride.

Carefully locking the door to the heads behind him, he slipped one of the two sharp points of the instrument into a small hole in the side of his phone. The little tray containing its SIM card ejected. He flipped it out, opened the porthole and dropped it in the river. He was on his own from now on.

As he climbed back up into the cockpit, he saw the ancient tower of Belém off to starboard and tuned in to Cristóvão's soothing patter. The mood was relaxed. Two screw-top bottles of rosé wine and one of vinho verde sat empty in a cardboard box. The skipper was refreshing glasses from newly opened ones. Henry reckoned that Cristóvão had long ago calculated the cost-benefit ratio between a generous flow of booze at three euros a bottle and the glowing online reviews which followed.

Chad and Karen were visiting from Milwaukee. First time in Europe, they couldn't wait to denounce President Trump, without even being invited to. In their thirties, they were honeymooners. Plastic glasses raised a number of times in salute. And then Ray and Angel, could you believe it, also newlyweds? More toasts. From Rhode Island, in their forties, and second time around.

Jed, the latecomer, proposed another toast. "Older, if not wiser!" Everyone drank to that as *Mystique* turned and set a course back to Lisbon.

Jed clearly intrigued the Americans. Retired from the music business, he was making his way around the world, taking things as they came. A London accent, with an undercurrent of something else, hard to place. Nobody else on board would spot it, but Henry did. Jed's bright blue eyes positively sparkled when Ray, a big-time music fan, asked him about his most memorable gigs.

"Man, some awesome ones in the early eighties." He paused for effect. "If only I could friggin' well remember them!"

The gang loved that. Angel whispered something in Ray's ear and he burst out laughing.

"I gotta ask you something, Jed. It's kinda personal."

"Anything, my friend."

"Angel wants to know" – Ray looked sheepish – "if you're Billy Idol travelling undercover?"

The cockpit erupted and Jed stood up, raising his hands in mock horror.

"You know what, folks? If I was, I'd have you all visit me back on my superyacht! Right after this!"

Henry tried to relax. He'd made his calls, gone offline and had time to decide which railway station to head for when they docked, and by which back alleys. He was ready for the run to London. The boat trip had helped, as had the wine. It had felt so normal after everything that had happened in the last forty-eight hours. Sitting with the others in the cockpit, he felt his head lolling forward. He needed to sleep.

Mystique shuddered as Cristóvão fired up the engine and turned the rudder for the final approach to her berth. The sensation that ran through Henry's frame took him straight back to the deck of the boat on the Thames the previous autumn, that invaluable lesson in counter-espionage. Mr Itoh, the young nurse, the backpackers, the older couple. All fakes. Colin's convincing maritime MI5 cast.

Jed sat opposite him, running a hand through his wind-ruffled hair, smiling at the sun. He had kicked off his trainers. One foot was oddly misshaped, hooked like a talon. He now had Henry's full attention. He was chewing rhythmically. Gum? Then he spat something into his hand and tossed the contents over the rail. Jed repeated the ritual. This time the wind had banked and blew something back onto the boat. Little black insects scattered on the white gunwale. Henry focused.

Fuck. *Semechki*! Russian sunflower husks.

The mate had taken the wheel and Cristóvão was heading forward to lower the mainsail. Henry followed him, offering help. As the two men folded the canvas down, he spoke urgently.

"Cristóvão, I need to get off *Mystique* before the others. Can you drop me somewhere?"

Cristóvão eyed him and shrugged.

"Relax, Henry. We will dock in ten minutes. And I am not permitted to land passengers anywhere except my berth."

Henry kept a smile painted on his face. Jed was looking their way.

"I've got a real problem here. Jed wants to hurt me. Hurt me badly. I just need a head start."

"Ah. I wondered if you knew each other. He's been interested in you the whole cruise. Watching. You two have a problem in London? He seems like a cool guy."

Henry looked pleadingly as they tied off the folded sail together. Cristóvão's face suddenly brightened. He threw his head back and bellowed with laughter.

"I get it. You bad man. You been screwing his wife!"

Henry nodded enthusiastically. Cristóvão clapped his hands in delight.

"Okay, here's what we're going to do. Sit on the left of the cockpit, by the open gate. I will come right by the old rusty ladder next to the ferry terminal. You see it now?"

Henry squinted ahead and nodded.

"I will slow right down, come as close as I can. You grab the ladder – and go! Then I will take my time back to the pontoon. I will give you ten minutes. Use it well, Henry."

Cristóvão grinned and made scissors out of his index and middle finger, indicating a shearing motion.

"You don't want him to catch you! Cut off your little dick!"

Five minutes later, Henry flopped inelegantly onto the ferry dock whilst two boat mechanics in blue overalls eyed him curiously. He'd lost one of his Oxford shoes landing on the first rung, and the bottom half of his pink trousers were soaked from *Mystique*'s wash, but otherwise Cristóvão's operation was faultless. The captain brought his boat alongside the jetty whilst pointing out a non-existent pod of dolphins in the middle of the river. The Americans were straining their eyes across the water and he'd even handed Jed a pair of binoculars to get a closer look. He stayed prone for a minute as he watched *Mystique* dawdle upstream towards her final destination. Just long enough to spot a furious-looking Jed hobbling along the length of *Mystique* before catching the glint of the glasses being trained on the ferry area. He sausage-rolled away from the concrete edge and headed inland.

Now he faced a choice. He could head directly to Santa Apolonia station and wait for the night train that would take him across Spain to the French border. Or make a quick detour to his apartment which was only five minutes away. The clock was ticking. And a lot of people would be looking for him. He dropped his remaining shoe in a waste bin and continued barefoot, drawing a few looks as he squelched onward. As he walked, he enumerated who was on his tail. The local police, certainly. Had João worked out he was on a boat? Then, whoever was tailing him to the British embassy. British? Portuguese? Russian? And finally, Jed. He wouldn't be alone, either, and he looked decidedly pissed off. Henry knew he was going to be very lucky to get out of Lisbon, whatever he decided.

He was out of breath as he flung open his apartment door. He timed his barefoot sprint up the stairs: fifty-two seconds. That gave him six minutes to do what he needed and be on his way. Jed would be ashore by now. And the police could arrive at any moment.

First, to the study. He found Priya's engagement ring and carefully placed the little green box in his jacket pocket. He would keep his promise to Sasha. Two indelible markers – one black, one blue – went into in his jacket pocket. He had made plans for those later. Finally, he placed his passport, credit cards and driving licence into a ziplock bag and dropped them into the bottom of a tall vase, replacing a spider plant on top of the stash. He wouldn't be needing them for a while.

Then he scoured the apartment for cash, stuffing whatever euros and pounds he could find into his breast pocket. He checked each room, including Sasha's. He would need every last penny he could find. Just in case, he pulled the bed that Sasha had occupied away from the wall and peered behind it. No money, but there was something else. An old, leather-bound book that he had seen before. Easter last year, the Russian church in London. He slipped it into his pocket without opening it. Checking it would have to wait.

Then he chose a photograph of his daughters from his bedside table. It was a favourite of his, the three of them together at Disneyworld. He took it from its frame and gently folded it in Sasha's book for protection.

He was out of time. He pulled on a pair of trainers, but that was it. He would have to travel light.

"London, here I come," he said to himself as he closed the apartment door.

Everything happened quickly, so quickly that Henry was never really sure of the order of events. It definitely started with him pausing by the communal utility room, halfway down the stairs. This was where he kept his surfboard and somebody had chained up a bicycle. It was always unlocked. Though he knew he needed to keep moving, something had compelled him to look down at the floor by the door. He saw a most unwelcome calling card. He wished he'd never clapped eyes on *semechki* husks. First time, the heavy mob at the Russian Church. Then Boris Aslanov's fateful shooting weekend. Russian Jed. And now here.

He consulted his watch and knew that, for so many

reasons, he had to crack on. But his hand was already on the door of the utility room. A motion sensor operated a basic ceiling light inside, but only after a delay. The pause was enough for him to poke his head into the dark – and gag. The stench of shit, then rust and copper, blood, overwhelmed him. As the light came on, the revolting tableau presented caused him to follow straight through with a gush of vomit that splashed his trousers and trainers.

His surfboard was propped up in a corner, resting against the wall at a seventy-five-degree angle with what looked like a naked, gargantuan ventriloquist's dummy strapped to it. Its rubber neck and barrel chest were tied upright to the board, smiling head lolling forward, tongue hanging out. The left eye had disappeared in a ball of purple contusion but the right one appeared to be open, a terrible, conspiratorial wink. Hands bloody and fingers contorted at unnatural angles, legs akimbo across the cold concrete floor, Sasha hadn't gone quietly.

Later, he was almost certain that this was when he doubled back up to the apartment and armed himself with the kitchen knife. He wouldn't have taken it before he found Sasha, would he? But with Jack and the Russian giant dead, he must have known he was next. Henry hadn't been in a scrap since cub scouts' British Bulldog fifty years earlier, but somehow the nine-centimetre-long razor-sharp paring knife in its wooden sheath had made its way into the pocket of his chinos. He gripped it tight as he opened his front door and turned left up the narrow stone stairs that ran up to the side of his building.

Nearing the top, he looked behind, down fifty steps. Nothing. Empty. Twenty more steps to go and the passageway opened into a quiet square with an orange tree in the middle, then the steep cobbled hill with its rattling funicular. He glanced down at his watch. His head start had vanished and he moved forward cautiously, taking one short step at a time, reading the bairro. The old lady was in her usual place up ahead of him, leaning out of her fourth-floor window, surveying the square. But something about her caused Henry to pause. Her usual vacant half-smile was absent. She was staring intently at something he couldn't see but now sensed viscerally. She was leaning forward to get a better view at whatever was at the top of the steps, immediately to his left.

Henry gripped the wall and pivoted himself around the corner, finding himself within touching distance of Jed. He stepped forward, putting Jed on his back foot. The Russian raised both hands in a defensive posture and stood like a boxer, left foot forward, limiting the amount of body exposed. He looked surprised.

"Henry, we just need to talk. You and me. Somewhere quieter. Back at your flat."

No longer an ageing London rocker, Jed sounded more like a cultivated Middle European art dealer. Soothing. Selling something. The two men stared at each other. Henry tried to control his own shallow breathing. His whole body tensed and he felt out of control.

"Fuck you, you murdering bastard!"

Jed sprang forward, right hand thrusting expertly towards Henry's throat. But he failed to connect. He looked shocked and took a pace back. Henry studied the blue eyes as they tried to compute something, something impossible, looking down to see white jeans turn to red.

"That's for Jack and Sasha."

Jed pushed himself forward again, using the wall behind him for purchase. Henry blocked the Russian's right hand with his left arm and struck out again, swinging the blade upwards to its hilt. This time Jed crumpled, his designer trainers slipping in the blood that was now slick on the cobbles beneath him. Curious. One of the shoes was built up.

"And that is for Pyotr Aslanov."

Jed's face had turned as white as his peroxide hair. Henry could never explain what he did next. It was singularly unwise. But he delivered his coup de grâce through a clenched jaw.

"Now, I'm off to find your fucking ABSALOM."

Jed said something in Russian and formed his right hand into a pistol shape, which he pointed directly at Henry's head, miming a well-aimed double tap. Slumped on the ground, propped against the wall, he was at Henry's mercy.

Henry forced a theatrically contemptuous laugh and looked around. He was about to make a short speech when he spied a large, leather-jacketed figure powering up the stairs towards him. No surprise there. Pavel. The old lady was still at the window, but now with her daughter next to her, the younger woman speaking urgently into her mobile phone. Time to look lively.

The bell of the little yellow funicular sounded nearby as it began its trundle up the hill to Bairro Alto. It would come alongside in a matter of seconds. Henry did something he'd always wanted to try but hadn't had a compelling reason to do, until now. The driver was concentrating on the empty hill ahead and a solitary passenger was reading the football results in *A Bola*. Henry gripped the wrought metal gate that was drawn across the passenger step and pulled himself up. Looking back, he saw Pavel had now emerged into the square. The funicular was travelling at a slow jogging pace and the burly Russian had his eyes on Henry, who gripped at the knife in his trouser pocket. He took two paces forward but then stopped and turned back to see his master prone on the floor. Jed must have called to him and now he was crouched over, one hand pushing down on Jed's thigh, the other holding his phone to his ear.

Henry had mapped out his escape and evasion plan by the time he alighted at the top of Bica. He abandoned his MI5 drills. If any of his hunters were behind him, then too bad. He could only dodge those ahead of him from now on. He was on his way to the international train terminus across town, but had mapped out two all-important stops first.

The travel section was kept in the third or fourth vaulted chamber of Lisbon's oldest bookshop. It was familiar to Henry, and its layout as a long brick halfpipe with a street entrance at the front and a small coffee shop at the rear, complete with discreet back exit, was perfect for his purposes. He found what he was looking for, a rail guide to travelling Europe on a budget. He turned to take it to the cash register but then thought better of it. The alcove was empty and he stood in the corner, back to the corridor, whilst he ripped ten pages from the book: three were line-drawn rail maps of Europe and the others described journeys through Portugal, Spain and France. Next, he scanned the shelves and found the decoy he needed. He carefully folded the loose pages inside a travel guide to Morocco and went to pay for it. He decided it was showtime, time for his am-dram skills. A reprise of an irascible Edwardian colonial policeman he had played in the theatre group's summer production sprang to mind.

The two young booksellers eyed the Englishman as he approached them. His straw hat was pulled low on the crown of his head. His pink chinos had a large brown stain across the crotch, only partially obscured by flapping white shirt tails. His shoes were mottled with something unpleasant. His eyes burned wild as he went into character.

"*Ola, ola, boa tarde, senhoras! Tudo bem?*" Henry spoke loud and fast. His Portuguese accent was dreadful.

"Do. You. Speak. English?" Henry spelt out his question, attempting to be as exasperating as possible. He knew the question was superfluous with young Lisboetas.

"Yes, indeed we do," one of the shop assistants answered with as much professionalism as she could muster.

"Well, I need your advice, young lady." He was laying it on with a trowel. "Is this the best guide you have to Morocco? You see, I am just about to set off and I really do need to know."

Now the other one answered.

"Gentleman, it's all we've got." She remained polite, but he had made his point. They would definitely remember the odd Englishman when people came to ask. Which they would. And also where he was going.

For his grand finale, Henry paid for the book by slowly counting out low-value coinage, confusing pounds with euros and muttering under his breath. Exiting via the small back door, he entered an alleyway with the Morocco guide clearly displayed in his hand.

The evening was darkening as he entered the square where he knew Portuguese Africans would be gathering in front of their church. A run of shops that traded in gold and silver or repaired mobile phones flanked Henry's objective. Two rails of bargain clothes stood outside it. He chose a pink-and-white gingham-print plastic laundry bag and in short order filled it with a pair of jeans, army surplus combat trousers, two check shirts, a sweater, puffer jacket, handfuls of counterfeit Calvin Klein underpants and socks. A rough blanket, beanie hat and canary-yellow flip-flops completed the purchase and, with a bulk discount, he was pleased that he got change from a precious fifty-euro note.

Clubbable Englishman Henry had stuck out like an increasingly sore thumb. He knew it was time for a metamorphosis before he got to Santa Apolonia station, but where to change? The doors to the curious church were open and candlelight flickered against the smoke-stained orange walls inside. It looked womb-like, safe, and a good place to kill a few hours before risking the railway ticket counter.

He had visited the church before. He knew its terrible story. Where in 1506, the wholesale slaughter of Lisbon's Jews was incited by two Dominican friars; hundreds of *novo cristianos* were beaten and burned alive in the square. Then where the auto-da-fé condemned crypto-Muslims, witches and diviners to death. Then the gathering place for enslaved Africans. A suitable place to set out on his quest for ABSALOM, he thought.

He slumped at a rear pew, listening to the end of Sunday evensong. The celebrant intoned a final prayer, bowing deeply whilst another priest swung a censer, the incense hanging over the altar like river mist.

As the congregants filed out, he made for an ornate wooden confessional he had spotted lurking in a side aisle. Checking down the nave, he was now alone in the church apart from the three priests who were packing away their accoutrements by the altar. He entered the dark box and closed the door behind him. There was just enough light to change by, and in no time he had transformed himself. Linen jacket and stained chinos were carefully folded away in the laundry bag, replaced with a puffer jacket, combat trousers and flip-flops. The beanie would wait until he left the church. Henry had an hour to spare so squatted on his haunches in the corner of the box. He had counted his remaining money by the little light dappling through the grille that divided the confessional in two, and was now using the marker pens to fashion tattoos on each hand. "*Amor*" and "*Odio*" looked good on his knuckles. And he was pleased with his attempt at a wolf tattoo on his left hand but was struggling to draw the Old Testament figure swinging from a tree on his right. Distracted, he didn't hear the other door to the confessional creak open.

"*O Senhor esteja no teu coracao para que confesses os teus pecados com espirito arrependido …*"

The voice was strong, deep and rich. The grille now darkened as the priest took his seat and waited.

Henry felt a spasm of fear, trapped and confined in the dark. He hadn't planned for this. Should he make a run for the square?

"Sorry, sir, but do you speak English?" he stuttered.

"*Ai, sim*. But in this house please call me Father."

"Of course. Sorry, Father. Your English sounds excellent."

There was a gentle, throaty rumble from Henry's unexpected confessor.

"I was born in Guinea but for thirty years I ministered in South Africa. Now when was your last confession, my son?"

The same instinct gripped Henry that had stopped him wearing his hat in church. He couldn't lie, but could justify a little dissembling. If his sessions with Nea weren't exactly what the priest had in mind, they would have to do.

"In October last year, Father."

"Go on, my son."

"Well, a lot's happened since then. So, your advice would be really welcome."

A disconcerting silence.

"Can I just check though; this is just between you and me? Like therapy. That sort of thing?"

Another long pause.

"My son, whatever you have done is to be confessed, and will forever stay with me and our God. This is the sacred seal of confession. But please understand, this is not a place for psychotherapy. You must confess willingly but also recognise a clear distinction between good and evil, between truth and lies, between sin and virtue."

The priest sighed and Henry knew he had made the right decision not to run. He felt safer in the dark, and the priest's voice was soothing.

"We now have to call this 'reconciliation'. The faithful are confused. My younger colleagues grew up on a diet of Freud, Jung and reality TV. They think listening is sufficient. But it isn't. We must also be judged. All of us. You see, the devil is out there. He is among us."

Henry left his corner and knelt on the step below the grille. He leant in to the priest and spoke softly.

"I think you are right, Father. I am sure I came face to face with him today."

"Go on."

"I have betrayed people. Manipulated them. Probably got them hurt."

Henry tried to find the words.

"Four are dead."

The priestly silence was deafening.

"I was trying to do the right thing. Help my country."

Henry's breathing was heavy.

"But I think my real reason is ego. Proving that I'm braver and cleverer than the enemy. Getting one over on them."

Silence.

"And I was bored. It's been like, like I'm in my own film. That's suddenly become all too real."

He paused.

"I also just wanted to be accepted by my own kind. Not be an outsider. But they're not my people. So, I've realised that's never going to happen. I need to rethink my life before it's too late ... and I don't know how long I've got left ..."

"It is good you understand yourself, your motivations. Is there anything else you wish to confess?"

Henry went deeper.

"I actually stabbed someone today, with a knife. In self-defence." He was stammering. "I was next on the list to be murdered. But I was also very angry. I don't know whether the man is dead or alive."

The deep voice spoke. Henry wondered if he thought him a fantasist or madman. The priest probably had a few regulars. But nothing in the rich timbre suggested that.

"My son, these are serious matters. I count at least three mortal sins. Pride, certainly. Envy – you are coveting something. And Wrath."

"That sounds about right," Henry sighed. "What do I do next?"

"For absolution you must now do three things. Firstly, show sincere contrition for your sins, to God. You must mean it."

"I regret that I ever got involved. And that any of my actions have caused harm. What is the second thing, Father?"

"You must commit to never committing these sins in future."

"My days of manipulating and lying are over."

"Finally, you must make recourse to the sacrament of penance through your actions. As soon as possible. You must right these wrongs."

Henry now spoke with a louder, firmer voice.

"That is just what I'm about to do, Father."

The priest was silent; Henry sensed a solution was coming.

"Tiago is the chief at the local police station. He is a member of my flock and a decent, honourable man. I think we should walk over together. Now. You explain the situation. He will be fair with you. And if you have information about these killings, the police should know."

"Thank you, Father. But there is only one way I can put things right. I need to get back to England without being caught. And then unmask who is behind this. That's the only way I can look the victims' loved ones in the face. I will sort this out or die trying."

As he slowly turned the handle of his knife in his jacket pocket, he thought of Mrs Aslanov and her girls, of João and Priya. Several minutes' silence followed. Finally, the priest spoke.

"I cannot compel you to go to the police as a condition of absolution. And you are clearly a determined man. You will leave the confessional first and I will stay and pray for your success – and for your soul. I do not want to see your face. Or be seen with you. *Mas, boa sorte, o meu filho.* Good luck with your journey."

"Thank you, Father."

"So, here are some final thoughts. Avoid main railway stations. They will be watched. And enter England by the back door. I spent several years at a monastery in the Mourne Mountains. A beautiful part of Ireland. Did you know there are over two hundred and fifty crossing points on the border up there? Impossible to keep an eye on all of them."

He didn't, and appreciated the priest's advice.

"So now, my son, I will absolve you. 'God the Father of mercies …'"

The two old ladies in shawls who sat cross-legged by the church porch were still there as he pulled open the wooden door. On his way in, they had shaken their tin cups at him, pleading for alms. Now, they gave him a pitying look and carried on their conversation. He stopped, pulled on his beanie and dug a handful of small change from his pocket. For a moment, he thought it might be refused as the women looked him up and down. He dropped the money into the pots and shuffled along the side wall of the church, the "*obrigadas*" of the women fading behind him.

A dark shadow, he passed silently through the narrow, cobbled lanes of Mouraria, across the deserted hilltop of Graça, and then dropped back down towards the river through Alfama. As he walked, he wondered how long the priest had stayed in the confession box after his departure. When he met Roddy and Colin, the golden rule was never to arrive or depart together. They usually gave him fifteen minutes' head start after he left, apparently the operational minimum. He assumed the priest was of the same school. Clearly a man of the Church, but also of the world. Henry looked at the stolen rail map as he walked, smiling as he realised he should have added theft to his burgeoning list of sins. A run across Ireland. That looked like it could work.

A police patrol car was parked by the entrance to Santa Apolonia station. Not unusual, but he advanced with caution. The station concourse looked deserted as he went through the open doors. The sleeper train to the French border was scheduled to depart in three hours' time and Henry caught sight of it waiting on the platform, lights out. But he also saw three uniformed policemen standing right next to it. And more worryingly, two hefty men in sports jackets, alert and watchful by the ticket office. His instinct was to double back out into the night. But he gripped himself and went straight to the station kiosk. Buying a large Sagres beer, he unscrewed the cap of the brown bottle and took a theatrical swig. He then bought the cheapest bottle of blended whisky and stuck it in his pocket, making sure its neck was visible. The uniformed police took a quick look at him and then went back to their conversation. As he shambled out of the station, he concluded that they had no interest in a semi-derelict. They had different prey on their minds.

Back out into the night, he picked up pace and headed north to a station on the outskirts of the city where, if he hurried, he could catch the last slow train up the coast to Porto. It was the right call. No police, no surveillance cameras, no ticket barrier, no fare to pay.

As the last lights of Lisbon faded behind him, he took stock. He would be the suspect in two murders. Three, if Jed hadn't made it. He had no passport or credit cards. Cash was short and he had to get back to London without contact with any authorities. Courtesy of Jack Somerset, deceased, he was the keeper of a secret that people would keep dying for.

As the train trundled northwards, he pulled his blanket across himself, gently rocked into a deep sleep.

14

GET HENRY

Pinchuk pressed down hard on the cotton wool swab as the doctor pulled the cannula out of his forearm. He lay prone on a reproduction chaise longue which came courtesy of the short-term rented apartment. The nearly empty blood bag, its final thick crimson residue clogging the bottom, hung from a makeshift infusion stand – a wire coat hanger bent over a curtain rod. Empty syringes of antibiotics lay on the coffee table.

"So, Colonel, I know you will not listen to me. But you are weak. My advice is to rest for one week. And the stitches in your leg could rupture at any moment if you are not careful. Do not exert yourself. You nearly died. You may not be so lucky next time. There. I've done my duty."

The doctor packed his bag and shrugged as Pinchuk

waved him away. He was dismissed. Pavel opened the apartment door, handed over an envelope stuffed with euros and watched his boss's saviour head down the stairs. The doctor knew better than to look back.

The Lisbon rezident sat on a high-backed chair next to Pinchuk. The colonel made an effort to sit up and his colleague deftly inserted a green velvet bolster behind his shoulders.

"So – what have you organised?" Pinchuk was terse.

"Lisbon airport watched by my team, Colonel."

"They'd better do a damn sight better job than yesterday. Bradbury spotted them a mile off, and now he's clocked their faces. MAURICE took a real risk with that signal from London, got him on his way to the British Embassy. All you had to do was drag him into a car. Rank bloody amateurs. Had to do it myself, nearly got me bled out like a stuck pig for my troubles."

Pinchuk winced as he shifted his weight.

"And what else?"

"Our Casablanca colleagues have their man in Moroccan immigration flagging airport arrivals for a Mr Henry Bradbury." The rezident seemed pleased with his new-found efficiency. One look from Pinchuk wiped the smile off his face.

"And the land crossings?"

The rezident looked blank, then worried.

"Good God, man! Watch the Ceuta and Melilla land crossings from Spain into Morocco right away. Signal that now."

The rezident nodded to the young GRU lieutenant sitting next to him. He tapped out urgent instructions into his computer. Pinchuk slumped back and stared at the plaster rose in the ceiling.

"We have to find this English clown before he does any more damage. And before the police get their hands on him."

Pinchuk spied the remains of his white jeans arranged on the back of a chair. The doctor had cut them off with scissors and they had a large brown stain down the left leg and a light-yellow patch at the crotch. Two narrow, parallel puncture holes penetrated the fabric at groin level, as neat as any vampire's bite.

"You know, those were my favourites. Dior. I paid at least a thousand dollars for them. Bring them over to me."

The young officer complied and was startled as Pinchuk cradled them to his chest. Minutes passed in silence.

"I must correct myself. I think Bradbury is not a fool. I had asked MAURICE to find us a British idiot. How hard could that be? There are millions of them! But MAURICE fucked up. He will pay for that, but later. I need him for now. He can earn his money for once. Get his delicate English hands dirty …"

Pinchuk studied the holes, carefully poking his finger through the openings made by Henry's kitchen knife, absent-mindedly plucking at loose threads.

"What have you done about the northern escape route?"

The rezident shifted awkwardly in his chair and Pavel took a step from the door in his direction.

"Well, we're watching Lisbon airport." He was starting to stutter.

"You told me that already. What else?"

"Your ABSALOM team arrives in London this afternoon."

"I know that. I ordered it!"

The resident and his junior exchanged glances. Pavel was now standing in front of them.

"Christ. Get a grip. Get a team on the intercity trains from Spain to France. Watch the Eurostar terminus in Paris – Gare du Nord. The channel ports – Calais and Boulogne. Signal Paris right now!"

This time the lieutenant didn't look for his boss's permission. The message was transmitting as Pinchuk finished speaking.

"I looked into his eyes. Bradbury is stubborn. And cunning. And angry. A bad combination. He said the name ABSALOM. Nobody must talk of ABSALOM. I think he is heading for home. We must stop him."

The Lisbon rezidentura were now nodding emphatically, as one. The terrible legend of Pinchuk was further strengthened by a message that now arrived on the lieutenant's computer with a ping. He read it in silence and then his eyes darted between Pinchuk and his boss.

"Lieutenant, I am tired. No games. What does it say? Spit it out."

"Colonel, our watchers report that the Portuguese judicial police have entered Bradbury's apartment, with a forensics team, and undertakers."

Pinchuk shook his head.

"Not good. We haven't found the message book that giant oaf, DYLDA, was carrying. If he hid it in the apartment, the police will find it."

The resident looked quizzical.

"Why would he be carrying a message book, Colonel? I haven't seen one of those since the old days."

Pinchuk knew he meant before the Fall – the fall of the Soviet Union.

"Somebody in the middle of this is obstinately old-school. Loved the Soviet Union. Refusing anything digital. It's a compromise I have to make."

The resident hesitated.

"Then shouldn't we signal Moscow that the operation is compromised, Colonel?"

He flinched as Pinchuk snarled back.

"Under no circumstances will we do that! Even if the police find it, they'll have no idea what it means. I think of everything."

The lieutenant broke the ensuing silence. Pinchuk decided he looked sullen. Not quite scared enough. He nodded to Pavel, who now watched the screen over the young man's shoulder.

"Another message from the surveillance team. They're removing a body. It seems it is taking six men to get it down the stairs."

Pavel was now breathing directly on the back of the lieutenant's neck.

"Young man – do they still do the night training exercise at the Winter Warfare School on Hatsavita mountain?"

The lieutenant nodded, eyes averted.

"Then you remember how we cover our tracks?"

"Yes, sir. We were taught to cut a fresh birch branch, then brush the snow back over our boot prints."

Pinchuk grinned.

"Exactly. This is now my job. Think of me as Russia's sweeper – her sweeper-in-chief. And please don't feel sorry for DYLDA. His mission was simple. A simple errand boy. How could you screw that up? But he did. He was already under suspicion for blabbing once to his English friend. My mistake was not to warn him about Henry. I didn't trust him not to give himself away, the Englishman is perceptive. And, besides, Henry's reporting back to his handlers on DYLDA was most useful to me. But I never considered quite how stupid he could be..."

Pinchuk seemed to be gathering strength, leaning forward.

"And now I have to sweep Russian snow over all the tracks that could lead back to ABSALOM. I've dealt with both DYLDA and my oldest English friend. I very much enjoyed my session with DYLDA. The other matter left me feeling surprisingly sad. That man made me who I am. I was actually a little fond of that difficult, stubborn old *dedushka*."

Pinchuk sighed, gathering himself before he continued.

"But the sweeping must continue. And that will include you and your boss here, if I feel the urge."

The room fell silent. Finally, Pavel spoke. He had taken the lieutenant's place at the laptop, who now stood next to the ashen rezident.

"Another message has come in, boss. The gossip in Bradbury's local bar is that the body is a young Russian. A giant. And that the police are talking amongst themselves about a British serial killer."

Pinchuk pointed silently to his leather shoulder bag that hung from the back of the front door. Unspoken, Pavel already knew what to do. The two other men were motionless, frozen waxworks. Pavel pulled out six passports, various colours and sizes. He fanned them out like a magician and offered Pinchuk his pick. The colonel studied them and then drew the dark red one from the pack. It said "Pasas" on the front underneath a shield emblazoned with a knight, sword raised above his head. Lithuanian. Then he spoke.

"The game is on. I will find Mr Henry Bradbury before anyone else. And I look forward to our rematch. Very much."

With that, he threw his soiled jeans across the room. The two men from the rezidentura, huddled together in the corner, now breathed again.

* * *

Henry woke with a start to a soft, warm, damp sensation on the side of his face. A small brown-and-white dog was snuffling at his left ear. He pulled his coarse blanket to one side and tried to focus. The spaniel was now poking its short snout into the plastic laundry bag that contained his worldly possessions. Without thinking, Henry took its collar, gently pulled it closer and stroked it. The night had been cold and the animal's warmth was just what he needed. The dog nuzzled him. Looking around, Henry spied its mistress standing on a gravel path that ran through the city park that had been his home for the moonless night. He had thought himself well hidden in a dense clump of bushes, but under the sharp blue skies of morning he could clearly see her cautious approach. And she could therefore see him.

"Zorro. Zorro. *Venha aqui!*"

She was Henry's age, dressed smartly in a Burberry coat and brown thigh-length boots. He stood up stiffly and gave a friendly wave, releasing Zorro who then quartered his way back to her.

"*Bom dia, senhora.* What a beautiful morning!"

But his attempt to exchange pleasantries was short-lived. The woman clipped on Zorro's lead and then started to step backwards carefully, eyes fixed on him. Back on the path, she dug inside her shoulder bag and carefully placed a plain brown paper package on the ground, pointing down and then making an eating gesture, moving her hand to her mouth whilst chewing. Then, turning smartly on her heels, she was gone.

Curious, he opened the bag to find a tuna sandwich, a pot of salad and a doughnut. Her lunch. Retreating to his lair, he sat on his blanket and devoured it.

The morning traffic of Porto was humming and the gate that he had climbed over six hours earlier was now wide open. It was nine o'clock as he carefully folded away his blanket and checked details on one of the increasingly grubby pages he had torn from the rail travel guide in Lisbon. A slow local train would take him across the Spanish border. Then one intriguing paragraph suggested an alternative to the intercity express service to France. Evidently the FEVE was a narrow-gauge line that meandered its way across Galicia, Cantabria and then the Basque country, roaring Bay of Biscay to the left and vertiginous green mountain slopes hard to the right. Now largely forgotten, it didn't even appear on Spanish railway maps. He calculated it would take him four days to complete the 783 kilometres. According to the guide, he would stop at 271 stations and pass through 248 tunnels. And, he guessed, zero cameras and few fellow travellers. Perfect.

The first day of travel was a novelty. Henry passed the time counting tunnels and watching the breakers, forests and graveyards slowly pass by. He aimed to count all 248 but lolled off at the fiftieth tunnel, falling into a deep, dreamless sleep. As expected, the carriages were barely used. The train stopped at countless small villages and remote halts. At the beginning, he found himself digging into his pocket at least twice an hour, unthinking, pulling out his inert phone and then sighing, before re-trousering the useless object. What was going on out there, beyond the mountains, in Portugal? Over the roiling sea in England? Had he actually killed Jed? How were his daughters? Would they now know their father was a fugitive from the law, on the run? He wanted to search the internet for a psychology self-help site to discover why the shadow had disappeared from his dreams so abruptly. He was sleeping soundly now. Given his predicament, where had it gone?

He dug around in his bag and pulled out Sasha's old book. He found his photograph of the children and carefully displayed it on the window ledge next to his seat. He had forgotten about the leather-bound tome. Getting out of Portugal undetected had taken all his concentration. Now he could study it carefully.

Gold embossed lettering on the front.

Библия

A Russian Bible. He would struggle without a dictionary, but so far, so good.

The hinge of the book was coming apart and stitched binding was exposed. He opened it gingerly. The title page named the publishing house and then read "Saint Petersburg 1917". The frontispiece consisted of a chronological list of eight names and then dates, all in different hands. Some prefaced with a military rank, all officers, all of them men of the Orlov family. The last entry: Lt. Aleksander Orlov, 2012. His eyes were drawn to the 1933, 1942 and 1953 entries. He wondered how often this book would have been a death sentence if discovered. And, as Henry was the latest owner, what would it mean for him now?

He turned page by page. After all, he had time on his side. He had a vague recollection of the King James version, enough to navigate around. He had reached the seventh chapter of the Old Testament and was about to take a break and stretch his legs in the aisle when he discovered something curious. The entire right-hand margin of a page was filled with rows and columns of handwritten numbers. Each row consisted of two sets of five digits, rendered very small and neat with a sharp lead pencil. The margin felt rough to the touch, rubbed worn, as if this wasn't the first time it had been used for this purpose. He counted three hundred characters on the page. His eyesight was poor and he could just read the letters if he strained. It reminded him of childhood trips to the opticians and the metal frame sitting heavily on his nose as test lenses were dropped in. This would have been the last line he could read before he started guessing.

He made a mental note of the page – Book of Judges, 13 – and flicked on.

Over the next three hours he found eight similar entries in the Old Testament. He tallied 3,120 numbers. Intriguingly, one row of numbers was underlined on each page. He guessed this was the key to crack the code but had no idea how it worked. He was just about to start on the New Testament when the train slowed to a halt as a couple held their hands out from a crumbling concrete platform. A solitary rusting sign behind them read "La Magdalena". The carriage was empty and he was disconcerted as they settled into the two seats opposite him. They greeted him and he smiled back. Dusk was falling and the train was heading into another long tunnel. The overhead lights in the compartment flickered.

In their thirties, they wore heavy coats and scarves. Old and scuffed trainers. The woman sported a plain headscarf and they carried four old plastic bags packed with what looked like a week's worth of shopping. He could see own-brand nappies in the top of one and bread rolls in another. Their faces were weather-beaten and Henry decided that they worked outdoors. The train rumbled deeper into the mountain.

This was Henry's first encounter with the etiquette of the little train. In his London commuting days, the unspoken rule was to sit as far away from other passengers as possible and avoid eye contact at all costs. Only speak to strangers to admonish them for playing loud music or putting their feet on the seats, if you dared. But over the four days crossing Spain, he came to realise – and appreciate – the unwritten code of the FEVE. For locals, this was a chance to meet others, gossip, complain about the cost of their shopping. He started to draw comfort from the farmers, fishermen and forestry workers who joined him, offering to share their food and stories. If the police boarded, he reasoned, they would be looking for a middle-aged man travelling alone. And whoever else was hunting him would think twice about breaking up the convivial conversation. Too many witnesses.

Henry's travelling companions opened a family-size packet of crisps and offered a handful to him first. He stood up and reached across the aisle and was surprised when the woman hooted with laughter and pointed at his waist.

"*Cravata!*" she said, in evident admiration.

He looked down at the Hereford College necktie that now held up his camouflage trousers, threaded through the belt loops of the waistband. He had bought them with his London measurements in mind and they kept slipping down. He laughed too. She seemed to have a keen appreciation of the need to improvise in adversity.

Conversation was slow and patient, drawing heavily on mime, but the three fellow travellers had time on their side. Henry gathered they were from Moldova, seasonal workers smuggled over to pick peas and beans. The work was hard but the money was good. They were billeted in a caravan with their three children. Henry introduced himself as Monty Crompton, an English travel writer on his way home. The man pointed to Henry's photograph.

"*Filice?*"

Henry guessed the correct response.

"Yes, my daughters."

The woman was clearly the live wire of the two. She pointed to Henry's clean-shaven, chubby face staring out of the picture and tutted in mock disapproval of the man sitting facing her. "*Barba*," she said whilst wagging her finger. Then she reached forward, gently tugging his beard, and the two Moldovans shook with laughter. Henry joined them. The touch of a kind stranger was a strange release for him.

Their curiosity piqued, after twenty minutes Henry found himself stepping down from the train and walking along a muddy lane with his two new friends. Night had drawn in and the kind offer of a bed in a shed where the single men slept was most welcome.

Luminata, his hostess, fed her children and farm dogs, three hulking mastiffs, and then served up a stew of pork and beans. Four of the single men joined them as they ate under the stars at a makeshift table, plyboard sitting on six columns of loose bricks. Wood crackled and spat in a brazier. One of the farm hands had worked seasons in Lincolnshire and spoke a curious English-Moldovan pidgin, innocent profanities mixed with East Midlands farm talk. He wore a Leicester City football top and pork-pie hat.

"Fucking good vittles these, mate. Deliciosa, Luminata!"

Henry presented his bottle of Scotch and, between the five of them, it was gone in no time. Farm-produced cider followed, flat, acid and strong. Conversation became easier as the evening wore on and Henry wondered if this was how new languages are born. Moldenglish, perhaps? That was his last thought as he pulled his blanket over himself and stretched out on the grubby cot by the barn door.

15

HOMEWARD BOUND

At dawn, the camp came to life. A cockerel paraded across the yard, resplendent in his crimson-and-green feather coat; hens scratched and took their dust baths. The three dogs guarded the gate, quiet but alert. Luminata had already lit the fire and had an enamel coffee can suspended by a chain above it. Henry's eight barnmates were seated around the trestle table, eating bread and ham in silence. As he joined them, he was acknowledged with a friendly nod, but that was it. Their hostess served them coffee and then called to her children. Two emerged from the caravan, a boy of about five and a slightly younger sister. Each carried an old work boot with metal toe cap, swinging them by the thick laces, smiling shyly. Luminata gave them a gentle instruction and they approached Henry. The girl hid behind her brother, who turned and pulled her forward. With great ceremony, they offered Henry a boot each. Bemused, he stood and received them with a bow. The children turned on their heels and ran back to the caravan whilst the table was banged with clenched fists of appreciation.

Henry removed his mud-caked yellow flip-flops and pulled on the boots. A perfect fit. He asked the man in the pork-pie hat to offer his thanks.

"Luminata says you can't fucking go round in them" – his companion pointed to his discarded sandals – "so, this is our present for you."

The table then went into a quick conference, the debate seemingly revolving around him. All eyes fixed on their guest. He felt as if his thoughts were being read, penetrated. He had hidden his secrets from Sasha, Nataliya, Aslanov and Jack Somerset. Occasionally from Roddy and Colin. But this felt different. His hosts had learnt wariness the hard way. And now the mastiffs had started to bark and push at the gate, straining to see something coming up the lane.

He pulled his beanie down low, over his eyebrows. He wanted to disappear. But he could now hear what the dogs had sensed a minute earlier, a slow-moving vehicle approaching the camp, gears shifting, engine labouring as the driver navigated the mud ruts. He tensed and Porkpie laughed. A green-and-white Land Cruiser lurched by the gates, emblazoned with the words "*Guardia Civil*". Its white bull bars were matted brown with dirt and its two occupants stared past the howling dogs at the breakfast table, dark berets moulded tight to their heads, eyes dead. The car slowed to an idle for a minute, then moved on.

"Have you just shat yourself, lad?" Porkpie's eyes twinkled.

"We'd already worked out you was on the run. Maybe from the police? Now we know. Lucky for you, them coppers were just on their way back to barracks – it's a cut-through they use."

Henry nodded wearily and shrugged his shoulders. He was learning who to trust.

"Listen, mate, we've all had our problems too. The police don't like us very much so we keep to ourselves. We don't have papers to be 'ere. Missus says you stay as long as you like. There's loads of work to be done and the farmer in't fussed who's in camp. We decide that. Make our own rules. And you're okay."

Henry inspected his hands for a whole minute. The palms were calloused and hard, the work of the surfboard and the sea. He was tempted. He could do the work, and here he felt safe and protected. But he had his mission – ABSALOM. And the hunters would be closing in.

"You're right. I'm in trouble. Serious trouble. Thanks a lot for the offer of a home, and for the boots. But my only way out of this is to keep on. There's someone I need to find. A bastard. And I can't do that hiding here."

Porkpie translated and the table nodded their understanding. As one, the men rose in early morning silence and Luminata wrapped lunch in a paper towel for Henry. Ten men formed up a makeshift guard and walked him back to the tiny station in a forest clearing. They waved their farewells as he boarded the empty train, then turned quietly towards their waiting field.

* * *

Henry stood at the newspaper stand by Santander casino and scanned the front pages. The proprietor was busy selling a page of lottery tickets to a young man and so he had time to browse, unobserved, unhurried. As well as the Spanish titles, there were the international papers. He wondered who even bought print papers any more, especially ones that were a day or two old. But there they were: *The London Times,* The *Telegraph, Daily Mail, Le Monde, La Stampa, Die Welt, Bild, International Herald Tribune.* The headlines were mostly about a mysterious virus leaching out from China, with the British front pages also carrying news of Brexit. Revolts in Parliament, the British government in crisis. But that wasn't what was on his mind this morning. Finally, he spotted what he was looking for, a Portuguese broadsheet. He studied it carefully. Virus news on the front. He opened the paper and turned to the inside pages. The owner of the stand was conversing with his other customer, buying him time. And there it was on page two:

"Briton Sought in Lisbon Double Murder."

At least that was Henry's rough translation. His former self stared back at him, a picture of smug-looking innocence. The mugshot looked like it had been taken from his passport, now sitting safely underneath a spider plant at his Lisbon apartment. Or had the police found it by now? The image was at least seven years old, clean-shaven, dark suit and tie. Heavy jowls. A lifetime ago and thankfully an unrecognisable version of the man who now dug into his pocket for a couple of euros to buy the paper. He considered buying all three offending copies to erase his presence in the city, but then thought better of it.

A quick rifle through the British press revealed nothing about him. Lottery transaction completed, the kiosk-keeper was now able to focus on Henry. He could feel it and it wasn't welcome. Time for him to pay and shuffle slowly over to a bench that looked over the promenade to the sea. He had put a sharp stone in his right work boot to force himself to affect an old man's limp.

Henry sat down heavily and faced a white stone balustrade, narrow beach and then a row of tankers and cargo boats. The giant ferry that plied the route to and from Plymouth was slipping into Santander harbour. It reminded him that home was four hundred miles over the horizon. England. England: one word, two syllables – they used to conjure comfort, safety, belonging. Now he said the word softly, under his breath, and gave an involuntary shudder. England had become an antonym of all that he remembered and wanted. A death trap, if his plan went wrong.

"Something is rotten in the state of England …" Henry mumbled. He caught himself and looked around. He was alone. "You've got to stop talking to yourself," he instructed in a low voice, smiling at his own in-joke. It was becoming a bad habit.

He studied the article, wishing he could just switch on his phone and translate the Portuguese. But he got the gist. "Henry Bradbury … 56 years old … judicial police … sought for murder … Mr Jack Somerset, 75, Cascais … Dr Aleksander Orlov, visiting Cais do Sodre from London … may have fled Portugal … international manhunt … dangerous … do not approach … call police immediately on 112 …"

No mention of Jed. He thought about this. Good news, or bad? Certainly good if he hadn't killed the Russian. One less sin on his tally sheet. But also bad – Jed would still be out there, and he knew he wouldn't stop until he caught up with him and finished their business to his cruel satisfaction. He could still see Jed's eyes – reptilian, inhuman, relentless, sharp blue. He checked himself: did any reptiles actually have blue eyes? He felt for the paring knife – still there in his pocket, a comforting, razor-sharp, blooded amulet. He creaked up onto his feet, took a last look at the distant horizon to the north, and hobbled back to the railway station.

* * *

Henry took his first limping steps into France and caught an unpleasant smell as he sat in the corner of the waiting room at Hendaye station. An odd mixture of blocked drains and sharply pungent cheese – perhaps overripe Roquefort? He shifted from one buttock to the other, surveying the near empty room, looking for the source, ancient prejudices about French plumbing flooding in. He stood slowly and then sank back down again, a ghastly exercise in self-awareness. The stench intensified as it wafted up to meet him. It was six days since his last shower in Lisbon and Henry stank.

He had reached the end of the line with the little Spanish narrow-gauge train, then limped over the border bridge, and now needed to meander across France, avoiding Paris at all costs. He was consulting his rail map, working out a route to Cherbourg docks, when a gang of six gendarmes strolled in through the station entrance, heavy doors swinging open like a Wild West saloon. Five men with a female officer in the lead. Three had sub-machine guns slung over their shoulders, all wore stab vests. They formed a semicircle around two Arab boys who were taking coffee, standing at a high café table. The woman seemed to be in charge, holding her hand out to receive their identity papers. Her colleague inspected them and called something into his lapel radio. They awaited a response, fingers covering trigger guards, legs braced. These gendarmes meant business.

He needed a plan, and quickly. The hall was quiet and the rest of the passengers were all white and comfortable-looking, decent luggage and well-scrubbed. He knew it would be his turn next. Two of the officers were looking directly at him and he was heavily outnumbered. They blocked the main exit, and the only other route out that he could see was onto the platforms and then along the open tracks beyond. He resolved to act this out. Getting into character, he pulled Sasha's Russian Bible out of his laundry bag and opened it to a random page. He sensed the gendarmes had finished with the young men in hoodies and were now sauntering towards him. He held the Bible open in one hand whilst scratching at his thigh with the other, vigorously, hand shaped into a claw, as if battling an unseen infestation. Then he intoned the first thing that came into his head.

"Speak of the grey one, the grey one heads your way … speak of the grey one, the grey one heads your way … speak of the grey one …"

Henry grinned wildly at the approaching officers and

the woman placed her hands on a pair of black rubber gloves that were tucked into her webbing belt. Then all six stopped dead, the two lead officers conferring quietly. He wondered if they had caught his scent. And he hoped that tackling a deranged, lousy manic preacher might not be what they had in mind when they entered the station. The extra laundry, all that paperwork. He had guessed right. At that moment, salvation appeared in the form of a tall black man sporting a crochet white skullcap and flowing djellaba, emerging from the station toilets, holding his young son's hand. Visibly relieved, the gendarmes turned and made for him, radios crackling as they re-formed into their intimidating half-circle.

16

BANDIT COUNTRY

The chips were lukewarm, congealed and smothered in tomato ketchup. But to Henry they were divine. The huge ferry windows were streaked with horizontal rain and the superstructure groaned as the ship pitched and rolled its way from Cherbourg to Dublin. Next, he tackled the half-eaten saveloy, pink and cold – sublime.

Henry had waited until the MV *WB Yeats*'s lounge bar had emptied of its handful of passengers, thankful that the early spring storm raging up the Western Approaches had dispatched all of them to their cabins, green-gilled, appetites dramatically suppressed as the boat shifted violently beneath their feet. Rich pickings for ravenous Henry as he finished plates of food that hadn't been cleared. He moved on to the next table and sat, remembering Roddy's advice on how to behave like an Oxford man: "Just act as if you own the place." A stone-cold lasagne sat on a tray, only two mouthfuls missing from it, together with a pint of lager, half drunk. Excellent. The solitary barman was passing by and Henry stopped him.

"Excuse me, but do you have a set of clean cutlery?"

The barman inspected him. Henry had strip-washed on the train from Hendaye to Bordeaux, contorting himself in the small washroom into his only change of clothes. In his own mind he was now fresh and dapper, but the man in the emerald-green waistcoat looked less certain.

"Sure, I will go and fetch them for you. And would 'Sir' be wanting anything else now? Bar closes in fifteen minutes."

Was that sarcasm? Henry couldn't tell. He blushed.

"Youse English?"

Henry thought about it.

"An excellent question. I used to be. I suppose I am ex-English. If that's a thing. At least until I sort something out."

The barman laughed. Short, plump, with a thatch of dyed orange hair. A gold earring in his right lobe.

"In that case I'll also bring you a fresh pint."

Henry was alarmed. His funds were running dangerously low.

"Relax, ex-Englishman. It's on the house. I've seen you minesweeping your way around the lounge. We can't be having that now, can we?"

The man headed over to the bar, his gait confirming that he had been at sea for a long time, professionally anticipating and countering each heave of the ship. Henry looked around. Pictures of a serious-looking Edwardian, dark hair and pince-nez spectacles, lined the walls. He guessed this was the great man himself. Framed quotes were interspersed. He read the one nearest to his table and chuckled.

"Education is not the filling of a pail, but the lighting of a fire" – William Butler Yeats.

The barman had returned with the beer and caught Henry's eye.

"There you go now. What's so funny?"

He perched next to Henry.

"Thanks very much for the drink. I'm down on my luck."

"No kidding."

He wondered how much to say, but he liked the Irishman and needed to talk.

"What's funny is that quote up there. On the wall."

The barman studied it.

"To be honest with you, I've worked this route for twenty years and never bothered reading any of this. Always assumed it was shite. But you sound like an educated man. Why is it funny?"

"I don't think Yeats meant to be funny. He doesn't look like a funny man in his pictures. It's just …"

He now had the barman's full attention.

"… I know a teacher. Sorry, knew a teacher. Recently deceased. He did just that. Didn't just teach his boys … stuff. He fired up his pupils. Ignited something. Someone. Set off a chain reaction. That needs to be stopped, before it's too late and blows the lid off everything."

A giant television monitor by the bar was showing a

24-hour rolling news channel. The ticker at the bottom of the screen caught his eye.

"… UNITED KINGDOM IN CONSITUTIONAL CRISIS OVER BREXIT … UNION IN PERIL …"

It scrolled continuously, ominously. The ship lurched, jolting him and forcing him to grip his glass. Beer spilled over the back of his hand. The Irishman got to his feet.

"Well, I've got to close up now. We're being told this storm is nothing compared with what's to come. This March is going to be rough. Front after front. Apparently, some ignorant sod of a butterfly flapped its wee wings off Africa and now we're all bolloxed!"

They laughed together as they collected the last glasses. It was the least he could do.

The fact that six hours earlier Henry had got aboard the ferry at all was a miracle. In fact, a series of miracles, that he had learnt first occurred in 1858 in a small Pyrenean town called Lourdes and, would you believe, continued to this day. He had a tract explaining the history folded in his pocket, a present from an elderly Dubliner whose ailing husband he had wheeled up the ramp and onto the ship. Henry had been sitting in the departure hall at Cherbourg docks, carefully observing the ticket office and a French immigration post beyond. It didn't look good. The odd foot passenger who approached the one out-of-season window that was unshuttered used a credit card. Would they accept the last of his cash? And the bored-looking French immigration officer was running each passport through a computer. The *WB Yeats* was due to sail in an hour and Henry needed to be on it. At that moment, a coach pulled up outside and a commotion ensued. Standing by the door, he saw a dozen folded wheelchairs being removed from the luggage compartment. A tour guide was organising things, peroxide blonde with a shrill Dublin voice. The operation was impressive. One by one, disabled pilgrims were helped down the steps and into their chairs by their able-bodied companions. He then spotted something promising. The guide held a transparent plastic folder, stuffed with passports and ferry tickets. The pilgrims formed an orderly line as they were wheeled into the terminal, probably about forty in total. An elderly nun, wheeling one of her sisters, started the singing, *Ave Maria*, just as she was passing him. In an instant he had joined the chorus *con gusto*, offering to wheel an old gentlemen who was swaddled in blankets up to his neck. His wife accepted Henry's offer with gratitude.

Henry extemporised in his best Dublin accent. "I'm glad that journey is over. Too long on a bus for my liking. It's been a grand trip but I'll be glad to get back home to Dublin."

The old lady couldn't agree more, and then asked Henry where exactly he lived. He had only ever visited Dublin once, a rugby international twenty years earlier.

"By the rugby stadium, a few streets away."

He wracked his brains and then it came to him.

"Lansdowne Road."

The pilgrim smiled and slipped her arm through his as he wheeled her husband towards the ticket inspector and immigration checkpoint. His heart was racing as he watched what the tour guide was doing at the head of their slow-moving convoy.

"Now, tell me, did you find what you were looking for in Lourdes?"

He looked down at her blankly.

"C'mon, did Our Lady help you with a cure?" she asked slyly, with a conspiratorial wink.

He guessed what the right answer was.

"Oh yes. I arrived with gout, terrible pain, and now it's gone. Completely fit as a fiddle. Look."

He performed a couple of vigorous high knees, much to the old lady's delight. Her husband had turned around, his turtle neck extending from the blankets. He spoke for the first time.

"Ah, sure that young fella can dance a jig! He could hardly walk when he got on the bus. Bent double. I noticed him. Just look at him now. Fair play to you, son."

Their neighbours in the queue murmured their approval as Henry beamed as hard as he could, all the while watching the blonde guide intently. The ticket inspector looked at the invoice but not the tickets, whilst the immigration officer disdained to take the passports out of the wallet and waved the group through. He had made it over the next hurdle.

Henry waited while the pilgrims were given their cabin keys, and then guided his charges to their deck and helped get the old man out of the chair and onto the bed. He wished them goodnight, promising to return to the cabin in the morning before the ferry docked in Dublin. They were grateful of the offer of help disembarking.

The old man waved him off.

"You're a fine young fella. Now get yourself to the bar and have a pint for me!"

Henry was closing the cabin door when the old lady stopped him.

"Declan says he can't credit the change in you. I want to tell my ladies at the church prayer group about what happened in Lourdes. Can you do it for us one last time? We couldn't believe our eyes the first time."

"Sorry. I don't follow."

He husband, prone in bed, helped out.

"She wants you to do your wee dance again."

He dutifully performed a vigorous ten-second high knee routine in the doorway, a routine he seemed to remember from a Bob Marley video. He was accompanied by gales of laughter from the pilgrims.

"God bless you. We'll see you in the morning," said the wife.

"Feckin' unbelievable," cried Declan, bent foetal with laughter.

Henry closed the cabin door.

* * *

A light drizzle was blowing in off the Irish Sea as Henry pulled up his jacket collar and turned left into Casement Street. His smartphone and even smarter watch were redundant and, despite having hitched a free ride on the MV *WB Yeats*, his funds were dangerously depleted. He again pulled his stunt at Dublin docks, helping the two pilgrims down the ramp before waving goodbye to the group and landing in Ireland unremarked. Or so he thought.

Henry had never had dealings with a pawnbroker in his life and, perhaps too readily, parted with his electronics for two hundred euros in crisp, fresh notes. Then, with a twinge of shame, he asked the jolly man leaning the shiny elbows of his suit jacket on the counter to appraise Priya's engagement ring. The jeweller held it up to what little natural light filtered in through the grubby window, making a well-practised show of wielding his loupe.

"It's a nice piece, in the original case too." The man tapped the little green box with his index finger, then left just enough time to unnerve Henry.

"Russian, I'd say. Antique too, from the markings. A family heirloom, is it now?"

Henry shifted uncomfortably and thought quickly, forcing himself to maintain eye contact.

"It was my great aunt Nataliya's. A lady from Saint Petersburg. We are clearing her house."

Satisfied, the pawnbroker was ready to make his offer.

"Tell you what, fella, the best I can do is a grand. A thousand euros. How does that sound?"

Now it was Henry's turn to pause for thought. The two hundred for the electronics would get him over the border to Northern Ireland and then back to London with little to spare. But the ring would buy him untold luxuries. In his past life the thousand would have gone unnoticed from his current account, enough to cover a few months of golf club membership. It now promised warm meals and soft beds for a good few nights. Sorely tempting; Priya would be none the wiser, and his mission needed funding. But then he pictured Sasha, the glowing slab of a face asking him to be his best man, tears in his eyes. And, together with the mysteriously marked-up Bible, Henry felt like the custodian of Sasha's past – and legacy. In this shadow world, these were his mortal remains.

"Sorry. No deal."

Henry sighed and put the ring back in its box.

"How about twelve hundred, my friend? That's my best offer."

"No thanks. More sentimental value than I'd realised."

The old brass bell tinkled as the door swung closed behind him.

* * *

Henry adopted his best Dublin accent as he boarded the bus heading north to the border town of Dundalk.

"What's your last stop, please?"

The driver scowled and shook his head when presented with a twenty-euro note.

"Dundalk bus station. But I've got no change, pal. Maybe go over to the newsagents there – you've got four minutes before we're off."

Henry looked across the wet street. He could probably just make it, but then he spotted two brace of security cameras ringing a metal post right by the crossing he would need to take. Since docking early that morning, he had adopted his MI5 counter-surveillance drills, carefully jinking around a series of ugly, watchful sentries arrayed above him.

A queue of would-be passengers was getting restless on the pavement below as he searched his pocket for every last coin he could muster. He found a handful of pounds and started counting them.

"Will you take British money?"

The driver was losing his patience.

"Listen, fella, are you in Britain?"

Henry shook his head, defeated for now. At that moment, a hand tugged at his grubby coat sleeve. It was attached to a bright-faced young woman sitting in the first row. Mid-thirties, purple-dyed hair, pretty but with a lived-in look and two laundry bags on her knee, identical to his. She dug in her coat and produced the exact change needed for the fare.

"Here you go. You can pay me back when we get to Dundalk."

He offered his thanks, his masked voice momentarily slipping into London English. The driver seemed to catch it, but his saviour was oblivious. She had her own story to tell as the price of the ride.

The driver accepted the coins and a ticket whirred out of the machine. It was slapped into Henry's open palm with what seemed undue force. She patted the seat next to her in invitation and he sat down next to his bagmate.

"Don't pay any attention to him. He's just a big ol' gobshite, that's all. I swear to God that I report him to the council every week. He's always picking on me. Harrassment, that's what it is …"

Her voice was hesitant, the sound of someone part-beaten into submission by life but with a spark of fightback smouldering somewhere inside.

The doors closed with a pneumatic hiss and the driver put the bus into gear whilst turning back to face Henry and his new companion.

"Listen, if she gives you any trouble, I'll stop this bus and put her off at the next stop. She's always a pain in the arse, so she is, especially when she's had a gargle – which she normally has by this time of the morning."

The woman flicked her index finger at the driver, who chose to ignore it and instead turned to face the road leaving for Dublin's northern suburbs. Henry automatically looked at his wrist – no watch – and then consulted the clock above the driver: 11.06. He could smell rich fumes wafting from his neighbour as she rummaged in one of her laundry bags.

"I'm Saoirse. And don't worry. I have had a few tins, like the wanker says, but then I calmed myself down with a smoke at the bus station just now."

He must have looked mystified.

"A smoke. Weed. A toke. Works wonders. And if it goes to shit between here and Dundalk, I've always got these."

Saoirse's voice was oddly beautiful, playful and tinkling. She shook a small brown pillbox with a white label strip around the outside with a slow, hypnotic rhythm. Like a maraca. With her translucent white skin, slight build and jet-black eyes, Henry thought of an enchanting fairy in a book that his mother would read to him. She leant her head on his shoulder and he didn't object. He liked her.

"These tablets are for my psychosis. Anti-psychotics, they are."

She searched his eyes for the look she seemed to anticipate from the revelation, and laughed when it didn't come.

"Christ, you might just be as mad as me!"

"You know what, I think I might be."

She nuzzled closer and told her story. Henry drifted in and out of sleep but caught the headlines.

"Four months sectioned in St James's acute unit,

alcoholic psychosis … on probation in three cities, Dublin, Drogheda and Dundalk, the Gardai are bastards, sure they are … not cut out to be a mother, some of us just aren't …"

Her children were in care, though she'd got presents for them in her bag and missed them so much … went to a day centre in Dublin every Monday and Thursday but lived at a women's refuge in Dundalk … all the rest of the girls addicts and selling their bodies, God help them, poor souls … would love to write poetry, if only she knew how to write …

All delivered in a happy sing-song with the odd squeeze of Henry's arm and surreptitious swig from something concealed in the laundry bag. The granite grey Dublin suburbs receded and rich green fields trundled by as she asked Henry who he was visiting in Dundalk. He reeled out his cover story in a brogue: Monty Crompton, itinerant travel writer, exploring the border country for an article. He tried to evade the question of where he was staying in Dundalk, but Saoirse was not letting go.

"Jesus, Monty, you can't be going round Dundalk on your own now! It's full of junkies who'll rob you blind the minute you step down from this bus."

The driver turned round for the first time since Dublin.

"She's right, you know. An educated-sounding fella like yourself needs to watch himself up there. They call it El Paso. Bandit country. All sorts cross that border – bad people and bad gear. She should know. Her family's made a small fortune out of it."

The driver laughed and Saoirse acknowledged the joke. Henry clicked. He wasn't in anonymous London any more. Since fleeing Lisbon, he had entered a watchful world, where knowing other people, and their private business, wasn't a luxury. It was a necessity.

After an hour, the bus was entering the southern outskirts of Dundalk and the pulses of rain had intensified. They passed a lay-by and Henry spotted two marked police cars and a black Land Cruiser. Carefully watching through the driver's wing mirror, he saw all three indicate and slip quietly into the road behind them.

"Saoirse, the Gardai have just pulled out behind the bus. Do you recognise them?"

Before he could stop her, she pulled herself to her feet and darted down the aisle to the rear window. The bus was now empty apart from a scattering of pensioners. This wasn't the counter-surveillance routine that he had planned and he regretted asking.

A minute later she returned, triumphant.

"I've taken a good look out the back and I know the fucking guards in the cars. I've definitely twatted two of them in the past. I was going to show them my arse through the window" – Saoirse smiled coyly – "but I didn't want you to think I'm common."

He held her hand and laughed.

"I don't think you're common. You're a special person and I don't think I've ever met anyone so positive about life. But did you clock the black car with them? Do you know them?"

Saoirse thought hard, then frowned.

"They're not guards. At least not police from around here. Both tanned – a dead giveaway in County Louth. A man and a woman. Him, fair-haired and good-looking, brown sports jacket, white shirt. Early forties. Her, hard-faced bitch. Hair up. Black padded jacket and mauve shirt. Sunglasses, and it's bucketing down. Also, something stuck on the dashboard that isn't right. Black box with a dome on it. Will that do?"

"That is brilliant, Saoirse. How did you spot all that?"

He felt her shrug against him as she pulled closer.

"I'm thinking we should be getting off at the next stop, just short of the bus station. The black car isn't right, and you're a bag of nerves. I can feel it. There's a shortcut through the fields across to town. We can stop in at the offie. You buy us some tins, I show you around Dundalk. We have a wee smoke and put all our troubles behind us. What do you say, Mister Monty?"

* * *

Henry took the opportunity to study their reflection in the off-licence window. With care. The beer cans fizzed pleasingly as they synchronised their ring pulls and tipped back the export-strength lager together. Through the improvised mirror the terraced street behind them looked clear of the marked cars and the Land Cruiser. Nothing out of place. Safe for now, but experience told him they wouldn't be far away. Saoirse was also staring at the shopfront, beaming as she caught his eye in their reflection.

"We make a right pair, don't we?" She laughed. "How long are you staying for?"

"Much as I'd like to stay here with you, I need to keep moving. Heading north, over the border. I'll let you into my secret. I don't much care for the police either. I thought

I was free of them, but it looks like they're catching up with me again."

"What have you done, Monty? Is it something awful terrible? You can tell me."

Henry took a long swig of beer. His stomach growled menacingly. He was preparing a careful answer when Saoirse spoke again.

"Whatever it is, I'm not worried. I've had all sorts in my life. I've learnt about men the hard way. You're okay, Monty. I can tell. And it sounds to me like you're starving!"

She patted his stomach and then began gathering her laundry bags.

"I've a mouth on me, too. Let's pass by the soup kitchen and then I'll walk with you up the Newry Road as far as the cemetery. Finish the cans and have a smoke. Then you crack on."

A few minutes later he was crouching down in the yellow-fronted community kitchen, loading the charity sandwiches and pies into his bag whilst Saoirse chatted happily with the lady in the housecoat who was clearly a regular volunteer. The conversation suddenly stopped dead. He tensed, fearing the worst. Saoirse was the first to break the silence.

"Mary, your back door, where does it lead to?"

He rose slowly, afraid to turn around.

"Jesus, Saoirse. More man trouble, is it? Is it that fella outside? With a woman. Or are they social services?"

Mary seemed unsure which would be worse but had clearly dealt with this before.

"Okay, love. They've walked by again. But they've copped on to you and your man. Come under the counter now. The back door's unlocked. The gate opens onto the boreen up to the graveyard. Stick close to that blackthorn hedge. It'll hide you. If they come in, I'll keep them gabbing on. Good luck to you both."

The pair were breathless by the time they settled on a moss mound at the dead centre of St Patrick's Cemetery. White gravestones and family plots spread in every direction, seemingly thousands of them. To the far northwest, the sweep of the Mourne Mountains marked the horizon. Then the Gap o' the North, the ancient saddle that would lead him into Ulster and then onwards to England. If he could just stay ahead of the hunters. Towering right above them, on a weathered wood cross, Christ in ecstasy, with three figures gazing dolefully upwards. A woman was on her feet – the Virgin Mary? Another female figure, prostrate, cradling a fresh bunch of flowers. Mary Magdalene? And finally, a man standing in prayer. Henry had no idea who he was.

The rain had stopped and he pulled hard on the joint that Saoirse had rolled and passed to him. The smoke was acrid and burnt his throat. He spluttered and gasped for air, then swallowed hard at his lager. That just made things worse.

Saoirse squealed with pleasure.

"You've not smoked before, have you, Monty?"

He wanted to give Saoirse her moment of triumph.

"That's right. I've no idea what I'm doing. You're going to have to teach me."

Saoirse looked delighted.

She pulled his old blanket out of his laundry bag, shook it out and carefully arranged affairs, moulding the grubby cloth into the contours of the soft ground at the virgin's stone-cold feet. Without thinking, he sat down.

"Lie back, Monty. I'm going to make this easy on you. Treat you gently, like the virgin that you are."

He looked around the deserted graveyard and did a quick risk assessment. He had a three-hundred-and-sixty-degree view from this high point, including the distant Newry Road. For now, he would spot an approach and could be on the track northwards quickly. The border was a few hours away but over tricky terrain for pursuers on foot. He'd had a couple of cans but felt alert. But what would the cannabis do to him, and his chances of escape?

He was about to stand back up when Saoirse gently pushed his shoulders back. He succumbed, finding himself staring up, prone, taking in the darkening blue sky and cascade of purple hair that brushed against his face.

"We're going to shotgun. Don't worry. You're in safe hands." That soothing, tinkling fairy laugh again. She expertly drew deep on the joint and held her pursed mouth against his, fluttering just above him. He yielded, taking in a lungful of pungent smoke. His head spun, and then it began. Gales of uncontrollable laughter. Effortless, natural. Not the forced laughter at some off-colour joke at the nineteenth-hole bar of his golf club. Or the polite appreciation at the end of a tedious dinner-party story. This was primal, orgasmic release. Saoirse glided in next to him and laughed along, a synchronised duo of heaving joy.

Finally, their breath started to return.

"What's so funny, Monty?"

Saoirse's question was greeted with a further convulsion before he could finally speak.

"People keep asking me that. The same question. And I've just got to the answer …"

Saoirse raised herself on her elbow and looked into his eyes.

"Everything about my life became ridiculous, Saoirse. I just wish they could see me now. Jane, my ex-wife. The boys at the golf club. Celeste from Talent, Respect and Inclusion. Roddy and Colin."

Saoirse stroked his beard.

"Look at me now. Living rough. Filthy. I haven't had a shower in weeks. Drinking strong, cheap lager and smoking dope in a graveyard whilst Christ watches over me. Eating out-of-date ham sandwiches. On the run from God knows who. And I'll probably be dead within the week. But I can't remember feeling more alive."

He started to laugh again, but a look from his companion stopped him in his tracks.

"Say it, Monty." Saoirse was now studying him intently.

"Say what?"

"And hanging out with a one hundred per cent-certifiable crazy madwoman. Banjaxed. Off me rocker. And, a bag lady too."

Saoirse kicked out at a plastic laundry bag to emphasise her point.

He put his arm around her and pulled her close.

"No. You've just given me everything I need to carry on. You're a good person in a bad world. A lot of people you meet drain you, run down your battery. You've done the opposite. Given me a full charge. Enough to finish my job, whatever it takes."

They lay together in silence. A full moon was rising,

picking out details of the graveyard around them that he hadn't noticed before. Gravestones cast a barely perceptible shadow and an owl hooted in a nearby copse. He started to drift away into a deep sleep.

A gentle dig to the ribs woke him.

"Monty. I've a question for you."

Henry roused himself.

"Go ahead."

"I know smoking wacky-backy can do funny things to people ..."

Saoirse paused.

"... but I've never heard of it turning a fine Irishman into a Brit, now. That's a new one on me. So, who are you, exactly?"

Henry sat up. The night had turned cold and he folded the blanket around Saoirse, sitting himself on the damp turf.

"Oh, did my accent slip? Sorry. I am English. But otherwise, you're a decent judge of character. Monty isn't my real name, of course. And I'm not a writer. But the rest is true. I know a terrible secret and I've got to get back to England to sort things out before more people get hurt."

"Like who?"

He pictured the evening by the fire with Nataliya that night at Martland Manor. And the cup of tea on Marylebone station, the last time he saw Nea.

"There are people I need to warn, face to face. Before whoever is hunting me gets to them. And then it's like a race – to solve a puzzle."

"What puzzle?"

He silently dug into his bag and pulled out Sasha's

Russian Bible. Saoirse reached out to hold the old book. Instinctively, he brushed her hand away.

"Better not to touch it. It's bad news, this thing. Like a curse. But I think it's the key to putting things right."

He hesitated.

"I don't want to tell you any more. You're the last person on earth I want to involve in this. The less you know, the better. There are already too many people I care about in danger."

The owl hooted and Saoirse sat up too, holding his eyes with an unblinking gaze. Her skin was the same luminescent alabaster as the statues that framed her. She used the blanket as a shawl, a timeless apparition.

He was about to speak when she tensed and crawled away from him on all fours, coming to rest behind a nearby gravestone that looked over the gatehouse down on the Newry Road. She signalled for him to lie down. After a minute, pigeons grunted in distant trees and then took to the air in a rapidly ascending panic. The faint internal light of a parked van flicked on as its back door creaked open on the distant road. Suddenly, three flashlights began sweeping the lower tombs and dogs began to bark as they jumped down from the van. Two or three of them.

He scrambled to pull on his boots and pack away the Bible and blanket. Saoirse was back next to him, calm and decisive.

"My uncle Michael lives right on the border. If you can get to him, he will look after you. If anyone can help you, he can. He was a senior officer in the army."

Saoirse must have caught his look of alarm.

"Not your army, you eejit. The IRA. Official IRA. *Óglaigh na hÉireann.*"

He heard her magical laugh. Like a spell, it calmed him. She gave him clear directions northwards, all off-road. Then she reached into one of her bags. The dogs were now passing by the gatehouse, baying. He guessed they were still on the leashes, for now; their windpipes sounded constrained and they were moving slowly.

Saoirse produced an old Polaroid photograph from a manila envelope. She blushed.

"I'm a bit sentimental, Monty. I always have my family snaps with me. Anyway, this is me and my uncle Michael. That's the name of his lorry yard" – she tapped the top right-hand corner of the photo. The colours had bleached over time but it clearly showed an elfin little girl sitting on the shoulders of a stocky, determined-looking man in a dark suit and black necktie. The beautiful smile was immediately recognisable.

"It's thirty years on but you'll still recognise him. He lives with my cousin, Frankie. He's not changed much, sure he hasn't. Just show him this and say I sent you. And tell him that I say you're all right. For an Englishman."

She squeezed his arm as he folded the picture away in Sasha's Bible.

"Just one other thing, Monty. No pretending you're Irish with them. No fucking about. Be totally straight. Otherwise, they'll suss you right away."

She smiled innocently, then winked.

"And then kill you."

They stood facing each other and kissed. Henry didn't want to leave but the barking was becoming more insistent.

She pushed him away and pointed to a track through the gravestones.

"Go on now. I'll head down towards the road. I can make enough noise to draw them off. And don't you worry, I've always had a way with dogs. I'll charm them. I'll be fine. I might even get to clatter a guard or two!"

He watched her disappear into the darkness as he pulled out his knife and turned for home.

17

ON THE ROAD TO FECK KNOWS WHERE

COUNTY ARMAGH, IRELAND, 18 MARCH 2020

It's come back. First time in weeks. Floating between the gravestones, getting very close. It smiled and then touched me. Not terrifying like before – comforting. A warm hand – not the ice I imagined. Looked a bit like me. Walked with it through the cemetery. Nea was right – much better to connect.

HB's Dream Diary
Saturday, 18 March 2020

Dawn was breaking over County Armagh as Henry tucked away his little dream notebook in a forgotten pocket of his combat trousers. He sheathed his knife and hid that too. The moon had given him just enough light to navigate by, but at some stage he had slipped into a small stream and gashed his left hand on unseen barbed wire as he extricated himself. An old sock that had staunched the bleeding now stuck to the wound it bound.

The route that Saoirse had given him mostly tracked alongside empty country lanes. The only clue as to which side of the border he was on came from an occasional road sign. Speed limits in kilometres in the Irish Republic and miles in Northern Ireland. He guessed he had crossed over the snaking line several times during the night but now woke to look down on his goal – Uncle Michael's farm, fuel depot and lorry yard. He had slept soundly on a raised bank, dutifully written up his dream and then started surveying the scene at first light. An old solid steel gate, heavily padlocked. Then ten foot-high chain fencing topped with spikes. Corrugated sheds and lean-tos around a hard standing. A whitewashed cottage with a stream of smoke rising vertically in the still, early morning. Two stock cars, cannibalised Frankensteins with no discernible pedigree, just "Frankie O'R" painted clumsily on the side.

He was in no rush. He lay flat on his blanket and studied the lane. Over the space of two or three hours – without a watch he was guessing – he counted two cyclists heading south, one tractor heading north and a dog walker crossing the field behind him.

Finally, at around noon, judging by the sun, an articulated lorry rumbled down the lane from the direction of Newry. Its green livery barely squeezed between the deep, brackened banks of the lane and he marvelled as the driver manoeuvred it around a sharp turn in front of the locked yard. An athletic-looking man in a tracksuit sprang down from the cab, unlocked the gate and then spun the truck into the yard as if he was driving a Mini.

Henry was watching the driver uncoupling the tractor when a spasm of pain hit his left knee, sharply spreading down his shin. A shadow descended on him from above and he made for his secreted knife. His bandaged hand hadn't reached his pocket when the stubby handle of a wooden stick came down on it. Hard. He yelped and rolled over on his back, shielding his eyes from the noon sun with his good hand. An older man with receding grey hair stood directly over him, stick raised above his head, ready to strike again, legs braced in black rubber boots. Dressing gown and striped pyjamas set off with a tweed flat cap.

"Uncle Michael? No! I'm Saoirse's friend."

The man peered down. Unreadable, piercing blue eyes. Just like Jed's. Henry heard himself sounding shrill.

"Please! Saoirse said you could help me. I'm in trouble. On the run."

Eventually Uncle Michael stood aside and signalled for Henry to stand. With as much dignity as he could muster, he rose and picked up his bag. His wound had opened again and blood leached through the grey sock. His captor now stood behind him and gave a forceful push between the shoulder blades that propelled him down the grassy slope. Henry kept his balance, but only just. The two men crossed the lane in silence and passed through the gate. The younger man appeared from behind the lorry and stared hard at him, locked and bolted the exit, and then joined the procession behind him. Panic set in as Henry noticed a heavy wrench swinging in his hand.

A hard-backed wooden chair was set down by the open coal fire in the kitchen, and another shove indicated that this was his destination. A strangely fashionable velvet armchair and three-legged brass-and-leather barstool were arranged facing it. He now knew he had been expected.

With Henry seated, Uncle Michael dropped down heavily into his chair. Henry took him in. In his seventies, heavyset – definitely the man in the Polaroid. His pyjama bottoms had ridden above his boot line, revealing one mottled white leg and one pink prosthetic. So, the walking stick wasn't just for Henry's benefit.

The younger man didn't sit but stood next to Henry. A clock ticked for what seemed an eternity. Finally, the uncle spoke.

"You. On your feet. Frankie – search him."

He sensed Frankie had done this before. Many times. He was fast but thorough. Soon his earthly possessions were lining up in front of him. Knife. Little notebook. Cash. Beanie. But he had overlooked one thing. Henry decided on a policy of being helpful.

"There's also a little ring box tucked away in my breast pocket. Easy to miss."

Frankie didn't respond, carrying on patting down each trouser leg.

Henry looked at the uncle for guidance, worried he had caused offence.

"You're wasting your breath. He's been stone deaf since he was a wee lad. The same Provo bomb that lost me my leg. The fucking bastards. But he'll understand you if you look him straight in the face. One of the best lip-readers around."

Henry nodded. Uncle Michael continued.

"And, you know what they say. Men with one sense missing make up for it with the others. So be careful now. He'll read you like a book. It's uncanny."

"That's it, Da. He's clean."

Henry sat back down as the contents of the bag were carefully arranged on his blanket. Old flip-flops. Bloodstained chinos. Linen jacket. Straw hat. Russian Bible. Photo of his daughters. Finally, the picture that Saoirse had entrusted to him. Frankie picked it up and handed it to his father. Henry thought he caught a fleeting smile cross the man's hard face. He felt relieved.

The younger man took his place on the high stool, wrench in lap. Uncle Michael spoke.

"So, who the feck are you? And how did you really come by this picture?"

Henry made a false start, before remembering last night's words of warning.

"My name is Monty ... no, no, sorry, I'm Henry."

Silent stares.

"Do you actually know who you are?"

He was tempted to explain his identity crisis but thought better of it. Nea might be interested in listening when he caught up with her in London. But he guessed trying to explain his current voyage of self-discovery and life-affirming experiences to the IRA might earn him a wrench around the back of the head. He composed himself.

"Your niece told me to be totally straight with you. So, I will be. But did she let you know I was coming? You seem ready for me."

His interrogators looked at each other in silent consultation. Then the older man spoke.

"No. That photo – that's her message. She did the right thing. We'll get it back to her." He slipped it in his dressing-gown pocket.

"It was your friends who let us know something was up."

Henry looked mystified.

"There's been a Dublin Special Branch car parked two hundred yards down the lane most of the night. A black Land Cruiser. It's still there now. And Gardai up and down the main road too."

Henry must have tensed.

"You can relax. At least whilst we finish our little chat. They can't come any nearer the border from the south. And forget what you read about the Troubles being over. Bollocks. The Brits wouldn't dare come down here unless they were mob-handed. A long column of armoured Land Rovers. And I would get a call as soon as they rolled out beyond the security perimeter of Newry police station and turned south. Then progress reports all along the way. We set up our very own Neighbourhood Watch long before anyone else thought of it."

He took a sip from a cup of tea that sat on a small table to his side.

"So, Henry, my favourite niece vouches for you. That's grand. But Frankie and I have grown up much less trusting. Why's an Englishman like you on the run? And who's after you?"

He took a deep breath and began his story. The old IRA man and his son mostly stared and listened. Occasionally they asked a professional question of detail or clarification. Each interruption pointed to a hard-won understanding of life on the run. Henry started to feel an odd bond of common experience. When the story finished, Frankie signed his father and his father signed back. An animated but silent conversation ensued. An index finger was occasionally jabbed in his direction but Henry was none the wiser. It felt like the silent deliberation of a hanging jury. He looked at the kitchen door to the yard outside. Six or seven bounding paces would get him there, but a metal wrench stood in the way. Frankie was shaven-headed and his broad shoulders and muscular forearms gave no comfort. And the yard gate was shut and locked.

Finally, Uncle Michael turned to address him.

"Now, that's been a fine old yarn. We liked it. Russian assassins. Brit spies." He paused. "We particularly liked your bad Englishman. What's his codename? ABSALOM. Eton. Oxford. That appeals to Frankie and me, so it does. Feeds our prejudices."

Frankie nodded in agreement.

"But who's to say you're not playing to the audience? Telling us what we'd like to hear?"

Henry shrugged and nodded.

"Sure, the Special Branch down the road tells me something's up. And the Brits wouldn't be mad enough to send somebody like you our way. It would be a suicide mission. But I need proof. Your bona fides, Henry. What have you got for us?"

He thought quickly. He had no physical evidence apart from the MI5 phone number in his little book. And they were hardly going to ring that. Otherwise, all his tracks had been meticulously covered. Colin and Roddy had been professional. He looked in desperation at the items arrayed on the blanket. Then an idea came to him.

"That's it! The Russian Bible there. I told you about it. Belonging to the SVR man, the illegal. I can show you. There's code written inside it. Some sort of secret messaging."

The two Irishmen signed each other, and Frankie picked up the leather volume and handed it to his father. The old man licked his finger and began to turn the pages, slowly. Henry watched carefully as Uncle Michael studied each of the pencilled tables.

"Frankie, fetch me that torch from the counter there."

He held each page open. They were printed on thin paper and when Uncle Michael shone the light from behind, the handwritten numbers were brightly illuminated, even casting an upward shadow on his hanging jowls. Eventually, he snapped the book shut.

"So, what do you think these entries are?"

"Some kind of code. I saw it being passed to the chap I was working, Sasha. Handed over by a priest at the Russian church in London. I think they're messages from Moscow. Meant to be passed to ABSALOM. The traitor."

Silence.

"At least that's my theory. If I can crack the messages then I find ABSALOM. And that ends all of this."

Uncle Michael put the Bible back on the blanket.

"That's going to be tricky for you. It's OTP. One Time Pad. In theory, unbreakable."

Henry must have looked disappointed.

"We learnt it from the Brits. They were kind enough to teach a couple of our lads in the seventies. Easy to sign up to the TA back then. They did a few Royal Signals courses, then we were in business. We used them ourselves. Very effective. The way it works is that only one other person will have the key to reading this. Your ABSALOM. If he exists …"

Henry didn't like the lingering doubt.

"The key must be exactly the same length as the original text and there can only be one copy. And that needs to be destroyed as soon as it is used."

The IRA man paused for thought. He smiled for the first time.

"I don't know why I am telling you this. But whoever sent out this Bible made one blunder. A real security breach. Should be shot, really."

Henry had to ask.

"Can you tell me how to crack this?"

Uncle Michael rose out of the chair and stoked the coals with a poker.

"I can't read Russian but I know my Bible. A good altar boy in my day, I was. The clue is in the verse. That's all I'm going to tell you. The rest" – he returned to his chair – "is for you to work out."

Now he silently consulted his son again. Hands cast into frustratingly mysterious forms, but then Henry saw Frankie make a C shape before he tipped it to his mouth. His father nodded and at that moment Henry guessed a new approach to the interrogation was coming. He needed to be more careful than ever. He was entering the danger zone.

Uncle Michael rose slowly from his chair with the aid of the stick.

"Time for a drink before I ask you your last question. The clincher, one way or another."

Henry watched him open a closet door in the corner of the kitchen. A full-height wine refrigerator, all chrome and glass, was hidden inside. He took his time finding the bottle he was looking for, stooping low in his dressing gown. Finally, he returned and placed it on the kitchen table. Frankie produced three crystal glasses, deftly removed the foil with a cutter and pulled the cork.

When the three men each had a glass in their hand, Uncle Michael chuckled.

"So, Henry, did you think we're culchies here, just drinking poitín direct from the still up here? Going blind on potato juice? We're good Europeans now. And shipping booze across the border, well ... it's been known to happen."

Henry smiled and raised his glass in wary salute.

"This is a Chablis Grand Cru, 2014. A decent year. Here's our toast now. *Tiocfaidh ar la*. Our day will come."

Henry followed his host, swilling the wine around his glass to release the bouquet before taking a mouthful. He'd had some odd experiences since he first met Roddy and Colin, but he decided this was the most surreal. Fine wine with the IRA, or retired IRA. He wasn't sure which.

"You know, I've dedicated my life to the struggle. To remove the border that's run right through this farm since 1921. Make Ireland a nation once again. Lost a leg. Three bullets to the back."

Uncle Michael paused and stared deep into the straw-coloured liquid in his glass. Something crackled and spat in the fireplace.

"Truth be told, funny, but it's given us a good living, that border. Not sure how I square that away with myself."

Henry considered whether this was a game, a clever ploy to relax him. Draw him out. But looking at the grey figure in front of him, clinging to his stick, he concluded he was about to hear a confession. He went for it.

"So, was it all worth it?"

Minutes passed in silence.

"I was meant to ask you your last question. But I don't see any harm in answering that first. Under the circumstances."

That sounded ominous.

"Frankie, can you please make us a round of sandwiches?"

His son rose silently and found a bread board and knife. His back turned, Henry and Uncle Michael became two men alone in the world.

"I don't want Frankie hearing this, but it's been preying on my mind. Between you and me, I'm not sure any more. I joined up in the sixties. A wain, really. Idealistic. We wanted a workers' Ireland. A red Ireland. Then the Troubles started. Us, the Stickies, blew up Aldershot barracks. All we did was kill some poor bloody women. Kitchen staff. Sickening. We gave up bombing and the Provos came after us instead. Fascists. We went to war with each other. That's the shame of it."

"Thanks for explaining that. And, by the way, you should be proud of your niece. She's one of a kind. In another life …"

The two men smiled at each other, understanding.

Uncle Michael pulled out the Polaroid again and studied it.

"This was taken at the wake for Saoirse's daddy. She must have been five when my brother was shot dead up in Derry. A volunteer on active duty. A brave soldier. But my niece has paid the price. The full price. We all carry our scars in this family. Only hers are inside her head."

Henry knew better than to probe further. But a troubling image had invaded his mind and wouldn't leave when asked to. He saw a teenager dropping down on one khaki knee, shouldering his rifle and taking aim. A boy from the Clyde or the Tyne or the Mersey.

"Really sorry to hear that—"

Uncle Michael raised his hand to stop him in his tracks. His eyes narrowed, shrewd.

"You've got a wee talent there, Henry. No need for holy robes or a Black and Decker drill. Not for you. You've got a way of getting the truth out of people. That's what will see you right."

At that moment, Frankie placed a large plate of sandwiches on the table and refreshed their wine glasses. His father briskly returned to business.

"Anyway. Here's my last question. All interesting so far, don't get me wrong, Henry. But you've yet to tell us something …"

Uncle Michael paused, an experienced, calculated silence that ratcheted up his prisoner's fear to a new plain.

"… something that you could only know from your secret world. Something that we could confirm ourselves."

Henry had one last card. He calculated the risk as he looked at Sasha's Bible. He had to get to London, so he played it.

"I know something about a farmer from somewhere here on the border. Ended up in witness protection in England."

He tried to remember exactly what Nea had told him about her case, the day they had their confessional in her office.

"Middle-aged bachelor. Lived with his mother."

Henry had been averting his eyes, staring into the fire. Wondering what more harm he was about to do. When he looked up, his interrogators were leaning forward, watching him intently.

"Henry, we're interested. Very interested. But speak directly to us. No looking away. A lot depends on how Frankie reads you now. You've got everything riding on this."

Henry fixed on Frankie's gaze.

"He was a police informer. Gave information on IRA smuggling over the border. Fuel and cigarettes. Here in Armagh. They got him out in the nick of time."

The two IRA men signed each other, urgently.

"Indeed they did. This sounds a lot like old Mrs Shaughnessy's boy. Always an odd fella. Not the full shilling. Now he's a tout with a price on his head, so he is. Cost Frankie five years of his life in jail."

Frankie continued to stare, now tapping out a rhythm on the calloused palm of his hand with the wrench. Uncle Michael spoke.

"And his mother died of a broken heart. Never saw her boy again, poor old girl. So, Henry, how do you know all this?"

Henry took his next risk and lied, straight into Frankie's face.

"My MI5 handler used to work on the resettlement programme. Told me the story over a drink. Not sure why."

A minute's urgent signing followed. Then Frankie spoke.

"Where is he? The tout. We owe him a visit."

He had got away with it.

"In a graveyard somewhere. Probably Swindon. Hung himself in a council house. Couldn't bear to live without his mother, apparently."

Frankie failed to hide his anger whilst his father gave a shrug of resignation.

"Ah, well. He got away. But we can take him off our list now. That story is just what we were looking for. You're telling the truth. Now, our side of the bargain. Frankie needs to pick up a load in Essex tomorrow morning. You'll be riding along with him."

Frankie jumped in.

"But I'm not sitting all that time in the cab with you in your state. The shower's upstairs and there's a tracksuit hanging behind the door. It's yours. And a bottle of TCP. Wash that wound. It's nasty. Don't want it turning septic and stinking my lorry out."

Henry got to his feet.

"One other thing: lose the Santa Claus. It's too fucking obvious now." Frankie made a theatrical gesture, hand waving around his chin. Henry wondered if that was Irish sign language, or just frustration.

"There's a razor and cream in the bathroom. But keep the tash. We like that."

Henry was about to make a gag about bachelor Frankie's preference in men's facial hair, but one look killed that thought stone dead. In fact, there was something worrying going on that he didn't quite get.

"The tash is an order. It will suit you. Now crack on. We need to catch the evening sailing. It's an Old Firm game tomorrow, so good cover. The ferry will be packed and the peelers will have their hands full."

Henry must have looked perplexed. Uncle Michael helped out.

"The Old Firm. Glasgow Rangers versus Celtic. Half of Belfast will be on their way over tonight. The Proddies singing poison at us. Us singing back at them. It'll be hard to spot an Englishman in all of that. And, by the way" – the old man rose and put the Russian Bible back in Henry's bag for him – "your story, for what it's worth, I reckon it's someone in Brit intelligence who put the police on your tail. Must have picked you up on cameras when you docked in Dublin. If it was just about the murders in Lisbon, the Gardaí would have lifted you right away. So, it's this book that they want to follow. London will have told the Irish some tall tale, asked them to follow you. Then they lost patience when you disappeared into the graveyard. Brought in the dog unit."

Henry started to pack his bag.

"I'm really grateful to you. I've got my plan thought through. For when I get to London tomorrow. But I'm still not sure why you're helping me."

Uncle Michael drained the last mouthful of Chablis and chuckled.

"We play the long game, Henry. ABSALOM is treasure for us. We'll store that away for future reference. I know it's just a word, a name from the Bible, but dropped into the right conversation it will go off like a three-thousand-pound fertiliser bomb. Right under the British Establishment."

Henry recalled Jed's murderous face when he had dared to say ABSALOM. The IRA man was right. And he also gave him an added incentive to defuse this by finding the traitor.

"And just in case you're worried about your Russian hitman catching up with us, you needn't. We can look after ourselves down here on the border. More than."

Uncle Michael banged the tip of his stick down hard on the flagstone beneath his chair, rose and shook hands with Henry.

"Now be on your way. We don't want to see you around here again. And that goes for being in touch with Saoirse too. She's had enough to deal with in her life."

* * *

After twenty minutes in the queue to board the ferry, Frankie turned off the engine and the two men sat in silence. At the IRA man's instruction, Henry was squatting in the footwell under the cab's passenger seat. He'd spotted two plain-clothes police officers waiting by the passenger gangplank thirty yards ahead, both middle-aged men in bomber jackets. As promised, the singing was intensifying as the passengers disgorged on the car deck. "No surrender … old Derry's walls … no Pope of Rome … on the one road … come out ye black and tans … armoured cars and tanks and guns …"

He reached up and tapped Frankie's knee to get eye contact.

"What's happening?"

"Sure, we'll be fine. Two peelers. One Catholic. One Prod."

Henry was mystified.

"How can you tell that?"

"I've been reading them since we joined this line and

they haven't discussed the match once. Sure sign, so it is. If they kicked with same foot, it's all they'd be talking about."

"Anything else?"

"They're watching out for someone call Henry Bradley. Would that be you, now?"

"Nearly. Close." He was thankful to Saoirse – if he'd lied this would have gone badly wrong.

"It seems you're wanted for murder, international arrest warrant. But they've got their priority orders from Box 850. Do not 10–26 under any circumstances. And apparently you are CCW. Master of incog. And an expert in HTH."

Frankie tipped his head back and laughed.

"What does all that mean?"

"I'll translate. MI6 in London seem to have the hots for you. So Da's idea checks out. No 10–26: that means orders not to detain you, just find you and keep you under close watch."

Frankie stared down.

"Funnily enough, you're being advertised as carrying a concealed weapon. And you're a regular Clouseau, what with all your disguises."

"Anything else?"

"Aye. The best bit. Lethal with the old unarmed combat."

Frankie gave a theatrical karate chop.

"That's quite flattering …"

At that moment, the lorries in front started their engines and Frankie put his into gear.

"That's us now. On we go. But Da asked me to offer you something for your trip. A memento of old Ireland. And, maybe, the peelers aren't so wide of the mark after all …"

He reached under his seat and pulled out a smart new tartan duffel bag, and passed it over to Henry.

"Take a look and tell me what you think."

Henry fished inside, tentatively. A brand-new wax jacket. Purple cashmere sweater and green corduroy trousers. Moleskin tan shirt and brown brogues. All in their factory wrappings.

"Thanks very much. It looks like you are kitting me out for a hunting trip. Even the sizes are right."

"Well, in a manner of speaking, that's exactly what you're off to, isn't it? Lucky we do a line in countrywear, with the usual border 'discount'. Thought a change of appearance might do you good for when you get to London. Now, take another gander, a little deeper in the bag there."

Henry felt under the clothes and his hands closed on something hard, metallic, wrapped in a plastic shopping bag. Also, a box with heavy, clinking content. He peered inside to see a semi-automatic pistol and carton of spare cartridges. The lorry moved slowly forward to the boarding ramp. He let out an involuntary whistle.

"So, Henry, you've got a big decision to make here. Da wants me to be clear with you. Full disclosure."

Henry stared into the bag, transfixed.

"We didn't get rid of everything on decommissioning. And that's a lovely little piece. A Colt Government. Old. From the seventies. But clean, mind."

Henry pulled the handgun from the bag and studied it, keeping his head below the windscreen. It felt heavy. Loaded? Black gunmetal with a brown grip. Its effect on him was hypnotic.

"What does that mean? Clean?"

"Identifiers filed off. But much more importantly, never fired in anger. No forensic history to track it back to us."

Henry balanced the weapon in his hand, finding its centre of gravity.

"So, Henry, listen carefully. We need to tell you something. You get five years in prison if you're caught with that thing. Automatic tariff. On top of whatever other jail time you get. In addition, if you were tempted to tell the police who gave it to you, you're as good as dead."

Henry slowly placed the gun back in its bag and made to hand it back to Frankie. The lorry was edging into the bowels of the ship as a loader shouted directions to the last few drivers to board.

"Hold your horses there, Henry. We want you to think this through, work the odds. You may know this, but on your average day's jaunt around London, you're going to be caught on five hundred cameras. Five hundred. With facial recognition. As soon as I drop you at that service station outside London, Spook Towers is going to light up like a fecking Christmas tree. Even without that stupid beard. No way around that. It will be a race against time. Twenty-four? Forty-eight hours? Before they catch up with you."

"That sounds about right. I'll be breaking cover. But I don't need a gun."

Frankie was pulling the lorry into its berth.

"Are you sure? Really sure? Think about it. Your Russian and his pals aren't going to make a mistake a second time, now, are they? Fair play to you, but your penknife trick won't work again. I've known a few fellas like him, you know. Behind the wire and on the street. Psychos. For him, it'll be a grudge now. Honour. Whatever he's got in mind for you won't be quick, or easy. And that goes for anyone else in his way."

Frankie let that thought hang as he turned off the engine. The boarding ramp was being raised as the ferry sounded its horn, long and deep. Henry wavered.

"Thanks. I suppose the Colt gives me a fighting chance. But I don't even know how to use the thing …"

His companion was pulling on his fluorescent jacket, ready to head for the lorry drivers' mess.

"We can find a field behind the service area we'll stop at on the A1. Lots of traffic noise so we can practise. I'll teach you how to get close. You'll need to be very close. Draw and cock it. Both hands around the pistol grip and then double tap. Two shots to the head or, if not, the torso. Drop it and be on your way."

Henry sat in silence.

"Dead simple, really. Nothing to it." Frankie paused. "Just a question of motivation, that's all. We've had a little experience, Da and me. And we think you're motivated, right you are. Now, I'm off for my tea. You lie low and have a wee think on it."

Frankie opened the cab door.

"I need the lesson. And the gun. Count me in."

"Top man. I'll bring you back a pie and a tea."

Henry watched as Frankie climbed the stairs, wondering what he had become. And what else he might be capable of.

18

TALLY-HO!

Henry was nicely camouflaged, sitting in the window of a third-generation Italian café on Sloane Avenue. Though his funds were fast depleting, he treated himself to a full English breakfast washed down with a mug of milky tea: two mealy sausages, three rashers of back bacon, black pudding, mushrooms, grilled tomatoes and baked beans. He had taken Frankie's advice seriously. The stopwatch had started ticking ninety minutes ago when he was dropped in North London. He noticed camera after camera on the Tube journey. A condemned man? This could be his last meal.

The cords and sweater matched well, and though the brogues pinched at the heel, they would wear in over time. If he had time. The jacket came with a nifty, detachable poacher's pocket on the inside. A perfect hiding place for the loaded Colt Commander that now gave him a disconcerting level of comfort. He'd tucked his knife, sheathed, in his left-hand sleeve, handle just poking out. Backup, just in case.

His perch gave him a direct line of sight onto the entrance of Nataliya's magnificent art deco apartment block. The vast building was set back from the main street with a one-way drop-off lane, emphatically marked "IN" and "OUT". Two black cabs waited, "For Hire" lights illuminated. A doorman in bowler hat stood at the ready to greet residents and visitors. It was now eight o'clock and Henry wondered how long he could wait. He had used a trip to the lavatory to assess the back of the small café. A fire exit was wedged open, giving access to bin storage and daylight beyond. That would be his best chance, if needed.

Waiting gave him time to consider Frankie's parting shot. It was still sinking in. Standing in that muddy field in North Yorkshire seven hours earlier, he had sung Henry's praises as he at first missed, then grazed, and at last poleaxed a football placed on a gatepost. He was a natural, apparently. Perfect stance and breathing, he could now take a head shot, no problem. But, as he was standing a mere seven feet from his target, something seemed forced, contrived. Frankie wasn't a man given to natural enthusiasm, so Henry wasn't surprised when the sly suggestion came.

Da wondered if Henry had thought through what he would do when he uncovered ABSALOM's true identity. Da was worried, really worried, that the Englishman's instinct would be to trust the Crown authorities to take things from there. Hand over the name, and walk away, confident that the British Establishment would do the right thing. But would they now? Would they bollocks. Not in our experience, for sure. They close in on their own, they do. So the question for Henry to ask himself might be as follows. If he really wanted to end this, and was sure of his target, might he not need to fall back on direct action – two skull shots, drop the gun, put his hands behind his head before the close protection team had time to draw theirs? A line under things and take his chances in court. And with what Henry knew, would they even want him telling his story? Probably not. Henry would be a prime candidate for a nice witness protection deal. A new start.

Plus, if ABSALOM was the sort of character they all imagined, Henry's sheer Englishness, together with his moustache and jolly new rig, would get him unchallenged VIP entry into any constituency surgery, party fundraiser or county show that circumstances required. Just get hold of a lanyard with any old photo ID on it – they never check them – stick on a blue rosette (sorry, they hadn't stretched to one of those in the care package, laughter) and smile gormlessly until the ten-foot line. Then "Boom Boom, Out Go The Lights". A great song, by the way. Little Walter. Here's a secret, Henry. In my younger days, that was my signature tune – the boys in the band in Dundalk used to play it when I bought my round in the pub. Still get a thrill hearing it, so I do. Well, not so much hearing it, of course. Feeling it vibrate through the floor.

Anyway, that's just an option for ABSALOM, Henry. Hopefully it won't come to that. But if it does, you're ready for it. We're just saying.

Henry's thoughts were interrupted by a black Range

Rover pulling up outside Nataliya's building. Hazard lights went on and the driver hurried to open the nearside back door. Muscular, short blond hair, familiar Boss jacket. At first, he couldn't make out the guest of honour, a slight figure shielded by dark glass and the tall vehicle. But as he mounted the steps unsteadily, the view became clearer. Skinny white jeans and close-fitting leather jacket, listing to one side. It could only be one person. Jed.

The Russian ignored the cheerful greeting and bow of the doorman, hobbling inside with a terrifying purpose. To compound matters, Pavel descended from the front passenger seat and took up watchful sentry by the door while the driver, who Henry now recognised as Ilya, resumed his seat, hands on the wheel. It looked like they were ready for a quick getaway. Henry watched Pavel produce the all-too-familiar bag of *semechki* seeds whilst he pulled back from the window and considered options.

Without thinking, he had already pulled the Colt from the recesses of the poacher pouch, cocked it and placed it in his outer jacket pocket, finger resting on the trigger guard. One round in the chamber, safety still on. The two old staff members and three other customers hadn't seen a thing.

His sole purpose in coming here, his first stop in London, was to waylay Nataliya, on her way out to give a language lesson or head down to Martland Manor, and warn her about Jed. But his role seemed to be evolving grotesquely; not saving his former lover, but sitting in savage witness of her end. She had warned Henry of the Grey One, yet there it was, standing in the lobby, lopsidedly waiting for the elevator.

He gripped the pistol hard, but felt powerless. A solitary red phone box stood ready across the street, about forty feet from Pavel. Worth the risk? He had no chance of remembering Nataliya's mobile number. And on closer inspection, it now contained a defibrillator rather than a payphone. So, no. And the frontal assault option? He guessed he wouldn't get within thirty feet of Pavel, never mind ten, before he was recognised. How would he do against two seasoned hoods with his few minutes of small arms training? Not well.

The trembling started. Henry just hoped Nataliya's daughter wasn't at home and that whatever Jed had in mind for the Russian teacher would be mercifully quick. But time passed slowly. The kindly old lady in a flowery pinafore brought him another tea and asked him if he felt okay. He said he was, but she didn't look convinced. He stirred a heaped tablespoon of sugar into his drink with his left hand whilst his knuckles were squeezing white on the pistol grip in his right-hand pocket. Pavel kept his position, staring, chewing, spitting, staring, chewing, spitting. The cycle seemed endless.

Then things happened quickly. Ilya turned the hazards off and the powerful engine started to purr. Pavel came to attention as the bowler-hatted doorman pulled open the heavy door and Jed blinked as he limped into the London sunlight, a look of triumph spread across his white face. Henry dropped a twenty-pound note on the counter and moved towards the door of the café, hand buried deep inside his right pocket. Then, in a blur, he found himself on the pavement, moving slowly but with purpose. The Colt carried seven rounds, two for each target plus one spare.

But who to hit first? Jed, if he could get to him. Henry was closing, and his targets hadn't looked his way; they were distracted. Seventy feet. Sixty. Fifty. Forty. Closing on an odd tableau, something not right. Jed had stopped and was holding the entrance door open, bathed in a rare smile. Almost saintly. Henry aborted in the nick of time, veering suddenly, thankful for the old phone box that gave him instant sanctuary. Closing the red door behind him, he peered through a grubby pane of glass, one of the few not plastered with adverts for the likes of Miss Whiplash, TV Tuition, A-Level Lessons, and Heel Boy!

Nataliya had emerged, far from dead but gloriously as alive as ever. Green eyes flashing, tossing her mane over a leopard-skin coat, tight across her full chest and hips. She wore high leather boots and bright red lipstick. Then she turned balletically, kissing Jed fully on the mouth, a long and hard clinch, hand caressing the back of his neck. She was taller than him. Jed had his arm snaked around her waist. Henry felt nauseous and had to look away. The box smelt of urine and span around him. He was a prisoner in a tawdry peepshow. He steadied himself with his left hand; releasing the iron grip on the pistol took all his willpower. His breathing felt erratic and his pulse raced. The defibrillator stared him in the face, its instructions bold and clear. Fuck. Would he be the first man to ever use one on himself? Then he found himself laughing, that same spontaneous, untrammelled convulsion that he'd experienced with Saoirse only two nights earlier. At the absurdity of his situation. And the release felt so good. He should make a habit of it. Sasha had warned him about Nataliya. So had Roddy. And now he knew the full truth.

Or did he really? How long had she been with Jed, working for the Russians? From the start, or a recent recruit? And did it really matter? The web of secrets was getting more visible all the time, dew settling on the intricate weave of its filaments, but he needed to focus on the predator waiting patiently in the middle, not the incidentals. Focus, Henry. He felt himself getting closer.

While he waited for the happy Russian party to pull out into the Chelsea traffic, Nataliya slipping into the back seat beside Jed, he made the pistol safe and committed the Range Rover's number plate to memory. Then he flagged a cab and headed north across Hyde Park. The next call was make or break, but unless he arrived to find Jed had got there before him, he shouldn't need the gun.

* * *

Henry inspected his reflection in the dulled brass plate of the Harley Street lift. Tanned face, cheekbones pronounced for the first time in years, military moustache. He was at least thirty pounds lighter than on his last visit. Hard to believe that only five months had passed since he had been in the same building, plucking up courage to get Nea's advice on how to stop spying. Standing with a handgun in one pocket and a book with Britain's greatest secret, tantalisingly close, in the other, Henry had no regrets. ABSALOM had given him all the therapy he needed, and more. For the first time, he had purpose in life. He was alive.

He didn't know what to expect as he approached Nea's oak-framed door. The front entrance to the Edwardian building had been wide open and the reception desk seemed abandoned, half-drunk coffee in a mug and an animated desktop screensaver lazily bouncing balls back and forth. Nobody in the waiting room, just an array of newspapers, headlines all variations on the same ominous theme: "Britain in Lockdown", "Life Put On Hold", "Time To Get Antisocial".

The chances were that she wouldn't be there. But this was his best shot. Forgoing the usual knock, Henry gently turned the handle, other hand firmly on the pocketed Colt. He'd checked the quiet street carefully when he alighted from the cab. And then waited for ten minutes in the downstairs reception, watching from behind the dusty gauze curtains for any "absence of normal". It was dawning on him that London seemed to be emptying out, but other than that, nothing to alarm.

The door creaked open and he found himself in the familiar anteroom, empty but with the fluorescent strip light switched on. Promisingly, the usual old transistor radio was playing; a woman wailing "No Time to Die" was being faded as a jaunty voice ended the programme. Henry decided that the music was a good omen and sat down on the settee. The door to Nea's consulting room was firmly closed, and he could hear a male voice, raised but indistinct. Six pips sounded on the radio and the midday news summary was beginning. Nea always ended her consultations promptly. If the door didn't open after two minutes, he would go in, unannounced. The BBC newsreader carried on in the background. "… Prime Minister says everyone should avoid the office, pubs and travelling … catastrophic epidemic … fast upswing in cases … in other news, a huge weather system is forming in the western Atlantic ... potentially the 'Storm of the Century' ... massive destructive power ... particular fears for South-West England ..."

Music was starting again and Henry took this as his cue. He cocked the pistol, checked the safety catch was engaged, and replaced it in his pocket, then made for the door.

It opened just before he reached it. A tall man with a full head of silver hair, Henry's age, stooped and with a defeated look, emerged with Nea right behind him. She didn't miss a beat.

"Ah, Henry, my next and probably final patient for a while, take a seat. I'll be with you in a moment."

The man mumbled something valedictory to Nea as she put a reassuring hand on his shoulder and then closed the door. He wouldn't meet Henry's stare.

They were back in the same old room, same old furniture, but with a lot of new material to pick over. Still, they fell back into their old routine. Nea curled up in the back of her armchair, shoes kicked off and legs underneath her. A few minutes' silence as she inspected him.

"Henry, you look like you've just come from a regimental reunion. What the hell's going on?"

They both laughed.

"Christ, Nea. Since I last saw you I've been a surfer dude, a pompous Oxford-educated expat, a travel writer, a Lourdes pilgrim, an Irishman, a down-and-out tramp sleeping rough ... and now this! My latest incarnation."

"You've packed a lot in. I knew your acting would come in handy, one day. But you seem well on it. And you look great."

Henry knew what he needed from Nea, but echoes in the room told him to go slowly. The last time he rushed it here, he'd ended up alone and terrified. And, anyway, he had some serious therapy to catch up on.

"A lot's happened. Do you remember my bad dreams? The awful dark thing? Well, it's all changed. People I cared for have been murdered all around me and I've been running for my life, cold and hungry. But the shadow's completely changed. Morphed into something else. I actually look forward to seeing it. Isn't that a bit odd?"

Nea put her fingers together under her chin, as if in prayer. But there was something softer about her now, more approachable. She tilted her head to one side, her elegant brown neck exposed. The evil-eye amulet studied him, unblinking. Henry so wanted her to smile. And then she obliged.

"Why do you think your dreams have changed, Henry?"

He didn't even bother to pretend to think about the question. Time wasn't on his side.

"No idea. I've written it all in my little book, but I can't find the pattern. The worse things have got for me, the sounder my sleep and the happier my dreams. Weird."

"So, what if the 'thing' in your dreams is in fact you? Or a different, hidden part of Henry, deep in your subconscious? That you couldn't connect with before? But perhaps something has changed over the last nine months, to bring you closer to yourself. What do you think? Does that make any sense?"

He nodded vigorously.

"You're so right, Nea. Shit happening all around. Dead

bodies piling up. Near miss after near miss. Stabbing someone within an inch of their life. Nearly pulling my gun twice this morning alone ..."

Nea looked off balance.

"But I've learnt who to trust, and how to trust, perhaps for the first time. And that's what is keeping me alive."

"We will need to come back to the gun and the stabbing later, but go on for now."

"Skipper Cristóvão and then that old African priest in Lisbon ... the lady in the park in Porto ... the Moldovans ... the barman on the Irish ferry ... lovely Saoirse ... Uncle Michael ... they didn't need to help me keep going, but they all did. Nothing in common with me, really. Sorry. I know these are all just names to you – I'll tell you the full story when we have more time. But they're the ones who brought me and my shadow together."

He paused for breath just as three vehicles with two-tone sirens blared along the street below. He instinctively touched his right jacket pocket for reassurance. Nea spotted the move immediately.

"What's in that pocket, Henry?"

He tried innocence.

"Sorry, which pocket?"

It wasn't working. Nea pointed directly. She wasn't going to take 'no' for an answer.

"Take it out and place it on the coffee table, slowly."

He shrugged and placed the pistol gingerly in front of his therapist, and then produced the box of spare cartridges and set them alongside.

They both stared at the weapon for seconds before he broke the silence.

"Bloody hell, I think I left it cocked. Sorry."

He made to move forward but Nea stopped him with a look.

"Don't touch it, Henry."

In an instant she had ejected the round, cleared the breech and placed it back into the magazine. She made it look like one single movement. Then, double-handed, she pointed the weapon into the corner of the room, elbows locked, squinting through the rear sight, adjusting her grip.

"That was professional, Nea. I think you've done that before."

The therapist placed the gun back on the table, between them.

"You guess right. A 1911 Colt. Design not much changed in a hundred years. Amazing stopping power, with .45 calibre. Weapon of choice in my unit of the US Army. I fired three thousand practice rounds with it on the range and in the killing room. Before I was allowed out on patrol. Also, how to draw it from inside an abaya. That takes a lot of practice."

Nea ran her right hand through her short dark pixie hair.

"So, how many times have *you* actually fired that, Henry?"

He held her stare.

"Five or six shots. But that's not the point. There's a professional Russian hitman, Jed, probably heading this way as we speak. With two of his friends. And with my ex in tow. I nearly shot him this morning, just couldn't quite get close enough. He could be in the building right now.

The bastard might be limping up the stairs as we sit here. The reception's abandoned and the building is empty. Just you, me and that Colt."

Nea picked it up and slid it between her coiled leg and the chair arm, turning her head to face the door.

"I think you'd better tell me your story, Henry. Everything that's happened, and what you're planning next."

Finally, he'd finished and was looking at the alarm clock that Nea kept by the armchair. Thirty-seven precious minutes had ticked by as she sat largely in silence. She'd only interrupted to ask a few questions about Jack Somerset, Roddy and the old Russian Bible. The only chapter he chose to skirt around was Ireland, Saoirse, Uncle Michael and Frankie. She didn't need to know that – and he might just have landed her in it with his retelling of her border-story.

Nea removed her glasses and rubbed her nose.

"That's impressive, Henry. You've shown a side of you that, well, frankly is a surprise. Though, thinking about it, you always had it buried inside. The determination, the resourcefulness. Quite the actor and exceptionally good at getting the truth out of people, when you let yourself go."

Nea broke off and, gun in hand, trod lightly to the main door, listening, checking the building for life. Then she returned.

"London's shutting down today. No more patients for me for a while. Funny how history repeats itself. Like the old days of plague, the cities are emptying of the rich, including all my patients. They're bolting for their country places, hoping that will keep them safe. It won't, of course. Everyone else has to stay put, hunker down, and pray."

Nea smiled.

"And most of us don't have the luxury of prayer anymore."

"I've not really followed the news. I went offline, completely analogue, for reasons of self-preservation. You're a doctor. Is this sickness bad?"

"Terrible. A very dangerous virus that transmits between people. No vaccine, no cure. The government doesn't get it. They're making it up as they go along …"

Henry considered what this might mean for his mission. He had to get to the point.

"I need your help to finish this, Nea. And I've nearly run out of time. You have to give me the new name of your MI6 officer. The one you buried deep in witness protection. Remember, you thought ABSALOM was her case? She can help with the code in the Bible. She's my only lead, but I'm sure she's got the last piece of the jigsaw. Please, help me. You're in danger. She will be in danger. I'm in danger. The Russians won't stop unless and until we identify the traitor."

Nea pulled her knees closer under herself and slowly shook her head, nearly disappearing into the corner of the big armchair. He'd seen this once before, and it didn't bode well.

"Why the fuck not, Nea? Forget your code of ethics. Her right to privacy. We're all going to be dead by the weekend if we don't do anything! And ABSALOM then gets to create whatever devilment he is told to by this book. Christ."

He pulled the Bible from his jacket pocket, brandishing it before slamming it down on the coffee table. Nea looked alarmed.

"Henry, I need to explain. I had a brand new client here, about a week ago. A businessman with acute porn addiction. Eleven hours a day online, looking for the perfect scene. That's what they do, never happy …"

He was losing patience and snapped.

"Why the bloody hell is that relevant?"

"He was quite convincing, but after twenty minutes enjoying telling me his darkest fantasies, he identified himself as an officer of the British security services. Not a pleasant experience. Certainly not a nice man."

"What did he want?"

"You. And my continued silence. He told me you were a dangerous psychopath on the run. Murder. Attempted murder. Sadistic torture. He questioned my professionalism. Why hadn't I spotted you a mile off?"

"And what do you think? Surely your porn addict has a point. The circumstantial evidence isn't great for me, is it? And I'm running around London with a loaded gun and a knife, ready to use them. Do you seriously think I'm right in the head?"

Nea smiled.

"I trust my judgement, Henry. You aren't mad, in fact you are showing remarkable resilience. And when I saw you appear in my doorway just now, well, I realised I've developed a soft spot for you."

He shifted uneasily on the settee and clambered back to safe ground.

"What questions did he ask?"

"When were you last in touch? Where I thought you might be? Were you more given to fight or flight?"

"And what about your silence?"

"He reminded me, in no uncertain terms, that I was lucky not to be in prison. Where, apparently, I belong. And that if I breached any of my terms, particularly contacting a single one of my old clients in witness protection, that is where I would end up. For the rest of my days. He would make that his personal mission."

Patient and doctor sat and studied each other carefully.

"What did he look like?"

He knew the answer. He just wanted confirmation of the worst.

"Slightly built, late forties, shot of dark hair. Unmistakably a British public school boy. Teeth too big for his mouth ... and a filthy imagination."

"I thought you weren't meant to judge. Anyway, that's Roddy Partridge. Or, more accurately, Rupert Samson-Brown. The MI6 officer who handles me. The one who reacted weirdly when I told them about Sasha's personal problems and Aslanov's offer."

"There's another odd thing, Henry. I know these people. They always work in twos. He didn't. And he was visibly agitated. Not their usual style."

"What do you read into that?"

"I think your friend is freelancing. Operating alone. At least as far as the British services are concerned. I think he might be working for the Russians. And under a lot of pressure to deliver for them. It's time for you to run to ground again."

It was his turn to shake his head.

"Nowhere to hide now. And I feel close, so close, to catching up with ABSALOM."

Nea paused. He sensed she was relenting.

"And what happens when you work out ABSALOM's identity? What do you do with that treasure? You'll have next to no time to act, with Roddy and the Russians close on your tail."

"Three options. Give the name and evidence to the British authorities. See how they react. Or go to the media. See if they publish. Or" – he hesitated and looked at the pistol in Nea's hand – "direct action. Get within ten feet of ABSALOM and deal with him myself. Which is why I would like my property back, please."

Henry indicated the Colt. Nea shifted in her chair. Moving from a defensive posture she placed the pistol behind her and leant forward, arms spread, palms open, facing each other.

"Henry, don't be absurd. You aren't an assassin. And you wouldn't be able to pull the trigger even if you could get close enough. Just think of the consequences. Your reputation. Your daughters."

"You said it yourself, Nea. Please don't underestimate me. A lot's happened in the last six months. I've changed forever. No more Bonners, the golf club, gong-chasing the OBE. I want a different country, a different England. One without a cancer at its heart. And I want revenge for the Aslanov boy, Sasha, Jack Somerset. I'll shoot the traitor in a heartbeat. Boom boom. So please, give me the gun."

Nea tensed. She fixed her eyes on him, but they had softened, now pleading.

"Look, I'm an advanced Krav Maga instructor. A very practical form of unarmed combat. I am small, Henry, but very fast. You really don't want to fight me. Hurting you would make me sad. And besides, I think there is a better solution."

"Go on."

"I've thought about it. You're right about the time we have. We have precious little."

With satisfaction, he noted the first-person plural. Nea straightened up, ready to declaim.

"Felicity Smith. Head librarian of the public library in Saint Morwenna, a lovely village on the north coast of Cornwall. Organises the chapel choir and runs the local pub quiz. Also, former head of MI6's Russia operations and the most senior female in the Service at the time. Ten years ago, accused of passing secrets to the enemy. Offered a stark choice. One-way ticket to Moscow Sheremetyevo airport. A long prison stretch at Her Majesty's pleasure. Or a new life amongst unlimited books and sea cliffs. And the chance to keep her generous government pension. I've never seen anyone go into witness protection so happily."

"Thank you, Nea. I'll head down there now."

He hesitated, then felt a surge of nobility.

"Please keep the gun. For your own protection. I should be fine. I've still got this."

He pulled the small kitchen knife from his sleeve, colouring up when Nea laughed.

"Not sure what good that will do you, Henry. But it might make you feel better. Here's my suggestion. I've got no patients, at least not for now. I'm an expert with the Colt and spent most of my adult life undercover, between US Army covert operations and then British witness protection. I can fade to grey, look after myself. You must go and do what you need to do. If anyone can solve this, you can. I have every faith. You won't see me along the way, but I'll do my best to stay somewhere close. Think of me as your new friendly shadow. Ready when needed. I can't guarantee always being there, but I will do my best."

Nea got to her feet and tiptoed to the door, gun in hand. He followed. Once she had checked the empty corridor, she came close to him, face turned upwards to his. Then they hugged on the threshold.

"Felicity knows me as Sue Nightingale. Use that name."

"Not Florence?"

"Don't be stupid, Henry. See you on the other side. We'll be fine."

19

THE GATHERING STORM

Bonners' visitor reception was busy when Henry arrived. It was only mid-afternoon but younger staff members were congregating in groups, laptop bags slung over their shoulders, discussing which pub would be best for their "last drink". A buzz of excitement. Their bosses were streaming from the lift bank, archive boxes in arm, heading across the lobby to the underground car park.

The receptionist remembered Henry and actually seemed happy to see him.

"Mr Bradbury! And looking so well, too. You handsome devil. So, there is life after Bonners? Do tell."

The two men laughed.

"Indeed there is, Lee. Indeed there is. And after decades of marriage ending too."

Henry wasn't sure why he said the last thing. Some sort of instinctive assertion of heterosexuality?

"Anyway, enough frivolity. Do you have a spare envelope, by any chance? I'm dropping something off for Priya Gupta in Board Analytics."

"There you go, sir. But I'm sure I saw her this morning. Would you like me to give her a buzz? Get her to pop down to see you? Such a lovely girl."

Henry suppressed a shudder as he thought of his final image of Sasha, battered and broken, tied to his surfboard. Priya would be less than delighted to see him and he felt the urgent need to get as far away from here as possible. He sealed the ring box in the envelope and handed it back.

"Thanks, Lee. The internal mail will do. And please don't call her. It's meant to be a little surprise."

Lee winked theatrically and dropped the envelope in a tray.

"Well, take care of yourself, Mr Bradbury. I probably won't see you for a while. The powers that be are closing the office and I'm not sure when we'll be back."

Henry was striding purposefully towards the swing doors when a hand gripped him by the elbow. He flinched and moved for his knife, before a familiar voice stopped him drawing it.

"Henry! My goodness. I hardly recognised you. You look so well."

The hand released its grip on his arm and now patted him on the back. Henry swivelled to see the familiar face of an old colleague. Nigel was probably fifteen years his junior, a born enthusiast and obsessive yachtsman.

"You disappeared off the face of the earth. We were

worried about you, looking like you were carrying all the troubles of the world on your shoulders when you left us."

Henry eyed the exit. He didn't want to prolong the conversation a minute more than needed but he also had to stay calm. As Colin liked to say, avoid a scene at all costs. Placing his travelling bag at his feet, he shook hands with Nigel with some vigour.

"I took some time out. I needed to. Leaving the City. Divorce. Life a bit of a mess …"

Nigel touched his arm sympathetically.

"But all well now, it seems. Amazing what a change of lifestyle can do for you."

Henry smiled as he thought of the Moldovan camp, minesweeping beer on the ferry to Ireland, shotgunning weed in the graveyard in Dundalk. If only he could tell Nigel the truth.

"Well, it looks like it's done you the power of good. There's hope for us all."

For the first time, he noticed that Nigel was wheeling two cabin-sized suitcases and, like everyone else, had his laptop bag over his shoulder. He wore an expensive sailing jacket with matching baseball cap, mirror sunglasses hanging from a string around his neck. He was fleeing London! Nigel answered the question before Henry could ask it.

"Isabelle's already headed down to North Cornwall with the kids to open up the cottage. I'm driving down now. Not sure how long we'll be there for, but I've just ordered three cases from Berry Brothers. Should be delivered tomorrow, so I'll be well provisioned for, I don't know, a week?"

Henry laughed along with Nigel's little joke, taking in his mottled red face, wondering how near the truth that might in fact be.

"It sounds like the locals down there are getting restless. None too happy with us lot actually using our own properties. Bloody cheek of it! We aren't lepers."

He nodded in theatrical sympathy.

"And I've got every reason to get down there sharpish. There's some enormous storm, Agnes, I think, coming in and I need to get my rib secured at the harbour. It looks like our coast will take a direct hit."

Henry made his play. Picking up his bag, he offered his hand to Nigel.

"Well best of luck getting down. Funnily enough, I'm heading over to Paddington myself. Hoping to catch a Truro train. Looks like everyone else has the same idea, though. I need to get to Saint Morwenna, to catch up with someone."

He turned towards the exit before he got the reaction he was hoping for.

"Woah. Hold up, mate. Come down with me. I pass right by Wenna. I've got the 911 parked underground. We'll squeeze in. Share the driving. It's a long schlep and I could really use the company. You can tell me all about life after Bonners and I'll catch you up on the office gossip. There's even been a murder, some Russian guy who'd only just joined!"

Nigel seemed positively gleeful.

"What do you say, Henry? Cornwall, here we come? Hurrah!"

* * *

The chapel clock was sounding nine as Henry stood in front of the solid oak door of the Pilchard's Head. The solitary bell oscillated over the roar of the ocean, louder or fainter with each strike. He paused to look at the pub landlords' notice stencilled in the porch.

"Mrs Daphne & XXXXXX Williams – Licensed to Sell Beers, Wines and Spirits to be Consumed On or Off the Premises."

The second name had been painted over, coat upon coat, thickly obliterated. He noted that with interest.

Opening the door, he was confronted with the fuggy warmth of the saloon bar. The smell of stale beer, dog and woodsmoke. Minutes earlier, he had pulled his jacket tight around him as he pushed against the Atlantic wind, bent nearly double, hurrying down from the main road where Nigel had dropped him towards the beckoning lights of the cove. The pub looked welcoming from the outside, rough wood boards painted white with its old sign creaking to and fro, a disembodied fish head sticking out of a pie, staring up at a full moon rising over a black sea. Apart from the licensee notice, one blackboard advertised the day's specials and another commended the pub's favourable winter bed and breakfast rates. But given Nigel's warning about the locals, he didn't know quite what to expect.

A huge Rhodesian ridgeback eyed him lazily as he unbuttoned his wax jacket and removed his cap. It didn't bother shifting from its prime position, a beautiful wheaten red, stretched out in front of the crackling fire. He could see four men playing darts in the public bar, pints lined up, following a timeless etiquette; silence as aim was taken followed by a burst of laughter, commiseration or congratulations as steel tip penetrated sisal. The saloon was empty and Henry was glad of the time to scan his surroundings. He had never seen so much brass in one place: a ship's wheel, countless chronometers, barometers, hunting horns and storm lamps. Tantalisingly, six bedroom keys hung from their hooks beneath the optics. None absent. From the look of it, plenty of vacancies, if they were accepting strangers in time of plague. Then he noticed a stack of five well-used library hardback books by the till. He strained his eyes to read a few of the titles on the pink and mauve coloured spines: *A Kiss to Remember*, *Would I Lie to the Duke?*, *The Devilish Deception*.

Henry was building a mental picture of Mrs Daphne Williams when he heard heavy steps slowly ascending from the cellar. He had perched on a bar stool, adopting what he felt was his most winsome smile, waiting for the landlady to emerge. First, a head appeared from below the flagstones. Blonde, pretty, early forties, not heavily made-up. Then the rest of her followed. A figure-hugging black dress set off with a large set of coloured glass beads that looked to him like the marbles he'd played with at school. Medium height and graceful, she smiled a greeting when she spied him. He had been quite unfair.

"Just give me a moment, my lover. Wasn't expecting anyone in tonight, what with the awful weather, and this illness doing the rounds."

She turned on the tap behind the bar and soaped up thoroughly, wiping her hands off with a tea towel. He looked carefully. No rings on her long fingers.

"Sorry. Just had to change the barrel. I've got to do

everything round here at present. Now, what can I be getting for you?"

He kept on smiling and held her eye. He was desperate for shelter for the night. And a discreet base for his grand finale.

"A pint of whatever you just put on, please. In a straight glass."

She pulled down on the wood-handled beer pump and filled a pint pot with suds before it started to run dark brown. Then she changed glasses and handed him a full pint, expertly poured with a perfect head.

He drew on it as his host unloaded the glasswasher.

"I'm probably too late for supper? Even a sandwich?"

She looked up with a weary smile.

"Sorry, love, I'm completely on my own now. Hubby walked out last year – utter bastard – as soon as our girl Clarissa went off to university. She's only sixteen but some sort of maths and computer genius, so Cambridge took her early. I was proud, but now I miss Clarrie terribly. And then the lovely Spanish couple who helped me with the kitchen and rooms went home to Malaga last week. All this blasted Brexit nonsense …"

She threw the dishcloth into the sink and leant her elbows on the counter, close enough for him to smell her perfume.

"So, what brings you to Saint Wenna? I haven't seen you round here before, have I?"

Time to tread carefully. He adopted his best Oxford persona, and accent to go with it. *Would I Lie to the Duke?* had stuck with him.

"My name's Monty, Monty Crompton. I'm a writer. Not

sure if you've read any of mine? Anyway, I've come down to research my latest novel. A love story set in a Cornish inn. A beautiful but lonely young widow left running the place. Late eighteenth century. I always like to spend time soaking up the atmosphere. Getting to know people, for my characters."

The landlady was leaning halfway across the bar now. She primped her hair. Henry wasn't proud of his dissembling, but this was mission critical.

"Can I buy you a drink? And sorry, I didn't quite catch your name?"

"It's Daphne. And I'll take a glass of prosecco with you, if I may."

Whilst she poured, he reached into his inner pocket and pulled out the little notebook, placing it purposefully on the bar. He tapped it with his forefinger.

"I keep my notes in here. Plan to stay for at least a week. Local history research in the library by day and write here at night. Perhaps I could test the plot with you too?"

She parted her lips and let out an involuntary gasp.

"Nobody's ever asked me to do anything like that before. I'd love to help. But where are you staying?"

He looked past Daphne at the full bank of room keys.

"Well, now I've seen the Pilchard's Head, and met you, Daphne, I was rather hoping to rent a room here."

At that moment an untimely cheer went up from the public bar, breaking the spell. The match was finishing. Daphne looked over, nervous, torn. She dropped her voice.

"See, I'd love you to stay. I'm bored off my tits here in the winter. And I could use the money. But my locals are going mad about this Chinese virus. Usually lovely lads, good as gold, totally obsessed with the surfing. But they've turned into a bunch of vigilantes. Crazy talk. Planning on blocking the lanes, turning back strangers and forcing people out of their second homes. Really sorry, Monty, but you can't stay here."

Daphne's eyes blazed with frustration.

Henry readied his last gambit.

"How about this? I'm also here to visit Felicity Smith, the librarian. She's an old, dear friend from university …"

Daphne looked more hopeful.

"I'm going to surprise her bright and early tomorrow morning. So, I'm not exactly a stranger in these parts, am I?"

"She'll be doing the quiz here tomorrow night, so don't you be stopping Miss Smith from her homework," she teased.

Useful to know. He was already planning his approach to the librarian. He would only get one shot.

"I'll pay you two hundred and fifty pounds cash for a week's bed and breakfast. In advance. And, even better than that, I can see you could really do with some help. A break, if only so you can take the dog for a long walk up along the cliffs. Have a little me time. Read a book. So, I'd be happy to work the bar, collect glasses, wash up, put out the empties, even tell you one of my stories."

The landlady was beaming. He was on a roll.

"Whatever you want, Daphne. Perhaps for the odd kitchen meal in return?"

She turned around, her hand hovering over the bedroom keys, still undecided.

"Listen, if you tell your locals I know Felicity and I'm the new help, I'll do the rest. I'll get them to trust me."

Daphne extended a soft hand and they shook on the deal.

"I'm putting you in the Ross Poldark suite. Best room in the house, Monty. Views right across the cove. A great place for you to write."

The match was over next door and a final round was called for. Uninvited, Henry slipped behind the bar and brushed behind the landlady. She squealed and playfully pushed him towards the back parlour where the darts team waited for their refills.

"No time like the present to get started. I'll show you what I can do."

The recesses of the public bar were dark and the four men gathered under the spotlight directed towards the dartboard, casting shadows as they cleaned the adjacent board of their chalked calculations and then sheathed their darts. Henry was pulling the third pint before they noticed the newcomer. Daphne hovered behind him, watching his technique in silent judgement. So far, so good. Then she placed a hand on the small of his back as four pairs of eyes rested on him.

"Gentlemen, this is Monty, my new help. Staying at the Pilchard's Head for a bit. Good friend of Miss Smith up at the library. He's a writer, so no swearing in front him, all right?"

Henry nodded in stern greeting, pulling the last pint. He decided not to smile but concentrate on getting the head just right, as he imagined was expected of his new role.

"There you go, chaps. Four pints. What do you think?"

The tallest of the group stepped forward to the bar.

He towered above Henry, full Victorian beard, hoodie, a bobble cap resting above searching eyes.

"Welcome, Monty. So long as you haven't just arrived from China." The man wasn't smiling.

Nobody laughed and Henry sensed the landlady tense behind him.

"In fact, I just got in from Carcavelos, the beach near Lisbon. I surf there until I run out of money. Then come back home, write a book, sell it, and back to my first love until I need to work again. And, please, swear away. I've heard it all before."

Daphne stepped in to help. "There you go, Big G. That sounds like a charmed life, doesn't it?" She was nervous.

The three other men looked to their leader for the next move. He seemed more suspicious than ever and Henry wondered if he had hammed it up a little too much. An occupational hazard that he needed to watch.

"So, you're a real silver surfer then, are you? I mean an old-school one, not a pensioner hunched over his computer, curtains drawn, watching porn all day."

The others laughed along. They liked that. Henry stared back, unsmiling.

"So, tell me Monty, what's the surfing like down there this time of the year?"

Henry had to get the initiative back.

"Best in winter. So, perfect now. A barrelling beach break, lefts and rights. Billabong Pro tournament every October. You must have heard of it?"

A banshee gust rattled the lead panes of the snug and the lights flickered. The smallest man of the group took a pace forward, lifted his pint off the bar and spoke up.

Squat, broad shoulders, with a thick blond thatch and neatly trimmed beard.

"I competed there a few years ago. Magic. A fantastic break when you get a swell from the north. Like Daffy says, you're a lucky man."

He was the first of them to smile, raising his pint in an awkward salute. Henry noted a potential ally.

"Jerzy. I own the hardware store. Hard-working Pole, when I'm not being dragged out into the cove by these pirates." They laughed.

At that moment, the giant dog padded silently through and joined the group, sitting on its haunches next to the man who was wearing an identical waxed jacket to Henry's, muzzle sniffing at waist height. Without apparently thinking, he reached in his pocket and fed it a treat, stroking it behind the ears.

"There you go, Scoob. Scared of the storm, are you, boy? I'm afraid it's only going to get worse." He turned his attention to Henry.

"I'm Vic, and Scooby here can smell my hounds on me. Occupational hazard of being the local huntsman, living with a pack of twenty of them. Funnily enough, this lot swear they can smell 'em on me too. And they're my only friends. Along with Scooby here."

The other three took an exaggerated step backwards.

"Probably why you never married, Vic." The last man patted him on the back. Younger than the others, he was slightly built with an aquiline nose and large, thoughtful brown eyes. His bright-yellow turban looked like it had been carefully matched with baby-blue tracksuit and designer trainers.

"Pleased to meet you, Monty. I'm Preet, Saint Wenna's very own village postmaster. But much better known around here as" – he paused for effect – "the Surfin' Sikh. Bit racist, I know, but I've been called far worse, and it seems to have stuck."

Daphne stood next to Henry, wiping down the highly polished oak bar top, a gesture of benign dominion. She whispered up into Henry's ear:

"Well done. You're in."

To his relief, the subject changed.

"Let's get our plan together. Lads, Agnes is out there somewhere, teasing us, taking her time. Building up her strength before landfall later tomorrow. They reckon overnight."

Big G led the others over to an antique Admiralty chart hanging on the wall, the long bony finger that is Cornwall shaded a mustard yellow, the surrounding seas a gentle blue and white. As the winds battered the cove, increasingly insistent, Henry couldn't think of a less appropriate colour scheme for tonight. Swirling blacks and frothy greys would be his palette of choice.

The men gathered in the dark corner, Big G every bit the polar explorer briefing his crew on a death-dealing mission. Even Scooby sat to attention, head tilted to the left, studying the map intently.

The mood had turned solemn.

"So, it's going to be proper gnarly out there for the next forty-eight hours. They're calling her the 'Storm of the Century' and most likely she'll hit full on somewhere about here …"

Henry's geography of the Cornish coast was sketchy,

but he knew enough to recognise that Big G was running his finger in an arc right above Saint Morwenna.

Jerzy spoke.

"Boys, let's give it a go! We'll never see something like this again. How about a dawny in the cove. Morning after next?"

Silence fell, then Preet shook his head.

"Sorry, chaps, but I'm not risking it. A full-frontal storm like this, we'll just get ragdolled. It could be the perfect tube, but might well be our last."

Big G turned on the torch on his mobile phone and directed it towards the southern coast of Cornwall, picking off villages as he spoke.

"Preet's right. Suicidal to try here. My missus would never forgive me. But the swell will make its way around Land's End and then the Lizard. Agnes will be mega on the other coast. First light on Friday, we'll try PK, Porthcurno, Levy or Praa. Agreed?"

The surfers were murmuring their assent, draining the last of the beer, when a furious gust sideswiped the Pilchard's Head and the sound of crashing masonry stopped dead the late-night proceedings in the public bar. Smoke billowed from the open fireplace across in the saloon, as soot part-extinguished the glowing logs. But two had escaped the down draught and lay glowing angrily on the old carpet, Scooby's spot in front of the fire.

Daphne cried out.

"Good Lord, the blessed chimney stack's come down!"

In a flash, Vic had a fire extinguisher in hand, Jerzy was filling a bucket from the bar sink and the two others battled to open the front door, opposed by the howling gale.

Five minutes later, order was restored and, with impressive organisation, the surfers had a plan in place. The external damage assessment confirmed that one of the chimneys had indeed blown clean off its moorings. They would return at lunch tomorrow. It wouldn't be safe to go up on the roof but Jerzy would bring plastic sheeting and plywood boards from his shop, enough for a temporary seal above the fireplace. Vic would bring plenty of old hessian feed sacks to be filled with sand from the beach. The pub was vulnerable to a storm surge from the cove, and the men were jokingly clear on one thing: the beer barrels down in the cellar must be protected from floating away at all costs.

Daphne looked exhausted and her regulars sensed it was time to go. Henry got into the community spirit and insisted that he would be on storm watch for the night, sitting in the saloon with Scooby, a big tumbler of Cornish spiced rum at hand and his notebook at the ready, should inspiration strike. The offer was gratefully received.

As the men stood at the door, preparing to battle their way back up to the village, Big G gave his parting orders.

"Remember, lads, you see anything out of the ordinary, anything at all, straight on to Saint Wenna Defence Force chat. That's what SWDF is there for. Watch out for strangers. Out-of-place cars at the rental cottages. People we don't recognise in the shops. And Monty, I'm deputising you onto the team, as of now." Big G laughed and pointed his index and middle fingers at his eyes. "So, ogles and ears open now. You're a writer, so I reckon you notice things. Just tell Daffy and she'll alert us. We'll handle the rest."

Within ten minutes of Daphne bolting the door

behind the SWDF and heading upstairs, Henry was fast asleep in an armchair, competing with Scooby for the loudest snores cutting through the gathering storm.

20

THE QUIZ

The bus shelter afforded Henry some protection from the screaming Atlantic, but he still kept a hand on the peak of his flat cap and could taste salt on his lips. His trousers were soaked by driving rain from the upper thighs downwards. Saint Morwenna's library was due to open soon, storm and plague permitting. This temporary perch was high above the village and gave a good opportunity to mentally map its topography, a new skill that he had come to realise was essential to good spycraft.

The only road in and out snaked down from the gorse-covered heathland behind him, the Truro bus terminating here. The little library lay just below, industrial Victorian red brick with an ugly post-war addition: a prefab with extensive glass skylight. Rainwater was pooling on its flat roof, dirty and grey. Beyond that, a cobbled street of shops, seasonal snack bars and cottages tumbled down to an empty car park and, finally, the beach with the Pilchard's Head perched just above it. The cove was ringed on three sides by steep cliffs, topped by a series of eerie brick chimneys and wheelhouses, graveyard of the once thriving tin mining industry. Then, out at sea, nothing but thousands of miles of jet-black roiling ocean, with only the odd wheeling gull, kittiwake or fulmar punctuating an unstoppable wall of approaching chaos.

It was a quarter to ten when he spotted a tall woman in a heavy raincoat and green wellington boots picking her way down a steep set of steps leading to the library, parallel to his vantage point. She wore a woollen cloche hat, tipped at an angle over a blonde bob, clinging to a handrail to keep her balance against the elements. In the rush of his last meeting with Nea, Henry had failed to ask for a description. But he knew that wouldn't have been much help to him now. A professional fade would have been part of the deal, live burial followed by resurrection. Born again as Felicity Smith. Anyway, there was nothing about this lady's poise and purpose that dissuaded him from a conviction that he was reaching the end of his quest.

Henry watched carefully as the librarian switched on the lights and then wheeled a trolley-load of returned books from the older half of the library to the newer annex. The chapel bell struck ten as he entered the vestibule, his face stinging from the freezing rain. He decided not to hurry, studying the noticeboard carefully, gathering clues. First to catch his eye was a freshly handwritten A4 sheet informing the library's customers that, due to dangerous weather conditions, the council had ordered its closure from 1 p.m. today. Another card, faded by sunlight, advertised the services of one Eric Crombie MIMC: Hypnotherapist, Mind Reader and Magician. Then a printed handbill: "Quiz Night at the Pilchard's Head, 8 p.m. this evening. £1.50 per person. Proceeds going to the Saint Morwenna lifeboat appeal." A gallery of children's paintings captured the village in happier times, all with the cove at the centre, set off with blue skies, gentle waves, and the odd rainbow and sailing yacht thrown in for good measure.

The librarian was working at the computer when he entered, an ancient desktop with a cathode ray monitor. She held a fountain pen in her left hand and had a lined notebook in front of her. Henry's age, a clear complexion, spectacles hanging around her neck, she was talking to herself under her breath before she noticed him. He surmised that this was someone who had lived alone for a long time.

"Good morning. I wasn't expecting anyone to brave the elements today. But nice to have company all the same."

She smiled, intelligent grey eyes and a confident, staccato BBC accent.

"Good morning to you. I'm actually here for work, so I'm afraid I can't let the weather get in my way."

The librarian looked interested.

"It's Miss Smith, isn't it? My name's Monty Crompton. I emailed you a few days ago, requesting a temporary borrower's card. I'm doing some research for a book set in Saint Morwenna and need to consult your local history books, if that's okay? Perhaps the message didn't get through?"

She scrolled down her emails and frowned.

"I can't see anything from you, I'm afraid. But no matter. You can borrow whatever you like. I'll show you what we've got. I'm afraid I've been told to close this lunchtime because of Storm Agnes. And then it looks like this virus is going to shut us down for months. So, you should borrow everything you need today."

She sighed and he surmised this place was now her life.

"That's really kind. Where's the local history section, please?"

Felicity got to her feet. Taller than Henry, with strong, broad shoulders and angular features. He noted that she had changed into a pair of sliders which she wore over thick woollen calf-length socks.

"It's just a shelf's worth, I'm afraid. Mostly ditchwater dull and badly written to boot, but I can point out a couple of books that are worthwhile. If you'd like to follow me, Mr Crompton ..."

"Please, do call me Monty."

"Of course. Call me Felicity."

He felt that he was being carefully appraised. Thinking back to his accidental confessor in Lisbon, he wondered if libraries, like churches, attracted more than their fair share of troubled men.

Sitting at a table by the biography section, he concluded that Felicity was right. After an hour's ploughing through a range of locally self-published books of old photographs with long-winded commentaries alongside, he had learnt little of interest. Just three things, in fact, duly transcribed into his notebook. Firstly, legend has it that a secret passageway runs from behind the old fireplace at the Pilchard's Head down to the cove. Only accessible at low tide, it was used by smugglers to hide contraband barrels of rum and brandy alongside tea and tobacco. Good for the novel, but perhaps also for a contemporary escape route, if and when required. Secondly, a veritable multidimensional maze of disused tunnels and shafts undermines the village, always ready to swallow up the reckless or simply unwary. Finally, one old mine, Wheal Dyowl, had a particularly gruesome history. Fifteen miners cut off by a roof collapse in an undersea tunnel in 1843. History is unclear as to whether they slowly died of starvation, drowned as the steam engine stopped pumping out the seawater, or simply vanished into thin air. No bodies were ever recovered, but to this day screams for help are still said to be heard when westerly storms power in.

"Are you finding what you need?"

He snapped out of his reverie.

"Just as you described, a lot of tosh but with a few gems hidden here and there."

Felicity smiled indulgently.

"Such as?"

"Well, I'm staying at the Pilchard's Head for a while. I love the story of the smugglers' secret passageway. And a chimney was blown over last night, masonry landing on the hearth. So, I might have a poke about behind the fireplace, just in case something's opened up."

Felicity nodded agreement and went back to staring at the computer screen, but soon she was frowning at the white luminescence, a look that Henry interpreted as impatience. She was jabbing her finger at the keyboard and he concluded that whatever command she was giving, the machine was roundly ignoring.

"The Pilchard's Head. God, yes. I'm pulling the weekly questions together here, for tonight. I've exhausted all the reference books in the library" – she swept her hand around, indicating the stacked shelves – "and now the bloody internet connection has gone down. And no mobile signal either. Is your phone working, by any chance?"

He shrugged.

"I had to give up on using my mobile and tablet. For health reasons. But I guess Agnes will be starting to knock out infrastructure, as well as pub chimneys."

Felicity nodded, misunderstanding.

"Probably wise. I could do with a digital detox myself. But I need a few more questions for tonight's quiz, and I'm blanking. Any ideas, Monty?"

This was playing out well.

"Okay. Here are three for you. A bit random, but see if they work."

Felicity brightened and made ready with her pen.

"Question one. In the wartime song, what sings in Berkeley Square?"

Felicity answered before he got the question out. She was competitive.

"A nightingale. That's a good one. The older teams will like that, getting one over the surfers and that annoyingly smug team of young doctors who nearly always win."

As she wrote the answer down, he studied her carefully.

"Okay. Question two. Name three prominent men who were schoolboys at Eton College and then Oxford University in the nineteen eighties."

Felicity put her pen down and stared at him.

"So, it could be prime ministers, members of the cabinet, businessmen, senior government officials, army generals, journalists …"

She sounded unnaturally hesitant, trying to work something out.

"That could be a long list to choose from, Monty. Do you have it to hand?"

Henry shook his head.

"But I spotted last year's *Who's Who* in your reference section. I'm happy to run through that, make a definitive list for us."

"That sounds like a lot of work. Why would you do that?"

He paused.

"Well, the internet's down. And I need to compile it anyway. For a research project I'm looking at."

Felicity wrote the question down, occasionally looking up at him and the library door.

"Final one. I think you'll get this right away. Name the Old Testament character, probably a narcissist, who found himself hanging from a tree, caught by his lustrous head of hair. Whilst his horse galloped away and his enemies appeared with spears."

He watched carefully as Felicity screwed the top back on the fountain pen and placed it on her desk. She was avoiding eye contact.

"Come on, Felicity. You must know your Bible."

She shook her head, looking down.

"Just give it a go. Hazard a guess."

Now she looked up, eyes blazing.

"Okay. Maybe write this down? It's Absalom. A-B-S-A-L-O-M. That should fox most of them tonight."

Felicity shut down her computer, turned off her mobile. Then she went to the door, hung a closed sign, and bolted it from the inside.

Back at her desk, they sat in silence for several minutes. The storm was intensifying, the rainwater boiling directly above them on the glass skylight. Then, speaking deliberately, Felicity was a barrister summarising her case for the defence.

"I've done everything you asked me to. Everything. I've kept my side of the bargain. Maintained cover for ten bloody years. *Even* when I happened to spot my brother's obituary in *The Times*. My only living relative. God, I cried so much. *Even* when Sue Nightingale disappeared off the face of the earth, with not so much as a goodbye. My only lifeline. Taken away. *Even* when I think about what damage ABSALOM might be doing to our country."

He hadn't expected this. Should he reveal himself? Or let her carry on, thinking he was one of her old colleagues?

"I didn't make a fuss, though you know as well as I do that it was all a clever set-up. Classic Russian play, ably helped by one of our own."

He sat taciturn, staring at Felicity's nose, Colin's old diversionary tip.

"Frankly, I was just so happy to see the back of your lot. That swamp, with ABSALOM sitting in the middle of it, biding his time. I couldn't wait to get away. Make a new start down here. Amongst decent people who can actually manage a whole conversation without lying once! Probably unfathomable to you. So, you can take that copy of *Who's Who* and be on your way. It's on me. I reckon you've got at least thirty candidates for ABSALOM in there. Best of luck. I'll let you out."

He sat immobile, thinking through Felicity's speech. It had been studied, not spontaneous. He realised she had prepared this long ago, knowing that one day this moment would come.

"I'm afraid I can't go anywhere, at least not until I identify ABSALOM. And, for the avoidance of doubt, I don't work for the British services. In fact, that couldn't be further from the truth. They'll be trying to find me as we speak."

Felicity flinched, eyes now wide with horror. She knew she had just made a terrible error. A hefty commercial stapler lay between them on the desk and her left hand was now creeping towards it.

"And, before things get out of hand, I don't work for the Russians either. On recent form, they'll kill me when they track me to Saint Morwenna. And they'll murder anyone else who knows about ABSALOM. Like you. And Nea."

Felicity looked quizzical.

"Sorry. Your Sue Nightingale. You see, I'm just a civvy, caught up in this, with no way of turning back. And I think you're the final piece of the jigsaw. Along with the coded messages I found in this."

He pulled Sasha's old Russian Bible from his pocket and handed it to Felicity. She turned straight to the frontispiece, then leafed through the Old Testament. He gave her the time she needed.

"We need to solve the puzzle together, and we've hardly any time left."

Felicity nodded as she opened a drawer under her desk and rummaged in it. Henry stiffened. Finally, she pulled out a metal tea caddy.

"Lapsang souchong. It's my special treat for moments like this. Smoky, black China tea. A taste I acquired when I was head of the Shanghai station. Lovely stuff."

She paused to think.

"We're on our own now. Just you, me, and all these books around us. No internet, like the old days. Very exciting, really. And, by the way, I want ABSALOM to get what's coming to him, probably as much as you do."

Felicity selected two teabags and returned the caddy to its home.

"Why don't you start by bringing over the *Who's Who*. Also, a copy of the King James version. There's a Russian dictionary in the languages section. And you'll find an old *Children's Illustrated Bible* in the kids' area. I'll get the kettle on. I think we've got some work ahead of us."

* * *

"Okay. First things first. What's your real name?"

Henry put down his chipped mug.

"Henry Bradbury. But I'm going by the cover of Monty Crompton. That's what Daphne and the regulars know me as."

Felicity smiled.

"Sounds like your porn-star name. Who helped you with that?"

"One of your former colleagues. Roddy Partridge. My MI6 controller, back when I got tangled up in this mess."

Felicity looked mystified.

"Real name: Rupert Samson-Brown. Eton College, 1987. Then Hereford College, Oxford. Read Russian. Fluent. And a complete arsehole."

Felicity nodded in slow agreement.

"I'm impressed you got his real name and bio. I'm no fan of his either. Rupert's the reason I'm here. We'll need to compare notes on him later. But I've got a more pressing question for now. How long do you think we've got, exactly?"

Two car alarms started to serenade each other in the distance, triggered by the buffeting winds.

"It depends on whether they picked me up on the way down from London. They would have been all over me in the City. I didn't have time to worry about facial recognition cameras. But I got lucky with a car lift down and I'm travelling tech free – no phone or tablet. Paying cash at the pub. Not sure about cameras here in the village. If anything, it's more likely that they'll be on their way down to deal with you. Finding me here will just be a bonus."

Felicity walked to the side door of the library and checked the padlock on it, shaking at the heavy chain.

"I suppose Sue Nightingale told you where to find me?"

He hesitated.

"She was unwilling. I had to press her hard. But she knows the net is closing in on us. She had a recent visit from Roddy – Rupert – and reckons he is working for the Russians, feeding them information."

"Absolutely true. And Sue made the right call. Out of interest, where is she now?"

He shrugged.

"She said she would try to shadow me down here. Be there when she was needed."

He looked out of the window, barely able to see anything through the horizontal pulses of rain.

"But God knows where she is. I wouldn't fancy anyone's chances of making it through this. I think you're right. We're on our own. And they could turn up at any moment. I told Daphne I would work the bar this lunchtime and I think I need to stay in character. I'll take the *Who's Who* with me, work on it when I can. Then back here after we lock up the pub for the afternoon?"

Felicity rose and walked to the windowless romantic-fiction shelves. Henry had noticed that these were the best stocked in the library. She pulled out a few hardbacks, studying them closely, one by one. Finally, she found one she seemed happy with, carefully removing its worn dust cover before replacing it between its neighbours. Back at the desk, she folded it around the Russian Bible. A perfect fit. *Lady Victoria's Passion by Moonlight* featured a curly haired woman in a laced-up bodice that looked two sizes too small for her, staring up at a tall highwayman in a black mask, tricorn hat tilted rakishly. She placed it carefully back on the shelves, admiring her handiwork.

"Best place in the world to hide an enormous state secret, in amongst all those heaving bosoms and rippling biceps."

They laughed.

"I'll come down to the pub with you too. I always pop in before the quiz, set things up. So that will look normal. And I'm not sure I want to be on my own here at the moment."

* * *

The surfers arrived at midday and got straight to work on the fireplace. Big G removed the fallen bricks while Jerzy measured the flue's irregular dimensions, expertly cutting sheets of plywood to size. Vic had arrived in a long-wheelbase Land Rover Defender, in fact more of a motorised dog kennel. It was packed to the gunnels with his foxhounds, howling over Agnes's growing might, competing with the roar of surf and gale. Released, they tore down onto the beach, noses down, tails up, searching in vain for a scent trail. Henry polished glasses by the window, watching Vic and Preet filling sacks with sand. Felicity had set up a card table by the pub entrance, laying out raffle tickets and photocopied quiz answer sheets while Daphne was making sandwiches in the kitchen.

Feeling guilty, he pulled on his jacket and cap, left the pub and went down onto the beach to help. The pack of hounds swirled around him, barking, jumping, large and lean, brown and white, in their element, with the elements. Henry certainly wasn't. Conversation was impossible, so he simply waved a greeting to Vic and Preet, then slung a sandbag over his shoulder, dropping it by the cellar trapdoor, laying the foundation of a flood defence. An hour later, the work was done and it was time for lunch. But first, Henry was given the honour of blowing Vic's hunting horn; a mime instructed him to sound it long and slow. The dogs somehow picked up the command and gathered in, following the three men right up to the pub entrance.

"They'll be fine out there. Won't wander when they

know their dinner's coming. They need their exercise, and besides, I reckon they'll come in handy later if these rumours are true."

Vic placed his horn on a table and shook the rain off his waterproof. Henry slipped behind the bar and pulled five pints. A stern look from Felicity signalled that a sixth was in order. Jerzy was vacuuming the carpet, working around a slumbering Scooby. Daphne emerged from the kitchen with lunch. She looked miserable.

"Bad news, chaps. And I'm really sorry, Miss Smith. I know you've gone to a lot of trouble over the quiz. But the Prime Minister's just been on the radio. We're closed down. Pubs, caffs, hotels, churches, weddings. You name it, you ain't doing it, at least not for the foreseeable future."

The group fell silent.

"So, let's enjoy lunch, have a few last pints. Maybe a chorus of 'Auld Lang Syne'?"

She was trying her best. Shock seemed to be turning to resignation. Then determination. Big G spoke.

"All the more reason to check out these strangers. There's something not right happening in Wenna and we need to get to the bottom of it. Jerzy, tell us what happened this morning."

"Okay. Three men came shopping, cash in hand. I've never seen them before. They knew exactly what they wanted. Rubber ground sheet, power drill, blowtorch, a hammer and cutting pliers, electric sander, two high-powered battery searchlights – usually just sell them for lamping rabbits. Bought all my drain cleaner and gaffer tape. And a load of cable ties. Said they were Lithuanians, builders, doing up one of the cottages."

Jerzy paused, taking a sip of beer.

"But they're not. They lied. I'm Polish, so I can spot Russians a mile off. The two young guys, heavies, made the mistake of speaking to each other about sulphuric acid, the concentration in the drain cleaner. Their boss, strange old guy with a limp, told them to shut the fuck up."

Big G spoke.

"Did they suss you?"

"Nope. I can act as English as you when I need to, my friend. And I watched them go. Not in a builders' van but a black Range Rover. Headed up towards the Truro Road. One thing I will say, if we want to have a word with them, we need to tread careful. All of us need to be there, with Vic's hounds and Scoob."

Henry caught Felicity's eye. Totally calm, under control, thinking hard, looking like someone who had dealt with worse things in another life. He breathed a sigh of relief.

Preet was next to report in.

"I had an odd emmet in this morning. Really odd. Very well-spoken little gent in a deerstalker. Binos and a camera with an enormous telephoto thing attached. Bought four pay-as-you-go SIM cards for cash, and an Ordnance Survey map that I've been hoping to sell for years. And then a set of kids' walkie-talkies that I had left over from last season. Seemed like my lucky day, until I thought about it."

Henry had to ask.

"Did he call you 'mate', by any chance?"

"Yeh. Lots. And it came out odd. Do you know him?"

Henry paused.

"Probably not. I just know his type. Did he tell you what he's doing in Saint Morwenna?"

"He's a storm chaser. Or so he says. Runs round the world photographing them. He seemed to have a right hard-on about our Agnes. Asked where a good place would be for him to get the best shots, somewhere with shelter, uninhabited, a place overlooking the village, with 'genuine Cornish atmosphere'."

Daphne shot him a glance.

"Oh no, Preet. You didn't, did you? That wouldn't be right, whoever he is!"

He shrugged.

"All I did was point out Wheal Dyowl on his map. Seemed to fit the bill perfectly. And I don't believe those old stories, anyhow."

Daphne shook her head and went back into the kitchen.

Big G took charge.

"Daffy'll let us use the pub for our base, at least until Agnes blows through tomorrow. No chance of the coppers calling in. They'll be too busy in Truro, pulling trees off the road and rescuing old biddies off roofs when the rivers burst their banks. We'll be left well alone here. And Jerzy's right. Safety in numbers. We'll keep an eye on the Truro Road and watch to see if anything happens up at Wheal Dyowl. And we need to find that black Range Rover, assuming they're still in the village. Did you happen to get the—"

A bang, and the lights went out, waking Scooby with a start. The group huddled in the storm's premature twilight, the only sound coming from Daphne's battery-powered radio in the kitchen. She rushed back in.

"Oh Lord, it's all happening. Monty, get those storm lanterns down and lit. I've just been listening to the local news. Power cut all over the county and the river's just taken out the Truro Road. Washed clean away down at Eight Mile Cross. No way in or out of Wenna. It's going to be a long night."

While Vic fed his hounds, the other surfers got to work. The small fireplace in the public bar was lit, doors and windows bolted and a patrol schedule agreed. Henry pulled Felicity over, taking the opportunity for a quiet word out of earshot of the others.

"This is really bad, isn't it? They're here, and we've no escape route. I guess Rupert will be setting up surveillance of the village and the Russians will move in soon? And I don't even want to think about their hardware. Christ. Perhaps we should stay here with the others?"

Felicity put a reassuring hand on his arm, speaking firmly.

"No, Henry. You've been right all along. This was my old game, so I know the rules. Find ABSALOM, and we end this. Stay at the Pilchard's Head, and we're all dead by morning. So, back to the library for us."

Felicity pulled herself up to her full height and addressed the pub.

"Monty and I are heading back up to the library. We've got some work we need to do. Urgent matters to deal with. We'll be fine out there."

Something in her voice, her face, brooked no argument. Hard as nails.

Daphne took Scooby's lead down from a hook behind the bar and clipped it to his collar.

"Understood, Miss Smith. But can you please take Scooby with you? It'll make us feel better. He's lovely and gentle here, but he was bred to take down lions. That's in his nature. He'll fight to the last. And also, Vic's hounds will pester the life out of him if he stays in the pub."

She handed the lead to Henry. Big G agreed.

"Take Scooby, please. And we'll check on you when we can. See you later."

21

THE FINAL PIECE OF THE PUZZLE

"God, I'm sitting here with palpitations. The heebie-jeebies. And you're so calm. How the bloody hell do you do it?"

Felicity put down two mugs of tea on her desk, the storm lamp uplighting her heavy jaw. Smiling, she went over to the games area, returning with a box, a thousand-piece jigsaw puzzle.

"By concentrating on the task at hand. And watching the clock. You really need to do the same, Henry."

Scooby sat by the library door, alert, head cocked, straining to hear over the storm.

Henry was mystified as she tipped the puzzle onto the desk and started to turn the pieces face up. Without being asked, he joined her.

"Are you a dissectologist, Henry? Do you like jigsaw puzzles?"

He shook his head.

"I've had ten years here, sitting at this desk, perfecting my technique. I do at least one a week. Very calming, therapeutic. And I think this one will lead us to ABSALOM."

He looked at the box lid, mystified. It was scuffed, Sellotape holding its corners together, the Houses of Parliament painted from across the river, the Thames in the foreground, blue skies encroached upon by ochre and blood-red clouds announcing the arrival of evening. Westminster Bridge busy with cabs and double-decker buses. Over the middle span, a silhouetted group of men striding purposefully across the river.

"I've worked out that the best way to solve a puzzle is from the outside in. Start with the straight edges, easier to find. Then gradually fill it in. It's such a good feeling when you drop in the final few pieces. So, what do we know? What are our straight edges? What do we really know?"

He followed Felicity, picking the pieces with straight edges, clipping them together. Henry understood the game.

"A good question. Let's start with who's here with us in Saint Morwenna tonight. They're known quantities. Rupert Samson-Brown. Heading up to the haunted mine. He got me in this mess in the first place. And then Jed and his two Russian goons, Pavel and Ilya."

He told Felicity his story. Recruitment by the Joint Russia Programme. Sasha's confession. Rupert's reaction. Oxford and his Pygmalion moment. Aslanov's offer. Rupert and Colin's argument. Lisbon and Jack Somerset's ABSALOM print. The murders and fight with Jed. The chase across Europe. Nothing seemed to surprise her as she worked quickly, building her own jigsaw boundary, attaching it to Henry's corner.

Then she spoke, reciprocating.

"Eleven years ago, the CIA had a walk-in at their Lisbon embassy. A Russian SVR officer with some goodies to sell. Strictly cash on delivery. He checked out and they got two meetings before he disappeared, vanished. When they passed it on to us, it landed on my desk. All a bit garbled but the gist of it was some files their man had seen in Moscow. High-level recruitment of a long-term British sleeper, codenamed, surprise surprise, ABSALOM. Blue-blooded Establishment type. A long-term play beginning at the end of the seventies, starting with a bit of youthful rebellion: Marx and Engels posters on the wall, *Das Kapital* read by torchlight under the bed cover – that sort of youthful nonsense, I imagine. And, of course, then it progressed, as it usually does. Their agent slipped easily into the service of new Russia. A slippery transition, but it turned out money, advancement and sex were more his thing than abstract philosophy."

He tried to catch up, working on his length of the border – dark, dappled river – as Felicity continued.

"The only other thing the Americans picked up was that ABSALOM was given the highest priority. Layer upon layer of Russian security. His own dedicated SVR team run by the officer who recruited him in the first place, a colonel kept out of retirement for the sole purpose of running him. More than unusual. Unique. I dropped everything when I heard that. Not that much to go on, but I started on the trail, looking for who was posted at the London KGB rezidentura between 1977 and 1983. At least the ones we'd identified. Someone who'd made the transition from KGB to SVR, who might fit the profile of a recruiter. Anyone still coming to London. After a few weeks locked away in the Registry, I'd whittled it down to one name and I felt I was getting somewhere."

Felicity had now completed the third border and clipped it on.

"That's when it all unravelled for me. And where Rupert Samson-Brown comes into the picture. Come on, Henry. I'm doing all the work here!"

He had finished one side of the puzzle and now started to build in from his corner, a bridge span topped with a gas lamp.

"Rupert was my number two on the Russia desk. A high-flyer, seemed like a big producer. Well thought of by senior management and whispered of as a future chief. He had two senior Russian sources, one GRU, one SVR. Or so he claimed …"

Felicity had completed the final border and clapped her hands in triumph, sitting back to admire their work.

"Look! We're getting there. I'll start working in from the top left corner. Blue skies are always tricky. Anyway, Rupert travelled around Europe – Helsinki, Prague, Lisbon – money belt stuffed with cash, meeting his most secret, most expensive sources. He always came back with something that seemed useful, sufficient to get him noticed. Two-star, occasionally three-star CX. Not chicken feed, but never quite enough either. More gossip than anything actionable. I should have seen the pattern, but hindsight is a wonderful thing. I've now had ten years' exile to stew over it, work out what happened."

The flat roof above them creaked, and drops of water sploshed down from the darkening skylight. Felicity fetched a bucket from the kitchen and then carried on with her story.

"So, I indoctrinated Rupert into ABSALOM. I needed his help, particularly triangulating things with his two Russian sources, testing out the name I had. And if things went wrong, Rupert would be my backup. But it didn't quite work out like that."

"What was the name, the KGB officer you identified? Did you get a description?"

Felicity had lined up all the blue pieces, arranging them by shade, from navy, through cyan to turquoise.

"Oleg Pinchuk. Sent to London in 1979 on his first mission. A graduate of their British training course, very prestigious back then. Disappeared off our radar for decades after that posting, but then he showed up again, spotted by chance in London – 2008, I think. A fluke of luck, but one of our long-retired watchers recognised him by his distinctive limp, passing on a street in South Ken. Right leg shorter than the other, apparently. Trailed him, lost him, but kind enough to file a contact report anyway."

Henry was starting on his first red double-decker bus.

"I can fill in a few pieces too. Your Pinchuk is my Jed. Murdered Jack Somerset and Sasha. Probably the Aslanovs too. I stabbed him in Lisbon but he survived and is still on my tail. Saw him two days ago in London. Tried to get close enough to shoot him but failed, and now he's here, in the village, somewhere close."

Felicity smiled sweetly, unperturbed, as if Henry had just confessed to having overdue library books.

"Wow, that's quite a download. A few new names to me, though I think Aslanov is definitely in the mix. Tempting to digress though it is, let's finish our Rupert part of the puzzle, then Pinchuk, then we'll come back to the others."

She looked at Henry's jacket which was hanging on the back of a chair, carefully assessing something, looking hopeful. Perhaps to see if one of the pockets was sagging?

"You don't still have a gun with you, by any chance?"

He grimaced and then looked sheepish.

"No, but I wish I had. Nea, Sue Nightingale, sort of confiscated it. I think she thought I was a liability."

"That's a pity. That could've have come in quite handy later tonight. Anyway, back to Rupert. Well, he spoke to his SVR source who'd heard of ABSALOM. Probably knew enough to work out his identity. And a great admirer of ABSALOM's handler, apparently. But there was a catch."

Felicity moved her jigsaw pieces around, grading the sky before pushing them together.

"The source would only spill the beans if he met me in person. Alone. And he happened to be in Helsinki the following day. Rupert had arranged a crash meeting at a hotel by the railway station. I should have spotted it a mile off, but I'd got the bit between my teeth. A cardinal error."

"What should you have spotted?"

"Rupert had always guarded his sources so closely. Why the sudden change of heart? And a meeting the next day? It gave me no time to follow protocol, get the local MI6 station to provide backup. I went in alone. It stank. It seems so stupid now."

"So, did you actually meet him? The Russian source?"

"No. When I got to the hotel, there was an envelope waiting for me at reception. A key to a left luggage locker across the road at the station. Nothing else. No sign of Rupert's contact."

"What did you do?"

"It's not unusual, a drop like that, dealing with a Russian professional. It's their standard operating procedure. Usually a way to check if you're alone or under surveillance. So, I went to the locker, expecting a note with further instructions of where the meet would take place."

Felicity looked triumphant.

"Hurrah. I've finished the blue sky! Now I'll start on the clouds."

"So, what was in the locker? I'm guessing not what you were expecting?"

"Correct. I found an Aspinal handbag with an airline frequent flyer tag attached. Gold card, with one of my work names printed on it. I took a quick look inside. Bundles of bank notes, pounds sterling. A Minolta miniature camera, the kind that used to be standard MI6 issue. And two undeveloped rolls of film."

Felicity paused and picked up three pieces, clipping them together to spell "No. 36 Vauxhall Cross". She pushed them across the desk.

"I think these are at the front of your bus. Give them a try."

A perfect fit.

"Escape and evasion procedure was clear, drilled into me from my first week on IONEC, the new officers' course. Maintain cover. Don't even think about contacting anyone. Get back to London station on the next flight, turn the bag over to the most senior officer on duty. Assume you're blown and under hostile surveillance. In other words, just get the hell out."

Henry got up and walked to a library window that overlooked the cove.

"It's pitch-black out there. No sign of lights, or life. If anything, Agnes is still strengthening, the trees are going wild. I'm surprised more haven't come down."

Felicity continued the puzzle in silence as he walked into the entrance porch, stroked Scooby and checked the bolts. As he looked up the hill, a bright light pierced the darkness, right above them.

"Felicity, is that Wheal Dyowl up there, by any chance?"

She came over and joined him, Scooby pushed his head between their legs, nuzzling.

"Oh yes. Not really a surprise. I don't think its spectral inhabitants carry a thousand-lumen flashlight. That would be Rupert. Pinchuk. His heavies. They're up there, planning their next move. Gosh. It's eight o'clock! Let's get back to work. Between us we've solved nearly half the puzzle!"

Felicity's outline of Big Ben was taking shape nicely and Henry was now working on a London black cab.

"It's history now, but my welcome party back at Heathrow immigration consisted of three Met Police Special Branch officers and two of the most unpleasant people I've ever dealt with, MI6 internal security. They must inhabit some awful dungeon under London station. I'd never seen them before. Arrested. Driven to a safe house, I had a week in hell. Telephoto pictures from Helsinki. Fifty thousand pounds in large denomination notes slowly counted out in front of me. Those photo rolls developed to give details of well-stocked bank accounts in Lugano in a range of my cover names. A sworn statement from Rupert that he had no idea that I was going to Helsinki, that my story was pure fiction. And some innocent questions from him, too. Why hadn't I requested backup? Why was I always trying to wheedle the names of his Russian sources out of him? And what was with my ABSALOM obsession?"

"So that's how you ended up here?"

Felicity sighed.

"I've only ever discussed this with one other person. Sue Nightingale, Nea, is a brilliant psychotherapist, just what I needed at the time. She was there for the last few days of my interrogation, picking up the pieces as my options were laid out in no uncertain terms. To this day, I don't know whether she was sent in to get me to accept the witness protection offer or was just being professional. Or even, a friend. But that doesn't matter now. They were never really going to send me to Moscow, and a trial would have been hideously embarrassing for them. But those long hours talking to her made me realise that I had to get out. Choose salvation. I'd joined MI6 straight from Cambridge, too young, believing in the mission, serving the country. But there I was, a fifty-year-old spinster, hardly any family or friends, living in a semi in Clapham, the burden of secrets hollowing me out, nobody I could confide in. I couldn't think of a single person who'd particularly notice if I disappeared. Dr Nightingale held up a mirror in front of me. And coming down to Saint Morwenna was the best decision

I ever made. She was on my side when I needed it. I only wish I could have thanked her."

They worked on the puzzle for a few minutes. Finally, Felicity broke the silence.

"So, that's Rupert and Pinchuk. ABSALOM's praetorian guard, death or exile for anyone getting remotely close. Right now, only half a mile away from us. Watching my little library."

She paused, then looked like she had made a difficult decision.

"In case you're wondering, the minute you told Rupert about Aslanov's offer to spill the beans, that was his death warrant signed. He was offering up ABSALOM. So, that sealed his fate."

Henry blanched.

"Nasty piece of work, old man Aslanov. But his poor son … I'll always have that on my conscience."

Felicity shook her head.

"You were thrown into our world at the deep end. I think Rupert had his reasons for picking you."

He shrunk into his chair, scared of what was coming, not wanting to hear what he suspected.

"What do you mean by that?"

She hesitated.

"It's of no matter, Henry. He clearly buggered up, read you all wrong. Picked the wrong man."

They both let it go.

"Great, we're getting closer, only about three hundred pieces to go. So, please tell me about Jack Somerset. And let's consult *Lady Victoria's Passion by Moonlight*. I feel this is all coming together nicely."

He told Jack's story. His boys. The familiar faces in the Eton College sixth-form photographs. His one-to-one tutorials. The German woodprint of Absalom hanging by his hair. Felicity listened carefully whilst working down the lower part of the clock tower.

"That is so very interesting. I think we've been missing a trick. Let me have a good look at those numbers in the Russian's Bible."

As he finished the river and started on two barges, time passed slowly. Page by page, Felicity ran her finger over the pencil lines. Then she found an old ink-stained wooden ruler in her desk drawer.

"Yes, I think we're on to something here. All the numbers have been repeatedly rubbed out and refreshed. You can see it. But the pencil line never moves. I think the answer to our puzzle is probably in the verse. Code names. I think somebody who should know better has really stuffed up here. Right royally."

"I thought that OTP, One Time Pad, is unbreakable."

Felicity's eyes narrowed as she stared at him.

"How do you know about OTP? I thought you were a civvy, amateur. Now I'm beginning to wonder."

He decided not to mention his acquaintances in County Armagh. Though Uncle Michael had worked it out too. He changed the subject.

"A question about ABSALOM, please. Who actually gives agents their names? I assume they're randomly generated by some clever algorithm?"

Felicity laughed.

"If only. It's much more primitive than that. I'm almost embarrassed to tell you. Same for us, same for the Russians.

It's the original recruiting officer who chooses the agent's cryptonym. Something that they can easily remember. Then they try to forget their agent's real name, erase it from their memory. But association inevitably creeps in. The Sovs were particularly crass, back in the day. They had a nineteen-year-old spy buried inside the Manhattan Project at Los Alamos, who they called MLAD, which means youngster in Russian. And the Cambridge Five. Anthony Blunt was TONY. John Cairncross was LISZT, his favourite composer. You get the picture. Clumsy. And now you're making me think there's something quite odd with the choice of ABSALOM, something that's been puzzling me."

Henry took the Bible from Felicity and leafed through its pages, lingering over the underlined numbers.

"What's that? The problem?"

"If ABSALOM's recruitment was in the late seventies, the Soviet Union was dogmatically atheist. The KGB was the most loyal organ of state. So why would Pinchuk choose an Old Testament character? How would he get away with it?"

"An excellent question, Felicity. And I think I know the answer. Jack Somerset is, or was, a clever clogs, a know-it-all."

"So, what are you thinking?"

"A prima donna, he needed indulging. Pinchuk and the KGB had to bend their rules and let him choose his agent's name, or it would have been toys out of the pram. And he must have chosen ABSALOM for a reason."

He lifted the heavy King James Bible, worked through chapter and verse until he found what he was looking for.

He cleared his throat, transported back to reading a lesson in church when he was fourteen.

"'But Absalom sent spies throughout all of the tribes of Israel, saying, As soon as ye hear the sound of the trumpet, then ye shall say, Absalom reigneth in Hebron' – 2 Samuel 15:10."

He searched on, his excitement building.

"This one's good. Listen. 'But in all Israel there was none to be so much praised as Absalom for his beauty. From the sole of his foot even to the crown of his head there was no blemish in him. And when he polled his head, for it was at every year's end that he polled it: Because the hair was heavy on him, therefore he polled it; he weighed the hair of his head at two hundred shekels after the king's weight.' Felicity, what do you make of all that?"

"One, your schoolmaster had more than just a professional interest in his recruit. Two, we're looking for a vain man with a full head of hair. Very high opinion of himself, likes to blow his own trumpet. Three, ABSALOM is biding his time, but as he activates, sounding that trumpet, all hell breaks loose. Which reminds me, how's your list of likely lads coming along?"

He looked at his handwritten column on a page ripped from his notebook which he had folded inside the *Who's Who*. He ran his finger down it, smiling ruefully.

"You weren't far off with your guess. I got up to twenty-six names. Then I whittled it down to a shortlist of nine, the boys that I can remember in the year photographs on Jack Somerset's wall. Sorry to say, it's pretty difficult to rule any of this lot out. In fact, they all make the profile."

Suddenly, he jumped up from the desk, startled.

"Fuck, Felicity. I just saw a face in the window, by the travel section."

Scooby was growling by the entrance, standing his ground, hackles raised. He wasn't going to back down.

"Calm down, Henry. Let's see who it is."

But he noticed that she had picked up the big stapler as he drew the knife from his sleeve. As they approached the door, they jumped as a heavy fist banged on it. A raised storm lantern suddenly illuminated five tired, wind-lashed faces.

"Daphne, boys, get in here!"

Felicity unbolted the door and Scooby laid on a display of pure joy, rear end wagging furiously as his mistress squatted to hug him.

Some old towels were fetched from the kitchen and the bedraggled night patrol made a vain attempt to dry themselves off. Vic's pack of hounds bayed outside, huddling for shelter in the lee of the Victorian half of the library.

Big G spoke for the group.

"We've taken a good look around the lower village, checked on the older folk and anyone who's on their own. Pleased to report everyone is okay. Lots of tiles and branches down, and it's only getting worse. Surf will be brilliant tomorrow morning, though. It'll make all this worthwhile. How are you two doing?"

The visitors looked at the jigsaw on the desk. Daphne chuckled.

"I thought you said you had some important business to attend to? Not passing the time with fun and games ..."

Felicity ignored the question.

"We're fine. But thanks for popping in. Shall I put the kettle on?"

"A nice offer, but we'd best press on." Jerzy hesitated. "We're having a bit of a debate about whether it's worth us climbing all the way up to Wheal Dyowl. I say yes, we still haven't found a trace of those strangers. I reckon that's where they are. But Daffy is dead against it."

All five of them seemed to be looking to Felicity for guidance. She spoke slowly.

"So, what do you think, Daphne?"

"Not being funny, but I'm the only one of us born and raised in this village, so I grew up on the old tales. The adults scared us silly of going near that place, even on the calmest summer days. So, the idea of wandering up on the cliff path through the worst westerly in living memory, well, my old mum would be spinning in her grave."

She shuddered.

The library went silent. Henry and Felicity searched each other's eyes, making their own terrible calculation. If the patrol went up the hill, leading a pack of foxhounds, they might flush out their pursuers, put them to flight. Or, just as likely, be efficiently slaughtered, one by one.

"I'm sure there's nothing up there, Daphne. Certainly not the fifteen ghostly miners, nor those little knockers that seem to keep coming down to pinch my library books."

The group laughed, nervous relief.

"But that path can be treacherous at the best of times. You all know that. And a storm like this could have blown away the grilles covering the disused shafts. If you want my opinion, it's a deathtrap up there tonight. Stay around the village. You're of more service by staying alive down here."

They nodded their agreement, grateful for the ruling, and headed back out into the night.

The team gone, they sat back down to the puzzle.

"That was the right call, Felicity. You headed that off well. Besides, the visit won't have escaped our friends' attention. A pack of twenty dogs? They'll be much more cautious now."

Felicity was finishing the angry clouds whilst Henry added the final pier of Westminster Bridge.

"Don't kid yourself. They'll be down here before dawn, I promise you that. Pass me the Russian Bible. We need to hurry now. Let's think about codenames. Oh, and you can have the honour of finishing the puzzle. Tell me what it feels like."

He picked up the last dozen pieces that would fit dead centre. By trial and error an image of nine men in dark suits, backs to the jigsaw painter, took shape, marching across the bridge towards Parliament.

He studied the image for a full minute, then gasped and seized the King James Bible. Frantic, he leafed through the pages. Felicity looked over, startled.

"Christ. Where is it? Here. This is it. 2 Samuel 15:10. 'But Absalom sent spies throughout all of the tribes of Israel …'"

He tapped on the men heading towards Parliament.

"Not spy, Felicity. Spies! Not singular. Plural. That clever old bastard Jack didn't stop at one recruit. ABSALOM is a whole programme!"

Felicity sat back and stared up at the rain hammering on the skylight.

"Bloody well done, Henry. You've finished your first

puzzle. Not sure if its beginner's luck, but you've cracked it. Now, make yourself useful: grab a pen and write down these names next to your shortlist of candidates."

Page by page, she ran the ruler underneath the pencil line, studying the parallel Russian text, translating as she went.

"'And Absalom went to his house, but did not see the king's face.'"

"'Let me tell you a riddle,' Samson said to them' – Judges 14:12."

"'So, David prevailed over the Philistine with sling and stone' – 1 Samuel 17:50."

"'The crowd pushed Alexander to the front, and they shouted instructions to him' – Acts 19:33."

Felicity translated five more lines, five more names, then closed the Bible. She looked amused.

"Well, sometimes we forget that the Russians have a great sense of humour. The choice of lines is really quite precious. You get what this is, don't you?"

He looked down at the nine silhouettes, framed in the middle of the jigsaw.

"Individual OTP messages meant for each member of the programme. The Absalom code for Jack Somerset. The Samson page for Rupert. Et cetera, et cetera. Sasha in the middle, acting as some sort of messenger boy."

"Spot on. Now, memorise that list and guard that page with your life. I'm going to return *Lady Victoria's Passion by Moonlight* to its rightful place, for safe keeping. Then, we need to get moving."

Henry pulled on his wax jacket and carefully folded the list into the peak of his flat cap as Felicity wrapped up against the storm. The chapel clock struck midnight.

"There's no way out of the village tonight. No power. No phones. Road blocked. We'll head down to the Pilchard's Head with Scooby. Hunker down with the others and try to walk out at dawn."

"And then what? Who do we go to? Who can we trust?" He was thinking of Uncle Michael's violent endgame.

"Then, we'll have a chat with a dear friend of mine, the one person from my old world who will know how to deal with this. And we can trust the professor."

22

SPEAK OF THE GREY ONE, THE GREY ONE HEADS YOUR WAY ...

SAINT MORWENNA, CORNWALL, 21 MARCH 2020

Scooby was first out of the library door, snarling and straining hard at his leash as Henry struggled to hold him back, battling against Agnes's furies. Felicity was locking up the library as he fell backwards, releasing his grip and landing flat on his back in a pool of water, glasses flying off into the night. Through the driving rain, he could just make out Scooby springing to head height, knocking a shadow to the ground, then a man screaming.

"*Chertova sobaka! Uberi eto ot menya!*"

Henry felt Felicity dragging him to his feet by the collar with surprising strength. She was shouting over the wind.

"There's a Russian there who doesn't much like Scooby. Let's make a run for it. Fast as we can ... down to the pub."

He started to sprint by the mêlée but could now make out two men trying to wrestle Scooby to the ground. The dog had his jaws locked onto an arm, shaking it violently. A man was screaming in pain. The other shape tried to straddle the dog and, to his horror, Henry caught the glint of a raised knife blade. Without pausing for thought, he flew at the figure. Through practice, Luis had hardwired Henry with his one forbidden routine – he delivered a fast left jab to Ilya's chest and then a right-handed cross to his exposed throat, the old one-two. A gargling noise, and the ruck collapsed beneath him. He felt something sharp pressed to the side of his neck, right against his carotid artery. He readied himself, but then heard Rupert's shrill voice cutting across the tempest.

"No, don't! We need them. Need to talk to them. Get them back inside. That bloody dog as well. Now!"

* * *

Hands fastened tight behind their backs with cable ties, thighs and legs gaffer taped to tiny wooden chairs in the children's corner, Henry and Felicity tried to avert their eyes from the flashlight shining directly into their faces. Ilya was binding a tea towel around his arm, pressing down on the puncture wounds inflicted by Scooby. Pavel was carefully laying out the contents of a canvas bag onto the rubber groundsheet with more than a little theatre. Rupert and Pinchuk watched on, evidently savouring the moment. They each held a pistol and Pavel sported an automatic rifle over his shoulder. Scooby was tied to a cast-iron radiator in the entrance hall, short lead, teeth bared.

"It's time to rock. So, what fun props do we have at our disposal?"

Pinchuk had chosen to deploy his Jed persona. It seemed it was a personal favourite.

"Oh, cool, the full works. Pliers. Claw hammer. Drain cleaner. Blow torch. And, yes, my favourite. An orbital sander with an extra coarse pad. It's going to be quite a party …"

Felicity interrupted, spoiling the Russian's fun, taking what Henry fervently hoped was a calculated gamble.

"I see. All quite intimidating, Colonel Pinchuk. In a terribly camp sort of way. But I couldn't help noticing your funny little Makarovs. Museum pieces, those. And what on earth is your young man carrying? It looks like a PPS-43 sub-machine gun. Went out with the ark. I know the SVR is hard up, but is this all they gave you? They can hardly rate you as a crack unit. More like an oddball historical re-enactment group, led by a geriatric ponce."

She gave a full-bellied laugh and Henry tried to join in, but felt sick, wondering where on earth she was going with this.

Pinchuk glowed white with fury. Rupert looked aghast, then tried to defuse things.

"The weapons are still perfectly workable, Felicity. So don't push your luck. Buried in a canister by the perimeter fence of Her Majesty's Naval Base, Devonport. Undisturbed for sixty years, until we dug them up yesterday."

Rupert took a sideways glance at Pinchuk. What he saw clearly wasn't reassuring.

"Look, we might as well just get things over with. Two simple questions for you. First, where's the code book, that tatty old Bible? Second, who else might know about ABSALOM?"

Henry cast his eyes to the floor, worried that he might be spotted giving the romantic-fiction shelves an involuntary glance.

Felicity wasn't letting go. Henry realised she had a plan, but was struggling to fathom it.

"So, what turned you into a traitor, little Rupert? A plain thief. Selling good people for filthy money. Or were you just born that way? Bad seed. You see, I know something of your family history."

To Henry's surprise, Pinchuk didn't intervene. He actually looked interested in Rupert's answer himself. He seemed to have regained his composure but it was Rupert's turn to lose it, falling for Felicity's precision guided taunts.

"No harm in telling you. You and your half-witted friend there, seeing as you're not going anywhere."

Henry now focused on Rupert's oversized teeth, wishing he'd knocked them down his throat in the pub, when he'd been given the chance.

"As you'd expect, I got tapped up for MI6 at Oxford, turned it down, or rather, deferred entry. Decided to take my chances in the ruins of post-Soviet Moscow for a few years. Idea was to make a tidy wedge rather than live on your public sector pittance. And also have some fun! It was the best time of my life. I still get a hard-on when I think about our parties with the girls we picked up at the Hungry Duck. You could do almost anything to them if you had hard currency, no limits. Same with your girlfriend, Henry. Nataliya Antonova Aleksandrova was most obliging once you scarpered to Lisbon and left her in the lurch."

Rupert paused and watched Henry carefully.

"Funnily enough, I was talking to my psychotherapist about it just the other week. She actually seemed quite shocked, and I thought she was a woman of the world. I think you both knew her. Nea Solomon. Sue Nightingale. Take your pick. God rest her soul."

Rupert made a show of putting his fingers together in prayer, looking up at the skylight in mock piety. Smirking, he continued.

"For the record, before the Russians get stuck into you, two things. Firstly, I'm no traitor. All I ever agreed to, or did, was to protect ABSALOM. Or more specifically, the line of communication. To this day, I don't even know who the bugger is. I've never given up anything else to the Russians, that was never part of the deal. My conscience is clear."

That did it. Henry launched himself forward in a futile headlong charge, little chair still attached, forced into a short-stepping waddle. Pavel and Ilya each grabbed him by an arm, firmly returning him to the children's corner. They were laughing.

"You utter wanker. What about the Aslanovs? Sasha? Jack Somerset? And what have you done to Nea?"

Rupert gave his toothy grin.

"All on you, my friend. If you'd just done what was expected, they'd all be alive today. You killed them, not me. Take that last thought with you."

Felicity spoke to Henry in a low whisper. She was staring into the dark recess of the biography section.

"Relax. We're going to be fine."

He couldn't quite see how, but he tried to comply,

hoping to God that Felicity knew what she was doing. Pinchuk and Rupert stood in front of them, Pavel and Ilya at their flank. Rupert signalled that he hadn't finished. He still looked furious, breathing shallowly, blood drained from his face.

"Just so you know, Henry, for the avoidance of any doubt, I hand-picked you. The MI5 profilers found six candidates who knew Sasha well enough, all suitable to be approached for our little cultivate-and-control operation. I had to choose one and I immediately realised you were my man."

He wondered where this was going.

"You see, I had to be seen to do something. That plod Colin was terribly excitable. This was his big find. We don't stumble over Russian illegals every day, so MI5 were throwing anything we wanted our way. Problem was, your friend Sasha was part of our ABSALOM chain, and a weak link to boot. So, your background file was a gift. Henry Bradbury. A lost soul. Personal life, a mess. State school and then a third-rate university. No sense of drive or purpose. One of life's born losers. I don't know how to put this any other way, Henry, but I chose you because I knew you would fuck it up."

Rupert paused for effect, grinning. Pinchuk stood at his shoulder, unreadable.

"And you know—"

Rupert got no further, his mouth exploding in a red spray of blood, saliva and flying teeth. His bottom lip was split clean in two, lower gums showing through. Pinchuk took a linen handkerchief out of his pocket, carefully wiped off the heel of his pistol, looking down at the smear of clinical waste with disgust. Pavel had Rupert by the arm, steadying him on his feet, arresting him mid-faint.

Apart from the deafening rain above, the library fell silent. Henry stared at Pinchuk in disbelief. Pinchuk stared at Rupert. Rupert's eyes looked vacant, unfocused, in shock. Felicity was now concentrating on the cookery and DIY shelves.

Then Pinchuk spoke, deadpan and matter-of-fact.

"I've had to deal with you people for forty years. And frankly, I've had enough. You, MAURICE, are the worst of a bad lot. You don't know for how long I've dreamed about doing that."

Henry found himself nodding in agreement, before a sharp look from Felicity stopped him. In fact, now Henry's fantasy had been played out in front of him, he was surprised at how queasy he felt.

"In Moscow, you were a degenerate. Up to your ears in debt to the mafia, a trail of failed investments, living in squalor with your disgusting Oxford 'chums'. You looked useful to us, pretty much the way you just described Henry, in fact. And over the years you've taken our money, stolen from your own country, betrayed it."

Rupert was starting to slump. Pavel wrenched him up by his elbow.

"And your crowning glory is Mr Bradbury here. I asked you to find us a British idiot. There's a nearly endless supply …"

Pavel and Ilya laughed in comic opera approval.

"And instead, you gave us Henry. I still don't know how he worked on Sasha, Aslanov, Jack Somerset, got them to spill their guts. Very impressive. Then he nearly killed me in Lisbon. Managed to evade the combined search efforts of Interpol, MI5, MI6 and the SVR, leading us all on a ridiculous chase across Europe. And best of all, I think he's worked out who ABSALOM is."

All eyes were now on Henry.

"I've actually got some professional respect for him. And, of course, for Miss Smith here. So, I've decided to make this quick, if they cooperate. With the code book, and their list of ABSALOM insiders."

Pinchuk reached down to the rubber floor cover, picking up the power sander. He ran the palm of his hand across the gritty disc. Evidently satisfied with its abrasive qualities, he started it spinning, slowly at first, then the holes in the pad began to blur as it picked up speed. He revved the motor.

"Speak now, or I will start to remove Miss Smith's rather plain face. I've got a feeling Henry will quickly reach his limit, much faster than his friend here. So why waste all our time?"

Felicity jutted out her chin and closed her eyes, serene. She could have been preparing for a spa treatment. Time slowed down for Henry. He'd read that's what happens in your last moments. He tried to go through his options, but all he could think of was his daughters. He had known this was coming if ABSALOM got the better of him, and perhaps that had been inevitable all along. Why hadn't he just gone to see them, rather than run? Would they ever know what happened to him, or would he and Felicity simply be dropped down a deep shaft, dead or alive. Looking at Pinchuk, Henry decided it would most definitely be a live drop. But then gone forever, joining the long-lost ossuary of miners deep below the village? Or, worse still, would Pinchuk just stage another murder-suicide? He had form. Henry couldn't bear that thought. He hadn't been a hero, but he'd tried to do his best, to learn, finally to do something worthwhile with his life. And his girls would never know. Their father, remembered as a maniac who tortured and slaughtered a gentle and much-loved librarian right after finishing a jigsaw puzzle with her.

Pinchuk took one step forward, the sander now a few inches above Felicity's nose, the rotating pad close enough to ruffle her hair, an insistent mosquito buzz just audible over the storm. He seemed to relish the moment, hovering the spinning surface just above one cheek, then the other, all the while smirking in Henry's direction. Henry sat transfixed, desperate to make eye contact with Felicity. But she just sat there, a beatific smile on her face. Suddenly, in his peripheral vision, he sensed a dark figure moving slowly from the back of the cookery and DIY section. He clicked. This could be the salvation that the librarian had already spotted. He thought quickly – his only option was to buy time. Act, perform, as if their lives depended on it, which indeed they did. Lie about Sasha's Bible, lie about the trail to ABSALOM. Use every last ounce of theatrical skill he could muster.

"I can't take this anymore. Please … please! This is sending me mad. Stark staring mad. Tell me what you want to know. And let's get it over with." He began to sob uncontrollably, shoulders rising and falling, then head thrown back in a bestial howl. "I just don't want to die like this. God, please help me!"

Pinchuk smiled a victorious smile before lowering the sander to his side. He took three steps back, joining the other men on the rubber sheeting. Henry was preparing his next line. His tormentors were all facing him, backs to the bookshelves. It took all his willpower to keep his red eyes averted from the shadowy figure lurking behind them. He readied himself for action, every sinew straining, ready to explode.

Then it happened.

Two sharp pistol cracks accompanied by a muzzle flash, bright orange flower bursts in the murk; then, thousands of gallons of storm water crashing down from the shattered skylight, raining glass daggers in a deafening torrent. Instinctively, Henry pushed his chair back, just clear of the flood. But their four captors took its full force, sent sprawling across the slick rubber cover, landing on the arrayed hardware, blinded by the gushing water.

Henry struggled to his feet, small chair still attached, just about keeping his balance as, bent double, he shuffled towards Felicity, still calm and composed. She spoke as the shadow revealed itself.

"Welcome back to St Morwenna, Dr Nightingale. So lovely to see you again."

Nea looked up to admire her handiwork, now a gaping void open to the wild elements. Wind screamed in and the spotlight crashed to the floor. Extinguished, the only light came from the dim storm lamp flickering above the jigsaw puzzle.

"Oh yes. Two of my favourite people in one place. Definitely worth the trip down from London. Especially to witness Henry's histrionics. Bravo."

Hunting knife in one hand, Colt .45 covering the groundsheet in the other, within seconds she had cut them free. In the half darkness, Henry tried to make out what was happening, readying himself for the next move. The four men were trying to get to their feet, but kept slipping, gasping drunks who couldn't seem to get themselves up. His pulse was deafening in his ears, God knows how many beats per minute. Pavel's Makarov had dropped to the ground and was spinning across the floor. The Russian bent down to retrieve it but stumbled and was sent reeling by two quick-fire kicks to the head, expertly delivered by Nea. Henry lunged forward and grabbed the weapon, bracing his legs and taking aim at the man now sprawled at his feet. Felicity was shouldering the old machine gun that Pavel had left on her desk, pulling back the bolt action. Henry heard the noise of the mechanism being released and made eye contact with her through the gloom. She nodded her head towards Ilya, silently indicating she had him covered. Looking over, he saw Nea had the Colt trained on the MI6 man.

The Russians were now rubbing their eyes, coughing, struggling to catch their breath. Rupert lay on his back, panting, his mouth a gaping hole.

Henry was the first to spot it. A five-litre plastic container of drain cleaner, ruptured when Pavel crashed onto it, lay bleeding out its contents, sulphuric acid washing into the dirty rainwater.

Henry, Felicity and Nea stood shoulder to shoulder, weapons made ready but now struggling to aim, battling overloaded senses. A strange phantasmagoria played out in front of them, a flickering magic lantern. Too late,

Henry spotted that a leading character had disappeared from the tableau. He shouted above the storm.

"Guys, where the fuck is Pinchuk?" They all swept the room with their eyes, straining to see movement, safety catches off, three fingers on three triggers.

Then Pinchuk was there in the entrance hall, on all fours, holding a snarling Scooby by the collar, a large canine shield, pistol pressed into the side of the dog's head. Scooby was struggling, trying to turn his muzzle to bite, adding to the mayhem whilst Pinchuk inched them both towards the library door. In the dark, it was impossible to discern captive from captor, man from beast.

Pinchuk was screaming now. "Lower your guns, or I'll put a round in this filthy animal. Lower them! Then just let us go." The other Russians were hauling Rupert to his feet, pushing him towards the entrance. Nea held her aim, arms locked, both hands on the pistol grip, a professional forward-leaning stance. Felicity and Henry looked at each other, then let their weapons droop to their sides, flaccid.

Nea shouted over the storm.

"Christ. I can't get a safe shot in."

Henry cursed.

"It's hopeless. We've got to let them go."

They watched helplessly as the grotesque party formed a single file, four coughing and retching men, scrambling blindly upwards towards the cliffs, arms extended to find one another.

Henry vaguely recalled a First World War poem. Softly, he spoke to himself. "In all my dreams before my helpless sight, he plunges at me, guttering, choking, drowning." That sounded about right, quite apposite.

Inside the library, the three of them folded their arms around one other. They were leaning in, head first, supporting, trying to get their breathing back under control. Somehow, they synchronised, inhaling and exhaling together. It felt hypnotic and Henry lost track of time. Then it came. What they feared most. Six gunshots, each one sharp above the wind. Delivered in quick-fire beats. Crack, crack... pause... crack, crack... pause... crack, crack. Three double taps. The unmistakable howl of a dying dog. Then silence.

23

A NEW DAWN

SAINT MORWENNA, CORNWALL, 21 MARCH 2020

The three of them breathed in the new day, walking up and out of the cove in thoughtful silence. Gulls laughed overhead and the scent of the early spring morning was released with every footfall, renewal. The ocean was calm, the air cold and still, the first fingers of sun tentatively creeping towards them.

Daphne had been in her dressing gown when they knocked at the front door of the Pilchard's Head. The surfers had already left for the Cornish south coast, hoping to find a way out of Wenna, but Daphne wasn't hopeful. Still no power or phone coverage. She was sorry she couldn't offer them any hospitality. Her eyes kept looking behind the three, to their side, and then searching their faces in turn. Then her shoulders heaved as she reached in her pocket for a handkerchief; she knew what had happened. Nea spoke.

"I don't know how to tell you this, Daphne. But I think Scooby is gone. We had some real trouble up at the library in the night. He saved our lives. But he paid for it. He'll be somewhere up at Wheal Dyowl."

At that, Daphne pulled her gown tightly around herself and took three determined paces towards the hill. Felicity placed a gentle but firm hand on her forearm.

"We can't let you go up there now. It's just not safe, but we'll get a search party organised when it's properly light. We're just so sorry."

The landlady sat back on the cold, wet step of her pub and stared out to the lightening ocean whilst three figures departed in silence.

The cliff path was narrow, too narrow to walk three abreast. The party was muted; Nea and Felicity spoke to each other quietly so Henry hung back a couple of paces, half engaged with his companions, half thinking back over his journey. How he got here. He wondered how often spies see all their questions answered, all the pieces neatly in place. Pretty much never, he concluded. He'd been very, very lucky.

And also lucky with the two women who strode purposefully ahead of him. Felicity had the machine gun hung from her shoulder, zipped under her raincoat, and Nea had the Makarov pistol in her pocket – she had kindly returned the Colt .45 to him. But he realised it was something else that had saved their lives as a team. And unmasked ABSALOM. Guts and brains. He felt proud to be walking out of Saint Morwenna with these two.

* * *

As the town of Porthmerrick came into view, now clearly visible in the growing light, Nea stopped sharply, raising a hand to halt her companions. In the distance, between them and their goal, two figures sat on a bench, facing the sea. Three or four hundred yards ahead, they were difficult to make out. Male or female, young or old? Not clear. The three were walking in the opposite direction to Wheal Dyowl, but even so, they now moved forward carefully, all eyes on the early risers ahead.

The bench came into sharper focus and two men took shape, one younger, one bent over a walking stick.

Nea stopped.

"They're not our friends from last night, that's for sure. But who are they? Any ideas?"

Henry strained. He couldn't find his glasses after the fight and the figures remained a stubborn, astigmatic blur. Felicity shielded her eyes from the rising sun, now hanging low above the sea.

"Goodness, I'd swear the old man is Professor Macindoe. He was the service's top talent spotter. And a legendary problem-solver. Always a freelancer, off the books, dealing with the most difficult operations. A genius, and a very brave man. I mentioned him to Henry last night. He's the only person I would trust with ABSALOM. And here he is, waiting for us. No coincidence, I'm sure of that."

"Is Macindoe a fellow of Hereford College? Translated Pushkin all those years ago?"

Henry was thinking back to that delicious confrontation with Rupert, that night on the frosty Oxford quad.

"That's the one. His academic career looked like a failure to the outside world. Stalled. But that was the price he paid for some remarkable service to the country."

They walked on, now changing configuration. Felicity strode ahead, her pace quickening, clearly anxious to speak to the professor.

Nea dropped back, hooking her arm through Henry's. It felt natural as they walked in step. Henry had to ask.

"Nea, why didn't you just shoot Rupert and the Russians last night, at the outset? Why take the risk of taking out the ceiling? We were bloody lucky that worked."

Nea stopped them dead in their tracks.

"That should be obvious, Henry. I'm a doctor, a psychotherapist, not an assassin. So, I wasn't going to kill them in cold blood. And frankly, four armed and highly trained men against me, the odds weren't exactly in our favour, were they? And it worked, didn't it?"

Henry nodded and made to move on, but Nea held him firmly anchored to the spot.

"Henry, I've something I need to tell you."

She pulled herself closer to him.

"I can't be your psychotherapist any longer. You see, it wouldn't be professional. Obviously, I can help you find somebody else to work with."

She must have caught his look of sadness.

"You'll be fine, Henry. You've just come through a trial that would have defeated all of those people you've always aspired to be. And you're a better you, a different you."

He was confused.

"Is it because of everything that's happened? You saving our lives last night? Or is it because I know too

354

much about you? Undercover operations, the witness protection programme … what they did to you?"

Nea stopped. Removing her glasses, she rubbed her nose and then kissed him, long and on the lips. He felt her arms around his waist and the warmth of her body. He felt dizzy, transported. He didn't want the moment to end.

"No, Henry. It's for a different reason now. You're a smart guy. Work it out."

They walked on.

"Hey, you two lovebirds! That's quite enough of that for this time of the morning. We've still got work to do, remember."

Felicity was well ahead of them on the path, smiling, stamping her feet against the chill. They caught up. Henry didn't know where to look.

"You two certainly aren't the first couple that've come together in field ops, so don't think you're unique. It's a regular hothouse for romance, in my experience. All that life and death stuff, adrenaline. Quite the aphrodisiac."

They stood together in silence.

"I'm very happy for you. But our job isn't quite over yet. Chop-chop!"

Henry was soon within visual range of the bench, even without his specs. Both men were clear now, in profile, stubbornly looking out over the ocean. He recognised Macindoe, leaning his chin on a wooden stick. And next to him sat Colin. This was beginning to make sense.

"That's my MI5 controller. Rupert's straight man. The sensible one. Well, I just hope he's straight."

That question hung in the early morning air as they arrived at the bench. Colin sprang to his feet, wreathed in smiles, facial tick nowhere to be seen, making space for the party to join Professor Macindoe. Henry demurred, preferring to stand after shaking hands with Colin and inclining his head towards the professor. Instinct told him to keep a hand on the Colt in his pocket.

The old man kept staring out to sea as he spoke.

"A beautiful morning, is it not? After a brutal forty-eight hours. In every sense, I suspect. The fact that you three are out and about suggests you survived. If not thrived. Would thrived be the right word?"

Henry spoke.

"Not sure about that, sir. But first things first. You and Colin aren't here by chance, I take it? Not staying over at the caravan park, out for your morning constitutional?"

Macindoe nodded.

"No, Mr Crompton, Mr Bradbury, not at all. We had reason to take an interest in Rupert Samson-Brown in recent days. Colin tried to keep a close eye on his erstwhile partner. The storm put paid to that, so I am afraid you were left to your own devices. But here we all are now. By the way, did your son Roddy ever secure his place at Hereford?"

His eyes twinkled as Henry stood, impassive.

"I've talent-spotted all sorts in my time, Henry, but I have to say you are a natural. One of the best. You missed your vocation, though it's never too late, don't you think?"

Henry was delighted, but resisted the temptation to show it.

"I am so sorry that Samson-Brown slipped through the net. I'd have sniffed him out a mile off. Unfortunately, I had a three-year visiting professorship at Peking University at the time of his recruitment. Quite a productive time in China, if you follow my drift. Anyway, these things happen. Whether we like it or not, back in the nineteen eighties Eton and Oxford were a ticket, like one of these 'Fast Passes' that I'm told people buy to jump the queue at dreadful American amusement parks."

The professor sighed and Colin pulled his mobile from his pocket, consulting a map on its screen.

"Last contact with Rupert's tracker was at 04.02 this morning. High up on the cliffs, right by somewhere called ..."

Colin enlarged the map and struggled with his Cornish.

"It looks like Wheal Dy ... Wheal Dy ..."

Felicity helped out.

"Wheal Dyowl. The Devil's Mine. Quite appropriate, given he was with Pinchuk and friends. None of them were in great shape when we last saw them. Quite a mess really. They've either gone to ground, killed each other or, most likely, fallen down a mineshaft, gone forever."

Macindoe looked at his wristwatch, then his eyes swept up the Bristol Channel. He could have been an old man waiting for a country bus, but instead a Chinook helicopter appeared in the distance, travelling at speed, skimming just feet above the waves, the whoosh-whoosh of its twin rotors unmistakable.

"Well, right on time. That will be the gentlemen callers from Poole. Loveable rogues who, for some unaccountable reason, relish the idea of squeezing into tight spaces, armed to the teeth, in pursuit of Her Majesty's enemies. Your Wheal Dyowl will make a pleasant change from the caves of Bora Bora, I imagine."

The helicopter began a low-level turn above the

distant silhouette of the mine buildings, describing a tight circle. Felicity screwed her eyes towards the west. She was decisive.

"We heard three double taps. There will be three bodies, guaranteed. One decent dog, two dreadful men. The question is, which men?"

Colin's phone pinged and he scrolled down the message, finally handing it Felicity. She put it in her lap and used thumb and forefinger to enlarge an infrared image. Henry and Felicity peered over her shoulder. The image showed three broken bodies at the foot of a cliff, contorted into shapes they shouldn't have been. Felicity zoomed in further.

"That's a positive ID. Scooby, Pavel and Ilya. So, Pinchuk and Rupert are still at large. No matter how hard your men think they are, tell them to go carefully. I mean it."

Macindoe nodded his agreement to Colin, who tapped out a message to the search team. For the first time, the old man looked along the bench and smiled, thinly.

"Now, Felicity, do you and your friends have anything for us? That makes all this worthwhile?"

"Henry, Sasha's Bible, please. Give it to the professor."

He had retrieved *Lady Victoria's Passion by Moonlight* as they left the library and it was now firmly in his poacher pocket. He must have looked reluctant. Colin intervened.

"Henry, we know we've put you through the ringer. I'm sorry for that. Rupert had me fooled, all of us hoodwinked. You were the first to work him out, though. Hats off. As soon as you told Nea your story, she was in touch and we were straight on the case. It must be difficult, but you need to trust us, me and the professor."

Felicity and Nea nodded and Henry pulled the book out of his jacket.

"And the ABSALOM list, Henry. Hidden in your cap. Hand it over." Felicity spoke firmly and he obliged.

Macindoe studied the code pages intently, cross-referring them to Henry's list.

"You've done a remarkable job, Felicity. Quite remarkable. We've heard echoes of ABSALOM for decades, but never got anywhere close. And never dreamt it was a full-blown Russian penetration programme, with Samson-Brown running interference for them. Blasted man."

Felicity corrected the professor.

"No, it wasn't me. Henry solved it. He got the confessions: Sasha Orlov, Boris Aslanov, Jack Somerset. Managed to stay alive against the odds, on the run. Then he worked out the puzzle. Not me. It's him you need to thank."

Macindoe nodded, handing the Bible and list to Colin. He struggled to his feet, Felicity helping him up.

"I need a quiet word with Colin, please. Indulge us for a moment."

The two men walked just out of earshot, conferring. Macindoe did most of the talking, Colin nodding in agreement.

Nea caught Henry's eye.

"I know what you're wondering. This rot, ABSALOM, is at the top. Who can we trust? Macindoe? Colin? But that's not the question, Henry, is it? It's whether you trust Felicity, her judgement here. I do, but do you?"

After a long pause, he spoke.

"You're right. In fact, I trust both of you, after what we've been through. I'm in, whatever happens next."

The two men returned and the professor elected to stand.

"So, you aren't going to see any dramatic arrests around the Palace of Westminster or up and down Whitehall. Nor any trials at the Old Bailey. In fact, you will see nothing of note. I hope that isn't disappointing for you, after all your efforts."

Henry was thinking of Uncle Michael's prophesy.

"But I want to assure you, this is not the end of the matter for these traitors. Far from it. They will be given no choice but to hand over their OTPs. We shall then unpick the details of the operation – anyone else involved, what damage has already been done, what the next move was meant to be. And next we clean out the stables, one by one. All you and Joe Public will see is the usual, the run of the mill. Resignations for health scares, family reasons … and if any won't go willingly, we can always dig out some scandal or another, sex or money. I think Colin and the chaps will have a decent file on each of them."

Colin studied the nine names, slowly running his finger down the list.

"Oh yes, Professor. We've got the full selection box here, sir. Shaggers, boozers, embezzlers. In fact, some of them tick all the boxes."

Colin laughed, but Macindoe didn't. He was staring straight at Henry, reading him.

"I'm afraid it's the way it works. Quiet, methodical but effective. ABSALOM is dead and we are burying him. Thanks to you three."

Nea and Felicity were now on their feet, joining Henry. Macindoe and Colin shook their hands in turn, taking their leave, but Macindoe hesitated.

"With this dreadful thing, this virus, what exactly are your plans? Where are you going to sit it out?"

Without hesitation, Nea spoke for them.

"Henry and I are staying put. Here in Saint Morwenna, with Felicity. We like it here. Plenty of fresh air. We're a team, and I couldn't think of anyone else I'd rather be locked away with."

Henry and Felicity both took a step closer to her in silent agreement.

Macindoe looked at Colin, who nodded his approval.

"That's exactly what we'd hoped for. In the not too distant future, I will have a new project for you, one you might be interested in assisting us with. Off the books, of course. Totally deniable. Hugely sensitive. A little dangerous too. We won't ask if you've kept the weapons you've acquired along the way, but I do hope you have."

Macindoe paused, drawing breath.

"I'm getting too old for field operations. So, the truth is, I couldn't think of three people I would trust more to continue my mission. You each bring something unique to the party. The perfect mix. Nea, you see right into people's souls. And pretty useful with a gun, and your hands and feet. Felicity, champion puzzle solver, prodigious memory, deep-cover trained. And you, Henry, actor, imposter and confessor. Between you, unstoppable. So, I'll be in touch when the time comes, but for now, please start training for your next mission. From now on, you are my new 'Occasionals.'"

Henry was about to ask what happened to their predecessors, but a look from Felicity stopped him dead.

In silence, the three turned back towards Saint

Morwenna. Henry suspected they were each wrestling with the same thing, trying to reconcile two worlds, parallel, concurrent, but, of necessity, separate. In the morning light, a village librarian, an itinerant writer of romantic fiction, and their doctor friend down from London. And then beneath, their dark reflections, their shadows beckoning them back in.

ABOUT THE AUTHOR

Angus Blair was approached to join the Secret Intelligence Service (MI6) whilst studying history at Cambridge University. He travelled widely across the Soviet Union and served in the British Army. An obsessive wanderer, he has notched up 121 countries and now lives between London, Lisbon and Cornwall. Blair has two adult daughters and a long-suffering psychotherapist.

Made in the USA
Monee, IL
20 December 2023

49981743R00208